DOWNHILL CHANCE

DOWNHILL CHANCE

DONNA MORRISSEY

A Mariner Original

HOUGHTON MIFFLIN COMPANY

Boston · New York

2003

For information about permission to reproduce
selections from this book, write to Permissions,
Houghton Mifflin Company, 215 Park Avenue South,
New York, New York 10003.

Visit our Web site: www.houghtonmifflinbooks.com.

First published in Canada in 2002 by
Penguin Books Canada Ltd.

Library of Congress Cataloging-in-Publication Data
Morrissey, Donna, date.
Downhill chance / Donna Morrissey.
p.   cm.
"A Mariner original."
ISBN 0-618-18927-0
1. World War, 1939–1945—Newfoundland—
Fiction. 2. Mothers and daughters—Fiction.
3. Grandfathers—Death—Fiction.
4. Newfoundland—Fiction. 5. Girls—Fiction.
I. Title.
PR9199.3.M6535 D69   2003
813'.54—dc21
2002027562

Printed in the United States of America

QUM 10 9 8 7 6 5 4 3 2 1

To my son, David Ford Morrissey,
and my daughter, Bridgette Adele Morrissey

And the rain descended, and the floods came, and the winds blew, and beat upon that house: and it fell: and great was the fall of it.

—Matthew 8:27

ACKNOWLEDGEMENTS

For their love and support during the writing of this novel, I wish to thank my siblings, Wanda, Glenn, Tommy and Karen, my dad and Aunt Shirley Dyke for her love of a sister.

Thank you to the Canada Council for the Arts and the Nova Scotia Arts Council for their financial support.

And for their critiques, research and time, I wish to thank my special friends Genevieve Lehr, Catherine Reader and Ismet Ugursal, my agent, Beverley Slopen, editors Cynthia Good and Susan Canavan, and my meticulous line editor, Mary Adachi.

NEWFOUNDLAND
FICTIONAL PLACE NAMES ARE IN ITALICS

WHITE BAY

ATLANTIC
OCEAN

HAMPDEN

CORNER BROOK

PORT AUX BASQUE

ST.
JOHN'S

ST.
ANTHONY

HARBOUR
DEEP

CAT ARM

*GOLD
COVE*

WHITE BAY

*LOWER
HEAD*

*ROCKY
HEAD*

CHOUSE
BROOK

*COPY-CAT
COVE*

THE
BEACHES

THE BASIN

HAMPDEN

N

CORNER BROOK

IT WAS A DIRTY OLD NIGHT that washed Gid O'Mara up on the shores of Rocky Head. Sheila's Brush, the old-timers called it, that late-spring storm that comes with the fury of February winds, transfiguring the desolate rock-island of Newfoundland into a great whale soaring out of the Atlantic, shaking and writhing as if to rid itself of the shacks, wharves and boats clinging to its granite shores like barnacles. Yawning with the leisure of an old tomcat, twelve-year-old Luke scrooped open the bedroom window, letting in a blast of sea-dampened wind that near put out the burning candle stub that flickered yellow over his older brother, Joey, lying beneath the blankets in their double bed.

"The old woman's going to skin you," Joey warned, the accordion he'd been lazily drawing a tune out of flattening back against his chest as he squirmed deeper beneath the blanket, pulling his brown worsted cap farther down over his ears. But Luke was already skimming his belly across the sill and dropping to the ground below. A swipe of rain cut across his face as he scurried to the lee of the house to break the wind, ducking below the lamplight spilling out through the window where his father, his cap rolled high above aging eyes, and his mother, a crown of greying braids besetting a brow forever etched with worry, sat watching the storm. A wave broke over the bit of bank that separated the string of six houses from the sea-pounded beach, and he gave a low whistle as seething white froth swooshed up around his feet, then slid back into the rioting black water.

Always he wondered what it would be like to live inland, away from the wet, wind and fog heaved at them by the sea, and for sure he would travel inland someday, as soon as he was old enough to get clear of his mother. But nights like this, when the storms were at their fullest, he wished for nothing. Hunching his head into his shoulders and jamming his hands inside his pockets, he crouched down besides a woodpile stacked against the house, and inched underneath the canopy made by the water-sogged canvas that covered it. Sea shelters, he called them, those dry hollows sometimes found in the tuck of an overhanging bank, or beneath the eave of a chicken coop, or behind the glass prism of frozen cliff water. He loved it, he did, crouching in weather, his mind lulled by the wind gusting past him, and the sea swarming up over the shore. And the gulls, sifting white through the dark, cried differently at night: tremulous, haunting cries that only the solitary deserved to hear.

Oftentimes, when curled in the bow of a beached boat or crouched within the warmth of a bough-whiffen—those little dome-shaped shelters he often made by weaving boughs into each other—and with the rain plinking all around him but never a drop dampening his skin, he slept. And as he crouched now, and a couple of fair-haired young-sters, their curls made limp by the drizzle, appeared out of the dark and stood in the spot of light thrown out through the window by his mother's lamp, he thought surely he must have fallen off and that the divinity presenting itself before him was but a sweet-scented dream. Then another boy, about the same age, appeared in the light. Luke blinked, then blinked again as a woman with a blanket wrapped shawl-like around her shoulders and a babe curled in her arms and a man with dark hair and a beard flowing down his chest appeared too out of the dark—all huddling into the spot of lamplight as if it might reprieve them from the storm.

In a land where the only visitors were fogbound fishers or the scattered husband or wife brought ashore to keep the bloodlines clean, this apparition growing in numbers before Luke became more and more extraordinary, and with a frightened yelp he tore to his feet, racing around the side of the house, hollering that Christ had returned, bringing with him the lost children of Abraham, and they was right outside, standing in the light of his mother's lamp. In less time than it took to spit, every man, woman and youngster from the six houses that made up Rocky Head were crowding out their doors and piling warily onto the bank. Luke was in the lead, and his mother, Prude, her hands clasped anxiously before her ample bosom, brought up the rear. They were as Luke left them; the children like shivering elfs, standing quietly in a patch of light besides their mother and father, their yellow curls tangled by the wind, a dull curiosity in their pale blue eyes and a stooped indifference around their scarcely clad shoulders. And when the smallest of them, no more than a toddler, turned to his mother and asked in a lilting voice and with the most sweetest of sounds, "Is this where we's going to live?" a gasp went through the outporters, and all eyes swung to Luke as they believed surely he must be right, and this bedraggled bunch were celestial creatures sent straight from the Divine Mother Spirit to land upon their God-forsaken shores—for such was the beauty in the melodic brogue of the child's Irish tongue, a brogue never before heard by anybody from Rocky Head. And when the father replied in the same sweetened tongue that it was up to the good people before him, because his boat had been lost to the sea, and everything they owned with it, the outporters stirred from their half-frozen states. Resisting their wariness of strangers, they reverently approached their God-given gifts, and divvying them up, half-carried, half-walked them straightaway into their homes and into their hearts.

Aside from Prude, that was. "No good comes from a night like this," she cried out as Luke ushered the boy the same age as he inside his own house behind Herb. And as was always with Prude's prophecies, it was met with a scowl from Luke as he nudged her, too, back inside. Standing on the stoop, Luke looked over to where Joey was following the bearded mister and his missus into Aunt Char's house and he wondered perhaps if it might not have been better to lead the young fellow into Aunt Char's house too. Then he, Luke, could sit and listen to the elders talk as well. But the sight of his conniving cousin Frankie following tight behind Joey, yet dragging his step over Aunt Char's stoop as he looked back curiously at the young fellow treading over Luke's, spurned all such thoughts.

"Stay weaseling where you're at, my son," he muttered, hopping inside and snapping the door shut behind him. And with a great might, he swung himself into the chair beside where his father was seating the young fellow at the table and, hauling it nearer, scrutinized more fully this token from the night's fury.

He wasn't as pretty as the younger ones, he thought, as his father turned up the wick in the lamp and his mother, crossing herself, scurried inside the pantry, reaching for a bottle of rabbit. What with his kinky brown-and-yellow hair plastered wetly to his skull and his eyes brown slivers beneath wide, heavy lids, he looked almost odd.

"What's your name?" Luke asked, and all hands stilled, listening for the brawling tongue.

The young stranger hesitated at first, his eyes rolling slowly onto Luke, then falling away timidly as he answered "Gid" in little more than a guttural mumble.

When nothing else followed, Prude scooped the bottled rabbit into a bowl, draining the liquor over it, as Herb stirred a spoon heaped with black molasses into a cup of tea and placed it before the boy.

"My name's Luke Osmond," said Luke, casting a discomfited look at his kindred as he gave his first ever self-introduction. "What's your last name?" he asked.

All hands quieted once more.

"O'Mara," said Gid.

"O'Mara. Not a namesake I ever heard," said Prude, placing the bowl of rabbit and a slice of bread before him. "And where's that talk from? I never heard tell of talk like that."

"Go on, old woman," said Luke impatiently, inching closer to the young stranger, "you never been nowhere to hear nothing."

"You mind, now," warned Prude, then, noting the boy's eyes fixed hungrily onto the bread, she nudged the plate nearer him. "Go on, take it," she said kindly. "Course, it's hard to eat with everybody staring at you. Here—sop your bread in the juice," she coaxed, pushing the rabbit breast floating in a bowl of liquor and pork scrunchions before him. "And leave off your nosying till he's done," she added sharply to Luke.

Luke watched as the young fellow dipped his bread crust into the liquor and then shoved it into his mouth. Aside from a queer head of hair, he had a face that was awful long and thin, and pasty in colour, and the eyes were threatening to shut at a second's notice as he struggled between chewing and staying awake.

"He's falling asleep in his tea, Mother," said Herb quietly.

"Sure then, let's put him to bed," said Prude, and Luke sprang to his feet, helping the young fellow up from his chair, leading him into his room. "And mind you keeps them legs in bed this time," warned Prude as Luke was closing the door behind him, "else, I nails a piece of two-by-four across that window come morn."

"Geez," muttered Luke, snapping shut the door. "Geez," he muttered once more for the benefit of his guest as he turned towards him but was astonished into silence as Gid, his wet pants already falling to the floor and still wearing his wet shirt, fell into bed, rolling himself into the blankets, his face to the wall. Shrugging disappointedly, Luke fumbled with the buttons of his pants, glancing at the window, his thoughts straying to Aunt Char's, but the threatening clucking of his mother's tongue sounding through his door stayed the notion, and kicking his pants aside, he crawled in besides his now sleeping bedmate.

He was still awake when Joey came home a half hour later. "They come from Ireland," he reported, his voice muffled through the room door. "They spent the last couple years down Harbour Deep and was looking for a new place to build when the wind hit. He says he was a carpenter back in Ireland."

"What's he looking for a new place for when he already come from Ireland to Harbour Deep?" asked Prude suspiciously.

"Now, Mother, just because he landed in Harbour Deep don't mean he got to live out his days in Harbour Deep."

"Nothing we got here they haven't got in Harbour Deep," said Prude, "unless he was looking for kin—and if he was looking for kin, why'd he spend two years in Harbour Deep when he found no kin there?"

"You're making a case," said Herb, the finality of his tone bolstered by the scrooping of his chair as Luke pictured him turning away from the talk and back to the storm outside his window.

"Mark my words—no good comes from them that's always shifting about," said Prude, her voice rising, and Luke, too, closed an ear. Ireland, he thought, his eyes beginning to droop, the place where men wears skirts and plays bagpipes—or was that Scotland?—and talks like they're singing. They never said nothing in the school books about people talking like they were singing. He flicked a dying glance at the back of Gid's head and felt a queer jealousy.

The next morning his eyes popped opened to the wheedling sound of his cousin Frankie's voice and the sweet lyrical sounding of Gid's as he said something about finishing his tay first. Scrambling out of bed, he hopped from one leg to another, hauling on his pants. It was just like Frankie, the sneaking, lying sliveen, to be the first one out this morning, trying to steal Gid away for his own, he was thinking, pulling a garnsey over his head. And leaving it riding high on his back, he tore out through his room door.

"What're you at, my son?" he growled, slewing his eyes from the knife-edged part of Frankie's slicked-back hair as he slouched against the doorjamb to that of Gid's mane as he sat at the table, chewing on a heel of bread. Gid's hair was fluffed off from his head like a seeding dandelion this morning, now that it was dry, but his eyes, noted Luke, were still drooping as if half asleep.

Frankie had straightened as Luke barged across the kitchen. "Going down to see the shark," he said.

"What shark?" demanded Luke, plunking himself down at the table and pulling his chair closer to Gid's.

"Back of the stagehead," said Frankie. "Uncle Jir dragged him ashore this morning—caught in his net, he was."

"You stay put—I gets you some bread, Luke," called out Prude from the pantry.

"How big is he?" asked Luke.

"Thirty feet," said Frankie.

"Hope now, thirty feet."

"Yes he is, my son; we was already down measuring him—two paddles long."

"Here, mind your talk and eat," said Prude, bustling to the table and pouring a cup of tea for Luke. "And stay clear of that shark; the last one come back to life and near took the arm of young Jack Dyke."

"You coming, Gid?" asked Luke, taking a loud sup of his tea. "Come on, then," he said as the young stranger nodded, draining back his cup. Taking one last sup, he clinked his cup alongside Gid's on the table and rose.

"What about bread, Luke—my oh my, have some bread," said Prude.

"I'll have it with me dinner," said Luke, shoving his feet into his rubbers and clumping around the kitchen. "Where's me cap, old woman—hey? Where's me cap?"

"Blessed Lord," whispered Prude. Luke screwed up his mouth at the look of fright on her face as she crossed herself, staring into the tea leaves stuck to the side of Gid's cup.

"Another flood coming?" he mocked. "Geez, old

woman." Snatching his cap off the foot of the daybed, he hustled Gid and Frankie out the door before him. "Women! Always bloody worrying," he muttered, slamming the door on Prude's cries. "Your mother read tea leaves?" he asked, chancing a look at Gid.

Gid shook his head.

"What's your name?" asked Frankie.

"Gid," answered Gid, his voice the guttural murmur of the night before.

"Say all your names," coaxed Luke.

"Gid O'Mara," said Gid, his eyes dropping shyly as both boys pierced him further with theirs, listening to each quavering syllable.

"Did you leave Ireland on a ship?" asked Luke.

"Yeah," said Gid.

"Yeah?"

"Yeah."

"Big ship?"

Gid nodded.

"What was it like on the big ship?"

"Cold. We was sick."

"Everybody?" asked Luke.

"Except Da and Ma."

"Da and Ma? Is that what you calls your folks—Da and Ma?"

"Yeah."

"Brothers! What do you call your grandmother?"

"Grandmother."

"Do everyone talk like you from Ireland?"

Frankie snorted, "Ireland! He's not from Ireland—he's from Harbour Deep—just down the shore," he muttered, leaving off Gid and sauntering towards the bank.

"Whadda you know?" sang out Luke, but Frankie had already ducked around the corner of the house and was letting out a sharp whistle.

"Ho—leee!" breathed Luke, lunging after him and coming up short, staring at the bank gouged out by the storm and littered with driftwood and countless clumps of glistening seaweed. Too, the tide was still in, and the grey, choppy water, muddied by the earth sucked from along the shoreline, seethed dangerously close to what was left of the bank. And no doubt the bulging offshore swells posed as much a threat to any poor mortal caught afloat its surface as did the wind-whipped whitecaps from the night before, thought Luke, looking out over the heaving body of water, half-mile wide to the hills on the far side, and as far out the bay as the eye could see—even on a good day. Today, a thick fog blotted out the horizon, and the banked sky rendered colourless what was visible in the dome surrounding them.

"You must've got some fright when ye lost your boat last night," said Luke, as Gid came up besides him. "You got sea like this in Ireland?"

"Yeah," spoke Gid in a half whisper, and its quiet drew Luke's attention back to him. He wasn't looking out over the sea at all, but along the shore the way he had come the night before. He shivered a little and Luke noted a small reddish birthmark puckering like a raspberry from his lower jaw, close to his ear. Catching his look, Gid lowered his chin, hunching his shoulder a little as he was apt to do, till the birthmark vanished amidst hair and shirt collar. Luke shifted his glance onto Gid's eyes, and was startled at the intensity with which they were fastened onto him. And like the pull of the moon to the earth, they drew Luke's attention to a muscle flexing out of control in the corner of one of Gid's wide, flat lids, lending him a pained look, and striking Luke with an urge to place his finger upon the pulsating flesh till it stilled. Balling his hands into fists, Luke shoved them into his pockets, shrugging indifferently as Frankie threw him an impatient look.

"Dare say he was scared. Bet he never gets storms like this down Harbour Deep," said Frankie.

"He's not from Harbour Deep, my son, he's from Ireland," said Luke, kicking a clump of kelp back into the sea.

"Yup, right."

"Yes he is; you heard him talk."

"So? He's still from Harbour Deep."

"Then, how come he don't talk like the ones from Harbour Deep?"

"Because he used to live in Ireland."

"If he used to live in Ireland, then he comes from Ireland, don't he?"

"Do he wear a skirt?"

"Geez, Frankie, they only wears skirts in marches."

"Do you wear skirts?" asked Frankie, turning to Gid.

Gid shook his head, eyes faltering between Luke's and Frankie's.

"Like I said—only in marches," said Luke, nudging Gid into a stroll along the bank.

"So, big deal," said Frankie, taking up stride besides them.

"Listen to Frankie," jeered Luke, "jealous because you're not from nowhere." Sauntering forward, peering sideways at Gid, he added, "I'm going up the Basin soon. By meself."

"Hope now, by yourself," scoffed Frankie.

"Yup. Walking up along shore; soon as I gets around to it. I'm going to buy a bottle of orange drinks—you can come if you wants," he said to Gid. "You know where the Basin is? It's up there, look," he said, turning and pointing to the opposite end of the bay that Gid had come from. "Can't see nothing today for fog. But when it's not foggy, you can see some of the houses. Close on to fifty she got; with a road going smack down the middle of her. They says they're going to have cars and trucks up there soon. You want to come?"

"Hope now, you're going up the Basin by yourself," said Frankie.

"Yes I am, my son. You'd be too scared to go."

"Yup, right," sneered Frankie.

"You can't listen to him, he's a liar," said Luke, dropping his voice as Frankie fell behind, poking a stick at a dead crab. "Real barrel-man, he is, and sly as a conner. Go on home, conner," he yelled over his shoulder at Frankie, and taking hold of Gid's arm, he hurried him farther along the bank. "Let's go see the shark," he urged, "and don't mind Frankie; his father drowned when he was a baby, and his mother's deaf as an haddock and don't come out her door and got him spoiled rotten. Do everybody talk like you in Ireland?"

"I was the one taking him down to see the shark," Frankie bawled out, and the crab come winging past Gid's ear, near nicking it.

"Ohh, you just struck him," said Luke, swinging around.

Then the sound of Prude's voice pierced the air as she came out on her stoop, singing out, "Luukee, Luukee!" Taking to their heels, both boys snatched hold of Gid's arms and bolted with him down the bank towards a rickety stagehead, standing half on land, half on water. Prude came bustling around the corner of her house, wringing her fist, and the wind flapping her skirts as she sang out "Luuke, Luuke, get back here, ye'll be drowned; mark my words, ye'll be drowned."

But the broad of their backs was the most she or any of the elders saw of the three boys that morning and during the following weeks. And with school having closed since early April due to the teacher from St. John's having a gall-bladder attack, there was more than enough time to squander. Climbing the hills, they took their new best friend to the top of the cliff that jutted out from the side of the hill, looking down upon the six painted houses, and the odd assortment of weather-beaten barns, woodsheds and outhouses that looped out from the base of the hill, circling back again, forming a communal backyard, webbed with pathways and overhanging clotheslines. There the younger ones shrieked to each other, ducking amongst the flapping sheets, mindless of the scattered goat bucking before them, and the elder's warnings of a tanning if they dirtied a spot on the wash with the black of their faces. And too there was the cluck-clucking of Aunt Char's hens firking the dirt by her stoop, and dogs barking and cats snarling, and always, always, the screaming of the snipes as they fought over fish entrails near the stagehead, and the plaintive cries of the gulls as they glided overhead, gaining momentum for the downward swoop over the surf.

From there they took him to all the best spots: Molly the horse's grave, where the lone hoof stuck two feet up out of the ground; the gutted-out motorboat that Aunt Char had pieced around with chicken wire and kept her pig in; Aunt Hope's well with the fancy tiled roof; Uncle Jir's new outhouse, painted white and padlocked, with real toilet paper inside. It was always best to wait for the tide to go out and climb up through the hole and have a crap and wipe with the real toilet paper, and jump back down through the hole again when the wave washed out. And, too, there was Chouse Brook with the biggest, fattest saltwater trout in all of White Bay. And when they were able to persuade one of the elders to lend them a boat, and beg for permission to row up the bay to Miller's Island, there was the old graveyard with a mother and daughter buried in the same grave and with the two black firs grown on either side of the headstone, imprisoning it no matter how much wriggling was done to try and pry it free. And always while roaming from one place to another Luke plied his new best buddy with a thousand "How big's Ireland, Gid? What other names do ye have over there? What do ye call your dogs, your cats? And what about boats? Sheep? And squid— do ye have squid?" And as Gid replied, Luke would pause, clinging to every guttural syllable that fell from his mouth, his eyes fixed intently onto the brown, drooping eyes as if willing them to open like mirrors, reflecting the journey that had spat this boy upon the beach before him.

But Gid's eyes held nothing. Partially opened at best, they would startle a little wider when called upon, as if having forgotten those around him. Coupled with his hesitant movements and halting speech, this habit proved him a rather dull companion. And on those occasions when he laughed, like when Prude's ram butted Luke in the arse, or when Frankie slipped on a wet plank and slid into his mother's well, it would burst from his throat in hysterical shrieks that would momentarily jolt Luke into wondering whether this favoured friend was laughing or crying. And while it was Frankie and his goading ways that caused Gid to grin the most, it was to Luke that Gid first looked, and Luke that he trailed behind like a lost pup.

"Yup, I thinks I might go to Africa in a couple of years," said Luke one evening, a week into Gid's arrival. He, Frankie and Gid were on the far end of the beach, out of earshot of the houses, weaving boughs through skinned alder poles they had laced around three young birch saplings, limbed and leaning teepee-like at the top, making for a good-sized bough-whiffen.

Frankie snorted, crawling inside the whiffen, "Yup, I dare say we'll go with you, b'ye. What you say, Gid?"

"If ye wants," said Luke. "Meet Bunga and the boys."

"Cripes," groaned Frankie, stretching out on the bough-padded floor, "he's going to meet a picture in his school book."

"Whoever's in the picture's not a picture, stupid," said Luke, tossing a handful of spruce needles in through the opening onto Frankie's face. "And it don't matter if his name's not Bunga; that's why you goes to places—to find out if Bunga's real, the same as we; or if he's no different than Daniel in the lions' den."

"Oops, he's getting smarter now," said Frankie, grimacing as he brushed the needles off his neck. "Cripes, b'ye, Daniel's a bloody Bible story, not a geography lesson."

"I knows Daniel's a Bible story," groaned Luke. "That's not what I means. Bunga's not a Bible story, but he don't seem much different from one. That's why I'm going to Africa—to make sure Bunga's not a Bible story. Hah, you'd be too scared to leave home, anyway." Holding out his hand for one of the boughs Gid was lodging on top of the whiffen, he asked, "What'd you think, Gid? You wanna come to Africa with me? Or you going to stay home with Fraidy Frankie?"

"I'd go right now if you wants," said Gid quickly, his breath scratching over dry, cracked lips.

Struck by this show of talk, Luke turned. As opposed to the indifference usually clouding Gid's eyes, there was a clarity to them at this moment and a fear that clung to Luke with the tenacity of a cat's claws skimming up the trunk of a tree. In time he would remember this moment, and think mostly to himself that surely it is in the light of the eyes that the soul shines forth, and that despite the previous three weeks of racing and playing about, it wasn't till this moment, staring through those two narrowly opened pathways, did he hold court with his friend Gid. But those were eyes reborn. For now, on this bright spring evening, he was struck once more with the intensity throbbing within the thinly built frame of this new friend, and as before, the little muscle to the corner of Gid's eye began flexing, striking Luke with the same crazy desire to lay a finger on the throbbing flesh till it stilled.

"Right," he said in a tone much rougher than he felt. Ducking inside the bough-whiffen, he elbowed Frankie to one side to make more room.

AS LUKE AND FRANKIE SAW TO GID, so too did the women reserve the fattest fish and leanest pieces of meat for the mister and his missus, whilst the men heartily constructed a shack to bide them over till something better could be had by winter. And there was quilt-making for bedding, and garments sewn over for the youngsters, and as festive an air as ever there was at Christmas, for it was a good Christian thing to harbour a family from a storm and make them a part of your home, and the outporters were as Christian as the angels traipsing across the pages of their Bibles. And their reward was the intrigue offered up by the O'Maras' strange new tongue and stories the mister told as he stood watching the men smear tar on the roof of his newly built shack, or sat roasting squids near a bonfire at night about the mist-peaked mountains in a far-off land, enshrouded by the yellow-gold rays of a sun that burned red each evening in the fiery skies of Killarney.

"Yeah, I knew we were in for it when I seen the white horses," O'Mara was often heard saying about the storm that brought him to Rocky Head, the yellow of a beach fire casting around him again the same hallowed glow as did Prude's lamplight the night he washed up upon their shores.

"The white horses?" the outporters would chorus in return. "Yeah, the white horses," O'Mara would reply, "that what looks to some as the curdling froth of the sea, but was made known to my father as white stallions belonging to the sea gypsies, making haste to cross the water before morn, and driving onto the rocks any poor boat happening to bear down on them."

"Sea gypsies," the outporters would murmur. "From Killarney."

"Aye, from Killarney," O'Mara would say over a nip of shine offered by the men as the women hushed the young-sters and inched closer to the fire to escape the distracting sounds of the sea washing upon shore behind them and the snipes calling overhead, "the land where your soul leaves your body at night and dances with the fairies upon the meadows, feeding upon the pollen. But then, there was no more pollen. And that's why we left our sweet Irish homeland, our house in the lee of the Sliabh Mish mountains—to find again the pollen for our souls to feed on, and keep us from becoming as barren as our dead piling up beneath the sod."

"Aye, to fale our bellies and save our sauls," mimicked Luke from up behind the stove one evening, peering out around at Joey, who was lying back on the daybed, idly playing a sea shanty on his accordion, and his father, who was sitting on the far end, mindlessly listening. The O'Maras had been living in their shack for near on two weeks now, and it was the rarest of evenings that Gid wasn't slouching up behind the stove besides Luke.

"You mind your mocking," warned Prude, her weight sending creaks of discomfort through the joists as she trod out of the pantry, a ball of wool in one hand and her knitting needles in her other.

"Aye, I'm not mockin', I'm talkin'," drawled Luke, "like the Irish, hey."

"Like the Irish!" scoffed Prude. "It'll be a fine day when you slips your tongue and mocks him to his face."

"Aye and wut a sheame that would be."

"It's more than shame you ought to be feeling," grumbled Prude, sinking into her wooden armchair. "I'd be wary of taking you around strangers, I'd be, for fear of what's going to come outta your mouth."

"Strangers don't bother me none."

"They should then, for there's more than one youngster that got lugged away by strangers."

"Yup."

"You forgets the one from Green Bay," Prude cried. "No bigger than yourself and lugged away by the foreign boats— never seen agin."

"Foreign boats," mimicked Luke. "You see any foreign boats around here, Joey?"

"Good thing you don't, else you'd be in her bowels by now, soaking in hot tar," snapped Prude.

"Hot tar!" Luke poked his head around the stove, staring at his mother, flabbergasted. "Now that's foolish, old woman; that's damn foolish. Did you hear that, Joey? Soaking in hot tar. Have ye ever heard of such a thing?"

"And worse, hey Father," muttered Joey.

"Yup—worse," said Herb, scarcely audible over the strains of Joey's accordion. Luke twisted his head around to him, questioningly. Mindful of Joey's closed eyes, his father tossed him a wink.

Luke grinned, winking back with a rush of affection for his kindly old father. "Come to think of it, I bet that'd feel real good—a soak in nice, hot, soft tar. What do you think, Father?" he asked, and groaned along with his father as Prude leaned forward in her chair, finger pointing.

"Be the cripes, I shouldn't bawl if you was," she warned, "for the paths around here won't be big enough to hold you soon, the way you're getting on these days."

"Aye, you'd bawl," said Luke. "Cripes, you bawls every time O'Mara tells his yarns—ye all bawls—even Joe."

"Young bugger," muttered Joey, shivering more deeply into his accordion and drowning out the rest of Luke's words, for indeed, Luke was right; each time O'Mara told his story, becoming more and more sentimental with each nip of shine, they all had a turn wiping a tear. As would O'Mara. Turning soulful eyes upon his saviours (as he had taken to calling them), he'd nod slowly at each and every rapt face as he finished of his storytelling by saying "And this is where the white horses brought me, amongst folks as blessed as the Saints of Ireland, and where strangers have become my neighbours, and neighbours have become my brothers." A tear would wet his eye, and the outporters would dab at a tear in their own, and Luke would shake his head in disgust at their snivelling, willing O'Mara instead to speak more of the white horses and their fairies, and the fiery skies of Killarney. For since the O'Maras' arrival, his taste for that which was foreign had grown more and more sweet, like the peppermint knobs his mother passed around at Christmastime, and left him craving for more long after the sweet had been sucked from his tongue.

"We'll leave for the Basin not tomorrow, not the next day, but next—Saturday, right when the sun's up," said Luke the next day, sitting cross-legged across from Gid and Frankie in the bough-whiffen. The strengthening May sun filtering through the boughs threw spots of light across the sceptical look clouding Frankie's shiny scrubbed face. Gid sat quietly, watching as Luke pulled a wad of rabbit wire out of his pocket. "We'll start making snares," he said, "pretending we's going rabbit catching—"

"Yup, that's what we'll do," said Frankie, pulling a pocket knife out of his pocket. "We'll walk partways up and set out a snare line in by the brooks. Uncle Nate said the rabbits is thousands in there."

Luke blinked, then burst out savagely, "You sliveen, Frankie, always trying to change things and making out you're not!"

"What's wrong with you, my son—I wants to go rabbit catching."

"Right, rabbit catching!" scoffed Luke. "I said we's going up the Basin, not rabbit catching. Never heard that part, did you?"

"Yup, well, I'd rather be snaring rabbits than getting skinned like one."

"See?" said Luke, turning to Gid, "like I told you—he's scared."

"I'm not scared—we'll get caught is all."

"How's we going to get caught?"

"It's too far."

"Too far. Two hours up, two hours down and two hours up there; six hours—no different than when we goes across the bay, trouting at Chouse."

"They'll see us on shore from their boats."

"See us? How's they going to see us if we hears the boat first and hides? Now you see here, Gid—you see how he does it? Every time you catches him, he comes up with something different."

"Oh right, my son."

"Oh right, my son; oh right, my son," mimicked Luke. "Fraidy Frankie. What about you Gid—you scared, too?"

"I'm not scared," Frankie cut in, a dirty look at Gid. "Why don't you just take Gid, then, you're so brave?"

"Because I'm asking you, too, scaredy Frankie."

"Right, my son."

"Well? You coming or not?"

"I said I was, didn't I?"

"Then you're going," said Luke. "And you?" he asked, turning to Gid.

Gid nodded.

"Then we's all going," declared Luke. He grinned towards Gid. "Bet you never went this far in Ireland by yourself, did you?" Gid shook his head, and it was then Luke saw the beginnings of a bruise purpling the skin beneath Gid's right eye. "How come you got your eye hurt?" he asked, peering closer.

Gid put a finger to his eye, as if having forgotten it had been bruised. "Da hit me," he said quietly.

Luke blinked. "Da hit you? How come your da hit you?"

Gid shrugged.

"You must know why he hit you," persisted Luke.

"I wouldn't listening."

"How come you wouldn't listening? Was you listening, then?"

"Huh?"

"Listening!" exclaimed Luke irritably. "Was you listening?"

Gid shrugged, both shoulders falling back, baring momentarily the reddish birthmark before hunching his shoulder and screening it again amidst hair and collars. Luke stared for a second, then grunted, "Lord, picking sense outta you is like picking knots outta wet rope. Let's get on with her," he ordered, tossing the coil of rabbit wire at Frankie. "We'll make a big pile so's they'll know we'll be gone for the day once we gets going. After you snips them, Frankie, me and Gid'll tie them."

They worked steadily for the next hour, the wind singing past the door of their shelter, and the water washing up over the shore a scant five feet from them. Yet, try as he might not to, Luke's eyes kept creeping back to Gid's and the bruised flesh thickening beneath. Too, there was a scratch across his throat that Luke hadn't noticed before. And was that not the same shirt he'd been wearing for near on two weeks now? And what of his hair? Wouldn't a good combing straighten some of the kinkiness?

Gid carried on, a studied look occupying his face as he slipped pieces of hay wire through knots, pulling nooses. Once, he looked up, catching Luke's scrutiny, and as was whenever anyone peered too keenly, his lids drooped, revealing the barest slivers of brown, causing Luke to question just how much of anything Gid ever really saw.

"Your da oughtna hit you like that," said Luke, startling Gid with the suddenness of his words. And ignoring the questioning look from Frankie, Luke uncrossed and crossed his legs against the prickling of the boughs beneath him, carrying on with his tailing as the sun began its descent beyond the hills.

That evening, eating supper, Luke looked to his father's gnarled hands as they wrapped themselves around a mug of hot tea. The worst he'd ever seen them do was rip apart a dead animal for supper, and even that was done in a careful, orderly manner, offering full respect, almost kindness, for the carcass about to be stewed and eaten. And when he saw O'Mara the next day, strolling along the bank, calling out liltingly to a couple of his youngsters, he looked at his small, almost womanish hands, gesturing fluidly as he spoke, and wondered how it was that such grace could bruise his boy's eye for not listening.

It was the following day—the day before they were to set off for the Basin—that the shine fell from the O'Maras like a cheap lacquer. Joey had taken himself to bed, and Prude was standing in her nightdress, unplaiting her braids before a mirror hung over the washstand, when the knock sounded.

"What's that—who's that?" she asked, her hand to her heart in fright. No one knocked on doors.

"Bide there," said Herb as Luke poked his head out from behind the stove.

"No, Herb, wait—go see through the window, first," said Prude, but Herb, was already crossing the kitchen, opening the door. Peering outside, he then quickly stepped back, opening it fully. The missus stood there, her dress torn, baring a bruised breast, her eye already swollen shut, a harsh burn marking the side of one cheek, and the blood spurting from her bottom lip, dripping thickly onto the crown of the babe she clutched to her bosom. She stared wildly at Prude, her breathing short and rasping over the night wind. Two others, trembling from the cold and whatever else that had touched them on this night, clung tightly to her dress tail, whimpering piteously in their naked feet and half-clad bodies.

"Glory be," cried Prude, one hand crossing her heart, the other reaching out to the missus. "What's happened, what's after happening, now?"

Joey came out of the room, pulling his suspenders up over his shoulders, his cap rolled down over his ears. "Shut the door, Father," he ordered as Herb stood out on the stoop, ushering the missus and her young ones inside.

"My oh my, I waited for this night," cried Prude, helping the missus into a chair. "Joey, get the brandy from the cupboard. Show, here, I gets a clean cloth. Luke, take the youngsters in the room and warm them in bed. Blessed be the Lord, what thing, what thing is this?"

Luke faltered, holding tightly to the warmth of the stove. He felt his mother's urgency in wanting the young ones warmed, as if comfort might ease the hurt this night had inflicted upon them. Too, it would free the missus to speak more openly without the younger ears listening, for it was already sensed by Herb, as he went back to jabbing at the fire with the poker, and Joey, as he kept his head down while passing the missus her cup of tea, and by Luke himself, as he stared with a sickening fascination at the exposed breast and the torn dress, that there was no wild beast prowling their doorstep on this night, no driven lunatic, no haunt exiled betwixt heaven and hell; but, rather it was a beast of their own nature that had caused the missus's dress to be torn. And it was this debacle of one turning against one's own and sending women and babies fleeing from their doorstep that caused Luke to cling further to the warmth of the stove. A chill rolled through his belly as he looked again at the sight of the missus's torn dress, like the time he had come upon Aunt Char's cat eating her newborn kitten, and then spewing it back up onto the door place, a bloodied, bone-sharded pulp.

But the stove offered poor shelter this night. The missus had no sooner taken a sip of the tea Joey had passed her, when the door was thrust open, and O'Mara staggered in, his eyes bloodshot with moonshine, and his face contorting furiously in the wildly flickering lamplight.

"Home!" he snarled, tilting drunkenly on his feet and pointing a finger towards the missus and her youngsters. And then, when Herb, still holding the poker, took a step towards him, O'Mara lunged. Both men went down with a crash, Herb on the flat of his back and O'Mara on top, hands clenched around Herb's throat. Joey, as if stunned by what was taking place before him, moved towards the men, slowly at first, as if through water, then with lightning speed as a cry from Prude cut through his benumbed senses. Grabbing hold of O'Mara's head from behind, he got him in a stranglehold, but O'Mara's liquor-skewed demonic strength was too strong for Joey's shocked, almost gentlemanly, defence, and Herb's eyes began to bulge, his face purpling from the pressure around his windpipe. Letting go of the stove, Luke stumbled forward, colliding against Prude, and for a second, they both held on to each other, watching in silenced horror this assault upon the one they beheld most dear. Never—not even a dog—had turned a baleful eye upon this gentlest of souls. And now, the sight of him as he flailed weakly at O'Mara, choked, strained whimpers escaping his gaping mouth, forged a sight that would forever brand Luke's eyes.

A hoarse cry from Prude freed Luke, and throwing himself onto the floor besides where the men sprawled, he grabbed hold of the fingers that were dug into his father's throat, and not able to budge them, bit into them as would a dog. Joey heaved harder on his stranglehold, cutting off O'Mara's breathing and forcing him to slacken his fingers from around Herb's throat. Shoving Luke to one side, O'Mara then grabbed hold of Joey's arm that was wrapped around his neck, and tried to throw him over. But with a sudden thrust of strength, Joey managed to topple O'Mara sideways off his father, then leaped to his feet, both fists curled. O'Mara staggered to his, and heaving drunkenly from one foot to another, stood wagging a finger at the lot of them.

"No one threatens me with a poker!" he roared. And then, jabbing at his missus and youngsters, "And no one comes betwixt me and mine. Now, get home!" Gathering the baby more tightly to her bosom, the missus rose from her chair and scurried out the door. The youngsters fled after her, and O'Mara, stumbling backwards, grabbing hold of the door jamb to steady himself, threw a murderous look at Joey, then lurched out behind them.

No sooner had the hinge snapped in place than Aunt Char, and others behind her, started running in through the door, having heard the commotion. "He's a lunatic!" Prude cried out as they all gathered around, helping Herb to a chair, and examining the bruises starting around his neck. "A bloody lunatic. The look on his face—ooh, he wore the devil's face, he did, bursting in through the door, and her sitting there with the baby in her arms, and the young ones too scared to open their mouths—the devil himself! And he was choking Herb, he was—with him pinned to the floor.

The black stranger—I seen it, I did; on the first day they come, I seen it, for what's a decent soul doing with his family away from his kin, unless he was drove out? And he was drove out of Harbour Deep too, mark my words, and I allows there's more than one place on this island he lived till he got drove out. My oh my, what are we going to do now, hey—we got the devil living amongst us, and his family needing us to keep 'em going? My oh my, I said it, I did; I said it."

Early the next morning whilst all tossed fretfully in sleep, Luke rose from behind the stove where he had finished the night and snuck out the door. The sea was without quiet this morn, its glassy stillness giving way to the ragged blue of a choppy winter's wind, and he was thankful; for there was a mar in the ordinariness of this morning, and he was not wanting to be alone with it. Wandering onto the beach, he kicked at a stranded jellyfish, then stood with the sole of his boot pressed hard against the purplish face.

"Luke!" It was Frankie. Appearing on the bank, he leapt down onto the beach, face scrubbed shiny and hair slicked back as though the sun was already shining and the bell donging for church. "What'd she look like, Luke, when she come to your door?"

"God, my son."

"She had her dress tore off?"

"Why didn't you come see for yourself, if you're that nosy."

"Mother caught me; geez, deafer than a haddock but she hears everything. Was her mouth bleeding?"

Luke jabbed at the jellyfish with the toe of his boot. "She was bleeding," he muttered, jabbing harder. The sound of a door slamming shut sounded from the O'Maras' shack and both boys swivelled their heads towards it. There was no one there. The heel of Luke's boot punctured the jellyfish and he jumped back, stomping it on the beach rock, freeing it from the dying flesh. "Let's go now," he said with a sudden urgency, turning to Frankie. "Up the Basin—let's go get our snares and leave now."

"Hope now, my son—we said Saturday."

"Who cares it's not Saturday."

"I already told Mother—"

"Tell Mother something else. I wants to go now—quick—before anybody gets up. Unless you's scared," he added as Frankie picked up jabbing at the ruptured fish. "Well—you coming or not?"

"What about Gid?"

Luke shrugged, his eyes fixed onto Frankie's. "Get some bread for later and we'll meet up behind the point," he said, tossing his head towards a curve in the shoreline a scant sixty or seventy feet up the beach. "Come on, my son, make up your mind," he all but shouted as Frankie stared back at him hesitantly, "because I'm going whether you comes or not—Fraidy Frankie."

"Right, my son. Better hope Mother's still in bed then, or she'll be up bawling out to Prude. Geez, my son," he yelled as Luke grabbed him by the shirt, his face a scant inch before his.

"You better bloody hope she don't, then," uttered Luke, his threat falling to the wayside as Frankie shoved him to one side. And muttering still, yet responding to the unspoken signal born out of familiarity, both boys turned, running towards their separate doorsteps. Letting himself inside, Luke quietly sliced off two pieces of bread, smeared them with molasses and, wrapping them in a piece of brown paper, shoved them into the baggy pockets of his cotton trousers. Scooping up the bundle of rabbit snares, he shoved them into his other pocket. Then he stoked up the fire to take the chill out of the house for when his mother got up, and snuck out the door.

He paused for a second, looking towards Frankie's house, then raced up the beach. Perhaps Frankie was already there. Rounding the turn, he dropped disappointedly onto his belly, staring back at Frankie's house, jiggling his foot impatiently. "Come on, Frankie," he ordered loudly, "come on." Pressing his chin onto folded arms, he stared unblinking at his cousin's house, willing him to appear around the corner. Aside from the thin trickle of smoke drifting out of Prude's chimney and the restless stirring of the wind and sea, the outport was quiet as death. Something moved near the O'Maras' shack and Luke squinted for a better look. "A rat, most likely," he muttered, then closed his eyes, allowing for the first time that morning the image of his father's face, purpling beneath O'Mara's hands and the half-bared breast of the missus as she sat bleeding and bruised with the baby in her arms and the smaller youngsters clinging to her dress tail.

A squawk went up from Aunt Char's rooster and Luke's eyes snapped open as Frankie came sprinting around the corner of his house, and alongside of him Gid, his father's .22 rifle bouncing awkwardly against his shoulder as he ran.

A flush darkened Luke's face as jumped to his feet, smashing his fist in his hands. "What the hell are you up to, Frankie?" he yelled savagely as both boys came panting around the turn.

"I found him, Luke, sleeping outside your place. He got his father's gun."

"You conner; you just wants to screw up our plan."

"No I never, my son—ask him—he was sleeping outside your place, by the hillside. He woke up as I was coming out the door. Ask him—go on, ask him."

"Ask him, go on, ask him," Luke mocked angrily, and was twisting on his heel, about to march off, when Gid spoke.

"You can carry it, Luke."

Luke turned then, looking first at the yellow-and-brown hair, more knotted than kinked, and the face, pale, splotchy, like day-old cream. He wanted to run, to shut himself inside his house and crawl up behind the stove and lay his head to its warmth. But his eyes found their way to Gid's and became rooted within the brown slivers, partially hidden beneath heavily padded lids. He knew now why they were thus, and as he stared, the sickening feeling came back again, the same as what he felt upon seeing the missus's bared breast and the half-eaten kitten.

"Come on, Luke," coaxed Frankie. "You can carry it like Gid says. She got a bullet in her—you can shoot it—"

"How come you got your father's gun?" asked Luke, his eyes still implanted in Gid's.

"Ma throw'd it out last night."

"After O'Mara went to sleep, right, Gid?" said Frankie. "And he won't wake up for hours, O'Mara won't—even pisses his pants whilst he sleeps. Gid just told me," added Frankie as Luke turned on him, suspiciously. "By then, we'll be back."

"We won't shoot it till we're on our way back—how's that, Fraidy Frankie?" Luke snapped. "And it's his gun, so he can carry it. Better hurry up, my son," he then growled at Gid, and falling back a step he beckoned for Frankie to start walking, and then Gid. Glancing back he noted the smoke spiralling darker and thicker from his mother's chimney.

She's up, he thought, and more fancied than heard her crying out, "No good comes from a night like this, mark my words, mark my words." He then hurried after Frankie, who was taking the lead, and Gid keeping up from behind, the butt of the gun bumping against his knees, and the barrel glinting fiercely in the first rays of the sun.

BOOK ONE

CLAIR

CROUCHING BESIDES HIM CLAIR WATCHED as her father, Job, pricked the tip of his knife through the hide of a young caribou, then drew it slow and easy across its belly, the hide singing back, and the blood spilling warm over his hands, staining scarlet onto the snow. Laying the knife to one side, he slid his hands inside the warmth of the carcass and pulled out the liver, pulsating purple in the afternoon sun, and threw it quivering upon a rock.

"Don't drop it," he cautioned as she lifted the flesh, still trembling in her hands, and ran to the cabin door, trailing a bloodied path behind her.

"Wait, Clair; wait right there," her mother called out and, snatching a frying pan off the stove, met her at the door.

That evening, at supper, Clair turned to her sister, Missy, a good six years younger than she, and said, "Mmm, tastes like berries."

"No it don't—do it, Mommy?" protested Missy.

"Yup; squashberries, partridgeberries, raspberries—all chomped together—like eating summer," said Clair.

"Mommeee—"

"Pass me the meat, Sare, I haves a bite of winter," said Job, long and gangly, his oversized features sombre as he pulled into the table besides them.

"Landsakes, you're going to drive her foolish, the both of you," said Sare over Missy's rising protests, the lamplight colouring their faces like apricots as she sat at the table with them. "Here, come sit besides me, my dolly. I cuts up your meat." She fussed as Missy knelt upon the bench besides her, her face haloed with curls. "Sure, no wonder she's always prattling about fairies when all she hears is her father and sister telling lies."

"Lies?" gasped Job, eyes popping. "I've never told a lie in me life."

"The banshees will take you," Missy warned, "and you won't even know it because it's winter and there's no bluebells to ring that they're coming."

"There, you've got her going agin," admonished Sare. "Eat your supper, child. You're smaller than the fairies tickling your dreams. You too, Clair, and never mind your father's foolishness."

Clair grinned as her father forked a piece of meat and pork scrunchions into his mouth and chomped down hard, his eyes widening with innocence as he turned them upon her. She didn't know it then, supping back on a strip of fried onion and kicking his leg underneath the table, that winter, as she knew it, would never come again. Thus it was with the same comfort as yesterday that she scrabbled out the door that evening, dragging a piece of canvas up over the hill behind her mother, and sliding back down with Missy, her mother and father taking the lead, their shrieks echoing through the crisp night air, and the snow stinging the red of their cheeks.

It was what they did most evenings here in Cat Arm, their winter isolate till the ice broke, and their father, finished with his yearly logging, took them back up the bay to their home in the Basin. "Enough," groaned Sare, part-ways up the hill for the third time, dragging Missy besides her.

"Come on, come on, me b'yes, downhill chance, down-hill chance," bellowed Job, walloping them on the behind much as he'd do with his old bone-wearied horse, Pearl, as he coaxed her, straining and snorting uphill, dragging a load of logs. "That's the way," he said heartily as they managed the top and fell to their knees. "Chance to catch your breath on the way down—come on," he ordered, directing them to fall in line behind him as he plopped down on his piece of canvas. And leading the way, he swooshed back down the hill, digging his heels into the snow so's to send it drifting back in their faces.

"Mercy," pleaded Sare as they landed in a pile at the bottom of the hill, and flopping back onto the snow, they stared up at the star-littered sky, listening as Job whistled shrilly up to the heavens, commanding the northern lights to dance.

"There they go, do you see them, Missy? See them, Clair? They're dancing. Smile big—show your teeth, for he's seeing us now, all lit up with his lights, and you wouldn't want him catching you scowling, else he'll think you're not proud of the little small corner he's given we."

"The foolishness of him," tutted Sare.

"Foolishness! You think this is foolishness!" exclaimed Job, expanding his arms as if to embrace the snow-blanketed evergreens, glowing white in the moonlight, and coating the hills that steepled two thousand feet above them. "Out of the garden with you, Mother—go on, out you go—that's right, on your belly," he roared, buffing the powdery fine snow off his mitts onto her upturned face. Squealing with laughter, she shielded her face behind her scarf and crawled towards the cabin.

After cocoa and crackers, and with her father puffing on his pipe by the stove, her mother gathered her and Missy around her lap as she always did before bedtime, and read to them from the Bible, showing them pictures of archangels standing over dreaming men, while thundering clouds gathered grey in the sky behind, and a tunnel of golden light led the pathway to heaven. The reading done, she bade them to her knees and listened as they said their prayers out loud. "Now I lay me down to sleep, I pray the Lord my soul to keep; God bless Mommy, Daddy, Sissy and all the starving children in the world, and the red men who died in the Congo." Then, with only the crackling of the fire and the creaking of the cabin beneath its snow-banked roof to hinder them, they recited the Lord's Prayer in silence.

Clair would speed through hers: "Ourfather whoartin-heaven hallowedbethyname thy kingdomcome, thywillbe-doneonearth asitisinheaven . . ." Once, she was awake when her father went to bed and she listened as he got to his knees and said his out loud: "Ooouurrr faatherr, wwhhhooo aarrrttt iinn hheavven" he whispered, so slow, so beautifully slow that each syllable was registered and words that she hadn't known were in there became isolated from their stream and took on meaning—or changed their meaning, like "lead-us-not-into-temptation" and not "leadusnot" as she'd always prayed. And all this time she had wondered why "snot" was in the Lord's Prayer.

It was when she lay in bed, muffled beneath a mountain of blankets, that she said her most important prayer, as if those spoken at her mother's knee were destined to go no further than the cabin door: "Dear God, please bring me a dolly, a real dolly." She would squeeze her eyes shut, bringing the darkness tight around her and feel her soul craving for the quiet of her mind as she concentrated on the curly yellow hair fluffing over the shoulders of the green lacy dress of her friend Joanie Reid's doll, and the marble blue eyes that slept when you tilted her back, and the little plastic hands that had crook marks across her fingers, just like her own. And when finally she drifted into sleep, she'd take with her the murmur of her father's voice as he'd assure her mother that all was well, and stoke up the fire in the stove for one last burst of warmth before he huddled besides the small wooden boxed radio, the volume low so's not to awaken them as he listened to the news about a place called Warsaw and a man called Winston Churchill. Then, the radio off and the battery removed so's it wouldn't ground out, he'd crawl into the bottom bunk with her mother, and tuck in for the night.

It was a week later, the night before they were to leave Cat Arm for their home up the Basin, that Missy had the dream. Awakening them all with her screams, she tumbled out of the top bunk onto the floor, frightening Clair that she'd broken her neck. Scrabbling to light the wick in the lamp, Job hurried back to where Sare sat on the floor, holding the now sobbing child in her arms.

"I had a dream, M-mommy!"

"Hush now child, and so you did," Sare soothed.

"The bluebells were ringing—"

"Ohh, now, it's only a dream—"

"And you were bleeding, Daddy, and there was spiders crawling out of your mouth."

"Precious Lord," Sare cried out.

"There now," said Job, bending besides Sare and stroking Missy's hair. "I'm not bleeding, see? And there's no spiders in the wintertime."

"You were lying in the m-mud, Daddy—and there was spiders."

"Shhh, how can something so young have such a dream?" Sare demanded almost angrily. "Go back to sleep, angel. Can Daddy get you some milk? Bank up the stove, Father, and heat her some milk with a bit of water. Do you want to climb in besides Clair again? There you go, back with your sister. This time get on the inside so's you don't fall out agin. Are you O.K., my angel?"

Clair wrapped her arms around Missy's trembling body as her mother passed her over and gently rocked her. By the time the milk was heated, Missy had gone back to sleep.

By morning Missy had forgotten the dream. Clair awakened to her shrieks as she ran tither beneath a clear, blue sky and a sun that shone loud on the white of the pan ice that dotted the face of the sea. Her mother was packing up the kitchen as her father loaded up the boat, and wolfing down the last of her pickled herring, Clair bolted out the door and up top of the hill, calling out goodbyes to the trees and the hills, and the stars that came out at night, and the northern lights now hiding from the sun. Her mother called out to her from the cabin doorway, ushering her onto the beach along with Missy and her father waiting besides the boat. When finally she was sitting on the short wooden bench spanning the belly of the boat, and her mother and Missy were fixed away behind her, her father leaned his shoulder to the bow, inching them off from shore, and leapt aboard a split second before the boat began bobbing out to sea.

Clair clenched her fists as the boat rocked beneath her father's weight, and stared down into the ever deepening water. Then the put-put of the piston blasted through the air, reverberating through the wooden bottom of the boat and up her legs and back, seizing her with excitement as they cut across the bumpy waters of the arm like a skidding rock. She looked back at her father, standing steady besides the motor, arms akimbo and his eyes squinting past the blinding white of the pan ice. He grinned down at her and she relaxed her grip, turning back to face the wind and the cool pinpricks of salty sea spray dotting her cheeks and stinging her eyes.

Leading out of the arm, they headed onto the heaving waters of the bay, a mile wide and forty miles long, the hills rising from grey rocky shores on either side, and hundreds more pieces of pan ice drifting towards them. Squinting as far ahead as the eye could see, Clair started to hum "aaaaaaaaaa," an effortless sound that started low in her throat, and broken by the vibrations of the boat, bleated through her mouth like the cry of a lamb. Big Island, a tree-covered gorge of rock in the middle of the bay, loomed before them, then fell to the wayside, bringing into sight Chouse Brook, whose name belies that river churning down the eastern hillside and spilling into the sea. Gold Cove appeared on the western side, thus named because of the goldenrod that ran rampant over its meadows in late summer, and then just ahead, Rocky Head, a small outport whose people were thought to be more than a little dull in thought, and whose youngsters were reported to be as brazen as a moulting goose.

It was the quiet that first struck Clair. The spew of youngsters that usually combed the beach, singing or whistling as they fished for tom cods off the stagehead, and fired rocks at all passing boats whilst ducking amongst the outhouses and woodpiles that lined the shore, were nowhere to be seen. And without the disruption of faces peering around their curtains the six or eight houses that lined the shore, their clapboard weathered a metallic grey and their windows glazed by the sun, looked to Clair like gladiator shields, this morning, protecting all therein from the lashings heaved upon them from the wind and sea. Only the winds were kind this day, and the sun an outside lure.

"Must be someone dead," Sare called over her shoulder to Job.

"Must be," said Job, steering them back towards the middle of the bay to get away from a clutter of pan ice floating towards them. But not before a stirring of shadow somewhere near shore caught Clair's attention, and scanning beneath a stagehead that stood out over the water on rickety legs, she glimpsed in its lee, and scarcely discernable from its shade, a fat, heavy-breasted old woman, her dress flapping around her stockinged legs from the wind, and her arms folded across her breasts. She turned from her scrutiny up towards the Basin, ducking farther back into the shade as their boat passed by, and if not for the white of her tightly wound braids showing through the dark, Clair might have questioned if, indeed, she had actually seen an old woman, or had witnessed, instead, the disembodied spirit of some long-lost fisher's wife.

The boat struck against a chunk of ice, startling Clair's attention away from shore and back to the rocking boat.

"Sit back down," Job warned as Sare half rose in fright.

"Lord, don't drown us, Father," Sare called out over the droning of the motor, "else there'll be no supper for you this night."

"There's a fate," her father chuckled, steering them clear of the ice and farther out to bay. "No rations for a dead man."

"I'm scared," sang out Missy.

"What's to be scared of, child?" said Sare. "See? There's Miller's Island, and just beyond is the Basin. Sure, you can almost see our house from here."

"Can I see the gravestone?" asked Missy.

"Soon, now; here, stand up a bit—my, she never grow'd an inch all winter—see over there?"

Steadying herself on her seat, Clair glanced towards Miller's Island with Missy, her eyes fastening on a granite headstone, a little ways in from the shore, and imprisoned between two full-grown fir trees.

"Tell me about the little girl, Clair," said Missy, leaning against her sister's back and wrapping her arms tightly around her neck.

"I keeps telling you."

"Tell me agin."

"A mommy and her baby girl, buried side by side," said Clair impatiently.

"In the same grave?"

"In the same grave."

"And the girl died first—because she was thirsty?"

"Because her body was parched from the fever."

"It was tiefie?"

"Typhoid."

"Her body couldn't hold water."

"She kept throwing it up. And her mother, too. And lots of others. And they brought them out to the island to bury them, so's to carry the sickness away from the land."

"Did she hear the bluebells ringing?"

"Ooh, Missy—"

"Did she?"

"Bluebells don't ring."

"Mommy, bluebells ring, don't they?" said Missy, leaving off her sister, and settling back besides her mother. "And supposing she'd slept sounder and never heard them ringing?"

"If there was such a thing, they still would've been ringing," said Sare.

"But would she still died if she never heard them?"

"I think so, child."

"But her daddy never heard them, right?"

"I guess they weren't ringing for him."

"And he'd just done burying his girl, when they brought him his wife?"

"And he dug up his girl, and laid her with her mommy. Then he buried them both."

"And then he planted the trees."

"One for each of them, and they joined together over the headstone, and grow'd as one."

"And now nobody can move the headstone, right?"

"Not even the sea."

"And the bestest blueberries grow there and nobody picks them—because of the roots."

"Back then they never, my dolly; for the faintest tinge of blue staining a lip would be sure to bring on a flogging."

"Tell me about the roots, Mommy."

Taking a deep breath, Sare launched into how the outporters believed it was the flesh of their dead that fertilized them berries, and their growth was a reminder to all hands left living that just as the roots of berry bushes nourishes the life above it, so, too, are people the walking roots of their own souls, and how it'll be their deeds that will judge the ripeness of their own resurrection someday. "No, my dolly, nobody picks them berries," said Sare, "not even today do anyone pick the blueberries on Miller's Island. Isn't that right, Father?"

"You shouldn't be telling her that stuff," said Job, steering them away from the island, the gruffness of his tone causing Clair to glance back at him.

Sare turned, equally as surprised. "What *stuff?*" she asked.

"It's what gives her bad dreams," said Job.

"Glory be, I always said you were squeamish—goodness, Job!" she cried out as he swerved the boat suddenly, knocking them to one side. Grabbing hold of her seat, Clair turned to face a four-foot mound of ice a hand's reach in front of her, the wind licking cold around its greeny blue contours and sweeping over her face with a chill that felt like fire. Swerving them still farther, her father let out an oath as the boat bumped against the big ice, rocking alarmingly before clearing it.

"It's all right, it's all right," he called out over Missy's screams and Sare's shrieks as he steered them closer to shore.

"Mercy, Job, didn't you see it?" cried Sare.

"It's what comes from talk of the dead," he answered, the gruffness back in his voice. "It's fine, my dolly, it's fine," he then said soothingly to Missy as she continued to sob. "You get a fright, Clair?"

Clair stared back at him, hands rigid onto her seat, shaking her head.

"That's the girl," he said softly. And ignoring Sare's eyes sharply upon him, he nodded to Clair, saying, "It's the strongest amongst us that hides their fears the bestest, my dolly; now leave off your talk, Missy, and watch for our house. See, there it is," and they all turned with relief towards the Basin lying straight ahead, with its painted clapboard houses dotting the side of the hill that encircled the bottom of the bay, and their house, one of the farthest upon the hill and as white as snow, looking down upon them. But it was the steamer that stole their attention—the sixty-foot passenger and cargo ship that steamed up the bay once every two weeks after the ice had thawed and was now docked by the company wharf. Usually the wharf was swarming with the outporters greeting friends and acquaintances on board, and exchanging news and items of interest as they waited for their parcels and newspapers to be unloaded and passed amongst them. Today, the wharf was empty. And aside from the gulls circling and shrieking overhead, the outport appeared more quiet than Rocky Head.

"It feels like Sunday," said Sare a few minutes later as they drew nearer and Job cut the motor, adding to the stillness of the air. "We haven't got the days mixed up, have we?"

"The steamer don't put ashore on Sundays," said Job. "Must be somebody dead. Bide now," he cautioned as Sare half rose, her hand to her heart, and straddling past her, he guided them alongside the wharf. A shadow blocked the sun. Looking up, Clair shrank back as an apparition lifted from her history book, stared down at them—his beret perched to the side and his green, baggy-pocketed coat opened to the wind.

"Good day, sir," said her father, tossing the painter up to the soldier as if he weren't at all perturbed by his presence and the Basin as quiet as death.

"What's he doing here?" asked Sare, a tremor in her voice as the soldier caught the rope, looping it around the grunt.

"I expect we'll find out," said Job, beckoning Clair forward. Taking hold of her waist, he helped her find her footing onto the ladder, then gently boosted her upwards. The soldier held down a hand and she hesitated, looking into a pair of eyes that crinkled almost as deep as her father's. Then as her mother clambered onto the ladder behind her, she grabbed hold of the hand and scrabbled quickly onto the wharf.

"Bad planning, perhaps?" said the soldier as her father climbed up on the wharf behind her mother and Missy. Her father looked puzzled for a minute, glancing towards the store that sat half on the wharf, half on land with its blinds drawn, and the fishers' boats hauled up onshore, signalling they'd already pulled their nets and were home for the day. "They've all gone hunting," said the soldier. "Overnight—or longer—so it seems," he added, beckoning towards the store and Willamena, the merchant Saul's daughter, peering through a corner of the blinds.

"Is this your first port of call?" asked Job.

"The last," said the soldier. "They're inside, taking dinner." Clair saw then, others dressed in garnseys and lumberjackets like her father's, darkening some of the port-holes and doorways as they passed by or glanced out through, none of whom she recognized.

"Job," said her mother, taking hold of his arm, her voice thick with worry, but he was looking past her, along with the soldier, towards a short, stocky man with a brown worsted cap pulled low over his ears and with a pack on his back, appearing around the corner of the store and walking hesitantly towards them.

"Your name, sir?" asked the soldier, his voice suddenly brusque as the fellow approached, and laid his bag at his feet.

"Joey," said he, softly.

"Last name?"

"Osmond."

"Where you from, Osmond?"

"Rocky Head, sir."

"Any more behind you?"

Joey shook his head, darting an apprehensive look at the steamer. As the soldier pointed to the foot of the gangway, ordering "Go on board, sir," Clair saw that he lifted his pack and walked towards it with a steady pace.

Missy started whimpering about her feet getting cold, and her mother tugged on her father's arm, coaxing him to come along now, and let's go home. And for sure he was about to do just that, but Clair saw, as he wrapped his arm around her mother's shoulders, holding her tight to his side, that quiet, lingering nod between her father and the soldier, as if they already were comrades in arms.

"There'll be a cheque coming to them every month," said the soldier.

"What cheque—" asked her mother.

"Take your sister's hand, Clair," cut in her father. And tightening his arm around Sare, he bundled her towards the road leading up from the wharf.

"Wait, Job, you're not thinking—"

"We leave in twenty minutes," the soldier called.

"No, Job, you're not going—"

"Shh, let's go home," said Job, hurrying her forward as her voice began to rise. "Hurry, Clair; follow your sister, Missy."

Clair started after her father, tugging on Missy's hand; but her legs felt stiff, numbed. The store door opened, revealing Willamena's sharp, pointy features. "The men's in on Faltner's Flat—by old Rushie Pond road," she hissed.

Job's step slowed, and Clair, despite her aversion to this old school buddy, turned to her as a drowning fisher to a buoy.

"Then, that's where you'll go!" Sare whispered fiercely. "You'll follow after everyone else."

Turning to neither of them, Job picked up his step again, leading Sare onward. And Willamena, her narrow eyes falling onto Clair, took on a look of hauteur and snapped shut the store door. Tightening her hold on Missy's hand, Clair hurried after her father. Aside from two mutts circling and sniffing each other's hind legs, the road leading through the outport was deserted. Yet, shadows shifted behind curtain corners as they walked by, and the occasional house-wife followed out onto their stoop, calling out to Job in hushed tones. But he paid no heed. Marching straight ahead, he half-carried, half-led the protesting Sare towards home, looking over his shoulder every so often to check on Clair and Missy, and the steamer tied up to the wharf. Missy began to whimper, and Clair, not wanting to disrupt her mother's pleadings, slowed her step to allow an easier pace. When finally they entered the garden gate, and untied the storm door, they bustled inside the house, and Sare gave way to straight-out wailing.

"You're not going; tell me you're not going!"

"Shh, you'll frighten the girls," he said, reaching for her.

"You can't go! You won't!" she shrieked, tearing away from him. "In the name of God, you won't leave this house and board no boat for some God-forsaken war."

"I won't hide, Sare," he spoke quietly. "It's a man's duty to his country, and I won't hide like a coward."

"You will, yes you will hide! And you won't be no coward, neither. Who says he's a coward that fends for his own family? Who'll fend for me while you're gone—and the girls?"

"Sim'll see to things."

"*Sim!*" Sare sneered.

"Please, Sare . . ."

"No! No—don't you dare beg me to leave you be." Clair clutched Missy's hand as her mother suddenly turned eyes clouded with fear onto them. Grabbing him by the arm, she dragged him towards them, crying with renewed vigour. "Look! Look at them! They're your girls! You said you'd never leave them, Job; you said you'd never leave them."

He closed his eyes as if the sight of Clair and Missy might prove too much. "It's not forever," he half whispered.

"You can't say that!" cried Sare.

"Yes, I can."

"No! No, you can't! You won't leave me! You'll be killed. Please—Job—"

Scooping her off her feet, Job carried her into the stairwell. "You'll watch Missy?" he said over his shoulder to Clair.

"Is Daddy leaving?"cried Missy as her father carried her mother up the stairs. Taking her hand, Clair led her to the divan besides the stove and they sat down, side by side, leaning each against the other.

"Is he, Clair—is he leaving?"

"I don't know," murmured Clair, but she knew, knew from the way he had tossed the painter up to the soldier that he was leaving, that his mind had already been set from before he'd even met the soldier—from somewhere back in the cabin when he'd sit in the dark, smoking his pipe and listening to his country's call. It was mixed up in there somehow, the mother country was, with the Lord's Prayer—

Our Father, our kingdom—no different than if God had descended the yellow pathway from heaven and given the call himself.

Scrunching back in the chair, she rocked with Missy, listening to her mother's muted cries floating back down over the stairs, and her father's soothing murmurs as he tried to quiet her. The cries turned to hushed sobs, then moans, and soon her father was hurrying back down the stairs. Crouching before them, he laid a hand on each of their shoulders, shaking them gently.

"I'll be back," he promised, his eyes milky chocolate in the sun slanting through the kitchen curtains. Pulling Clair into his arms, he held her tight. "You'll take care of your little sister," he said into her hair. "Make sure you does your homework every night; you're going to be a grand teacher someday. And practise your reading, because for sure you'll beat out Willamena in the reading contest again this year—and that'll be something to write to your old daddy about: showing up the merchant's daughter. And go get Uncle Sim to come help your mother. And don't ever forget—" he leaned back, his eyes more soft than she had ever seen them "—I'll be back. No matter how long it takes, I'll be back."

"But, where're you going, Daddy?" asked Missy, her voice still on a whine.

"To help other fathers fight in a war," he said, cupping her chin and dropping little kisses on her nose. "You be a good girl and listen to Mommy and Clair, and when I comes back, I'll be bringing you presents."

"Can I come, too?"

"No, not this time. Remember your prayers—and say an extra one for Daddy."

"But I wants to come."

"Shh, now, you'll make Mommy cry agin, and that's not a good girl, is it, Clair? I got to go now. You'll see to her, Clair?"

Clair nodded, not knowing what she was nodding to, knowing only that there were no daddies in wars, only soldiers who shot and got shot, and whose bodies got blasted by bombs that spilled their guts upon the ground no different from that of a slaughtered moose.

"Hey!" He cupped her chin as he had Missy's and his breath, like spiced tobacco, grazed her face, all warm and sweet. "Everything's going to be fine. I'll be going to England. There's no fighting there, and perhaps there never will be—if they sees how many of us are willing to fight for her shores. And I'll be right by the sea all the time, looking over here towards you and Missy. All right, my dolly? So you better keep watching for them northern lights, because when you sees them dancing, you knows it's me standing on the other shore, whistling. All right, my dolly?"

She nodded, her throat too tight to speak.

"And mind what your mother says," he added more quietly, his eyes moving slowly, tenderly, over her face as though memorizing its every curve. "We're the walking roots of our souls, that's what we are, and we got to nourish what's underneath. You remember that, no matter what happens, a man's got to do what his heart tells him—else what's underneath will wither and rot like last year's spuds. And of what good is resurrection then? You understand me, Clair?" Her mouth quivered and he pulled her against him, his chin rough on her forehead as he rained kisses all over it. Then, he was on his feet and lunging towards the door, his muffled sobs hoarse in his throat.

"Daddy!" Clair ran after him and stood on the roadside, watching, as he marched down the road towards where the boat was waiting at the wharf. The wind brought his tobacco smell back to her and she curled her toes in her boots, clenching her fists by her side, wanting to run after him, but caution overtook her and she turned instead to the windows all around her. There were no faces, but she felt them watching; watching after him as he walked to war whilst they hid behind their wives, and the tuckamores in on the downs. She felt a burst of pride then, as she watched after his wide, strong back. And it looked as if he must have felt her onward nudge, for his step picked up and he started swinging his arms as if he were already a soldier, a daddy soldier who could never hurt anybody, and who could never be hurt, for after all, hadn't he prayed the Lord's Prayer every night, with all the words slowly spoken and their meanings soft and clear? Squeezing her eyes shut, she lifted her face towards heaven and promised never again to pray for a doll with fluffy yellow hair and blue marble eyes that slept upon tilting, only for all wars to end.

Her mother's wailing sounded through the doorway, and taking a last, longing look after her father's back, she ran back through the gate and inside the house. Sare was running down over the stairs, her cries taking up with Missy's.

"Your father's gone, child," she cried, running to the window. "He's gone, he's gone, damn him, damn him!" and collapsing onto a chair, she dropped her head into her hands and sobbed freely.

Clair struggled to move, to run to her mother, but her feet were rooted, her eyes fixed on her younger sister, crumpled onto the floor, her fluffy yellow hair sticking to the wetness of her tears, and her blue marble eyes half closed as she tilted back her head, sobbing, "Mommy, Mommy, Mommy!"

"Hush, hush, you dreamed it, Missy," cried Sare. "And now he's gone, he's gone."

"Clair," wailed Missy, holding up her arms, and Clair held back from the little hands reaching up for her, almost afraid to look for the crook marks across the fingers that would bind Missy to the doll in her prayers. And that night, the first since Missy had been weaned from her mother's breast and placed in her older sister's bed, Clair lay apart. And later, when Missy started thrashing and moaning in her sleep, Claire awakened and refused at first to touch her sister. Missy's moaning grew louder, and chiding herself for being foolish, and not wanting to awaken her mother, Clair finally reached over, jiggling her awake.

"The little girl, the little girl," cried Missy.

"Shh, you'll wake Mommy."

"She's not dead, Clair. The banshees took her—"

"Hush, now, Missy—"

"No, I s-saw them," sobbed Missy. "It was a changeling they buried. The banshees put it there. And the little girl's not dead. She's living with the fairies, Clair. She never h-heard the bluebells ringing."

"That's nice, Missy, that's nice. The fairies made everything nice. Shh, now, you'll wake Mommy."

"Is Daddy coming back?"

"Shh, he's coming back. Now, go to sleep." And minding her father's words, she laid her cheek against the damp of Missy's, rocking her.

CHAPTER TWO

ANY SIGN OF WILLAMENA?" called out the merchant Saul one sunless September afternoon as Clair qualled to the lee of the store, watching the great belly of the sea rise and fall with the wind.

She crouched lower now, enclosed from view behind a stack of lobster pots, idly listening as the merchant grumbled noisily about his daughter's laziness to a couple of loggers just tying up by the wharf. It was how she mostly liked it since her father left the past five months; qualled away by herself, somewheres, so's not to hear their gossiping tongues. Indeed, those first few weeks it was as if he were being waked the way everyone crowded into her mother's kitchen, bestowing upon her every move the same subdued excitement one rendered the freshly bereaved. No doubt her best friends, Phoebe and Joanie, and the others hers and Missy's age were quick to move on; the lure of the sunfish that ran aground on the beach or the bright pink of Joanie's new skipping rope quickly taking over from any intrigue found in her mother's kitchen. Not so were the elders as quick to stray. And their talk was unkind—as was warranting any man confronting self-sustaining, brave-hearted mortals with the limitations of their own courage. And no fear of boredom, for with each new nuance that got spun on the spot, the grey shrouding Job's enlistment had taken on the vibrance of Joseph's coat, with each tuck of the sleeve or turn of the collar reflecting the whims of its fashion-conscious narrators.

Clair startled—her attention snagged by Saul's latest recount of the war.

"Twenty miles wide across the sky they said the bombers was stretched out, and forty miles long, sir," he called out. "There's not much of London left standing after that."

London. Bombed. Clair whipped her head around the lobster pots, staring out at the merchant. Her father's letters had assured them that England would never be attacked, that there were too many of them guarding her shores for such a thing to happen, and that the most he and Joey had to do was dig holes, march and stand guard, and that he'd soon be coming home, and wasn't it good that he'd signed on as a soldier after all and was able to stand besides Joey and the others and stave off attack on the mother's shores?

"Be the lamplighting geezes, I wouldn't want to be sitting under that cloud, buddy, when they was droning overhead, dropping bombs," said Johnnie Regular, his tone thinner than his wiry frame as he hunkered down by a grunt, pulling out his tobacco pouch. "Another telegram come, did it?"

"Not yet today—I managed to get a bit of radio this morning," said Saul, burying his hands inside his new seal-skin coat as he strolled from his stoop towards the loggers, who were all three sitting or squat by the edge of the wharf now, rolling tobacco. "She come as a surprise to me. From what they been saying, I figured the only fighting our boys would be doing would be over a poker game."

"Yup, sir, I wonders about Job," said Johnnie. "I allows

we'll have something on our hands if anything happens to him—Sim says Sare's too sick to get out of bed most days."

"Fool, he is, to go over there," blustered the second logger, Ralph Blanchard, his thickened features raw with the wind. "Hard enough to stay alive on our own shores with things the way they is—let alone going the frig over to foreign shores and offering yourself up to be shot at."

"Yup, it's a strange thing, war," drawled Crowman, called so for his thatch of black hair and hawk-like nose, and known for his moseying over thought. "Some says we're all at war, that we signs up every time we goes in over the barrens and gets caught in a snowstorm with nary a tree or the sun to guide us out—or out on the water getting squat by pan ice in a fog. They're getting enough meat, are they?"

"Sim's seeing to that," said Johnnie. "Leastways he is for now. Willamena said she was talking to him the other day; sounds like he got a lot on his plate with taking care of Sare and his mother crippled up, and the both of them calling on him night and day."

"That's not true," Clair protested silently, but held her tongue, listening as Saul commended the loggers for having the sense to stay at home.

"For ye're good family men and here's where ye ought to be—taking care of your own—not over there, getting killed in somebody else's dirty business. And it's not just we that opt to stay home in this one, for none of the Americans went, either. Let the ones who wants to fight go ahead and fight, I say, and leave them that don't out of it because them ones over the seas, they're forever meddling and fighting with their own kind, and you'd think after how tired and broke they all is with the big one just over, they'd be sick of it by now; yes, sir, sick of it—how much blood can the soil hold? There she is, then," he added abruptly, the grey of his eyes as barren as the pelt on his back as he caught sight of Willamena, heavily bundled against the driving cold, striding down over the hill towards them. "I'll be off. Good day to ye, b'yes, and thank the Lord for the warmth of your fires when ye goes home this evening."

Clair half rose, wanting to leap from her roosting place and follow after him, but despite the quivering in her stomach to get up over the hill and into the post office and hear further news of London, she was willing the extra five-minute wait so's to avoid Willamena's tart tongue—even more acidic now since the reading competition.

"Yup, for sure now it's we he thinks about," Johnnie Regular was muttering, raising a brow after Saul's back as he walked away. "Right sick with worry, he is; I allows he'll knock a month's grub off our credit after this, what you say, Crow?"

"A man's got to pay for his fancy furs somehow, I suppose," said Crowman. "Hey, Ralph, boy. And I dare say you'll be looking pretty enough in furs too, you gets made foreman someday."

"Be the frig, I'm a thief too now, is I?" said Ralph.

"Yup, that's what you'll be when you gets made foreman, buddy—a thief," quipped Johnnie. "I says you're looking right good, my son—first a coward, now a thief."

"Coward!" muttered Ralph, flicking his butt over the wharf.

"Heh, that's what the soldier was calling ye, then," said Willamena, her shrewish eyes darting to the men as she bustled up to the store door. "Cowards, hiding behind the women's skirts."

"Be geezes, I'd like to been there, brother, when he was calling me a coward," blustered Ralph. "I would've told him a thing or two about cowards. As far as I'm concerned all them that puts on a uniform is the cowards—too frigging lazy to get off their arse and go in the woods and hunt a bit of meat for their wife and youngsters—they leaves it to we to do it for them. Well, they can call me what they wants, brother, but as far as I'm concerned, Job Gale's the frigging coward, deserting them that needs him the most."

One of the lobster pots crashed to one side as Clair rose and walked straight-backed across the wharf. "What knows ye about courage," she bit back from saucing the fishers, "when ye've never left the soil ye were born on?" She wanted to hiss at Willamena, "Strife-breeder! Always spreading yarns."

But pride stilled her tongue. And aside from a tsk-tsk sounding from Willamena, silence followed her wake. It was as her mother said—they were the roots of their own souls, and the likes of Willamena and Ralph would strangle themselves some day with their twisting, misshapen tongues. Time would show who was the coward. And what of this uncle who would blaspheme the soil of his brother's stoop for their worthless praise? Hadn't she heard her father call him a bastard once when she oughtn't to have been listening?

Coming upon the post office, she ran up to the door, poking her head inside. Alma, the postmistress, was sitting with her back to her, raising her hand for silence as she rapidly jotted down the message tapping its way through the telegraph. Spotting the great big book that looked like a Bible, lying opened on top of the counter, Clair anxiously crept forward, reading from the position of the last person who had read the entry. It was today's—about the bombing:

The feeling and reaction of the ordinary citizen is a mixture of fortitude, valour, anger, and some fear. Casualties are heavy, but Londoners are carrying on despite the hell being thrown upon them. Children are being evacuated, and thousands are cleaning up the city, putting out fires and continuing business as usual and showing they are able to stand proud. But concerns rise as the German war machine turns its attention to the rest of Europe . . .

"Here, you knows your mother don't want you reading this stuff," said Alma as the tapping stopped. Shoving herself heavily to her feet, she pulled the book to one side, staring disapprovingly at Clair. "And tell her there's no mail today. Go on now," she ordered kindly, her glasses slipping down the broad bridge of her nose as she reached for her nib pen and ink bottle.

Clair trailed towards the door, staring back over her shoulder as Alma sat herself back down, dipping her pen into the ink and copying the message into the big book. Another warning look from Alma over the rim of her glasses, and Clair pushed out through the door, trailing the rest of the ways up the road. Just as well her mother didn't allow for the news, she thought, for despite the anger quickening her step earlier, the closer she got to home, the heavier became a weight that had been slowly settling itself around her shoulders. There was a bitter truth to Willamena's words. Since the day her father left, her mother had given over to a sullenness that was becoming more and more so each day she awakened and Job wasn't lying besides her. It felt to Clair as if the sun had been sucked out of her world, leaving only the dark—a cold, miserable dark that covered her mother's tears every night and bared her swollen face each morning upon arising. And even Missy, who'd already retrieved her step since their father's leaving, and who was wearing once again the sun's rays within her sheen of curls, appeared dulled to Clair, shadowed by the want of a prayer she feared God had already tallied.

Her mother was sitting in the kitchen window as Clair neared their gate, staring out over the muddied flower bed beneath the kitchen window where Job had planted a bed of sweet williams, already in bloom, the day they had moved into the house. "It's your morning gift, Mother," he had said that morning as they lingered over breakfast, laughing and chatting over molassy bread and tea, and savouring the fruity sweet scent of the blooms that wafted through the window.

"And kind you are to be always thinking of me, Father," her mother gaily replied.

"Aye, it's to keep you thinking of flowers when you're scrubbing me dirty socks and soaking the skid marks off me underwear," replied he.

"As if scent could do away with such a thing," she scoffed. "Now, seal blubber might do the trick."

"Well, well," sighed Job, "and here I was thinking how nice the flowers smelled, when it's a seal's carcass I ought to have dragged to your window."

"For goodness' sake, Job, is the stink of your dirty socks worse to you than the stink of a rotting seal's carcass?"

"No, my love, 'tis neither stink that bothers me, because I been smelling them both all me life. It's the other man's stink that smells the worse, and it's your fine little nose that got to labour over mine."

"Then, I thank you for the flowers, sire, but, if I'd known they were to cover the smell of your poop, I dare say I wouldn't have felt so proud watching you plant them."

"Now, now, Mother, it's the thought that counts," Job sang out over the burst of giggles from Clair and Missy over their mother's bad word. "I dare say I could've gone out and planted you piss-a-beds for a stronger smell if I'd thought on it," he added with a wink as Missy and Clair burst into more giggles, leaving their poor mother shaking her head and pointing a scolding finger as she tut-tutted warningly about how he carries on so with his talk of pee and stink, when it was flowers they'd started out talking about, and the shame of him with his girls listening.

Wanting now a sense of her old mother, Clair skipped up to the window, smiling. Sare smiled wanly down at her, and Clair was about to push in through the door when her uncle Sim, as thin as he was tall, and stooped, as if by burden, appeared around the corner of the house, the black of his brow deepening further the air of depression that pulled down the corners of his mouth, rendering a dull look in his small, sunken eyes.

"You was suppose to fill the woodbox," he snapped.

Clair pulled back, her mouth contorting. "I always do's it, don't I?" she snipped. "And there's no need for you to be coming by here any more, either—" The rest of her words were silenced by a rap on the kitchen window and her mother's footsteps sounding across the kitchen floor.

"He was talking about us," she muttered, brushing inside as her mother opened the door. Turning, she stood staring accusingly at the uncle over her master's shoulder.

"I swear, she's always forgetting things," said Sare apologetically. "I suppose Grandmother's doing fine?"

Clair grimaced as the uncle's nostrils suddenly twitched, catching the smell of hot bread. And like the sly old dog ambling towards a nap till a whiff of something from the pot stops him in his tracks, his ears perked and his shoulders slunk as Clair imagined his plotting whether it best to hang his head and beg, or to lunge upon his hind legs and fill his chops afore anyone had a chance to stop him.

"She's not been good," he mumbled, shaking his head discouragingly. "Her hands is too crippled to even do a bit of baking."

"Dear soul. Tell her I'll send Clair up with a pot of bread after it's baked. I'd come myself, but—" Sare broke off, gazing down over the hill towards the wharf "—since Job left, I guess I haven't been going out much."

Sim nodded, his stoop becoming heavier as old Mrs. Rice, swaddled in layers of skirts and shawls, looked their way. Stifling a snort, Clair stormed into the kitchen.

"Ohh, I can't stand him," she burst out after her mother had made her goodbyes and was closing the door.

"You listen here, my lady—"

"He's so *sleiveen*, Mommy!" she all but shouted. "And he's talking about us; he's telling everyone he's doing our work, when it's me bringing in all the wood and chopping splits."

"It matters naught to me," said Sara wearily. "Let him have his say if that's what pays him. For as long as your father's gone, we needs him, and I won't stand for you saucing back."

"I can bring in the wood and water. We don't need him."

"And cut the logs, too? Mercy, Clair, it's more than bringing in the wood and water and chopping a few splits that needs to be done. There's meat to be had, and God knows what'll happen to this roof after another winter."

"We can get somebody else to do it."

"I won't argue it," cried Sare, pressing her fingers against her temples. Clair quieted, struck by her mother's pallor, made more so by the curls tumbling around her face without their daily constraints of combs and clips. "Can we not fight?" she pleaded tiredly to her daughter. "I swear I haven't got the will these days to keep a junk of wood in the stove—and now you've got me worrying about what people are saying."

"Ohh, they're not saying nothing," said Clair, her tone becoming contrite. "You want me to make you some tea—I'll make you some tea."

"If you wants," said Sare. Sinking tiredly onto her chair, she turned to the window.

"Where's Missy?" asked Clair, taking two cups down from the cupboard.

"Up to the grandmother's, I expect."

"She's going up there a lot, isn't she?"

"Since her father left, she has. I suppose it's a good thing—the grandmother don't get much company, poor old soul." Sare turned to her. "There's a bit of stew left in the pot—why don't you have some?"

"You want some, too?"

"No. Just the tea."

"I'm not hungry, either."

Laying a cup before her mother, Clair sat aside her, wrapping her hands around her cup, absorbing its heat as she watched her mother do the same. "Soon be summer," she said. "You want to plant more flowers?"

"Your father was the gardener."

"It was you that was raised on a farm."

"So I was," said Sare, turning back to the muddied patch outside her window. "But it weren't planting that I learned."

"Tell me agin—about when you met Daddy," Clair begged, knowing how her mother liked to talk about such things.

"Oh, Clair," sighed Sare, her eyes that usually danced with merriment when flooded with such memories now dulled, emptied, beggared by grief.

"You were a girl, not much bigger than me," prodded Clair.

"Just a girl."

"And he was a dear, handsome man," whispered Clair with an exaggeration that had often merited her kisses on the nose in the past, or a playful pinch on the cheek as her mother snuggled into such beloved memories with a warble in her voice, and her father sat across the table from her, interrupting her story with saucy grins and winks. A piteous look befell her mother's face now as she allowed her eyes to fall onto his chair, emptied and pushed tight against the table since he had gone, his canvas bag stuffed with dirty clothes she hadn't had a chance to wash. Yet, it was the scent of him she wanted, and despite her reluctance to graze such tender fodder, she pried her tongue from the roof of her mouth.

"Yes, he was—" she began.

"He took you from your house, he did."

"Yes—"

"And it was a hard house."

"Oh, Clair—"

"And you won't ever say why."

"I said so to him."

"Was it haunted and that's why it was hard?"

"Lord, you do go on."

"But why won't you ever say?"

"It's because *they* were hard," cried Sare, her eyes clinging to Job's chair, her mouth trembling as her words spilled forth. And unwilling to quell an insurrection that so aided her now in her misery, she stared hard at her girl. "The backs of their hands was how they taught us," she cried bitterly, "and the sharpness of their tongues. They near killed us they did, with their hands and their tongues. And when they weren't swiping at us with those, they lashed out with their belts and their buckles and—and whatever else lay close by." She grimaced, her face turning ghastly, but her grief, finding vengeance in past laid injustices, lent fuel to her outpouring, and her words fell more wildly. "They were all bigger, they were, and wont to strike out at whatever didn't strike back. And I was the smallest. A split-arse girl, they called me. And there was always reason to strike—the cold, or the soggy wood, or the storm door that slammed with every gust of wind, or every damn bird that shat on the house as it flew overhead. Ooh!" She stopped, clutching her fist to her mouth, her eyes widening in shock. "Blessed child, now look what you've done. And I promised Father I'd never be hurt by their lashings, again."

And Clair, aghast at her mother's revelations, recoiled as she tried to imagine the horror of a daddy hitting his little girl and calling her vile names, and that little girl being her mother, with soft curls dancing all around her face, and her eyes wet from tears as she spoke of such things—as they must have been then, when they were striking her. She understood then, why it was that her father always rose from his chair and circled behind her mother as she come to that part in her story, twirling a finger through one of her curls as she skipped past those horrible deeds and spoke happily of him, instead—of when he had found her on the beach, her knee bleeding from where she had slipped and scraped it on a wet slab, and her cheek bruised from the morning's beating.

Pulling her chair closer to her mother's, Clair patted her hand, smiling hard, knowing that her own brown curly hair was much like her mother's, and her eyes, as her father often said, were the same as the ones in her mother's mirror. What comfort her mother could draw from her daughter's likeness at this moment, she didn't know, only that her father once said it was an ointment to gaze upon the slight crook in her and Missy's noses and to know that it had been borne from his. "He came in a horse cart, didn't he?" she whispered.

Sare nodded, choking back a sob. "To buy strawberries for his mother. I was just fourteen. He spoke like the poet when he squatted besides me."

"What words did he say?" asked Clair.

"Silly words—as he always does when he's feeling that way."

"The tender misery of crushed girlhood," quoted Clair, her eyes soft upon her mother's.

"Goodness," said Sare, coming back to her daughter with some surprise. "I hadn't thought I'd said that."

"It's what he whispers when you leaves them out," said Clair.

"Is there nothing you miss?" Sare exclaimed incredulously. Pushing her untouched mug of tea to one side, she rose, her hand to her forehead. "Take up some stew for you and Missy. I'm going in on the daybed for a bit. It's the devil of a headache I've got. And mind you never tells anybody what I just said—about the beatings," she added sternly. "It's your father's wish." Walking briskly into the stairwell, she disappeared into the seldom used sitting room, caressing her cheek. Clair watched, a cold lump in her stomach as she imagined a father's hand striking such a thing. And shifting over to her mother's chair, she slouched back against the window, gazing after her.

"Unburdened gentleness," she mouthed. "That's what you saw when you looked into his eyes. And then he built you a house, and married you. And everyone talked, with you being so young, and he walking away from his sick mother, leaving her to Uncle Sim who was just as indulgent with complaints. And no one come to visit after me and Missy was born, because of the misery, they said, with all of us talking at once, and Daddy would grin as they walked out the door, shaking their heads and muttering about how it sounded like they'd just been in a barn with a dozen nanny goats running about, baying over sweet hay."

Sighing, Clair stared morosely around the kitchen. But for the moaning of the half-boiling kettle on the damper, there was silence, a hard silence, bursting with yesterday's noise.

"Here, Missy, get off the railing," she recalled her mother's voice ringing out from a last winter's eve. "Mercy, Clair, go catch her; she's sliding down the rail agin."

"Did you catch her?" called out Father as Missy swooshed off the bannister, her bottom plummeting into Clair's belly with a whump! "Then go get your book and start your reading."

"Blessed mercy, Clair, help your sister off the floor—did she hurt herself? My Lord, she's forever falling and crying."

"Like one other I knows," said her father with a playful pat at her mother's rump as she hurried by with the broom, "always falling and bruising and bawling."

"Now, Father, I'm never one for bawling," laughed Sare. "Sit at the table and let me get you your tea—for sure you must be thirsty from all day at the wood. And mercy, Father, catch her," she shrieked as Missy dashed out of the stairwell and sprang onto her father's lap. "Mind you, child, you're going to break your neck if you tries that again. Start your reading, Clair."

"Read louder," said Father over Missy's squeals, "because I allows you're going to win over Willamena in the reading competition again this year. Won't she make a grand teacher, Mother? And she'll write to us everyday from her desk in the city, won't you, my dolly?"

"You're always filling her head, Father. Pass me that child if you can't stop her squealing."

"And such a pretty head it is," said Job, smiling fondly at Clair. "Stand back in the corner now and practise making your voice louder, for it's a good strong voice you'll need to be a teacher. Sare, you listening to her voice?"

"I'd like to, but for this one," said Sare, peeling Missy off his lap and clapping a hand over her mouth.

A sudden screech cut through Clair's dreaming and she sat up with a start as Missy burst in through the door, bounding across the kitchen, pink cheeked from the cold and bundled in caps and scarves.

"It's Grandmother's birthday, it's Grandmother's birthday," she chanted, skidding across the floor with muddied boots and slamming into the cupboards.

"What's wrong?" Sare cried out, running out of the sitting room, her hand to her heart.

"Ohh, it's just Missy! She's the noisiest thing, Mommy, she's fine," said Clair, yanking her younger sister back to the door by the hood of her coat.

"It's Grandmother's birthday, Mommy, aren't we baking her a cake?"

Confusion clouded Sare's eyes.

"You don't have to, anyways," said Clair. "How come you always got to make her cake?"

"We always makes her cake, and I can help," said Missy, tearing away from Clair and snatching her mother's apron off the sink. "Uncle Sim lets me help all the time. He says I'm the real little woman."

"Bet he likes that, somebody else doing his work," sniffed Clair. "Get your boots off," she ordered, pulling Missy back from the sink.

"Let me go, Clair."

"You're getting water everywhere."

"Uncle Sim said you're brazen. I can help, can't I, Mommy?"

"Uncle Sim—" sneered Clair.

"Ohh, Clair—take off your boots, Missy," said Sare, and trudging across the kitchen, she cleared some dirty dishes to one side on the sink, and pulled a mixing bowl out of the top cupboard.

"Last night I dreamed we made the biggest birthday cake ever," chattered Missy, kicking off her boots and scraping a chair over besides her mother, "and that's a good dream, isn't it, Mommy?"

"Yes, it's a good dream," said Sare, staring mindlessly at the mixing bowl. Throwing down her hands, she sighed heavily, patting Missy on the head. "Mercy, your chattering got me all fuddled; we can't mix up a cake when there's bread in the oven. Clair, dish up some of the stew for your suppers and sing out to me when the bread's done. I'm going upstairs to lie down."

"When are we going to do the cake, then?" cried out Missy.

"In the morning," said Sare decisively. "I'll mix it up in the morning, and we can take it after school. You'll feed her some stew, Clair?"

"I'll feed her," said Clair, putting away the mop she had wiped up the water with. "Come, Missy, put your chair back to the table, and we haves some supper."

"I don't want no supper." Missy glowered, still standing on her chair, watching as her mother crept slowly up the stairs.

"Don't start whining," said Clair impatiently, taking the lid off the cast-iron pot resting on the damper. "You're always whining these days, Missy."

"I'm not whining," protested Missy.

"Don't go bawling, either—"

"I'm not bawling, either!"

"Yeah, you are; you're always bawling," said Clair, and was about to say more but was deterred by the quivering of Missy's little petalled lips as she stepped off the chair. "Come, let's eat our supper," she coaxed instead.

Shaking her head, Missy sat at the table, clamping her mouth shut as Clair sat across from her, feigning relish as she dug her spoon into her stew. "How come Mommy always got a bad head?" she asked finally.

Clair shrugged. "She just has a bad head, that's all."

"Why don't she take aspirins, then?"

"They makes her stomach sick."

"Why don't she take brandy, then?"

"Uncle Sim carried it all up to Grandmother. Is she still picking her nose—the grandmother?" asked Clair, crooking her little finger and shoving its joint up her nostril.

The pout gave way to a giggle. "Uncle Sim says one of them days she's going to pluck out her eye for a booger."

"Humph, wonder he don't pluck it out for her," said Clair.

Missy giggled again. "He says she's crosser than a cat."

"That's what they're like—two cats with their tails tied together. Tell you what, Missy, why don't you get your books and we does our homework. Go on, now," she coaxed. "And after, you can tell me a story."

"You'll come to bed same time as me?"

"After I brings in the wood."

"And we can tell more stories?"

"Long as you don't wake Mommy."

After homework was finished, and the bread taken out of the oven and buttered and cooling on the bin, Clair coaxed Missy up over the stairs and into her pyjamas. "We'll just let Mommy sleep," she said, lying on the bed as Missy crawled beneath the blankets.

"You get undressed," said Missy.

"I got to bring in the wood," said Clair. "Hurry on and tell." And for the next half hour Clair listened as Missy prattled about fairies combing the hair of little girls when they slept, and how the banshees were angry because the fairies took away their wails and now they couldn't give warnings of death, and how everyone was now living to be a hundred, two hundred, and even five hundred years old, and no more little girls and their mothers would ever die again.

Adding a few details of her own to the story, Clair waited till Missy's voice began croaking sleepily, and feeling a little of the comfort she had always felt from her sister, from before her father went to war, she kissed her cheek, whispering good night, and that she would be back soon as she had the wood stacked for morning.

"But I don't want to sleep by myself," murmured Missy.

"I'll be up soon."

"But I don't want to sleep yet."

"Shh."

"I'll be quiet."

"No, Mommy hears *every* sound—and they makes her head badder. Be good now—I won't be long." Running lightly down over the stairs, she pulled on her coat and boots, and donning a cap a pair of mitts, she went outside and brought in the splits for the morning's fire. Then, listening by the bottom of stairs and hearing silence from her mother's room, she crept into the sitting room and hunkered down before the cabinet, lifting out her father's radio and rehooking the wires.

"Shut it off, Clair, shut it off!" her mother had cried out that first time she had set it up and was tuning in to the news.

"But I wants to hear about the war."

"I can't hear about it," her mother had shouted. "Turn it off, child, turn it off!" And she had run from the room with her hands barring her ears.

Listening again for any sound coming from her mother's room, Clair switched on the radio, quickly lowering its volume as a tinny male voice sounded through the static:

> . . . to snapshot the past several months, we have seen the spread of war to the Balkans; we have seen the Russian army advancing over a carpet of their own dead; we have seen hundreds of Soviet planes hurling a rain of bombs upon Finland; we have heard Britain declaring she would meet Italy on land, sea, and in the air; and now with Germany's bombing of London, we can start believing indeed that this is no phony war; that indeed, Prime Minister Chamberlain may be right with his prophecy that we are entering a phase of war much grimmer than the world has ever seen. . . .

"Grandmother, Grandmother, we made you a cake," chanted Missy the next evening, barging inside the grandmother's house, Sare behind her, carrying a cloth-covered dish. Clair dawdled, closing the door on the cool fall evening and wrinkling her nose against the fetid smells of Vicks and cod-liver oil as she stepped into the smothering, wood-driven heat and the dimly lit room before her. Fire glimpsed through the cracks in an old rusting wood stove, flitting over the grizzled head of an old woman as she bobbed herself awake.

"Look at it, look at it!" Missy was chanting, tugging on the fatty underside of the grandmother's arm. "We got candies on it."

Shrugging off Missy as if she were a bothersome fly, the grandmother propped herself up on doughy white forearms, blinking herself out of her heat-induced stupor. "What'd ye lose your way?" she grumbled at the sight of Sare and Clair, her jowls quivering in the splotches of firelight and looking to Clair like yellowing pork fat.

"Job wouldn't be pleased if we forgot his mother's birthday," said Sare, laying the dish before her and pulling Missy to one side. "He always made sure we baked you a cake."

"Job!" snorted the grandmother. "He cared a lot now for his old mother, he did. The most I ever seen of him was the broad of his back—" Clair rolled her eyes towards the dirtied windowsill, cluttered with jars and nails and screws as her mother took a chair, listening sympathetically, apologetically, guiltily to the grandmother's drone about her crippling rheumatoid arthritis, and her heartless son, Job, hardly ever coming for a visit since his father died, leaving her dependent on the lazy oaf of a first-born who was always hove off like a lord in his room despite enough rain leaking through the roof to drown them all.

"But I'm a good help," cut in Missy. "See, Mommy, I washed all the dishes last night, didn't I, Grandmother?"

"That's a good girl," exclaimed Sare, finding relief through her daughter's largesse. "I'm so glad she's of help, Grandmother. I never thinks of her as being big enough to do housework, but I suppose I wasn't much older than her when I had a back-load of chores. It's just that she's so small for six years—my, I swear she haven't grown an inch this past year."

"Uncle Sim says small people works the hardest," said Missy, "and he drags over the woodbox for me to stand on so's I can reach better, right, Grandmother?"

Another snort from the grandmother. "As long as it leaves him with nothing to do," she said, casting a cross look towards a closed door to the other side of the stove.

"Is he in his room?" asked Missy, darting towards the door. "Uncle Sim, Uncle Si-im!"

"Goodness, Missy!" said Sare, darting after her, but the door was already drawing open and Sim shuffling out.

"What's she getting on with now?" he mumbled, a stoop overtaking his shoulders as he slewed his eyes onto his mother.

"Oh mind now, you don't have to put on this evening, Uncle Tom Langford, it's wares, not work that's waiting," said the grandmother, pulling the dish towel off the cake. "I can't even get him go to the store and get me some flour," she said to Sare, "and I been wanting a bit of hot bread for two days."

"That's because she was going to bring a pot," said Sim, looking crossly at Clair.

Clair started guiltily as her mother turned to her. "Don't tell me you never ran up with the bread last evening."

"I forgot," she exclaimed.

"Forgot!" said Sare. "Well, sir, she got the mind of a sieve. Never mind," she ordered as Clair opened her mouth to protest, and turning to the grandmother, she threw her hands up helplessly. "I'll send up a loaf by Missy soon as we gets home—I swear, I don't know what I'm going to do with her."

"She never had no splits brought in either," said the uncle testily, his nostrils so splayed, it appeared he had sunken to his ancient beginnings.

"I brought them in after," declared Clair, and lapsed into silence as her mother shot her a warning look.

"She did bring them in after, Uncle Sim. Mercy, how she makes such good grades in school, I'll never know. Certainly, she's no worse than her father for keeping things in his head. I tells her all the time, that's who she takes after, her father. Well, we should be going now," she added abruptly, laying a hand on the grandmother's, "and I'll send up that loaf the second I gets home. I should be sending you a loaf every time I bakes— Lord, I never thinks of such things, and it's the least I can do for all the time Sim spends bringing wood and water. There, then, I'll send you a pot—perhaps two—every time I makes bread. Job wouldn't like it knowing his mother was wanting for a loaf of bread, would he, Clair?" But Clair was taking no note of the grandmother's sour look, and had fixed her eyes onto the uncle as he searched amongst the dirty dishes on the bin for a cup, wondering how the blazes this sneaking low-life had been able to divide one loaf into thirty.

"Suppose he gets killed; who's going to fend for ye then, if he gets killed?"

"Goodness, Grandmother, it's thinking of him coming home that keeps me going, not his being killed," her mother exclaimed. "Clair, you ready? Come, Missy, leave off Uncle Sim and come."

"Stop long enough for tea, I suppose," said the grandmother. "Sim, make them tea, for it's not often I gets company, and if it wouldn't for talking to the stove, I'd forget I got a tongue most days."

"My no, I can't wait for tea, Grandmother. Missy, come on. Clair?"

"Sim, you making tea? Look, he's already making it; sure I never sees nobody, nobody."

"I should be sending Missy more; she's home all the time getting underfoot. That's what I'll do then, send Missy more often to keep you company. Would you like that, Uncle Sim?"

"As long as she sweeps a floor, he'll like it," said the grandmother, attempting a smile, but so long had she brooded in foul nature, her mouth twisted sideways instead, reminding Clair of a broody hen straddling a nest of thorns. And when Sare shook her head, backing away from another offer of tea, this time from the uncle, the grandmother's voice rose nasally. "Why'd you wait till she was leaving before putting the kettle on?"

And when the uncle snapped back, "She can make up her own mind whether to stay or not," the scorn in his tone was as much from his own testiness as from the grandmother's needling. Indeed, thought Clair, escaping into the clean fall air, and letting go her pent-up breath of Vicks and coal heat, it would be hard for even the uncle to know the source of his own testiness, for he wore the grandmother's ill nature the way a mean-spirited rider rides a contrary horse, with neither of them figuring from whence the ill nature stemmed.

"For goodness' sakes, Clair," her mother chided, catching up with her, dragging Missy by the hand, "the least you can do is say goodbye."

"He never brings in the wood," she all but shouted. "I always brings in the wood—and I chops the splits, too."

"Are you still onto that?" Sare exclaimed in astonishment.

"He's always scheming!"

"He haven't got the sense for scheming. Now, you listen, here, my lady—"

"Daddy said he's a conniving bastard!"

"Mercy, Father in heaven! Do you sleep beneath our bed? I allows when your father gets home, we'll have to put a bell around your neck like we done the goat once, to keep track of its whereabouts."

"Missy ought not to be going there," said Clair, snatching up her younger sister's hand as her mother caught up with her. "He's only wanting her to do his work."

"There's nothing wrong with Missy sweeping a floor."

"You're bad, Clair," said Missy, yanking away her hand. "She's bad, isn't she, Mommy?"

"Ooh," huffed Clair, and running ahead, she burst in through the house door, kicked off her boots and skulked into the sitting room as Missy and her mother came in after her. The radio behind the glass doors of the cabinet caught her attention, and she turned from it in a huff. What mattered about a radio when you weren't allowed to turn the thing on? Marching into the stairwell, she started up over the stairs, but a sharp cry from her mother brought her running back down and into the kitchen. She was leaning over the bin, her fingers to her temples, and a loaf of bread on the floor from where she had dropped it, taking it out of the bottom cupboard.

"What's wrong?" cried Clair, running to her.

"It's—it's this head-*ache*," Sare moaned, pressing her fingers more tightly against her temples as if she might press out the pain itself.

"I can get the bread, Mommy," said Missy, snatching up the loaf. "I'll take it up to Grandmother."

"It comes on so sudden," said Sare, massaging her brow. "And then it near makes me sick. Ooh, it's nerves, is all. No, here," she said, taking the loaf from Missy. "You run up with it, Clair. Missy, you bide here and get your books, else it'll be late before you gets home agin."

"But you told Grandmother I was going to bring it up—"

"I'll do it, Missy," said Clair impatiently, taking the bread from her mother. "Get your books like Mommy says."

"I won't," shouted Missy.

"Missy!"

"Shut up, Clair!" And turning from her sister, she bounded up over the stairs.

"Leave her be, leave her be," exclaimed Sare, sinking tiredly onto her chair besides the window. "And you don't be long, either, Clair."

"Needn't worry about that," muttered Clair, and pulling on her boots, she let herself out the door and through the gate. She turned as she started up the road, hoping to reassure her mother with a quick wave. But Sare's face appeared only as a spectre of white through the window in the evening light.

CHAPTER THREE

I N TIME THE FISHERS STOPPED TALKING about her
father. And Willamena found new scandal to report. Even
Missy stopped asking when their father was coming back.
And most disturbing of all to Clair was her own thinning
memory, when she closed her eyes sometimes to think of
him and couldn't bring his features up close. During those
times she'd sneak into her mother's room and rub her nose
into his good church coat hanging in the closet, breathing
deeply of the spicy tobacco smell that clung faintly to the
wool, and read and reread his letters. And now even they
were coming more seldom, and were shorter, speaking of a
routine that she couldn't connect with him, of his marching
and digging holes and cleaning guns and training and more
marching. And the 57th regiment he'd been assigned to in
England was renamed 166 Nfld. Regiment since he arrived
in Scotland, and he was training all over again, this time to
be a field regiment as opposed to heavy artillery, which
meant that he might be moved from Scotland soon, to somewhere that someone deemed his family ought not to know,
because full sentences of his letter had been cut out. But that
was a good thing, he continued, because now with Japan
having bombed Pearl Harbor and the Americans finally at
war, it was more important than ever for him to be a soldier,

fighting along with everyone else for a freedom that was rightly theirs, and he'd never felt so proud. And Joey was like his little brother, he'd often scribble, following along by his side, day after day, and only seldom venturing into town after the girls. And he missed them terribly, he'd always close his letters by saying; at least those pages she, Clair, was allowed her to read. Always there was a page her mother slipped into her apron pocket and took out later in the sitting room or in her bedroom, and read in the comfort of solitude.

And there was the radio. Those hushed evenings with her mother and Missy in bed, it was her favoured companion. Yet not even there in the rapid-fire voice of the broadcaster as he talked of the earth being pulverized, and the millions of soldiers killed and lamed, and the earth being torn asunder as the war circled the globe, could she find a picture of her father. Not even when this blight creeping over the world torpedoed a ferry leaving Newfoundland, killing 137 Newfoundlanders, 2 of them cousins to Johnny Regular's wife, Rose, could she conjure up an image of her father as a soldier. It was as if he had died. As if he'd never been. And when once she managed to pull a fragment of him out of a dream, he became diffused with the million others from the broadcaster's report, and lay dying with them on a soil torn asunder.

"I hope the Newfoundlanders does better in this one than they done at Beaumont Hamel," Johnnie Regular's boy, Rupert, said to a couple of older boys, just out from a history lesson two years into the war. "Yup, 753 went to battle, and 68 comes out alive—I wonder who trained them to shoot?" he asked as they gathered behind the school around a scuffed-out field, kicking around a soccer ball. Clair was standing nearby, scarcely interested in her two best girlfriends, Phoebe and Joanie, as they turned admiring eyes onto the older boys, yet managing a haughty look whenever one of them turned their way.

"Just as well they never come back, from what I seen of that fellow down Port Ray," said Phoebe loudly. "Leg cut off to a stump and half-blind. Can we play?" she asked, sticking out a foot, pretending to trip Rupert.

"Go play with your dolls," said Rupert, nudging her to one side, missing the ball coming at him.

"Legs short as yours, you can use some help," said Joanie, stopping the ball with her foot as it rolled towards her.

"Here, let it go," ordered Rupert, cutting in front of Joanie and kicking the ball back to the other fellows. "Get home with ye," he huffed at the girls, running back onto the field.

"Yup, 753 men goes out with guns, and 68 alive the next day," said the eldest fellow, Eddie Jones, from in by the church. "Now what kind of fight do ye think was that?"

"A fool's fight is what," said Georgie Blanchard, Ralph's son, red-faced from running down the ball. "You take a man from his own place and put him in someone else's— and in a different country at that, mind you—and what kind of sense do he got? None, brother! And they had none to start with, going the frig over there in the first place," he added, a sly glance at Clair, then kicking the ball hard towards Rupert.

"That's true, that's true," called out Rupert. "I used to listen to me old grandfather talk about them men that went to war. Strong as bears he said they was—and matched them, too. Remember old Sammy Jones—ripped his knife across the throat of a bear?"

"Yup, and he with the bear still pawing at him," said Georgie.

"Yes, now, that's a likely story," snickered Phoebe as Georgie ran past her. "Come on, let us play," she egged him on, running alongside of him. "Girls against the guys. Come on, Clair! Joanie!"

"So, what's a fellow like that doing getting killed in less than a day, and he with a rifle in his hands and hundreds just like him standing all around?" said Rupert. "Foolish is what it is, going off and fighting in places you knows nothing about."

"Perhaps he should've stuck with his knife and left his gun at home," offered Clair.

"Yes, now I knows Sammy Jones was too stunned to shoot a gun. Is that what you thinks?" sniped Georgie. "Well, I can tell you a thing or two about Sammy Jones; he was nobody stupid, and he was no frigging coward, either—"

"Perhaps it's you who thinks he's a coward," cut in Clair, ignoring the warning look Phoebe was darting her way, "else what're ye all the time talking about it for?"

"Oh, come on, let's play—girls against the guys," cajoled Phoebe.

But Clair was already walking off, her back stiffening as Georgie went into a rant about how "it's like the old man says now; 'twas men going off leaving their own behind to be fended for was the cowards, not men like Sammy Jones who stayed on his own land, ripping apart bears that threatened him and his family."

Dark looks followed Clair the rest of the week at school; or at least, she imagined, for she never took time to check herself, or talk with Joanie and Phoebe much, to find out. Enough to keep her mind on her school work and to help her mother with the cooking and cleaning at home, than listening to the likes of Georgie Blanchard going off half-cocked like his father. And besides, Phoebe was forever making eyes at Georgie these days, and the sight of Clair was quick to darken his face and bring a snide retort, making it more and more awkward for Clair to be hanging around the back of the school with Phoebe during recess or after school.

Home felt equally as uncomfortable, what with her mother's chatter turned silent, and her face never smiling as she moped from room to room, upstairs and down, fidgeting with a cleaning rag or, most likely, lying across the divan with a bad head and hushing both Clair and Missy over the slightest sound. The days rolled into weeks, and the weeks into months, breakfast, dinner and supper, school, homework and bedtime. It all came and it all went, day after day, month after month. Dull, grey, colourless months. Except for Missy. Chattering, twirling and preening she pranced around the kitchen, mopping, sweeping and dusting—like the winter's lamb that, born out of season and brought inside to be warmed by the stove, reminds everyone with its babyish bleating and the sweetening smell of last summer's hay lining its bed, that somewhere outside, spring, like the cocooned butterfly, awaits the warming sun's rays to release its bloom. But, Sare, mired by the dead flower stalks outside her window, was not to be wooed by thoughts of spring. And Clair, pulled by a side of herself too newly formed yet to know, scoffed at this target of her blinder self.

"For the love of it, Missy, you don't throw stuff on the floor," she scolded, picking up the broom Missy had flung to one side as she skidded into the kitchen.

"I never throwed it—I lodged it near the wall and it fell," protested Missy. "You want me to open some bully for supper, Mommy?" Sare was standing at the sink, slicing a loaf of bread for supper.

"If that's what you wants," replied Sare. "Do you want bully, Clair?"

"Yes, we wants bully," said Missy. Diving for the bottom cupboard, she came up with a can of bully beef. "Here, help me get it started," she demanded, prying the key off the lid, and scaling back the label.

"Get Clair to start it for you."

"No, I wants you to start it."

"Give me the can, Missy," said Clair, but Missy held the can away from her grasp. "I wants Mommy."

"I'm just going to start it for you—"

"No!"

"For goodness' sakes, pass it here," exclaimed Sare, dropping the knife and taking the can from Missy. "And no more fighting, *please*."

"Is your head bad, Mommy?" asked Missy as her mother squinted, trying to fit the key onto the little metal tip sticking up from the side of the can.

"Mercy," she muttered impatiently as the key slipped through her fingers. Snatching the key off the floor, Clair took the can from her mother's hands. "Here, let me do it."

"You're bad, Clair," shouted Missy. "I dreamed Daddy smacked you last night. I did, then," she countered as Clair groaned. "And my dreams comes true, don't they, Mommy? Don't they?" she asked, gazing imploringly at her mother. "And I was dreaming about you, too," she added, her voice softening, "you and Daddy—and he was buying lots of presents for you, and hats and ribbons—"

"You're lying," said Clair.

"No, I'm not. It was a real dream, and you were bad, Clair, and Daddy smacked you—"

"Mommy—"

"It's true—and he was in a box, Mommy, and he was trying to stand up—and he was singing out to you."

Sare's eyes fastened onto Missy. "What kind of box, child?"

"Don't listen to her," said Clair.

"A pantry box—"

"A pantry box?"

"Like a small pantry and I was singing out, 'Daddy, Daddy, Daddy,' but he wouldn't answer me—"

"Perhaps he couldn't hear you—"

"But he did hear me. He was looking right at me. And— he was scared."

"Mercy," moaned Sare, clasping her hands to her mouth. "All right, Missy, that's enough. No more dreams, now."

"But, Mommy—"

"No more dreams, Missy," Sare all but shouted, her voice trembling. And running into the stairwell, she flew up over the stairs.

"Now, see what you've done?" said Clair. "You've made her cry. That's what telling lies does . . ."

Clair's voice trailed off as a look of utter misery turned down the corners of her sister's mouth. Far was she now from the lamb bleating for its teat. Trailing into the stairwell as she was, the sheen of her hair burying itself in shadow, she more resembled the butterfly whose wings had fluttered briefly, and finding only winter, was withdrawing into the dark whence it came.

"Missy—"

But Missy was fleeing up over the stairs. Clair sighed as she heard their room door close ever so softly. She slumped against the window, laying her forehead against the cool of the pane, seeking out the withered remnants of the sweet williams that lay beyond it, encased within a film of October frost. The cold of the pane brought an ache to her forehead, and she held back her head, hearing only the ticking of the clock. Unlike those early days when her father had just left, the house was no longer pressing with yesterday's noise, as if it too had forgotten its maker.

Summer came, then winter again. As if to compensate for their refusal to allow their men to take up arms, the women from the Basin had responded ardently to the British government's requests for knitted caps, mitts and socks to send to the soldiers overseas. Shearing, carding, spinning— the entire outport had turned into a sheep farm overnight, with the baa-ing of the sheep, and the burring, creaking and clacking of spinning wheels, Clair thought as she walked down over the hill to the store. Except for her mother's house. She looked over her shoulder. Aside from the thin trickle of smoke drifting out of the chimney, the house appeared deserted, with its closed doors and draped windows.

"We never sees your poor mother," said Johnny Regular's wife, Rose, in a rough tone that forever accused, whether it was to babies or men that she spoke. It was a dirty fall day, wind, drizzle and fog, and Clair was about to duck inside the store to pick up some tea and soap. She paused in her step, nodding politely to Rose and Alma, the postal clerk, as they picked amongst the dozen or more turrs Ralph was tossing up from his boat onto the wharf, murmuring some-thing about her mother being fine. But it was onto Alma her eyes were fastened, as they always were whenever she caught sight of the postal clerk these days, hoping for word or a letter that might be lying in the post office, that had thus far escaped notice, and was now in her pocket, waiting to be delivered. The last letter had been several months ago, cursing the African heat blistering his back, the sand-blasted sirocco wind, and the flies that drank more of his tea than he did himself, and how glad he was finally to be entrenched in the rain-soaked soil of Italy. Perhaps the fellow Joey had written? her eyes asked.

"Strange he haven't wrote for this long," said Alma, her eyes barely discernable above a gaily coloured scarf twisted thrice around her neck. "The young fellow from Rocky Head is just as bad; they haven't heard from him in a while, either—not since they got to that place in Italy—Cassino, I think's is the name of the place."

"A lot of fighting going on there," said Ralph, tossing up the last of the turrs. "Read it in the newspaper that come off the steamer last week."

"You'd think he'd write," said Rose, "with your poor mother in such a way."

"I say now there'll be a bunch come all at once," said Alma, noting the look of concern on Clair's face at Ralph's words. "With the way the mail is, and coming from all the way from over the seas, you never can tell. Sure Darryl Day's wife, over in Trinity Bay, she got forty letters all at once when her husband went over to the first war—and that was the day he stepped off the boat, back home agin. He keeped them all, he did, and brought them home with him when he come. Imagine that, now. Funny things, my dear, war does to a man. And I allows that's what your father'll do, just climb off the boat someday, with the rest of his letters sticking out a shirt pocket. Who's that coming up there?" she asked abruptly, squinting past Clair to a boat moving towards them, some distance off.

"Looks like that young fellow Frankie from Rocky Head," said Ralph, wheezing heavily as he tossed the last bird onto the wharf and climbed up the ladder. "For sure he's the only one to come up here, rough frigging water like this."

"Yes, and balls, brother, after spotting that submarine."

"Aahh, a seal, more likely," scoffed Alma.

"That's what they probably thought on that ferry that got torpedoed," said Rose. "And we knows what that got them. Sir, you got the set of ears," she exclaimed as the store door was shoved open behind her, and Willamena, a heavy shawl wrapped around her shoulders, poked her head outside, her features appearing doubly pointed as she peered through the blowing snow at the lone figure in the boat cutting steadily towards them.

"Not that hard to hear you, Alma maid," piped Willamena. "How's you doing, Clair?" she asked, her interest heightening at the sight of Clair attempting to sidestep her way into the store. "We hears your mother's some sick."

Clair shrugged, "She's not sick—"

"That's not what young Missy says, then."

"She gets a bad head, that's all," said Clair, standing back impatiently as Willamena guarded the entrance to the store.

"You'd think you'd quit school and help her out if she's that sick. Nothing the school board can do if you quits to help your mother—that's what I done—quit to help Dad."

Clair was struck silent with surprise. "I'm—I'm getting my grade eleven," she finally stammered.

"Oh, yes, that's right," said Willamena with feigned seriousness, "You're going to be a grand teacher someday. That's what your father was always going on about, wasn't it?" Taking stock of Alma and Rose's rapt attention, and

Ralph approaching them from behind, pulling his cap up over an ear the size of a conch, Willamena took face to ask what they'd all been querying about for months now. "According to young Missy, your mother's getting a bit low-minded, is she?"

And as was when she had crouched behind the lobster pots listening to them badmouth her father, Clair rose to her full height and was about to turn on her heel and march back up the hill again, if not for Saul pulling the door open farther, his eyes as hard as two grey beach rocks as he stared fixedly at his daughter.

"With those looks, you'd think she'd be trying to bring the customers in, not freezing them to death on the stoop," he said past her to Alma, and Clair bit back a satisfied retort as a flush reddened Willamena's face.

"Tasty figs grows on trees no matter how blight the blossoms," Willamena snapped at her father, flouncing back in the store, but not without a backward glance at the young fellow from Rocky Head who was now tying up at the wharf.

"And what's a duff without a fig, hey, maid?" said Alma, as they all crowded in behind her, stomping the snow off their boots. "That fellow Frankie looks in the need of a good prune. I don't suppose she got plans for he, now, do she, Saul?"

"Yes, watch out now I goes with someone from Rocky Head," said Willamena haughtily from behind the counter.

"They're a working people, and that's something they can teach some of we," said Saul, tightening his apron around his waist. "Tend to her," he ordered Willamena, beckoning towards Clair standing silently at the counter.

"A pound of tea and a bar of soap," said Clair as Willamena sauntered towards her, but her order was washed out by the door swinging open and Frankie pushing in through, a burlap sack tossed over one shoulder, the salty smell of the sea clinging to his heavy winter clothes, and with a bold smile that demanded acceptance as much as willed it.

"You're back already," exclaimed Willamena, scampering over to the far side of the counter, greeting him.

"Good day, good day to you, sir," said Saul.

"Not what I'd call a good one," replied Frankie in the broad, flat talk of the Rocky Head crowd as he nodded pleasantly to those standing around, "but there's more than a few companies of turrs out there."

"That's what there is then, brother, thousands," said Ralph, taking a seat atop the apple barrel. "And poor, too, they is."

"Broody as an old hen to buff," said Rose. "That's not more knitting you got brought up," she asked as Frankie rolled his burlap bag onto the counter.

"Yup, that's what she is, then," said Frankie.

"Sure, how do the women find time for buffing birds with all the knitting youse is doing?" said Alma. "My, look at that stitching, Rose," she added, mauling through the pairs of knitted socks and mitts Saul was emptying from the bag onto the counter. "Tighter than Aunt Sulaney's, I think."

"Yup, too bad it's for government purposes and not our own," said Frankie, an admiring eye upon his goods as he doffed his cap, patting down his slicked-back hair with the knife-edge part. Spotting Clair, he stepped back, sending her a smile of such charm that it tinted her cheeks and brought Willamena scurrying towards her once more, demanding her order.

"No doubt, sir, there's a market somewhere," Saul was saying, holding open the burlap bag as Alma shoved the knitted goods back inside. "There's more money being won in this war than land; the merchants of death don't die with wars. Find the goods, I always say, and the rest is in your pocket."

"Fancy words, them is," grunted Ralph. "How come all it gets me is store bills to stuff me pockets with?"

"What's on the bills stuffs your gut, don't it?" retorted Willamena, coming back to the counter with Clair's tea and soap. And ignoring the sudden flare of Ralph's nostrils, and her father's look of warning, she sidled up to Clair, laying the goods on the counter, asking loudly, "Do you got money?"

Clair blinked. Money! Aside from the scattered copper, she'd never seen money, and never in the store where everything was always marked down and deducted from her father's work, or his army cheque since he'd gone to war.

"Well, they're over their limit," said Willamena, pushing the bill book at her father as he stared at her, equally as perplexed. "I told that to Sim twice this week when he was here carrying up stuff to Sare."

"He—he don't carry up stuff to we," said Clair, hearing naught but the shuffling of Frankie's feet, and the sudden quiet from Alma and the others.

"I knows what I'm marking down," said Willamena. "And what do you know anyway about what he brings to your mother when you're in school all day?"

"I gets the groceries," said Clair. She turned confusedly to Saul as he reached past Willamena, pushing her bagged goods in front of her. "Well—do we owe more—?" she asked, faltering as her tongue thickened in the sudden dryness of her mouth. And scarcely hearing Saul's reply that he'd fix it up some other way, she took the bag off the counter and walked hotly out through the door.

Decidedly, in a soul still clean with youth, there is nothing of the dirtied greys to temper a judgment, but a clarity that shows decisively what is white and what is not white. And this—this theft of the uncle's, bringing the shame of charity to her father's name, along with the lies he told of his labours on his brother's stoop—seeded scorn in Clair's brain, a scorn that watered itself with rage, anguish, fear and other ills that, left alone, become too monumental to disperse within and is charted into that darker unknown self. And as is with most things that grow, it seeks light. And whereas before this encounter over her father's credit it had flowered into thoughts of pulverized bodies rotting the ground they'd plundered, it now took the form of the living. And as a duckling follows whom or whatever its eyes first light upon, so did the uncle become the harbinger of the rot festering in Clair's mind.

Missy was kneeling upon a chair, jabbing a junk of wood into the stove when Clair burst in through the door. One look at the scowl on her sister's face and Missy clanked the poker across the stove and, scampering off the chair, dove for the stairwell.

"You wait there," yelled Clair, kicking off her boots and diving after her.

"Clair's after me, Clair's after me!" said Missy, the thrill of the chase sounding wildly through her cries as she scrabbled up over the stairs.

"What're you after doing now?" sighed Sare, trailing out of her room, a few garments of dirty clothes hanging limply from her hands.

"Clair's after me," shrieked Missy, darting behind her mother, clinging to her skirt.

"She's blabbing off to Willamena at the store agin," yelled out Clair from the bottom of the stairs. "I've told her and told her not to go blabbing off to Willamena at the store."

"No, I never!"

"Yes you did."

"I never blabs!"

"Yes she did, Mommy, and there's something else too—" But Clair's accusation was cut off as her mother's wearied look was suddenly replaced by one of fright. Dropping the garments of clothing, she came running down over the stairs, her eyes locked onto a curl of smoke drifting from the kitchen. Clair's insides quickened and she darted into the kitchen after her mother.

"Are you trying to burn us down?" Sare cried, snatching the burning-hot poker off the floor and scuffing at the charred spot on the canvas. "That's just what your poor father needs to come home to—his house burned to the ground."

"It's Missy's fault."

"No it wasn't!" hollered Missy from the stairwell.

"Don't start that agin," sighed Sare, laying the poker back on the stove, and sliding the stove top in place. "I allows it'll break your father's heart the way you've been fighting, and especially after him asking you to help take care of Missy, Clair—mercy, the singing out, the singing out—I swear I can't stand it; it's like the claws of a bird gripping my temples."

But Clair was not wanting to commiserate with her mother's pain right now. "He's stealing from us, Mommy," she shouted. "Uncle Sim's stealing from us. He's marking down stuff on our store bill and carrying it to his own place." She paused as her mother turned on her, a look of surprise chasing away her pained look. "We're already over our limit for this month," she added more quietly, "and we still got another week before Daddy's cheque comes. Saul said he'd fix it up, but that means he'd be giving us food, and—and Willamena was there—and everybody else, too—" She faltered as her mother stared helplessly around the room, her hands falling to her sides.

"What're we going to do, Mommy? I can go get him."

"Nothing. We do nothing," said her mother thickly.

"Nothing!"

"It's how your father would have it. It's not the first time your uncle's done this—your father knows. He's turned his back on account of his taking it up to his mother—and that's what we'll do, too. Lord knows, we can't afford it now, but it's how your father would have it—we'll do with less, that's all—that's what he's doing over there, somewhere—half starving himself to death—and we're nowhere near that."

"But it's stealing!"

"It's how your father would have it," Sare returned sharply. "And I'll not hear more about it. And you're not to take it up either—promise you'll not say a word. Promise," she demanded as Clair stood tight-lipped with anger.

Ignoring her mother's command and the trembling in her hand as she raised it to her brow, Clair turned on her heel and stomped to the window, staring hard outside. The divan creaked as her mother lowered her weight onto it, then there was silence. Loud, smothering silence. And the ceaseless ticking of the clock became louder as it struck down at her from the kitchen wall, interrupting all thought and holding her bound in this stayed moment with her mother. Her eyes sought out the flower patch, frozen beneath its blanket of snow and ice. Yet, there was a root down there somewhere that would respond to the first rays of the sun's heat and grow new life from those frozen stems. She turned a little, glimpsing her mother now sitting forward and holding her hands towards the stove, drawing its heat. Hadn't she said they were the walking roots of their own souls? Was not she the one who seeded this home? Was she not, then, its root? Where, then, was the warmth now needed to nurture its growth? And in that moment when the ills of the day began to fold in, crimping all thought into weariness, she looked to her mother's reflection vaguely outlined in the window and whimpered in a voice unlike her own, "How come you don't knit socks for the soldiers?"

There was a silence at first, then the shuffling of her mother's slippered feet as she rose from her place of rest. "Is that what they're asking," she whispered, "why I don't knit socks for the soldiers?" When greeted by silence, she commanded, "Answer me, Clair."

Clair pressed shut her eyes, wishing she could undo the moment.

"Perhaps it's you who's doing the asking, then, is it?" asked Sare. And as Clair refused to speak, she took another step towards her daughter, taking hold of her shoulder. "Then, it's you I'll answer to," she said, the trembling leaving her hands and the fall light glancing greyly off her eyes as she hauled Clair around more fully to face her.

"It's because my husband *is* a soldier, that's why I'm not knitting," she said, her tone clipped with bitterness. "And if I've got to do without him while he fights for all of them, the least they can do is put socks on his feet. You hear me, young Clair? I sent my husband, I did, and they're sending socks. Wouldn't I gladly change places with them that knits socks and their own husbands sitting across from them? I'll knit enough socks to warm the feet of a thousand men when Job comes back to me. And I'll knit enough socks and mitts to

warm the feet and hands of every frostbitten soldier in all of
Europe when they brings my man home. But for now, for as
long as I breathes, not knowing if he's dead or alive, I'll do
nothing. I'll mourn him gone. I'll mourn his every breath
that he takes without me sitting alongside of him to hear it.
You tell them that asks why I'm not knitting socks, you tell
them I'm a miser that walks these floors—a miser that prays
with every breath she takes in, and curses with every breath
she heaves out. You hear me, young Clair? I didn't choose to
offer him that holds my heart. And that gives me no right to
sit in charitable company and hope. And I feels no shame.
God forgive me, but there's a stinginess in my soul and I'll
play no part in this gambit. Now, is that what you asked me,
child? Is that what you wanted to hear from your poor
mother this day?"

Clair sank back nearer the window, cowed by the coldness of her mother's words, and Sare, as if hollowed by the
expulsion of so much, sat back down onto her chair, the
trembling creeping back into her hands. And not knowing if
what her mother had said was good, or if what she, Clair, had
said to trigger the circumstance was bad, Clair never took
time to figure. Turning towards the stairwell, she fled up
over the stairs and into her room.

Missy was half beneath the bed with only her legs sticking out, talking some sort of nonsense talk. Moping to the
window, Clair stared out through, yet saw nothing, absorbed
as she was in her own gloom. A loud shriek caught her attention, and she looked down to see a couple of youngsters
fighting over a rubber ball, and a parent running to separate
them. Her glance strayed towards the houses grading down
the hill to the wharf, their windows yellowing as the evening
lamps were being lit, and adults and youngsters alike darting

over their doorsteps and that of their neighbours, and dogs
yapping besides them, and clotheslines screeching, and
Phoebe running up over the bank to Joanie's house. How
busy everything and everyone looked with their singing out
and running about. For certain she was no longer a part of it
now—she no longer felt a part of anything. A soul hanging
in the expectancy between the inhale and exhale of her
mother's breath, between the tick and the tock of the clock
that reigned absolute from the kitchen wall.

"Come tell me a story, Clair," said Missy, peering out
from beneath the bed.

"What're you doing under there?" mumbled Clair, still
gazing out the window.

"Looking for fairies."

Clair sighed.

"I have a new story—a better one. But I'm only allowed
to tell it in the dark," said Missy, her voice dropping to a
whisper. "Come on, Clair, come down with me," she coaxed,
lifting up the bedspread, her eyes an enormous blue, her hair
a mussed-up cloud of yellow, and her little pink mouth
curled into a silencing shhh as she bade Clair to enter.
Wordlessly, Clair dropped to her knees. Crawling beneath
the bed with Missy, she wondered how on earth such a tiny
little thing could maintain such vibrance of colour in a house
forever darkening with despair.

CHAPTER FOUR

T HE SCHOOL DOOR SWUNG OPEN, letting out the blue-white light of a half-dozen lanterns and the shrieks and laughter of youngsters and adults alike as they sang, danced and cheered to the foot-stomping jig of an accordion.

"My God, haven't he come along and paid ye's yet? Sure, the soup's half-gone," Alma called out, poking her head outside the door and peering through the blowing sleet at the bunch of men huddling and kicking their feet to keep warm. Clair edged around their backs, trying to get nearer the door.

"I seen his head through the window when I was walking by," said Johnnie Regular, his breath oozing the sour smell of shine as he passed the jug to Ralph. "I allows he's still counting it out."

"Heh, he's paying us in coppers then," said Crowman, "or else he's forgotten how to add and subtract."

"I say that's what's after happening, brother, and he's scared of giving a copper too many," said the fellow Pinkson from over the hill. "What you say, Ralph?"

"Not much I knows about that," wheezed Ralph, the shine burning his throat. "I'm foremen over his logs, not his frigging books."

"Go ask him if he wants a dose of salts," said Alma,

"perhaps it's making his stomach bad having to part with his money."

"Perhaps it's we needing the dose of salts," drawled Crowman, nearly trampling over Clair as she tried to worm her way around him, "standing out here, freezing our arses off, waiting to get inside and pay for a bowl of soup made with our own grub."

"Hah! When ye spends all day peeling spuds and chopping up beef with a dozen youngsters hauling on your skirts, ye can come inside, too, and warm yourself with the women in the kitchen," said Alma over the rising titters.

"And who's going to bring home the meat for ye to put in the frigging pot," sputtered Ralph, "if we spends all day standing in the kitchen, yakking? Frig, the women sees the world through a needle-hole, they do."

"I'd rather be looking through one than trying to squeeze me fat arse through one—like them that stuffs their guts on the backs of the working man," goaded Alma. "And looks like we got another one to put up with now; Willamena just got engaged to the young fellow Frankie from Rocky Head. Imagine that now," she said over another rising of titters, "the merchant's daughter marrying someone from Rocky Head." Craning her neck to see over the heads of the men, she asked, "Show, is that young Clair standing amongst ye?"

"I'm—I'm looking for Missy," said Clair, as the men stood apart, letting her pass.

"She's inside," said Alma. "Go on in and get yourself out of the cold, and tell Rose I said to give you a bowl of soup. No need for ye youngsters to stay home from the time just because your mother's not coming. How's her head?"

"It's fine," mumbled Clair, squeezing past the postmistress's portly figure. Immediately she was into a wide, open room. Ducking towards a table piled high with coats, she screened herself, watching a group of square dancers kicking up a storm in their Sunday best. The light of the lanterns hanging along the walls bounced sharply off the faces of the women (and those men who had been able to beg or pay their way in), illuminating their good-natured smiles as they ended off the jig. Others bustled to and fro, bringing soup from a small pantry to long tables lined with white cloths. Phoebe and the other girls Clair's age were standing around the heat-reddened, cast-iron stove, their faces flushed from the coal heat and laughing excitedly as they taunted a group of boys, sitting at the table, eating soup.

Clair grinned, struck with a sudden urge to be standing with them, wearing her own pretty blue Sunday dress, when Georgie Blanchard strutted from a back room and made to grab after Phoebe. Clair drew back, not wanting to be seen, then turned her attention onto a crowd of youngsters running pell-mell before her, the boys with their white shirts rolled up to their elbows, and the girls with their new ribbons hanging down their backs amidst ringlets and braids and ponytails, and amongst them, Missy, dressed in her old brown corduroys, a woolly red sweater, and her hair, more tangled than an abandoned crow's nest found in a chip pile.

Ohh, Mommy will kill her, thought Clair, and was about to rush over and grab her, when Willamena and Frankie suddenly appeared out of the pantry, their arms crooked into each other's, and sipping on glasses of blueberry wine and everyone crowding around them, laughing and talking and examining what must've been an engagement ring on Willamena's finger. Clair peered curiously at the couple. Willamena, wearing a new red dress, looked almost pretty with her hair piled high on her head and a rhinestone necklace sparkling around her throat. And the fellow Frankie, grinning and nodding at those extending good wishes around him, looked just as grand in his black suit, his face scrubbed shiny clean and his hair slicked back smoother than a wet otter.

She felt like a shabbily dressed mummer in the glow of Willamena's rhinestone necklace. A flush worked its way up Clair's neck and she shrank farther behind the coats so's not to be seen. "Here, Missy, come here," she whispered as the youngsters suddenly darted nearer her, jumping up and down and swinging each other around in their best imitation of a square dance as young Jim Bushey, his face beefy-red beneath a crop of carrot hair, sat on a footstool, scrooping on his father's accordion.

"No! Let me go," yelled Missy as Clair's hand popped out from the shadows, snatching hold of her arm.

"Shh, come quietly," begged Clair, her cheeks tinting, and closing her ears against her growing protests, she dug her fingers into her younger sister's arm, dragging her mercilessly out into the porch where the fellow Pinkson was heard exclaiming angrily, "A bloody quarter! Sir I could go after he now, and turn him upside down like a dirty pair of pants and shake him till his pockets empties out."

"That's right, b'ye, you'd think he'd be inside toasting his girl's wedding; not out here robbing ye," Alma agreed loudly, and catching sight of Clair and Missy behind her, she ushered them outside, then pushing the fellow Pinkson to one side as he backstepped, near tripping over Clair.

"The bloody thief is what he is!" Pinkson sang out, shaking his fist after the merchant who was hunching deeper into his coat as he disappeared into the sleet and dark. "The bloody thief!"

Missy whimpered, turning to Clair in fright as Ralph turned snarling onto the fellow Pinkson. "What about your store bill—old man, you got that settled up, didn't you? I suppose you eats more than a quarter's worth of grub every month. He gives you plenty, there."

"Gives!" scorned the fellow Pinkson as the men's anger grew louder. "I likes that—*gives*. He don't *give* we nothing. He gives we what we bloody works for, and after six months' work, you'd think we'd have more than a bloody quarter to jingle in our pockets. Sure the women makes more than that picking caplin off the beach."

"The women!" snorted Ralph, starting towards the door. "What the frig they got to complain about? They gets all they needs when they needs it."

"It's the sound of a jingle, Ralph, b'ye, that a man likes to hear coming from his own pockets every once in a while," said Crowman, clapping him on the shoulder, "even if he do take it out and give it to the youngsters to give right back to the merchant. At least he feels like it's himself that's doing the giving. Show, look, you're near trampling the young ones," he added, catching sight of Clair and Missy, huddling near the school, staring up at them. "Get along home," he said kindly, "not fit to be outside." Casting him a grateful look, Clair led Missy around him, darting past Ralph as he teetered over them, bellowing, "Be the frig now, if the youngsters cares whether they're taking it from the merchant or not. As long as it's sweet enough to rot their teeth now, that's all they thinks about."

"How come you're arguing agin we, anyway?" asked Al Rice. "He's stealing from you, too—unless you're planning on doing the same thing someday." Clair ran with Missy as Ralph swerved around, grabbing hold of Al's collar.

"I ain't no frigging thief!" he roared, "I works for my dollar like every man here, and I ain't going to frigging stand here apologizing if I becomes a frigging boss!"

"No need, Ralph, b'ye, no need," said Crowman, taking hold of Ralph's arm. "The merchants been robbing us blind since our fathers were shitting yellow. Nothing we can do to change it this night." And then Johnnie was holding back Al.

"Good say, Crow, b'ye, good say," said Johnnie, patting Al's back coaxingly. "What say we all goes inside, else we'll be spitting blood if the women gets ahold of us—fighting this early in the evening."

"I won't be talked about," blustered Ralph as the men led him towards the school door. "I earns my living like every man here—be frigged if I'll have it said any other way."

"Sure you do, b'ye, sure you do," joined in another, "We're all just joking, that's all, just joking."

"Who's hogging the shine? Let's all have another drop; sure we don't look pretty enough yet to go dancing; it's red the women likes in our eyes, not spit."

"I won't be talked over," argued Ralph, louder than the others.

"No, but be Jesus, you'll be walked over if you soon don't get outta the way," said another, jostling through the men to get inside. "I been standing out here long enough."

Holding tight to Missy's hand, Clair hurried through the sleet towards home, glancing over her shoulder as the men stomped the snow off their feet, crowding their way in through the doorway, handing over their quarters to Alma. Missy kept twisting around as well, slipping and sliding as she partially hid behind Clair's back to escape the wind. Her step slowed as the last of the men disappeared inside.

"I wants to go back," she yelled as Clair, head bowed to the blowing sleet, dragged her onwards, oblivious of her cries. Fighting to keep her balance on the ice building up on the road, Clair managed to get her, kicking and fighting through the gate, then latched it, barring her escape.

"Now listen, Mommy's really sick tonight," she cautioned.

But Missy was already bursting in through the door, yelling: "Mommy, Mommeee!" and skidding across the kitchen, she came to a halt where her mother was lying back on the divan, a damp cloth folded around a bread poultice resting across her forehead.

"Shh," Clair hushed, running after her, but her mother was already rising.

The bread poultice had slipped to one side, and she was whispering, "Don't yell, ohh, don't yell."

"But I wants to stay at the time," said Missy.

"You can," said Clair, closing the door and slipping off her coat. "But first we cleans you up, all right?" she said soothingly, carrying a pan of water from the washstand to the table.

"Mommeee!"

"I said shh," said Sare, opening her eyes and squinting like one jarred from a deep sleep by an unexpected light. They widened as she fixed them onto Missy's dirtied clothes and hair. "Mercy, were you at the time looking like that?"

"I'm going back."

"First, let Clair wash your hair, my dolly."

"Noo," cried Missy and swinging away from her mother, darted towards the door.

"No you don't," said Clair, catching her by the sweater and dragging her to the table. "It won't take long—come now, we'll make you real pretty and then you can go."

As Missy yelled, Sare, her face pinched with pain, came to her feet, pleading, "Ooh, angel, don't yell, for I swear, I'll be throwing up agin tonight."

"See, it makes Mommy sick when you yell; be a good girl, now; come on—"

"Let me go!" said Missy, shoving against Clair. "Lemme go, lemme go!"

"Stop it!" ordered Sare. And surprised by the sharpness of her mother's cry, Clair let go of Missy, and Missy, losing her balance, stumbled sideways, knocking against the table and sending the pan of water spilling to the floor.

"Now look what you've done!" said Sare, and Missy's face whitened as she looked from the spilled water to her mother's face. With a cry, she ran for the stairs, but slipping on the water, she again lost her balance, teetering awkwardly. Snatching hold of her shoulder, Sare held her upright, but, whether to catch her from falling, or to catch her from escaping, Missy never paused to consider. Opening her mouth, she let go with a scream that sent a grimace across her mother's face. Releasing Missy, Sare clasped her hands to ears.

"Stop it, stop it!" she said, but Missy, believing she had done wrong and seeking absolution through her tears, held back her head and screamed all the harder. Another grimace distorted Sare's features, and reaching out, she smacked Missy across the face. Stunned, Missy collapsed into a wide-eyed silence. That this mother could be capable of administering harshness was in itself a moment of incredulity. That this harshness could be turned upon her—who, in even her most devilish of childhood antics had received nothing more then a playful pat on the bottom—was a blow more crushing than the hand of a thousand demons. Stumbling backwards, she reached out to Clair as a crab would a rock beneath a swooping gull. But Clair, as stunned by the slap as Missy, and with a growing nausea in her stomach, saw too late her sister's reach of trust, and moved, instead, to her mother, who was turning as ashen as the dead, and whose body was beginning to sway as if she might faint. She reached for her, but at that moment a rap sounded on the door, and the uncle inched it open, peering inside.

"Uncle Sim, Uncle Sim!" Missy cried out, the tautness of her body dissolving into convulsions of sobs as she ran to her uncle.

"No, Missy, wait here," Clair cried out, but Missy was already throwing her arms around the uncle's legs, wailing, "Mommy hit me, Mommy hit me," and for the first time since she'd found out about his thievery, Clair was caught standing a scant foot before this uncle, staring into the shadow made by the peak of his cap, to where the scarcest glimmer of light marked the pits of his eyes. Her lip curled with loathing as he laid his hands possessively on the crown of Missy's sobbing head. But it was Sare who held the uncle's attention, leaning towards him, as she was, holding tightly to the hand that had just struck her child, its pallor like the sleet clinking against the window pane.

"What's she done, now?" he asked with a weariness that could as easily been born of Sare as of Missy. But it was the sight of his ears perking back that Clair was keen to catch, and with her lip curling farther, she stepped protectively before her mother.

"Missy knocked over a pan of water," she said, and before she had a chance to declare that the spilt water was of no consequence, and therefore there was no need for him to stand around a second longer, Missy tore around to face her, her blue eyes grappling at Clair's heart.

"You made me, Clair!" she cried, her voice swollen with reproach at this second breach of trust.

"Goodness, Missy, it's not the end of the world," said Sare, wringing her hands, her voice equally as reproachful as Missy's. She smiled, more shamefully than apologetically, at Sim, pressing her fingers against her temples. "I'm at my wit's end with her today, Uncle Sim. She won't get her hair washed."

"She was just about to," said Clair, holding out a hand with which to persuade Missy away from the uncle. "Come, Missy, we'll get it done fast, and then I'll take you to the time."

But, Missy, already embraced by suffering, drew more comfort from her sister's remorse than her offer of good will, and clinging tighter to her uncle's waist, sobbed breathlessly, "Leave m-me alone, Clair, you l-leave me alone."

"She can come with me if she wants," said the uncle, "her grandmother can help her."

"We don't need nobody helping us," snapped Clair.

"Goodness, Clair—"

"Well, we don't! I'll take her to the time."

"I w-wants Uncle Sim to take me. And I wants Grandmother to help me wash my hair."

"It's your mother's say," said Sim.

"Won't it be too hard for the grandmother?" asked Sare, hesitantly.

"She washed it before!" sobbed Missy.

"Yeah, only your bangs—" began Clair, but was stopped by a raised hand from her mother.

"Perhaps the grandmother can do something with her, Sim. I knows I can't stand to hear them fighting, and it seems that's all they does these days."

"A good smack don't hurt sometimes," muttered the uncle, slewing his eyes to Clair. But Sare heard nothing of Clair's angry snort, feeding as she was upon the uncle's sanctioning of her deed. "Perhaps I can get you a cup of tea before you go?" she offered, her shakiness giving way to relief. But the uncle was wearily shaking his head, the cup of tea an encumbrance to already laden shoulders.

"I just come to check the wood box—"

"I already done it," cut in Clair.

"Clair—" but Sare's voice faltered, her strength failing her. "Bless you, Sim, but Clair's already filled it."

"There's no splits," he noted.

"I'm doing them now," said Clair, and her look fell pleadingly onto her sister. "I wants you to help me, Missy."

"I'm going to the time!" shouted Missy.

"Goodness, hush your crying then, silly girl," said Sare. "Here—come let me wash your face, then you can go to Grandmother's if you wants."

Ignoring the hand her mother held out to her, Missy snatched a face cloth off the wash bin and scrubbed at her face.

"Mind you scrubs off that pout," said Sare. "Come here, child, and give me a kiss, for I can't stand seeing you cry, and I swear, I won't get a wink tonight for thinking about you."

Eyes glowering and head down, Missy allowed her mother to clasp her hands around her tear-stained cheeks, kissing each one passionately. "My, the mess her hair's in," she murmured, finger-combing a handful of curls away from Missy's forehead. "And the fuss she makes when we got to wash it, Uncle Sim— I don't know what we're going to do with her. Now, are you going to be a good girl for Grandmother?"

Missy pulled away, refusing to speak, and picking up her mitts from where she had tossed them earlier, stalked out the door ahead of her uncle. Clair watched through the window as she struggled up over the iced garden path onto the road. She turned once, glaring back at the house, the usually cherubic face so disfigured by scowls that Clair felt an impulse to grin at its comic likeness. But then Missy's eyes caught hold of hers, and even from afar, and with the dark of the evening between them, their coldness reached a place in Clair's heart that the night's wind had not. And with a knowing that comes like the darkest hour before dawn, where its presence is more thought than felt, Clair grasped that the little coaxing or prodding that had always in the past been sure to bring a smile or a sense of giving over to that twisted little face was a thing no more. With a backwards glance at the house, the uncle caught up with Missy, and taking her hand, steered her towards the grandmother's.

"Old bastard," muttered Clair.

The sleet turned to rain during the night, and by morning the pale yellow of the late winter's sun cast a brighter light on the saturated outport. Clair was up early, washing her face besides the washstand when the door burst open and Missy came flying in, her hair a tangled mass of curls, and the corners of her eyes still gooked with sleep. "Mommy, Mommy," she sang out, slamming the door shut, and with a murderous look at Clair, sped over to where her mother was standing near the bin, sipping a cup of tea.

"I had a dream, I had a dream!" she cried out. "It's about Daddy."

Sare faltered, a fearful look clouding her face. "No more bad dreams now, child," she whispered, reaching down to stroke the cheek she had slapped the night before.

"No, Mommy," said Missy, shaking her head, her curls dancing prettily around her face. "It was a good dream—a real good dream—Daddy was laughing."

"Ooh, tell me, then," exclaimed Sare, laying down her cup and squeezing Missy's shoulders.

"He was picking flowers," said Missy, bowing her head like one taking a curtain call at the school play, "big, pretty flowers."

"Goodness," exclaimed Sare.

"And he was giving them—to—to—"

"Don't change things, now!" cried Sare.

"To—me," said Missy, giggling.

"Isn't that nice," said Sare, hugging and kissing her girl. "And what else did he do?"

"Nothing else."

"Then, what did he look like?"

"Like Daddy, silly."

"His clothes, Missy, what was he wearing?"

"Soldier's clothes—and he was clean."

"Clean! My, it's you that's silly," said Sare, giving her daughter a little shake as Missy burst into giggles again. "Now, remember everything—was it a field or a garden that he was picking flowers in?"

"A field, a big field. And the grass was blowing all around his legs."

"Oh, the sweetness of her; isn't she an angel, Clair?" she asked as Clair came to stand besides them. "Were there others picking flowers with him? Think carefully, now."

"Nope. Just Daddy."

"Did he speak?"

"Nope. He just laughed."

"Dear mercy, was there anything else?"

"Nope."

"Are you sure?"

Missy nodded, a pleased smile charming her face.

"There now, what a good girl. Sit up and have your cereal with Clair. Did you hear that, Clair?" she asked, seating Missy at the table. "Wasn't that the nicest dream? Here, my dolly, have some more sugar in your cereal. You want some more sugar, Clair?"

Clair nodded, smiling as her mother dumped a spoonful of brown sugar into her bowl and Missy's, and then a dollop of butter. She sought out Missy's eyes, searching for a smile in return.

"Uncle Sim said you're bad," hissed Missy.

"You don't listen to him," said Clair, "he don't like me."

But Missy was not to be had and began eating her cereal with nary another look at Clair. Clair sighed, but was unable to keep the smile from returning. It was the rarest of mornings when her mother was up before her—and making breakfast. And now with Missy's dream, it felt as if her father had been for a visit during the night.

A sharp cry from her mother cut short her thoughts. Sare was holding tight to the back of the divan, her face constricted with grief.

"Mommy!" Clair leaped off her chair, running to her.

"He's dead!" gasped Sare.

"Mommy—"

"Yes, he's dead, Clair, I can feel it."

"No, he's not, Mommy," said Missy, running to her mother. "He's picking flowers—for you."

"Sweet child!" Then Sare broke down sobbing. "That's w-why you had the d-dream, he's dead, I know he's dead."

"He's not dead, Mommy," cried Missy. "He's not dead;

he was laughing, and he was giving *you* the flowers, not *me*."

"No, Mommy," said Clair shakily, her worries returning like the devil's haunt, "he's not dead, I knows he's not." And catching the distress in her eldest girl's eyes, Sare bit off her sobs, attempting to straightening herself.

"There now, I've upset you both," she cried. "It's a poor mother I've been. Oh, God, help me," she wept anew, sinking into the depths of the divan. "I just can't care about anything since he left. I try and I try, but I just can't care about anything, and I don't want to; God help me, but this feels worse than death," and she began to weep harder, her body shaking, her hands trembling as they covered her face.

"Mommy?" whimpered Missy.

"It's all right," said Clair, touching a hand to Missy's shoulder, and despite their mother's final descent into hopelessness, she felt indeed it was all right, for had they not been circling around and around in a timeless void for the past two years since the day their father left? What weariness to be moored within the expectancy of a moment that never realizes itself, a spiral that cross-threads, carrying them neither upward nor downward. Now, finally, those threads had righted themselves and she felt freed and as willing to follow her mother into the throes of despair, as she was into heights of ecstasy. Just then Alma pushed in through the door, waving a white envelope and blabbering excitedly that it was a letter from Job.

"See? Daddy's not dead," shouted Missy, pulling on her mother's arm. "I told you he's not dead."

"Dead? Well, I never thought of that," said Alma, her face sobering. She held the letter higher as Missy dashed towards her, hand outreached. "But it wouldn't come in an ordinary white envelope if he was dead, would it?" She looked questioningly to Sare, whose look of sudden rapture had now turned to stone.

"Give it to me," said Missy, reaching up to grab the letter.

But Alma shushed her away, walking straight to Sare. "I'm going to open it for you," she said. "You stay where you are, Sare, and you, too, Clair. Missy, come stand besides your mother. Although I knows in me heart it's good news because your name is handwritten and not typed, and they wouldn't send bad news like that in handwritten letters. I should know because I receives enough government letters in the mail to figure that one out by now."

"Alma—"

"Yes, yes, I knows, maid," said Alma, slitting her fingernail beneath the glued flap and peeling open the envelope. "Give me time, give me time; sure me hands are shaking worse than yours," and unfolding the white sheet of paper, she went quiet, a tuck furrowing her brow as she stared hard at the lettering.

"Alma!" Sare near screamed. Alma's face burst into smiles. "See? It's just as I said. They wouldn't send news in a handwritten envelope if he was dead. He's alive, my dear, and had someone writing the letter for him—"

With a cry, Sare flew out of her chair, swooping the letter out of Alma's hands. "Oh, sweet mercy, he's coming home," she moaned, her eyes flying across the page. "Clair, Missy, he's coming home! He's coming home!" She stared at them, astonished, crumpling the letter to her breasts.

"Yea, Daddy's alive, Daddy's alive," chanted Missy, jumping gleefully around the divan.

"Yup, he's alive, all right," said Alma. "I knowed that soon as I seen the handwriting. Sure, I never even thought he might be dead."

"Ooh, blessed Lord," and it looked as if Sare would collapse into a swoon, but steadying herself, she waved Clair to one side, uncrumpling the letter, her eyes flying across the page. "He's been wounded, but he's all right and is resting in a hospital," she read with mounting excitement. "He'll be home as soon as he's able." She swung towards Alma and clasped the surprised woman in a tight embrace. "Thank you, my dear, oh thank you for bringing me such news."

"I knowed you'd be excited," said Alma, her arms flopping awkwardly by her sides as she endured Sare's embrace. "That's why I runned with it as fast as I could."

"God bless you, you never got much of a chance to say anything, the way I was getting on," said Sare, hugging Clair tightly to her side. "My, Clair, isn't it grand news? Missy, Missy, come here, my love," and dropping to her chair, Sare gazed lovingly into her younger girl's eyes. "You're an angel, a sweet blessed angel, that's what you are," she whispered. "She dreamt about him last night, Alma, didn't she, Clair? Took word to him, she did, and now he's found a way to bring word back to us. It's nothing short of a miracle! A blessed miracle!"

Clair nodded, grinning at Missy. Miracle or no, her father was coming home, and Missy's dream was their first sign of that fortunate event, and for that, Clair was as eager as her mother to heap upon her the praise worthy of the saints. And indeed, Missy's returning smile captured for Clair again the sun's rays within her sheen of curls, evaporating fully the shadow that had been engulfing all of them since the day of her father's departure.

"Yup, it's good news, for sure," said Alma, taking time to check around the kitchen now that the excitement was dying down. "I always runs around with the mail when something important comes. I figures everyone wants good news as quick as possible. You girls not going to school today?"

Sare gasped, coming to her feet, "Of course they're going to school. Clair, Missy, your cereal. Oh, it must be cold by now." Ushering them both to the table, she near waltzed Alma out the door, asking after her poor mother.

"Grand, my dear, she's grand," replied Alma. "Up with the birds and more chipper than the youngsters."

"What a good thing for you," sang Sare. "You take her my regards, won't you, and come back for tea—the both of you, especially when Job gets back; he always asks after your mother, he do," and then she was closing the door and turning back into the kitchen with the broadest of smiles. Letting out a whoop, she squeezed her arms around herself, dancing around the kitchen, her head tossed back, eyes closed, singing foolishly, "He's safe and he's coming home, he's safe and he's coming home, oh thank you, sweet Jesus, thank you, sweet Jesus."

"Now, you help Missy get off to school, Clair, and I'll make some rice pudding with raisins for your lunch—you'll like that, won't you, my dollies? And I'll make up some extra for us to take up to the grandmother and Uncle Sim. They'll be happy to know your father's coming home."

"You go," said Clair to Missy, her smiles giving way to a grimace as she pulled on her coat.

"My, Clair, you knows you're not going to pout on this day of all days. You go to school now, and hurry straight home after. In the name of the Lord, child, we owes it to the grandmother to tell her ourselves, for she's the one who gave him birth, and for that alone, she has my prayers."

Waving goodbye to her mother watching after them through the kitchen window, Clair pushed out through the

gate, breathing deeply of the balsam-scented air of late
winter, admiring how the sawdust spread golden mats
across the last fingers of snow arching across door places
and backyards. A drop of water dripped from a passing
cloud and splattered against her eye, squiggling her vision.
Dancing crazily before were her the greens of the
surrounding hillside, the reds and blues of the clapboard
painted houses, and the indigo of the far-flung hills
cradling the rocking blue sea—the sea, the waterway that
would soon be bringing her father home to her. And she
ran after Missy towards the schoolhouse, slowing her step
as she came abreast Phobie and Joanie, singing out to them
that yes, yes, her father was coming home. And wasn't it
grand that summer would soon be here and they could all
go swimming again down on the sandbar at the mouth of
Wild Bear River and beachcombing down by Copy-Cat
Cove? And yes, for sure they'd be going back to Cat Arm
come winter, to sliding beneath the stars, and whistling to
the northern lights, and bribing old Pearl uphill with a
downhill chance. Ohh, it was an impossible thought!

CHAPTER FIVE

THE DAY OF JOB'S ARRIVAL dawned a brilliant clear sky. Up with the chickens as she had been since the day of the letter three months before, Sare rustled through the house like a spring breeze, dusting, polishing, tidying, having days before scrubbed down the floors, walls and ceilings, and painted and touched up chairs and skirting boards and window benches, and a hundred other varied and sundry tasks that the house had been begging for since the day of Job's departure. The neighbours waved cheerily as she stood in the window, polishing and smiling out at them as they passed by, lugging their buckets of water or heading for the wood trails with their axes and bucksaws. For despite the scorn that had been heaped upon his departure, the outporters had been buzzing for days about Job's return, and wondering amongst themselves—and to Sare, now that she was getting out a bit more—what stories he might have to tell about the war and other things that come with travelling over the seas.

Clair skipped lightly down over the stairs, not wanting to miss a second of this promising day, and came to a standstill as her eyes lit onto her mother standing before the bin. It wasn't so much that Sare was whipping up a pudding this morning before the sun had yet to rise, but that she was doing so dressed in her red satin skirt that she only wore on Christmas Day or Easter Sunday, with an edging of white petticoat slipping a little below the hemline, and her white, high-collared blouse with the pearly buttons. And gracing her neck and earlobes were the rhinestone necklace and matching earrings that Job had given her for her birthday that first year they had married.

"You're the early bird this morning," said Sare gaily, wiping up a floption of flour and water she had spilled onto the bin. "For goodness' sake, Clair, are you sleepwalking?" she asked as Clair continued to stand, wide-eyed.

"You're wearing your Christmas clothes," said Clair.

"Is that what I'm wearing?" said Sare, cracking an egg and stirring it into the mixing bowl. "And I thought it was a skirt and blouse."

"But it looks silly—everybody will stare."

"What's wrong with that? Your father's coming home today, child. Why wouldn't you want to be dressed grandly on the day your father's coming home?" She swung proudly past her daughter, her skirt rustling around her stockinged legs as she pulled a cake pan out of the bottom drawer of the stove. "Now, you get yourself some breakfast," she said, waltzing back to the sink, "then, go wake Missy. I wants you to wash her hair so's it'll be nice and fresh. You knows how your father likes to smell her hair after it's all washed and fresh. And then you can make your bed, and put on your nice dress and the new stockings that I bought you for church last month."

"But it's Saturday," said Clair. "I'm not walking down on the wharf dressed like Christmas on a Saturday. Everybody will be staring."

"Goodness mercy, Clair, are you going to stand there arguing about what day of the week it is? Your father's coming home. Now go get washed and get your breakfast like I asked you."

"But I'm not wearing no Sunday clothes on a Saturday—"

"Well, sir," sighed Sare, standing arms akimbo, "Saturday or no, you'll go get dressed like I asked you. If the good Lord can see fit to bring your father home from across the world, then I see fit that we be dressed respectably to greet him when he gets here, because for sure, it's a day of all days, isn't it, with your father coming home? And isn't that when we wears our best clothes—on the day of all days?"

Clair moped to the washstand, staring morosely at her mother in the mirror, knowing better than to argue with her when she was on about the higher moral of things. But as grand as it was that her father was coming home, she wasn't going to be wearing her Sunday clothes on a Saturday for Phoebe and everybody else to be pointing and staring at. A shuffling outside signalled the uncle, and coupled with her mother looking like a Christmas wreath, a sourness tempered some of the joy of the morning. The door opened and she saw before the uncle entered, the thoughtful look bringing life to his otherwise dulled eyes, for wasn't it one's make-up to sniff out that which was new? To juggle a closing door against the bounty of another? And now with his brother coming home to warm his own hearth, what right had he now to the fresh loaves of bread and sweet puddings, and Missy's labours to cleanse his bin? And for sure, thought Clair, drowning her face in a handful of water, he'd have to find some other poor mortals to steal his grub from now that her father had come home.

"I'm going to tell Daddy," she silently promised herself as her mother, brushing bread crumbs off her hands, greeted the uncle with smiles.

"You're up and about early," she declared, closing the door behind him. "Come in, come in, and have a cup of tea."

"No. No tea," said Sim, his eyes sinking onto the sliver of lace edging below her skirt.

Sare, quick to follow his look, stepped prudently behind a chair. "I was just arguing with Clair about how silly it must seem to be dressing up on a Saturday," she said. "But it's Job's homecoming, after all."

"Are you coming with us to see Daddy, Uncle Sim?" asked Missy, running down the stairs and over to her uncle.

"The wind's off the water," said Sim, patting the back of Missy's curls. "The grandmother asked if she can wait up with her," he said to Sare, scuffing his feet on the piece of cardboard she had laid as a mat before the door.

"My goodness, no," exclaimed Sare. "Job would want to see her on the wharf, waiting for him. Tell grandmother she's a dear, and Job will be proud to know how well his mother's been keeping company with his little girl, but, blessed heart, he'll miss her if she's not waiting on the wharf for him, won't he, Clair?"

Clair scratched a smile across her face as she looked to the uncle, but it was onto Missy that his eyes were fastened, and it satisfied the jealousy breeding in her heart to see the look of disappointment settling over his wrinkling old face, for she had been a good bone, had Missy, always there to be played with, to do the dirty dishes, and to buffer the heat between him and the grandmother. And for sure, thought Clair—her happiness this morning extending a rare moment of charity towards the uncle—in a house as darkened with pettiness as her own had been in despair, Missy's would be a precious light to lose.

"I'll come tomorrow, Uncle Sim, won't I, Mommy?"

"Of course you will. And tell Grandmother, Job will be up, too—and me and Clair. It's the least we can do, now that the good Lord has brought us all together again—to show ourselves as a family. What do you say, Clair? My, Sim, are you sure you won't stay for tea?"

"No, no, I'll be going."

"Bless you for thinking of us. And now that Job's coming home, you won't have to bother with us any more. God knows you've seen us through these past horrible years. I swear, I don't know what we would've done without you."

The uncle bowed in the face of Sare's praise. "I'll go with ye when the boat comes," he said gravely.

"That's all right; we can walk ourselves," said Clair impulsively.

"He's family, and Job will want him there, too," said Sare, eyeing her daughter sharply. "Bless you, and give Grandmother our love," she called out as the uncle, with scarcely a glance at Clair, let himself out the door. The second the latch clicked, Sare spun onto her eldest girl.

"You'll mind your ungratefulness! I allows your poor father's heart's going to be broke if he hears how bad you behaves towards his brother after all he's done for us this past two years."

"He does for his self," muttered Clair.

"He'd have to walk on water before he'd get a kind thought from you, and even then, I swear you'd be checking the soles of his feet for stilts. Now, go get dressed, and don't argue no more about the clothes I got laid out, because you're wearing them, supposing I got to dress you myself. Missy! Missy, come here, child, I washes your face and combs your hair. Go on, Clair, up over them stairs!" she ordered, pulling Missy to the washstand. "Landsakes, the tangles," she complained, trying to draw a brush through Missy's hair, "it's a wonder you got any hair left on your head. Where's your ribbons? Have you got any ribbons? Clair, have a look around her room and find me some ribbons. I swear I've used a yard of material making ribbons this past year and I still can't find one when I needs it." Backing up to the stairwell, leading Missy by a ringlet, she called out, "Clair, Clair, are you looking for ribbons, or you just going to spend the day moping? I swear your father's going to have his hands full with the two of you once he gets back."

"I listens," said Missy, as Sare bustled her back to the washstand, wetting the brush into the wash pan. "Clair's ignorant."

"For the love of it, Missy, where're you learning words like that—and saying them against your sister?"

"Uncle Sim tells them to her," shouted Clair, tossing two yellow ribbons down from the landing.

"No, he don't," shouted Missy.

"Yes, he do," Clair shouted back. "He's a bloody black-guard."

"Clair!" Sare ran back to the stairs, wielding the hair-brush like a tomahawk, but her eldest was already disappearing inside her room, slamming the door behind her. "The sting of my hand is what you're going to feel, young lady, if I hears one more word," Sare yelled up over the stairs. "I swear I don't know where the two of you is getting your bad manners, because it was never a thing allowed around here. My, is that the pudding? Well, sir, I forgot all about the pudding, and it's black currant, your father's favourite. Ohh, I allows it black as the cinders. Clair? Clair—get dressed and get down over them stairs and help me this morning."

Clair trudged down over the stairs, her face darker than a rain cloud as she pressed down the skirt of her plaid Sunday dress, watching her mother bustling to and fro in a rustle of silks and petticoat. When finally the pudding was scraped, and Missy's hair was brushed and tied up with ribbons, and they had all eaten breakfast and with the dishes washed and floors swept and waxed and buffed, the booming of the steamer sounded up over the hill.

"He's here," cried Sare, running for her coat. Sim, his hair wet back off his forehead, and wearing his Sunday jacket, tapped on the door, poking his head inside. "I allows you're going to have to hold me down," cried Sare running to meet him, "because I swear my feet just wants to up and fly. Missy, Clair, come on, let's go. And watch out for the ruts in the road so's you don't get mud on your new stockings— Missy? Clair?"

The wind grazed damp and soft against Clair's cheek as she lagged behind her mother, uncle and sister, her coat wrapped tightly around the tail of her Sunday dress, partially hiding her new white stockings. Head down, she avoided those peering through their windows at Sare, or hanging off their back steps, calling out greetings as they, too, hurried through their housework, preparing to run down over the hill and greet the steamer. Luckily, Phoebe and Joanie and everybody were taking advantage of a Saturday morning and burrowing more comfortably into their beds, mindless of Job Gale or any other soldier coming home this early in the day, sparing Clair the sight of her friends, at least, watching her walk down the road on a Saturday with her Sunday clothes on.

"Small comfort," she muttered, then turned her glance resentfully at the uncle's back as he took hold of Missy's

hand, no doubt appearing to all those looking as the doting
uncle. And were not his shoulders more drooped than
yesterday—testimony to the burden he'd borne these past
years? And did not his grave look and Sunday jacket lift him
above the ranks of the rest of the Basiners this morning,
earning him a share in the excitement of her father's homecoming?

Lordy, she bemoaned, pushing away her thoughts of
gloom—her mother was right—this was a day to treasure,
and here she'd gotten herself into a snit because of the
uncle and a few garments. But gloom redescended as her
mother queened towards her, her head slightly tilted beneath
her green feathered hat, her eyes more sparkling than the
rhinestones adorning her throat and earlobes, and her coat
partially opened, showing off the red of her satin skirt and
the gleaming whiteness of its lacy, hanging petticoat. Plus,
at the last moment before leaving the house, she had tinted
up her lips and cheeks with a little rouge—worse than Joanie
Pinkson's doll.

It struck her then that since the day her father had
walked away from her, down over the hill to the waiting
steamer, and she had run inside to find her mother sobbing
broken-heartedly, and Missy crumpling onto the floor,
holding her arms up to Clair, that she hadn't again thought
of the doll. How so should she think of it now—on the same
day as his return? And in such a manner? For upon thinking
of the doll, she had turned her eyes skyward, and imprinted
upon the cloud-tossed blue were the marble blue eyes in a
stoic pink face, and painted lips that never moved, and
glossy, curled hair and painted brows. The image hung there
as did the hands of the clock in her mother's kitchen, awaiting the breath of an ocean's breeze to infuse it with life.

With a sudden gust the sky shifted, no longer the robin's-egg blue of a second ago, but deepening to shades of indigo and mulberry, lightening, then darkening. As her father's features replaced the face of the doll, they shifted too—his eyes, squinting, gazing, his cheeks dimpling, his mouth widening, narrowing—nothing stilled, nothing stationary. She shivered as that same gust now curled itself inside her collar, causing her to tighten further her coat as she turned her glance down over the bay to where the steamer was quickly approaching.

They reached the wharf and looked over the heads of their neighbours at the black hull of the ship as it neared, heaving and dropping on the swells from an offshore storm, and with a flock of snipes and gulls screaming over its stern. It wasn't just her father's homecoming that was spurring people out the door this morning. The steamer's first visit of the year was always too fortunate to miss, what with the parcels of all shapes and sizes being unloaded and passed around before finding their rightful hands, and the passengers from up and down the bay getting off and milling around the wharf to stretch their sea legs and calling out to those they know and sharing bits of news about politics and friends before launching off again.

An old couple huddled at the far side of the wharf near the store and Clair peered more closely as the wind swiped the hood back off the old woman's head, exposing her tight white braids. She instantly remembered that it was the same old woman that she had seen standing in the shadow of the stagehead the day her father brought them home from Cat Arm. And the brown worsted cap pulled down over the ears of the old man standing besides her left no wonder in her mind as to who these people were and their reason for making the trip from Rocky Head on this most hopeful of days. Holed by the cuddy in a boat bobbing up and down on the water behind them was a young fellow with longish blond hair tucked behind his ears and straying down over his shirt collar. Emptying out bilge water with a bicket, he sat with his back to the wharf, seemingly oblivious of the dozens of people swarming around and casting curious looks his way, but there was a tautness to his shoulders, and as Clair watched, she sensed as strongly as if she were sitting in the boat alongside of him that this was more attributed to the dozens of pairs of eyes boring into his back than his act of bailing out bilge water. She knew because the same tautness was stiffening her shoulders as she stood with the glaring white of her Sunday stockings luring, undoubtedly, the attention of every man, woman and child standing behind her.

Frankie moved out from the crowd and stood talking with the elderly couple, and Willamena, brushing past Clair, ran over to join him, linking her arm through his. Spotting Crowman slouching against the side of the store, Clair pushed away from her mother and sought shelter in the shadow he threw off besides him. A dog trotted by and Missy sprang after it, and the uncle after Missy so's she'd not get her stockings dirty. Her mother stood by herself for the moment, and Clair noted that even Crowman, who was renowned for his absent-mindedness, couldn't help but be attracted to the sight of her mother. If not for the Sunday clothes, her presence might have blended with the others and one might not have noted the trembling of her mouth and the expectancy in her eyes, like the bared soul of a virgin maid upon the eve of her first love. As was, the wind-fondled garments resembled a foreign flag fluttering around her legs, enticing all those who neared to stare and query whether scorn or respect was the appropriate tribute to this exotic outlander, or whether to turn away from the beguiling appeal of the bride and satisfy their intrigue through secretive, sideway glances instead.

Not so was Clair flapping in their faces. Scrunching as tightly to the side of the store as its walls would allow, her coat tightly drawn around her, and the white of her stockings greyed by Crowman's shadow, she more resembled a flag at half-mast on a windless day. A shout sounded from up on deck as the last rope was tied and the gangway lowered, and Sare, forgetting once again those standing around her, pressed forward, cottons and satins fluttering around her legs, searching out the faces of those leaning over the ship's railing. Heavily clothed figures stared back, their gaze skipping over the upturned faces of most of the people and fastening their scrutiny onto Sare's, as intrigued as the Basiners by this coloured spectre straining towards them, her eyes eagerly searching theirs, so urgent, so tremulous, one feared she would succumb to convulsions before discovering that which she so frantically sought.

Then Alma was shuffling besides her, taking her arm and steadying her as she bumped into a youngster in her haste to get closer to the gangway. "My dear, come—stand back a bit, and give him time to disembark."

"I don't see him," said Sare, her tension breaking to half sobs as she allowed Alma to lead her away from the centre of the crowd, closer to where Clair was standing by the store.

"How can you expect to see anybody in this mob?" said Alma. "Look, there's Missy—and Sim. Watching her like a hawk, he is. My, you had some help there since Job left. Sim, come here, my son, and hold up Sare. I takes Missy. How old is she—eight? Nine? Running around like a two-year-old, she is. Here, Clair, come take your sister's hand. That's the girl," she said as Clair left Crowman's side, reaching for Missy.

"Mommy, Mommy, do you see Daddy?" sang out Missy, pulling away from Clair and dancing around her mother. Clair trembled with excitement too, straining to see over the heads of the men and women as they crowded before her. No doubt they were all here now, she thought somewhat contrarily, and no doubt from the eagerness of their smiles as they strained towards the boat, they were all thinking mighty fine of themselves—for were they, too, not heroes? Had they not warred against starvation and frostbite on his—their neighbour's door stoop—thus allowing him to war on the stoop of another?

"Job!"

The cry was from her mother. Clair wormed into an opening and caught her breath. He was there—all six feet and gangly—standing at the top of the gangway with a package of sorts in his hands. And his eyes fastened onto her mother. Daddy!

The crowd parted, allowing Sare a clear path towards him. Missy darted after her, but the uncle snatched her back. Clair wanted to reach out, to take her sister's hand, but her own remained lifeless to her side as her father started walking down the gangway. His step was slow, bow-legged, like all those at sea for many days. And there was a limp, a decided limp to his right leg. His wound. Most everyone quietened as he slowly made his way down amongst them— even her mother came to a standstill, watching him, one hand covering her mouth, the other her heart. He had come back. Her father had come back. And not the coward they had made him out to be, but a man. A proud man.

"It's home you be, agin, Job, my son," someone called out, and others spoke too, welcoming him. But his eyes touched only Sare, standing with both hands to her mouth now, and the tears streaming down her face. Someone let out a whistle as they drew nearer and Alma's whoop was heard above the rest as Sare broke into a run and threw herself into her husband's arms. Holding the cloth-wrapped bundle he was carrying to one side, Job buried his face into the curls that the wind had torn free of the green-feathered hat, and held her tightly to his chest.

It's a hat, thought Clair of the bundle he carefully held to one side, as was in Missy's dream—a hat for her mother. Or seashells. Or flowers—

Everyone quietened again as Job pulled back from Sare, raising his head to look around at them. As if he recognized Missy's whines, his eyes swept towards her and Clair's insides quickened as he gazed over Missy's head and onto her—but then, just as quickly, beyond. Moving Sare aside, he held the bundle more firmly before him and started walking, his step a slow, dragging limp.

She knew—without looking she knew—whom he was walking towards, whom he was holding the bundle out to. Amongst them all, there were only two others waiting with the same look of longing on their faces as was on hers and her mother's—and onto her father's too, as he searched them out. She turned, following him with her eyes towards where the old man and woman from Rocky Head stood side by side, watching, waiting. Their look turned into a pressing urgency as they stared from him to the ship's railing, and back to him again, the same look that she, Clair, had seen upon her mother's face a dozen times as she had sat at the kitchen table, staring out at the muddied garden, waiting, praying, begging for a word, a sign—

A breeze lifted the cloth off the bundle, exposing a brown wool cap atop a few other articles of clothing. Emitting a little cry, the old woman began to fold. The old man swayed, his arms reaching around her, his eyes straying from her father to the railing, from her father to the railing, searching, searching, for that which still could be. Yet, they knew. From the way their bodies had already begun to shrink into each other, they knew. Had known since long before the boat had docked and her father stood before them, holding out to them all that remained of their son, for how can death to a part of you be held unknown?

A whimper escaped Clair as her father pressed the bundle into the old woman's arms, and she clasped her hand frightfully over her mouth, looking down lest the sound be tagged to her. A hand touched her elbow, gently nudging her to one side and Frankie moved past her. Reaching out to the old man and woman, he laid his forehead against theirs, all three leaning into the other.

"Luke!" Her father called down to the young fellow still sitting with his back to everybody, the bicket now resting by his feet. He looked around slowly, and she saw the tears glistening on his face in the paltry noonday sun. Kneeling down on the edge of the wharf, her father reached inside his shirt pocket, pulling out a bronzed medal with a striped ribbon dangling from it. The young fellow refused to move at first, preferring to hang his head instead, allowing his tears to freely fall. Then, wiping at them, he rose, holding up his hand for his brother's medal.

A medal of honour, thought Clair. Of war. Oh, sweet release that it wasn't her accepting the medal from some young man wearing a brown worsted cap, whilst the others watched her tears glisten in the noonday sun. A murmuring of sympathies poured forth from the Basiners, and Frankie stepped to one side as Sare approached the old couple, the joyousness of her eyes tinged with shame as she turned them upon their grief. Bowing, she then wrapped her arms around the woman's shoulders, embracing her. And grasping the man by the hand, she held it to her cheek, made wet with her tears of mingled joy and suffering. Job laid an arm around her shoulders and they watched silently as Frankie helped the elders down over the wharf into the boat. Luke was already heaving on the flywheel, and puffs of blue smoke soon rose into the air, spreading the pungent smell of gas across Clair's nostrils as he released the clutch and they putt-putted away from the wharf, back towards Rocky Head, Frankie at the stern, Luke qualled down by the motor, and the old man and woman huddling together, facing the empty seat between them and the bow.

"Job, the girls," said Sare, and Clair's heart constricted again as her father turned towards her. But before her eyes had a chance to connect with his, the uncle stepped before her, bowing slightly as he held out Missy's hand.

"You've seen to them?" her father asked, his tone grave.

"A brother's lot," said Sim, voice equally grave. Her father nodded, then bent over, gazing lovingly onto Missy.

"Hello, Daddy," said Missy boldly, yet holding tight to her uncle's hand.

"Why, she's shy of you," exclaimed Sare. "Goodness, she was only six when you left, just a baby. She hasn't grown much, has she, Father? And here's Clair. Clair, come speak to your father."

He rose, moving towards Clair, and her knees trembled. Struggling to breathe, she lifted her eyes to his, about to open her arms in welcome, but a sudden grimace distorted his face. She held her ground, watching, instead, as her mother, hearing the small cry of pain that had escaped his lips, take hold of his arm, staring imploringly onto his face.

"Job—"

He nodded reassuringly, yet wrapping his arm more tightly around her shoulders, leaned onto her as if she were a living crutch. Finally he was limping towards his eldest girl, his eyes heavily lined and blinking oddly as they sought hers.

She'd never known him to blink oddly before. And his eyes, ooh, those lines, almost as if they were deepening and withering as he neared her. And that dear gentle face that once smiled the tenderest of smiles was now taut in a gaunt jaw. But it was his eyes that revealed the most, for when she finally looked, wanting the milky brown of her father's eyes, she saw instead two frozen, muddied shells. She closed her eyes and felt his lips, chilled, unmoving, touch her brow, and a shiver cold enough to solidify a thousand galaxies curled itself around her heart.

Her mother saw only life, felt only his warm flesh beneath her hand, heard only the whisper of his breath, the taste of his salt-sweetened skin, the smell of his unwashed hair. And when he let go of Clair and drew his hand across the rippled mass of Missy's curls, and haltingly peeled back his lips into a smile, Sare threw her arms around his neck and began sobbing with the abandon of an unchecked babe. Then she was drawing Clair before him again, and lifting Missy up with both arms for him to see better, and Missy, mindful of her ribbons fluttering in the air, and those around her reaching out to soothe a wind-tossed curl, smiled sweetly at this man whom she vaguely remembered as Daddy, and clutched her arms more tightly around her mother's neck.

"They're so shy of you now," sobbed Sare, letting Missy slip to her feet and taking hold of his arm. "Come, we takes you home and gets you a nice hot bath. I swear, from the smell of coal on them clothes, you must've been sleeping in the coal bin." Then, caring naught for those standing around, hoping to have a word and shake his hand and welcome him home, she wrapped her arms around his waist and led him homeward. Clair followed behind, and Sim, holding Missy's hand, followed behind her. Others trailed along as well, but Sare invited no one to walk alongside of her, and the second she was home, she marched him straight through the house and up over the stairs, calling over her shoulder for Clair to stoke the fire and start heating up water for the washtub.

Clair never saw her father for the rest of the day. Nor the next, aside from brief glimpses and quick smiles that passed between them through the room door as Sare waltzed in and out, bringing him tea and toast and puddings, or whatever else she happened to be boiling, baking or stewing for him that day. His wound was a piece of shrapnel imbedded in his back, which made it difficult for him to walk, sit or stand in an upright position for any length of time. "He's plumb exhausted," Sare told everyone that dropped by. "I allows I'm going to make him sleep for a week before I lets him out of that bed." And then she'd hum her way through fixing him a meal, dabbing her finger into his tea to make sure the water was just right, and smearing his bread with molasses and baking it in the oven, the way he mostly liked it, and making up bangbellys, his favoured teacake, made out of pork fat, molasses and flour.

"Blessed Father, Missy, I allows I'm going to tread on you if you're not careful," she said often enough during those first days as Missy trailed behind her from the sink to the stove, from the sink to the table, from the sink to the stairway. "Why don't you go visit with your grandmother, or sit at the table besides Clair and copy some writing like a good girl? Clair, take her, will you, dear. I sees to your father's breakfast."

"She won't let me do nothing with her," muttered Clair, equally as tempted as Missy to shadow her mother and peer inside the room for a glimpse of whatever was taking place in there.

It was on his eighth day home, a Sunday, that Job got out of bed. Clair was waiting at the kitchen table with Missy, both wearing their hats and coats, the church bell donging through the early morning air, as they waited for their mother to come down over the stairs and accompany them to morning service. It was their father that came. His face was smoothly shaved and his hair looked silken clean, winging off from his head at frightful angles as he stomped down over the stairs and limped into the kitchen, hooking his braces up over his shoulders. He stopped at the sight of them, and as Missy began to giggle, staring at his messed-up hair, he managed to grin in his old foolish way. Clair's heart flip-flopped. Her mother had been right—it was only a rest he needed. Yet, before the thought had properly registered, he was shoving his naked feet into his boots, hauling open the door and marching outside.

"Job!" Sare called out, running down over the stairs, still pinning on her hat. "Job, where you going?" She ran out the door, Missy and Clair behind her, stopping at the gate, watching as he marched up the road, one foot steady behind the other, despite the dragging limp of his right leg, and taking no time for those others strolling along the same path with their hymn books in their hands. Straight up Bob's Hill he walked, and through the wooden door leading inside the small white church sitting on top of the hill behind his mother's house. Within the minute he staggered back out and headed towards home, buckling beneath the weight of the pew his grandfather had built some eighty years before, one end on his shoulder and the other dragging the ground at his heels, looking much the same as Jesus must have done trudging beneath the weight of the cross on the road to Calvary. Ignoring the questioning look of his neighbours, Sare's astonished protests, and the wide startled eyes of his girls, he dragged the pew in through the house door and, setting it down in the centre of the kitchen, went outside to the shed and came back in with his handsaw, a hammer, and bucket full of nails. Closing the door upon the gaping faces of his friends and neighbours, he lodged the jagged teeth of the handsaw to the back of the pew, a quarter from the centre, and started sawing.

"For goodness' sakes, Job—"

"Leave me be, Sare," he ordered.

"Job, the girls—"

"Take them to church. There's plenty more places to sit."

"Job, stop—your mother—"

But he listened naught. Bending one leg onto the seat to steady it, the other stretched out behind him for balance, he continued pushing and pulling, pushing and pulling, the blade ripping through the splintering wood. Sare watched helplessly, her face wincing against the shrill scrooping of the saw as it hit upon a nail. Shooing Clair and Missy towards the stairwell, she turned back to her husband again, eyes pleading, and her hands fluttering before her like a cornered hen on the brink of flight.

Job saw nothing. Sweating and grunting, whether from pain or labour, he sawed. And Sare, overcome by the shrill whining of the saw biting through nails and knotty wood, and half frightened by the sight of her husband ripping apart with his bare hands what the saw wouldn't cut, collapsed onto the divan and became quiet.

Missy began to whimper, allowing Clair to hold her from behind as their father, the pew now hacked into pieces, picked up his hammer and some nails, and in the space of an hour, with all three watching, built a single seat from the pew. Then, tossing out the kitchen chair next to the window, he sat the pew-chair in its place, and turning to them all, spoke the only words Clair ever heard him speak again about the pew-chair. "It'll do me as good here as there." So saying, he sat sideways on his new seat, leaning one elbow on the table, the other on the windowsill, and with a fine covering of pew dust settling on his forehead and shoulders, he stared vacantly past the faces outside his window, lighting his pipe.

CHAPTER SIX

IN GROUPS OF THREE OR FOUR they came, and some-times five and six, as visiting strangers from nearby outports were equally as curious as family and friends to hear from a man just home from war on a continent that most had never heard of, despite it being their pilgrim ancestors' starting point. And too, there was the pew-chair.

"War's a hard thing for a man to put behind him," said Ralph, leaning against the wall, staring warily at Job, as Crow and Johnnie sat at the table alongside of him. "They says some never gets past it."

"Oh, now, Johnnie," chided Sare, pouring more tea into Crowman's cup, "as soon as his back gets better, he'll be as good as new agin, won't you, Job? Pass me your cup, Johnnie. And how's Rose?"

"Rose is fine, maid, just fine," said Johnnie, "and she says to tell you she'll be up soon as the crowd starts wearing thin." He looked to Job, sitting one elbow on the windowsill, the other on the table as he puffed on his pipe, looking from one to the other through a smoky haze, like a curtain, thought Clair, curled up on the divan, a book before her face so's to hide her fascination as she watched her father along with the men.

"One thing I'd like to bring up, Job, b'ye," said Johnnie, shifting his splinter-thin frame uncomfortably in his chair, "and that's—well, it's what Rose was asking about just before I come over, and that's—well—she was wondering b'ye, how you feels about all we, when you was the only one to sign up?"

"My, Johnnie, what a thing to ask—" began Sare, but even she, always alert to answer any question that befell Job since his return so's to spare him the trouble of talking, lapsed helplessly before the tumult of emotions riding over the faces of the men at the surprise question. Lowering her book, Clair peered closely as her father stopped puffing on his pipe, looking to each of his neighbours as they in turn looked to the bottom of their cups, shuffling uncomfortably, their own thoughts bristling to be heard. But they had argued and reargued their own take on affairs, and were more keen now to hear Job's. And as he lowered his pipe and leaned towards them, their shuffling stopped.

"War ain't no place for a thinking man," he said quietly.

The men nodded in turn, each pondering the sense of what had been spoken, and anticipating more, but Job was sitting back in his chair again, puffing on his pipe as before.

"That's right, b'ye," burst out Ralph, "and like we was saying after you left, it's not just on a bloody battlefield that you finds war either, because we signs up every time we goes in over them barrens and gets caught in a snowstorm with nary a tree or the sun to guide us out. Or, even when we goes out on the frigging water and stands a chance of getting crushed by pan ice—or—or lost in a fog, sometimes. That's war, ain't it—fighting to stay alive?"

"Yup, sir, brother," said Johnnie, with a nod. "Thick as pea soup, sir, it was the other day."

"My, if sitting in a boat in the fog is the same as going to war, then I guess we've all been fighting since we were gaffers," said Sare, looking up from the blueberry grunt she was slicing, a touch of scorn riding her brow.

A flush of red stained Ralph's neck. "There's times I said me prayers, buddy, water lopping over the boat and you can't see the shore for swills. I dare say Job can nod his head to that."

"I don't say it's nice all the time," said Sare, "but I allows it's a comfort in having rode those same swills a hundred times before, and knowing that when you did get home, there'd be a cooked meal and warm fire waiting."

"And a comfort to ye on shore knowing we was bringing home turrs for the soup," snipped Ralph.

Raising his hand to silence Sare, Job spoke in the grave tones that had accompanied him home from the war. "And a comfort it was, b'yes, in knowing Sare and the girls would be cared for. I slept easier knowing that."

The men fell into silence and Sare moved quietly, placing the sliced loaf before them, "Here, have a piece," she invited, her tone much softer. "Hurry on while it's warm. It's the last of the blueberries for a while. I swear, I can't wait to get in on the barrens this fall. Crow, you're not saying much."

"Well, I was just thinking," said Crowman, helping himself to a slice of grunt, "fire minders is what we must be, Job, b'ye, them that stays behind to mind the fires. There always got to be them that stays behind to mind the fire."

"You can call yourself what you frigging wants now, Crow, my son," said Ralph, jamming his hands in his pockets, the red on his neck stirring up again, "but I ain't no frigging fire minder. I'm a logger and a fisher and whatever else it takes to run me own life, and no one's going to be calling me a coward cuz I wouldn't jump on no boat and sail the frig overseas."

"Goodness mercy, Ralph," cried Sare, "you riles up faster than a surly dog. No one's calling you a coward—"

"There's them that thinks so," said Ralph.

"Now, b'ye—" cut in Crowman.

"No, don't b'ye me," said Ralph, "it's like I said before, I ain't fighting nobody else's frigging war when I got me own to fight. I've gone in on them barrens with a full storm on, tracking caribou, and the worst I got out of it was cold feet. And I'd do it right now if there was one that said I wouldn't."

"Would you now?" asked Sare sharply, and Clair felt the cold grey of her eyes as she turned them onto Ralph.

"Sare—"

"No, don't stop me, Job, I've been hearing this kind of self-talk since the day you left, and if you thinks, Ralph, my son, that by walking in over them barrens in a storm and coming back out agin—just to show you can—makes you a hero, well then, perhaps it does, but it minds me of a young-ster walking along top of a picket fence just to show off. And if that's what a hero is, then that's what Job's not. He didn't go to no war to show himself big to me or those around here. He went for his country, and all those fighting to keep it ours. And if some of them comes back with a leg missing—or, some never comes back at all—then he knows it was a manly thing he give himself to, and not some foolhardiness. And you might as well hear this too, whilst you're standing there, Ralph, and that's this—Job don't hold no man lesser or higher than himself, and it would please him if they give him the same respect. Now, have a piece of grunt to go with your tea," she said, plonking the breadknife onto the table.

Crow and Johnnie looked uneasily betwixt Sare and Ralph, but it was to her father's hands that Clair kept watch, and saw almost before he started, his fingers beginning to tap on the table. Sare noticed instantly as well and, without further ado, held out her arm to her husband, addressing the men in a clear even tone. "It's time for him to get his bandages changed and then have a nap. Talking about the war always wears him out—that's why I don't allow it. You men finish your tea now," she added as Job began easing himself out of his chair and onto her arm, "while I helps him upstairs, and perhaps ye can come back again when he's feeling stronger."

There was a chorus of agreements and Clair hid her face as her mother walked past, her father leaning heavily on her shoulder, into the stairwell. Hearing their step on the stairs, she tossed her book to one side and crept after them, peering around the bannister, watching as her father bent over from the waist, his breathing coming in harsh, fast gulps, and his face turning redder than anything.

"Shh, easy, breathe easy, my love," her mother murmured, and Clair pulled back so's not to be seen again— as she had that first time, during his second week at home, and she had rushed to her mother's side, frightened that her father was choking or dying of some horrible fit. A look of absolute forbidding from her mother had frozen her step, but not before her father, in the midst of his anguished breathing, had also seen her. Collapsing onto the step, he had dropped his head between his knees, shuddering as his breathing became more even and he was able to look at her.

"Come here," he had whispered hoarsely. And her mother had stood clicking her tongue disapprovingly as she crept fearfully up the stairs, bowing before him. "Look at me," he had whispered, and she had raised her head, forcing her eyes onto his. They were almost the same as before in the soft light of the stairwell, chocolatey brown and warm. But there were those lines, those wretched lines that entrenched the skin below them like bloodless cuts that forever warned of the pain he was suffering within, a pain she knew that was as separate from the shrapnel in his back as was a shoe from the foot that wore it.

He smiled, the cuts deepening, and taking hold of her arms, he pulled her towards him, his breath sour on her face, and his chin scratchy as he rested it on her brow. "It appears them stairs have gotten higher since I left," he said hoarsely. "Now I knows how poor old Pearl felt down Cat Arm, dragging them loads to the top of the hill. But she never broke for rest, did she?" he added, pushing her away a bit. "Hey—this old wound's going to get better," he said deeply, a grin torturing his face as he prodded her shoulder, forcing her to look up at him. "Even old buggers like me gets a downhill chance. And them—spells—are just part of it. It didn't frighten you none, did it?"

She shook her head.

"That's good, then," said he, "that's good. Great teachers can't be scared. You're still going to be a great teacher someday, are you?"

She nodded.

"Tomorrow you'll read for me?"

"Yes, Daddy."

He nodded. "Tomorrow, then. Perhaps it'll remind me I'm home agin," he mumbled, his voice falling off. She stared at him questioningly, but he was already rising, his breathing becoming more and more normal—as it was becoming now as she stood in the stairwell, peering around the bannister more carefully this time, watching as they began ascending. The men rose, quietly leaving, and creeping back out of the stairwell, Clair gathered up their teacups and cleaned the half-eaten grunt off their plates.

DESPITE HER FATHER'S SICKNESS, there was joy to their mother's step during those first few months he had returned. Scurrying around the kitchen, cooking, baking and cleaning, she spoke with a song to her voice as she chattered continuously to Clair and Missy to pour some water for their father, for sure he must be thirsty, to fetch some sugar for his tea, for sure it must be too strong, and pass him a bit of shredded cabbage. My, Father, it tastes some sweet this year, and for the love of the Lord, Missy, go out in the garden and play, because I swear you're forever beneath my feet these days. And for a while during those long summer days when she'd come back from picking fireweed at Purple Flowers, or beachcombing down by Copy-Cat Cove with Phoebe and Joanie, and seeing her mother squat in the flower bed, wearing her faded pink hat and weeding the sweet williams whilst her father sat puffing his pipe and watching through the open window, it felt to Clair as if things truly were going to be all right again, and it was only a matter of time before the piece of shrapnel in her father's back healed and they'd be climbing aboard the boat, heading for Cat Arm, making angels in the snow, and whistling up to God, reminding Him of their small corner. Even Missy stopped traipsing behind her mother, and acting skittish around her father. And best of all, since their father's homecoming, the uncle scarcely came around any more. And when he did, there were few words exchanged, except for those of Sare's as she covered the brothers' quiet with chatter about the grandmother's arthritis and how her and Job keeps meaning to drop by, but that the pain from Job's wound goes right down his leg, crippling him worse than the grandmother. "The poor dear," she added during one of those visits, "she's been cooped up for as long as I can remember. Do you think she minds it much—not getting out?"

"It's hard on her, for sure," mumbled Sim.

Clair, settled comfortably on the divan, looked up from her book in surprise as her father replied rather brusquely, "Ahh, Mother! She was always for the house, crippled or not."

"Might be," said Sim. "Still don't make it easy, none—always needing someone at hand."

"You knows it must be hard," murmured Sare sympathetically, pouring more tea into his cup, "always having to be on hand. It can't give you much of a life."

The uncle's head sagged. "I won't leave her. It don't matter much now anyhows—I feels older than she."

Sare tutted, but held her tongue as Job leaned forward, pointing his pipe stem at Sim. "There's always been ways if you wanted to," he said in a no-nonsense tone. "Father never trapped furs all them years for nothing. There's money tucked away, enough to pay for a serving girl if ever you wanted to go off."

"The grandmother has money?" questioned Sare in some surprise.

Sim shifted uncomfortably. "Be some serving girl now, to please Mother."

"You were never one for not pleasing yourself," said Job.

"My, Job . . . ," started Sare, but Job was turning back to his window, the smoke puffing faster out of his pipe, and his turned back signalling he had already left the room. Clair's book had fallen to one side and she half rose—her eyes narrowing as she turned them onto the uncle's sagging head and drooping shoulders. He had money? Yet he'd stolen from them? Her loathing from the day she'd stood before Willamena and the others near choked her, and she might've spoken then if not for her mother catching the explosion about to take place within her daughter and stepping forward with a raised hand of warning. And still she suffered to speak, and might have, if not for Missy thumping across the hall and swooshing down the bannister, calling out, "Uncle Sim, Uncle Sim, are we going raking today?" And flying across the kitchen, she landed in his lap, her arms whipping around his neck.

"Here, child! My, she's the ticket," exclaimed Sare, turning from Clair and hauling Missy off her uncle's lap. "Go—outside—and wait," she ordered, pointing her finger towards the door.

"No, I'll wait for Uncle Sim," said Missy, hopping impatiently.

"There now, and he hasn't even finished his tea," said Sare as Sim rose, readying to leave.

"The sun'll be down soon," he mumbled.

"I allows that's a job for me and Clair before long," said Sare, "raking up the yard. Mind she's no trouble, Sim."

"I'm going to stay for supper—all right, Mommy?" Missy sang out, running out the door.

"Mind you watches yourself," Sare called back. "Sim, send her home if she doesn't watch herself. My, she's one for her grandmother, she is, Father," she said, closing the door behind Sim and trailing back to the kitchen. "If we could only get that one to go visit every once in a while," she added, frowning Clair's way, a touch of warning still riding her brow, "but I don't bother trying any more. I allows if I never made her go with me sometimes, she wouldn't know she had a grandmother."

"Cut from the same cloth," said Job, and the tightness in Clair's throat lessened a little as his lips curled into a smile around the stem of his pipe, despite the disapproving tut of her mother's tongue. "Perhaps she can read to me," he then said, making her heart leap a little, for it was rare that he asked her to read since he came home, and she always had a story ready, chance he should ask. Today it was Missy's story of the banshee stealing the little girl and putting a changeling in her place and taking the little girl into the woods to become a fairy. She had taken to writing down Missy's stories since her father had returned, giving her another excuse to dawdle across the table from him and not be driven out the door or up over the stairs by her mother. Running to her room to fetch her scribbler, she smiled, listening to her mother's chatter ringing through the house with the charm of a songbird as she talked with her father, her melody drowning out the ticking of the clock, and drawing them forward into winter. And yes, Clair agreed, upon running back down over the stairs, it was time to start raking the garden before winter come and they still hadn't parted with last year's leaves. And my, won't it be grand when they were able to pack up the boat and motor down to Cat Arm again, when Father's wound got better, and throw on a pan of fresh liver and go sliding down the hill again at night, and whistling for the heavens to dance? Yes, for sure it would be, for sure it would be.

And no doubt it would've happened, Sare was to lament in time to come, had it not been for the trek Job made with that young fellow Luke from Rocky Head that horrid night.

It was a late evening and well over a year since his return when he appeared more pained than usual by his wound.

Sare was leading him up over the stairs to bed, and Clair trailed behind, sickened by the low moans escaping him.

"The lamp, Clair," her mother spoke over her shoulder. "Put out the lamp." And Clair had darted back to the table, about to blow out the lamp when a sound from outside caught her attention, followed by a quiet tap on the door. She cupped her hand to the window, staring outside. The houses were blackened all around, and the sky dark with cloud. The tap sounded again, softer than before, as if it feared awakening the souls sleeping within, and then her eyes drew in the tall figure hunched besides the door.

The uncle, she thought, darting across the kitchen. Something's wrong with the grandmother. Pulling open the door, she started back in fright at the unknown face before her, darkened as much from a beaver cap pulled low over his brow, its flaps hanging loosely around his ears, as from the dark. "My name's Luke—Luke Osmond. I'd like to speak with Job Gale," he said with a quiet that belied the sense of urgency directing his hands as he pulled off his cap and held it as a shield before him. Luke. The one who had sat in the boat, his back to those around him. Till her father had called his name. He shifted, the red of his mouth feverish against the paleness of the lamplight, and the blue of his eyes pleading his words.

She shook her head, shrinking back. "He's real sick tonight," she said apologetically.

"I won't take long," he said as she prepared to close to the door. A movement upon the road caught her attention and she noted Frankie standing there, fumbling with his cap the same as Luke was now doing.

"He can hardly walk," she said more loudly, her eyes addressing them both. And despite her curiosity, firmly closed the door. She stood for a moment, listening to Luke's footsteps as he walked out of the garden, back upon the road. A murmur of voices, then silence, aside from the rapid beating of her heart and her anxious questioning of whether or not she'd done right. Her father's step sounded heavy on the ceiling and she turned the lock. Trailing back to the divan, she slouched upon the pillows, reliving again the image of Luke on her stoop. Already it began to feel as though she'd imagined the whole thing.

Minutes passed, not many it seemed, for her father's step was still dragging around upstairs, when another sound came from outside. This time a shuffling, and leaping to her feet, she ran lightly across the kitchen, knowing it was the uncle.

"He's sick," she half whispered, unlocking the door and opening it, but the uncle brushed inside like a squall of wind, treading across the kitchen towards the stairwell. He called out, "Job! Job, they wants to talk to you, b'ye—the ones from Rocky Head."

"He's in bed," Clair cried out, running after him, mindful of Frankie standing out by the gate, his hands dug in his pocket, and Luke nowhere in sight. "You hear me," she cried out, grabbing hold of the uncle's arm as he called out her father's name again.

"He can speak his own mind," snapped the uncle, flinging off her hand and turning on her as if he might strike her.

"My Lord," exclaimed Sare, coming out on the landing and gliding partways down the stairs. "What is it, Sim? What do they want?"

"The fellow, Luke, from Rocky Head—he's down at the wharf, waiting to speak with Job."

"On the wharf," said Sare. "Job can hardly walk this evening—"

"He was at the door but she wouldn't let him in," cut in the uncle, a sour glance at Clair. "Now he's gone back down on the wharf."

"Then let him come tomorrow," said Sare, "when Job's feeling better."

"He's got a queer mind; he won't go around people."

"And neither will Job, not with his back the way it is." She broke off as Job came out of the room, pulling on a heavy work shirt. "You're not going out the door this evening, Job Gale. You listen to me," she warned, as he began limping down over the stairs, scarcely able to conceal his pain. "That young fellow can come up here more easily than you can go down there. No, no, you listen," she cried out, ignoring his pleas that he was fine as she clung to his arm, following him into the kitchen. "It's worse you're getting, not better. It's not right that they come for you this late, anyway. Did you tell them he was sick?" she demanded, turning onto Sim as if he were the cause of the commotion.

"Better than dead," said Sim, and Clair glared at him all the harder as the fight oozed out of her mother like a torn windsock.

"It's all right, shoo, it'll be fine," said Job, limping to Sare as she crumpled onto a chair.

"I don't mean to be uncharitable," she whispered, bowing into her hands.

"Course you didn't," said Job, stroking her cheek. "Course you didn't." He nodded as Sim grunted impatiently at the door, then rose, wincing as his legs took his weight, and the final band of constraint holding Clair in check snapped.

"Bet you didn't tell them how sick Daddy was, did you?" she hissed at the uncle. "That's because you wants to hear about the war like everybody else."

"Clair," warned her father, but a horse bursting out of a barn thinks no more of his return to his stall than he does the bog holes and ruts of the terrain he's about to blaze across.

"He's a bastard, Daddy," she shouted, and oblivious of her mother's leaping to her feet, forbidding her another word, she shouted all the harder. "And he stole from us when you was gone. He used to mark things down and keep them for hisself and the merchant had to give us stuff! Yes, you did!" she continued scornfully as the uncle turned a savage look upon her. "Saul's the one who told me—and he give us charity to cover what you stole!"

"She lies," snarled the uncle, raising his fist in anger towards Clair. "Nothing but sauce is all I got from her, no matter the work I done, lugging wood and water—anything I took was to feed the young one. Lord knows she spent enough time eating at the house."

But Clair was quiet now, the uncle's tirade as he slunk back to the door scarcely audible. It was her father taking her attention, corralling her into a new twist of torment as he shook his head, lowering it into his hands as had her mother but a minute ago.

"You get yourself up over them stairs, young lady," her mother ordered, reaching her arms around Job's waist. "Not another word. Get on now—get!" And Clair crept towards the stairwell, no different from the uncle stealing out the door, her stomach seething with sickness.

Cowering at the railing, she closed her eyes as her father whispered harshly, "Did he leave ye enough?"

"Yes, yes, more than enough. There's nothing for you to think on there, Job Gale, and I won't allow it. And there was nothing that was given that wasn't tallied back—you can trust Saul on that one."

"Tell me the truth, Sare."

"It's the truth, every word of it the truth. They lacked for nothing, the girls didn't, and me neither. And we've paid back; not a cent do we owe—I seen to that."

"I should never have left."

"Ohh, you can't think that, now. It was a good thing you done. No matter what, I've always known that."

"You don't know."

"Know what, my dear?"

"What I've done. What I've taken from them."

"From who, Job?"

"And I've nothing to give them—not even the truth," he more groaned than said.

"No, no don't leave," said Sare as he began for the door, "What're you carrying, Job—oh, my dear, let me come with you. I'll dress warm—" But he was shaking his head, pushing her behind as he stepped over the stoop and, with a last tortured smile, closed the door.

"Ooh, poor soul, poor soul," Sare whispered, running over to the window.

Creeping up the stairs, Clair darted to her window, looking down upon her father as he leaned his weight upon Frankie's shoulders and began walking down the hill. Scarcely visible through the dark, he turned, looking back at her mother, no doubt, as she watched over him from above the flower patch, and gathering his strength, he waved reassuringly, smiling all the while. It was then she, Clair, understood that in the absence of humility, only shame can lower a head so, and as did her mother when caught decrying the bereaved whilst selfishly nurturing her living, and her father as he tallied his deeds against himself, she hung her head, denouncing the extra torment she had brought upon them, and desired the weight of her blankets in which to bury herself. But her eye strayed back to the window, lured by a neighbour's light falling upon the uncle. He was dodging a step or two ahead of her father and Frankie, and her mouth curled in contempt. "Old bastard," she whispered. "Old bastard!"

It was an hour past midnight when he returned. And towards dawn when his screams started. Jolting awake, Clair sat up in her bed, horrified by their guttural rawness. Leaving Missy plunging beneath the blankets like a frightened mouse, she sprang out of bed, dashing out of her room and across the landing to where his door stood ajar. He was lying on his back, his fists clenched to his throat, and his head twisting from side to side as the screams rippled harshly out of the depths of his guts. Her mother was half lying over him, shaking him, holding him, and yet his screams kept coming— loud, raw and hard. And when she failed to awaken him, she lay across him, crying, "Scream, my love, scream it out, scream it out." And when finally his eyes sprang open, staring wildly at the ceiling, and he peeled back his lips, gritting his teeth, striving to hold back the utterances still rasping out of his throat, she cried louder than he, "No, don't hold it, don't hold it, be sick, my dear, be sick all you wants."

Her cries gave way to a gentle humming as his body slowly quieted, and soon it was only the sound of his breathing, along with her murmurings, filling the room.

Creeping back to bed, Clair pulled Missy up from hiding beneath the blankets. "It's fine," she said, wrapping her arms around her to still her trembling. "It's fine. Daddy's fine."

But it wasn't fine. It wasn't fine at all. The acid that had begun seeping into his stomach somewhere over there across the seas, had been eroding all this time, its gnawing felt only by him as he sat day after day, aiding its corrosion. And now the burning pain of its rot, once broken through, continued its discharge, night after night, stripping his throat and numbing further his eyes as he arose each morning and limped down over the stairs to his chair besides the window, filling and refilling his pipe as he puffed and puffed, tapping his foot and staring vacantly outside.

"I thought your headaches were gone with Job coming back," said Alma one frosty Sunday morning after she'd invited herself for tea at their breakfast table.

Clair picked at her fried dough and baked beans, yet despite her feelings of discomfort, and those, she knew, of her father over yet another visitor, she was relieved for the disruption of the interminable silence that was growing more and more loudly around their mealtimes since the night screams started.

"Yes, maid, they did," her mother was saying, tearing off more dough and dropping it into the frying pan, "but they've started up agin, now. I allows I'll never get clear of them. Is it next week Willamena's getting married?"

"Yup. I never thought I'd see the day when a merchant's daughter would be marrying someone from Rocky Head," replied Alma, "but it's what the merchant says now—with Willamena's looks, they're not lining up. And they says he's like her father, the young fellow is, out for the dollar. What about you, Job? I suppose it'll be some time before you gets back to work?"

"I dare say," said Job around the stem of his pipe.

"Mercy, it's what everyone's asking of him—as if he's the maker of his own health," said Sare, her tone becoming a little crotchety. But then catching herself, she turned on a smile and flipping the touten out of the pan onto a plate, she laid it before Alma, asking pleasantly, "How's your mother doing with this cold? I allows it'll never warm up again."

"My dear, she's wonderful grand." Alma gave a short laugh. "I got to say, Job, b'ye, it's not something I ever wanted to ask about for fear of sounding stun, but all this time you been home, me and mother been trying to figure out what a piece of shrapnel is. Then I finally out and asked Will Brett the other day and he told us it was a piece of steel. So here I goes, sounding stun agin," she added with another laugh, "but what me and Mother can't figure out now is, how'd you manage to get a piece of steel in your back?"

"Well, bless the Pope, how'd you think!" Sare exclaimed. "From an exploding bomb, maid. He was in a war, you know."

"My, yes, I knows that," said Alma, water swamping her eyes as she swallowed too big a piece of the dough, "but it's hard to tell what something's like when you only sees bits of it in pictures, hey, Job? You knows, b'ye. I suppose you never seen a battle tank till you got over there. It must've been some bad having them all around you—they looks so big— what was they like?"

"We don't talk about the war," said Sare sharply, laying a protective hand across the back of Job's chair as he began puffing harder on his pipe. "How's that's touten going down?"

"You fries a good one, Sare. I got to say, I can't stand Mother's. She don't fry hers in pork fat, she uses butter and it loses its taste without pork fat—too dry. But it's easier now, keeping the fog at bay in a easterly wind than trying to change Mother's ways. Well, sir, you're some quiet this morning," she interrupted herself to say to Missy. "What's you scared of, your father?"

"Scared!" exclaimed Sare as all eyes turned to Missy, who, in turn, looked up from her plate to stare wide-eyed at her father. "My, Alma, why'd you say that?"

"Maid, that's what Willamena was saying in the store the other day."

"For the love of the Lord—Job's been home for more than a year—and the little thing's been good as gold."

"You knows Willamena," said Alma.

"The mouth of a guppy, always gulping for air and spitting back the same," cried Sare, looking fretfully at the look of concern replacing the vacant stare in Job's eyes. Leaning across the table, he laid his hand over Missy's, peering into her face.

"Is that true?" he asked, his grave tones somewhat roughened as he strived for softness. Clair caught her breath as Missy raised her eyes to his—this stranger with the tortured smile who sat staring relentlessly out the kitchen window day after day, and screamed like a devil in her mother's bed night after night.

"Missy?" asked Sare, fondling one of her daughter's curls.

"Shh, leave her be, Sare," said Job, but Missy, emboldened by an encouraging smile from her mother, stared back at her father, shaking her head from side to side.

"I'm not scared," she declared.

Job's mouth twisted into the semblance of a smile as he sat back in his chair, but his back was rigid, thought Clair, as rigid as it had been that first night she had burst into his room and found him screaming on his pillow. And his fingers, the nails chewed to the quick and bleeding in spots, shook as he refilled his pipe from his tobacco pouch. She remembered when he would squat before the motor in their boat on the way to Cat Arm, greasing up the piston and oiling the flywheel, those same fingers so swift, so strong and so very, very sure. And now, with their chalky colour and chewed nails, they more resembled the blood plant, whose roots, once ripped from the earth, gnarled outward, bone-white, and its sap the colour of blood as it dripped from its ragged tips.

"She's still getting used to me being back, I think," he said, and raising a clawed hand, he tweaked a lock of Clair's hair before lighting his pipe.

"Of course she is," said Sare, patting Missy's hand as if she had just done something good. "There, you've finished your beans. Put on your boots then, and take these toutens up to your grandmother—I told her I'd be sending her up some this morning." And wrapping a tea towel around a plate piled high with fried dough, she stood waiting as Missy slipped off her chair and into her boots. "And tell her I'll try and get up later the week," she said, opening the door, "and mind you don't spend all evening—you got homework to do. Clair, why don't go with her?"

"I'm not finished," said Clair, quickly bending her head and scraping her fork across her beans.

"My, she dawdles," sighed Sare, closing the door behind Missy, and then noticing Job beginning to tap his fingers, she hurried to the bin. "Alma, there's still a few toutens left—why don't take them home to your mother."

"No, no, maid, no need for that, it's enough I dropped in for tea; I wouldn't want to rob you of supper, too," Alma protested, but Sare was already wrapping another tea towel around the few pieces of dough left on the plate.

"Don't be silly," replied Sare, holding out the plate to Alma as one would a coat to a departing guest, "we've been eating them all morning. Be sure to give your mother my blessings—and Job's, too."

"Yes, yes I will," said Alma, rising reluctantly. "I suppose when this cold weather's over with, Job, b'ye, Mother'll get up to see you."

"I minds her well," said Job, laying his pipe in the ashtray. He began to rise, his body creaking like an old rocking chair. "And Alma—" he managed his full height "—tell her they sounds louder than Bear Falls in springtime."

Alma blinked, then broke out in smiles. "Ohh—the tanks! Lord, that's some roar, then. I'll tell her that, my son. And you take care of yourself, now. And you too, Sare," she said, allowing Sare to lead her to the door, "you looks awful white to me."

"The winter sun," said Sare. "Tell your mother we looks forward to seeing her."

"That I will, that I will, my dear. Later, now."

And then Sare was shutting the door and hurrying back to Job as he started his slow, painful walk across the kitchen, his breathing becoming faster and harder. "Here, hold on," she said, offering her shoulder, "and if anybody else comes knocking," she called over her shoulder to Clair, "tell them your father's gone to bed for the day. For a month we should be telling them," she grumbled, "give you time to get your strength back, and perhaps I will start telling them that, perhaps I will."

Her father, as if remembering her presence, turned to her with a little smile as he made his halting way into the stairwell. She smiled back, watching after him, and the second he was out of sight, the smile fell from her lips. Pushing aside her plate of beans, she turned to where he'd been sitting and shifted onto his chair. Taking his pipe from the ashtray, she lifted it to her lips, and then leaning one elbow on the table and the other onto the windowsill, she looked out over the muddied patch of garden, allowing her eyes to empty, to see what it was that emptied eyes saw as they looked for hours in a day, as quiet as a mouse in a flour can, staring, staring, staring at some distant point that held no shape or colour.

He began spending more and more time in his room. Napping, as Sare put it. And perhaps he was, thought Clair, for he seldom slept at night any more. Always, whenever she awakened, and it was frequent, she heard his low, aching voice and her mother's nurturing softness as they both talked their way through the hours, staving off the night screams, for he didn't seem to be bothered by them during the day, and his sleep was much easier. And keeping true to her word, Sare kept careful vigilance at the door, allowing no one in but her girls, and to them she'd stand with her finger to her lips, becoming more and more frantic in her need to silence their footsteps.

She seldom rested, scurrying around the house on tiptoe as she did the dusting and sweeping, and speaking to her girls in low, urgent whispers, forever bidding them to do the same till they were both hushing and shushing the other. Meantime, Sare's world became smaller, perhaps even more tortured than Job's. Seldom had she stepped outside before, except to pin the clothes on the line and do a little gardening. Now, she had Clair hang out the clothes so's to avoid them that leaned over the fence to have a chat, and too, she closed her curtains, begging Job to do the same with the window he sat so silently besides, hoping to stave off the curiosity of those who strolled by half a dozen times a day, hoping to be the one singled out to break his silence about the war and achieve the heroic role of becoming poor Job's saviour. And as before Job's return, her headaches became more frequent, for so intent was she on silence that the sighing of the walls and creaking of the beams oftentimes deepened her headaches, sometimes keeping her slouched on the divan for hours, with a pillow stifling her moans, and a bucket to catch her retchings.

In time, as Job refused to recognize any of them waving at him through the window, and Sare continuously disallowed any of them to come inside and sit at their table any more, the neighbours' compassion dwindled. What show had he now of courage, they asked of each other, when fear from a far-gone feat still seeped from his body like the elusive blue gas of the will-o'-the-wisp? And believing he had truly gone mental, they became impatient with Sare's insistence that he was just tired and disgruntled when she pretended not to hear them knocking on her door, and so considered it their moral duty to ensure Job was not a threat to his family or the outport. Thus, the hounding of Clair and Missy—who they likened to two anaemic calves gone white in the face and spindly in the legs from being holed up in a stall all day with two sickly parents.

"Sure, how's your poor father today, my dear?" the fishers, the women and mole-faced store clerks would ask as they put their jiggers, laundry baskets and store books to one side, and leaned over their nets, clotheslines and counters, calling after Clair as she went along her way, and "My, it must've been some awful thing that happened to him in the war to make him scream and go on like that—do he talk to your mother— you know, at night. He was such a good father before he got sick, and now, my, my, he must be awfully low-minded—"

As she had before her father came home from the war, Clair took to staying at home. Drifting up to her room, she'd sometimes lean against her windowpane, staring out at the open doorways of her neighbours' houses, hearing their easy laughter and watching the youngsters and adults alike running in and out, and Phoebe and Joanie and Georgie and the others sneaking off down the shore or through darkened paths up over the hills. And as was before her father's homecoming, she felt caught, trapped within a sphere of light that illuminated only the darkness funnelling it. And the dark grew as a film over her eyes, swiping the colour from the world outside her window and tinting her thoughts with a vindictiveness she couldn't trace, for what had her neighbours to do with her father's malaise, or her mother's need to protect?

Yet, one thought kept pervading all others; for all their talk of being fire minders, they had been quick to abandon the hearth when the fire inside had cooled to ashes.

It appeared of small consequence to Missy.

"Mommy, I'm going to Grandmother's," she'd say quietly most afternoons, within minutes after arriving home from school.

"You're not being any trouble, are you?" Sare would ask, and Missy, with scarcely a reply, would lay her books on the table, and hurry out the door. And with their father so sick, Clair was as relieved as her mother by the quiet of her sister's absence. But watching her creep out the door, her face more solemn with its loss of baby fat, and the mane of curls more tidied with buckles and combs, Clair sometimes ached for an echo of the former Missy who had chattered her way around the kitchen, sweeping, dusting and cleaning, her hair growing wild around her face. Sometimes, during those rare afternoons when Missy wasn't up visiting Grandmother, Clair would sprawl across their bed, her cheek resting against Missy's, pondering out loud if maybe everybody wasn't right, and that perhaps they might all become low-minded, as her father had, and sit for hours in a day, staring out the window, more and more like the dreadful apparition that he was now.

Missy would listen for a while, her childish shrieks and laughter long since sobered by their mother's quietening finger, and would beg Clair in a voice that had become as whispery—almost weepy—as their mother's, to stop speaking of their father, and talk instead about fairies singing in the forest, and riding the whitecaps over the ocean till they found the land with the largest of all meadows and the grandest of all bluebells to curl up in at night. And when Missy had gone, and her mother lay resting in bed, Clair would lie on the divan, watching her father as he sat sideways on his pew-chair, one elbow resting on the table, and the other on the windowsill, staring out the window for hours, days, weeks, as if impaled upon the hell-scorched eyes staring back at him from his reflection, whilst the flankers from his pipe burned an arc on the canvas floor around his feet, and the weight of his mind burnt a hole through his entrails.

"Don't he say nothing, not even to your mother?" Phoebe asked one windy, sunny day as Clair, during one of her rare outings, sat on the steps outside Joanie's house, waiting for Joanie to finish her dinner so's they could go swimming down on the sandbar.

Clair shrugged.

"Don't you listen?" asked Phoebe.

"No."

"Sure, why won't you listen sometime?"

"Because I don't want to," said Clair.

"Aren't you scared?"

Clair gazed distractedly at Phoebe's long, coppery hair, wishing the wind would lift it as it had on other summer days, and wrap it around her face, and she and Joanie would laughingly flattened it down with their hands and braid it into fat pigtails and tie the ends with skinny alder twigs that were still supple and dripping with sap, and then tickle and tease each other, and romp through the timothy wheat, playing hide and seek, the way they always used to—before her father went away to war. But the wind was mindless of Phoebe's hair on this day and merely sifted a strand across her brow, a strand that was quickly plucked back and wedged behind an ear, baring nosy, grey eyes that flitted from side to side as they searched out Clair's.

"Why should I be scared?" asked Clair, her voice dulled, her mind already wandering, knowing the answer.

"Scared that it might be something in his blood."

"What might be in his blood?"

"Mental, b'ye, you knows. When someone goes mental for nothing, it might be something in his blood. Then that might've been passed on in your blood and you could turn mental, too, when you gets older—and your youngsters."

Phoebe's voice had dropped to a whisper, but she might as well have been silent, for Clair was leaning forward now, her body quiet, and her eyes a little dazed as she drifted into some distant place that would become a place of refuge in years to come.

"I didn't mean to make you angry," Phoebe called after her, her voice deeply affected with regret, as Clair rose. But Clair was beyond hearing as she strolled up over the hill towards home, head down so's not to encounter any more concerned souls dawdling on their step. Pausing at the gate, she watched her father watching through the window at her mother squatted in the muddied patch of garden, her straw hat shading her eyes from the sun, and ever so often glancing up and smiling at him as she ripped out weeds and grass from amongst the sweet williams. Clair smiled at him too, and calling out a greeting to her mother, went inside, kicking off her boots.

"Not gone swimming?" asked her father. He turned to her, his eyes cocoa brown in the sun.

"Too windy," she said, noting that the pained lines that usually marked his face were absent today, their shadows flushed out by the brilliance of the light, and pulling a half-used scribbler and piece of pencil off the bin, she sat across from him in the splotch of sunshine, and idly began to write. Her mother's spade chinked against the rocks in her flower bed, and a thousand dust mites swam lazily through the air. Missy was off somewhere, no doubt visiting with Grandmother, and all was fine really, thought Clair, pushing away the nagging words of worry Phoebe had whispered in her ear.

"What are you writing?" he asked, after she had done a page or more.

"I told Missy I'd write her a story," she answered, smiling, knowing the effort that it took him to ask.

"Perhaps you might read it to me."

"Right now?"

He nodded, turning finally to smile at her. Her heart melted, as had his eyes in the hot July sun, and going to the farthest corner of the kitchen, she took a deep breath and began reading in a clear, strong voice, the story Missy had been telling her for some years now.

"My, Father, you got her going with the stories agin," said Sare. "Isn't she the reader—and what stories Missy makes up. I keeps telling them, they're like you for telling the lie, but it's a funny thing that a lie becomes a story simply because it's written down. Shall I make you tea, dear? Clair, sit besides your father, I makes us some tea."

Clair sat back down. With her mother's charm, and the warmth of her father's eyes, and the sunshine spilling through the window, it felt like the old days. And as they sat sipping tea together, it was easy to forget that Missy wasn't sitting with them, and indeed, hadn't been home for suppers for weeks now, and that her father, though he was sitting with them, nodding to their chatter, even smiling, had ceased hearing their words long ago.

It was nearing midnight, and Clair was easing away from the sweat of Missy's back, when a loud cry sounded from her mother. Scrabbling out of bed and cautioning Missy to bide where she was, she ran across the hall, carefully opening the room door as her mother's cries grew harder. She was as she had been that first time Clair had run into her room—the night her father's screams had started—half-sitting, half-lying across him. Only she wasn't soothing him on this night as she had been, then, but shrieking crazily as if it were her, Sare, being tormented in sleep. Clair stepped farther into the room to understand why he wasn't soothing her mother as she had him, why it was that he lay upon his pillow, his teeth clenched, his head stilled.

"Mommy," she whispered as her mother's shrieks became more harsh.

"He's dead!" cried Sare, squirming atop of him as if to awaken him, and Clair saw then that his eyes were not sleeping at all, but glazed pits, staring straight ahead, as if shackled to some horrific image that not even death could intercept. And his hands, those big strong hands, were tightly clenched across his chest, as though protecting him from a war that finally killed him, three years after the shelling had stopped. Holding her hands to her heart, she watched as her mother, now whimpering like a hurt puppy, crawled all over him, crying fretfully as she tried to find comfort on a breast awash in the coldness of death.

SIX MONTHS LATER, ALMOST TO THE DAY, on a sunny September afternoon, Clair and Missy walked home from school and found their mother curled up on the bed of sweet williams, her cheek cushioned against the purple-and-pink petals as if she were napping, her hat shading her eyes from the sun, and a curious, almost flirtatious smile frozen on her face. Sinking onto the dirt, Clair reached blindly for Missy's hand, her ears deaf to the rising hysteria sounding from her sister, and a sense of the unreal overtaking her. Holding out a finger, she traced the curve of her mother's smile. Anyone watching might have been heartbroken to see one so young maintaining such control in the face of her mother's death. In shock, they might say, or too frightened to honestly believe her mother was really dead along with her father, and that she and her sister were truly orphans now. Or perhaps even that she had lost her senses, like her father, and that it wasn't the war after all that took poor Job Gale's mind but a sickness of the blood like they'd been thinking all along during his last year.

It was this last thought they would have held true if they were privy to the absurdity consuming Clair's mind at the moment, for it wasn't herself she was thinking on at all, or her younger sister, Missy, and that they were both orphans now. But a deeper intrigue to her at that moment, as she traced her finger around the curve of her mother's smile, was the memory of the grimace that had so distorted her father's face as he had lain upon his pillow. How was it, she wondered, beginning to rock ever so gently, that it was her mother who went smiling into the arms of death, when it was her father who had so craved its comfort?

TWO WEEKS LATER Clair sat in the same perplexed silence in her father's pew-chair, clutching a sobbing Missy to her side, as Sim stood before them, his words falling around her like a cold rain as he declared himself their guardian. He told her that Frankie, who had married Willamena, was offering her a job to teach down Rocky Head—at least for the next six weeks till they found a real teacher. Meanwhile he and the grandmother would be moving into this house to take care of Missy, for there wasn't enough room in his old house for himself, the grandmother and Missy. Too, Clair herself would be needing a room after she finished with her teaching spell down Rocky Head, and she couldn't very well live on her own yet. But wouldn't she be wanting to leave for teaching college the following year, after she finished grade eleven, the way her father always said she would? Then it made sense that he and the grandmother move into the house so's there would always be somebody here to take care of Missy—and the grandmother's house could now be used for a woodhouse, given the roof was rotting off.

"But—but I'm not a teacher," Clair whispered and it was only as the uncle kept talking and Missy kept crying had she realized that her words were spoken silently; and even if she had shouted them, there was no one to listen. They were gone. Her mother and father were both gone.

She repeated the thought to feel it, but felt instead the same dizziness that threatened to overcome her once, when she had jumped two feet over a split in a canyon wall, with the thunder of churning water echoing up from the darkness a hundred feet below.

That she could feel anything was a surprise in itself, for since the night of her father's death, it felt as if a calming had descended over her insides, allowing nothing of the horror around her to penetrate, and even allowing her to smile reassuringly at Missy as they had walked hand in hand behind their mother on the way to their father's burial. And it was as if her senses knew, for the calming stayed with her, right up through the six months leading to her mother's death. And now, sitting here before her uncle Sim, listening to his pronouncement of her fate, the calming had shifted, surprising her with the feelings of fright it allowed in, when it was pain she had been fearing the most.

"But I'm not a teacher," she repeated, this time louder, again startled by the tumult of emotion awakening throughout her. Like one awakening from a sleep, she looked around the room and saw all that had been taking place this past while, and her body was rising in revolt. And most of all against the rot of her uncle's ways as he stood before her, the peak of his cap overshadowing all else, and his stoop no longer present now that the neighbours were gone.

Vulture! she uttered within. Nay, not even a vulture, for they have the grace of flight. More the slinking dog again, a weasel, crawling on its belly, waiting for the hen to stray so's it could suck itself full of the victuals of another's labour.

"Don't matter you're not a teacher," he was saying as Clair rose from her chair, eyeing him defiantly. "They only goes to grade six down there, anyway—and it's only to hold the youngsters over till the real teacher comes. Count it lucky that they picked you."

It was to the uncle's good fortune that Missy, at that moment, let out a long, shuddering sob, and Clair, seeing the misery in her eyes as she looked from her to the uncle, felt her heart wrench—and not merely for Missy's suffering but her own as well. For it was the uncle's side Missy was harbouring besides, and it dawned on Clair with the foreboding of a winter's storm that hers would be a lonely path indeed, for it was not Missy's fortune to suffer again as she had done these last two years. No. The hearth had long since chilled for Missy, starting the day their father had left for war, and their mother had forsaken all around her. And even she, Clair, had helped shush her into silence.

A shudder tore through Clair. She drew back from the uncle, hissing at him, "I won't ever live in this house with you!"

"Clair," Missy sobbed, but the uncle was already taking her by the arm, leading her towards the door.

"She'll be back, you ought not worry about that," he said roughly, his efforts to be consoling echoing loudly through a house that had heretofore been tendered in silence. And it was to this house that Clair's eyes clung as she sat, gripping onto the wooden seat of the motorboat beneath her, trying to shut out the sight of Missy sobbing and clinging to the uncle's hand as the two fishers from Rocky Head shoved the boat off from the wharf. Stark white against the grey of the sky, and with its wreath of colour circling beneath the kitchen window, it far more resembled a tombstone marking the death of a life she had once known than the home where Missy would continue to live—and which she, in six weeks, was supposed to be coming back to.

A crow swooped before it, like a black tear falling from the heavens, and holding tight to her seat as the piston popped to life, reverberating through her wooden seat and jarring up her spine, she turned to her sister with a last plaintive cry, "I'll come back for you, Missy, I promise—it's just for a little while. Be a good girl, now, and don't forget to wash your hair—don't forget." The putt-putt of the motorboat drowned out her cries, carrying her farther and farther offshore till the great September sea stretched out between them and Missy was but a fairy, glancing over her shoulder and waving as she followed the uncle up over the hill.

Miller's Island loomed to the wayside and Clair startled towards it as she heard her father's voice sounding over the wind and the sea: "Aye, my dolly, it's the bravest man that hides his fear the bestest," and then the boat pitched wildly, sending a stinging spray of mist into her face as it stubbornly fought to stay in alignment with the shore. And turning calm eyes onto the curious ones of the fishers, she wrapped her scarf more tightly around her throat and looked seaward towards Rocky Head.

CHAPTER SEVEN

I T WAS FRANKIE THAT MET HER down Rocky Head. Hair
slicked back by the wind and buffing his hands to keep
warm, he stood on the beach next to a stagehead on rickety
legs, half on land, and half out over the water, wearing a
concerned look on his face as he waited for the boat to drift
ashore.

She remembered again his bold smile the first time she
had encountered him, displaying an eagerness for acceptance
as well as charm. And despite the fact it was her now, landing
on his shores, she saw again in the quickness of his smile that
same desire for acceptance. That it should be from her, an
orphan freshly begotten from the gates of the graveyard into
a bed feathered by his benevolence, she was too fatigued to
think. But upon clambering over the side of the boat, her
knees buckling as she stood before him, partially from fear
and partially from the gruelling trip on rough waters, she
shored herself up. For in those moments of life's great
surprises, as with the death of her mother and father, time
offered her no respite to reach inside and lift out the mottled
web of feelings tangling her insides, only a nudging onward,
as with her father the day he walked down over the hill to the
waiting ship, knowing that to sit is to chance entwinement to
a bed pillowed with naught but springs of barbed wire.

"Welcome," said he, his handsome white teeth subdued by a quiet smile. "I worried Nate might've capsized the boat and drowned ye's all."

"It—it was a bit rough," she managed, as he helped her out of the boat.

"Yup, that's what she did pick up, then," said the bearded logger, Nate, hopping onto shore behind her. "And some of us might've figured that out by the cloud, if our eyes weren't glared by a pair of pretty city shoes," he added ruefully, glancing at the shiny, wet gaiters buckling nearly up to Frankie's knees.

Frankie grinned, grabbing hold of the thole-pin and helping Nate haul the boat farther up on shore. "I hope you don't think us disrespectful," he said, turning back to Clair, his grin sobering, "asking you to come work for us so soon after—well, your loss. We would've understood if you'd said no."

Clair nodded, stepping aside as Nate bent over, fixing a wet plank beneath the keel of the boat. "Is you afraid of getting them pretty boots wet?" he called out, looking up at Frankie impatiently.

"I hope they gets everybody's attention at the meeting the way they're getting yours," Frankie grunted, kicking the plank in place.

"Heh, no doubt they got a pretty tongue, but it's the one in your head I'll be more interested in hearing from," replied Nate, giving the boat a last extra wrench, "providing it talks straight with us, that is."

"Better watch him, miss," called her second escort, Calve, still hunkered down by the motor in the boat, "for he's like the merchants, he is, curling his tongue into whichever cheek got the sweetest pudding."

"Pay no mind," said Frankie, taking her arm and guiding her towards the bank. "Nate, you got her suitcase? The women can't have heard us, else they'd be down to meet you by now," he added, nodding towards the six half-painted houses standing resolute to the wind and shrieking gulls. The screeching of clothesline pulleys and the cries of youngsters sounded from beyond and Nate nodded encouragingly, hoisting her suitcase onto his shoulder. "They're taking in the clothes—getting ready for the meeting in a few minutes, to talk about the vote."

"You're welcome to join us—Willamena will bring you," said Frankie as she turned to follow Nate.

"Willamena!" exclaimed Nate, peering sharply at Frankie. "She's coming to the meeting?"

"Geezes, Frankie, how's we suppose to speak our minds with Willamena there?" said Calve.

"It's honest concerns we'll be raising, b'yes," said Frankie. "It don't matter who's there when it's honest concerns. Besides, it'll be a chance for Clair to meet everybody at once. Better hurry on—I sees the Lower Head crowd coming."

"I don't know," said Nate. He glanced at the half-dozen or so men and women walking up the shore from a scattering of houses a little distance off. "They don't put much in a company man, no matter what his stand."

"Company man," snorted Frankie. "Sure now, I'm a company man. I was born and raised here same as everybody else."

"Aye, you was fine till you went and faulted yourself," said Calve.

"Like Luke says now, it's who buys a man his shoes we ought to be looking out for," said Nate, tossing a wink at Clair.

"Luke," groaned Frankie, casting his eyes up over the tree-coated hills. "Either I brings him out of the woods and tames him or banishes him to Chouse altogether."

"I allows that's one meeting I'll work on skipping," said Nate, heading for the bank. "Follow along, miss, I takes you to the women. And no matter what Frankie says, I'm not sure if the meeting's a good place for you to meet everyone. We argues down here about the colour of the fog, but this vote is a likely good reason to get everybody stirred up—and right it should when nobody knows rightly what it is they're voting for. What do you say, miss?" he asked, slowing his step as Clair stumbled over her footing.

"I—I'm not sure," said Clair, catching up with him.

"Nobody is," said Nate, carrying on his way. "It's one thing to say, yeah, we're voting for Confederation, but what's that? All we knows is the ways we got, and brother, that ain't too appealing either; never a cent to call your own. But rather the devil you knows, they says, and that's Frankie's job now, seeing how he's hooked in with the merchant—to convince us of the one we knows."

Scarcely listening, Clair nodded, keeping half a step behind, growing more timid as they neared the growing bedlam of shrieking, screeching and singing out from the houses beyond. "When's the vote?" she asked, hoping to quell her fluttering insides.

"Another six weeks. Have you decided yet?"

"Oh, I . . . I haven't thought about it much," confessed Clair, and Nate slowed his step, turning to her.

"Of course you haven't, young miss. We feels for your bad fortune." He nodded awkwardly, and Clair, biting down on her lip, moved past him. Kindness could overtake her right now, and she was to be their schoolteacher, not a snivelling schoolgirl. Nate fell quiet, picking up besides her and leading her onto a path between a woodshed, with six-foot logs to one side, and a two-storey house shading the other side. Her mind darkened as she pondered for a second just how much Willamena had parleyed to the Rocky Head crowd about her and her mother and father and all that had happened. But there was no time for further thought, for just then she came to the back of the houses and Clair stopped, staring in wonder. A flat patch of grassland lay before her, about sixty feet across to the woods rising straight up, and the houses and woodsheds arcing around it, forming a communal backyard that was webbed with well-scuffed pathways, and criss-crossed above with tiers of clotheslines running from windowpanes to door jambs, to limb-bared poplars—reminding Clair of a game of cat's cradle gone wild. The lines were half filled now, with flapping sheets and towels as the women hung out of windows or doorways, reeling in their lines, and snapping the clothes from the pins and dropping them into baskets at their feet.

"Here, here, get away—get away from the sheep," a worried voice bawled out, and Clair swung her eyes past the flapping sheets and chattering women to a baa-aaing sheep as it scurried this way and that amongst a bunch of tormenting youngsters and clucking hens that blocked its path. Straightening up from the cramped door of a henhouse, her dress tight around her barrel belly and its hemline flicking with the wind around her heavy, stockinged legs, was the old woman with the white coiled braids, the same who had hid amongst the shadows beneath the stage-head that day, watching her boy walk away to war, and who had stood on the wharf that day her father had come home, waiting his return.

"The birds is going to get ye! The birds is going to get ye!" she bawled out, setting across the patch, pointing the finger of doom down at the youngsters scattering at her feet.

"Who's the birds gonna get now?" asked Nate, hastily stepping to one side, Clair quick behind him, as the sheep scuttled out past them.

"Well, sir—" faltered a voice from above, and Clair glanced up to see a red-headed woman, a few years younger than her mother, looking down upon her, a wide grin broadening her freckled face.

"This is our new teacher," said Nate, and then others were looking her way, and the clotheslines stopped shrieking, and the youngsters stood still in their boots, and the old woman came up close, checking her over through little grey eyes imbedded amidst a mesh of wrinkled flesh.

"Bad day to be taking you on the water, ain't it?" she asked.

"Ah, you worries for nothing, old woman," chided Nate, resting the suitcase down by his feet. "I'd say she's as good a sailor as the best of them."

"Nay, you got no sense, you got no sense," the old woman sputtered. "A wonder you wouldn't drowned, hey maid?" she asked, her foreboding tones giving way to a gap-toothed grin. Caught unawares, Clair grinned back.

"And now that you've met Prude, you might want to meet the rest of the clan," said Nate, nudging her arm and directing her attention to the redhead. "That's her eldest—and my wife—Nora. And her over there's her sister Beth," he added, pointing to another, slightly younger woman with the same crinkly brown eyes. "And Beth's husband is Calve, the fellow in boat with us—my brother—and she's Aunt Char," he called out to a scrawny old woman with a wispy white bun clinging to the back of her head as she swept the hens off her stoop with a straw broom. "She's Prude's cousin. They was raised as sisters, and over there, staring at us from behind her sheets—and that's the most you'll ever see of her—is Prude's youngest sister, Hope— Frankie's mother and deaf as a haddock and scarcely moves outside her door since the day her husband drowned." Nate turned to her, his chuckle partly sympathetic, partly musing. "He drowned same day Frankie was born—that's why yonder fellow there got such shiny boots—she been spending every day since, scrubbing his face and everything else he got, and baking him pies."

"Nate!" hushed Nora.

"Not as if she can hear us," said Nate.

"Still," said Nora. "And you got our new teacher mesmerized," she added, turning to Clair. "Was it rough on the water? We got worried with the wind picking up."

"I'm used to the water," said Clair, struggling to keep her voice from quavering. "I—we always went to Cat Arm with Father in the fall."

"Cat Arm—now there's a spot," said Nate, ruffling the back of a toddler's head as he lurched by. "Perhaps we can go down for a cook-up while you're here. Now, as for them scallywags," he added more loudly, eyes resting fondly on the young ones as they stared shyly up at Clair, "you can start picking them apart in the morning, for sure they'll all be at their seats before the bell rings." A movement in the darkened hallway to his right gave shape to Willamena. "And I suppose you knows who this is."

"I never even heard the boat," said Willamena, coming out on her stoop, eyes squinting over Clair and reminding her of some nocturnal creature coming too suddenly into the

light of day. Then, with a slight tilt of her head, Willamena
clasped her hands before her in the manner of the merchant
when putting on appearances for a stranger just walking into
his store; only in this case, it was the people of Rocky Head
she must be parading before, thought Clair, because for sure,
she, Clair, would have to travel the high seas and be crowned
Queen of All Heavens before Willamena would ever allow
her such footing. And indeed, it appeared as if the crown had
already been fitted, so grand was the manner in which Willamena spoke.

"I suppose, my dear, Frankie told you how bad we all
feels about your poor mother? It's only for six weeks anyways
that we'll be needing you, but I allows it'll be a great help for
Sim and his poor old mother to have you staying down here
for a few weeks while they're shifting in. Do you think you
can handle it—the youngsters, I mean?"

Clair shrugged, smiling at the young faces staring up at
her. "I'm sure," she said, settling her gaze onto curious blue
eyes beneath chopped red bangs.

"Frannie!" warned Nora. "Better watch her," she added
to Clair, "else she'll be in your room, helping you get dressed
in the mornings."

"Yes, and I think it's time we all started getting dressed,"
said Willamena, "if we wants to get to the meeting. Bring in
her suitcase, Nate, b'ye, it's getting late," and with a royal tilt
of her head, she stepped back over her stoop.

Clair's stomach plummeted. Dear God, not Willamena
and Frankie's, she prayed, the shock of such a thought
sending more tremors through her still-quivering sea legs.
Casting her eyes frantically around the patch, she must've
appeared to those watching like a young doe stepping
unexpectedly into the light of a campfire. Nora's eyes

caught hers—and Beth's—and was that sympathy they beheld? Or pity? But unlike most animals of the wild when encountering a foe, there was no time for resorting to that unlearned manner of response that might send one fleeing into the storm from one's own shadow. Years of being accosted by prying and well-meaning neighbours alike and her training to stand firm her ground in defence of her ailing father and mother had taught Clair well to screen her impulses. Shoring up once more her weakening legs, and with a last nod to the women whose eyes she felt sure were encouraging her, she stepped warily into the camp of her opponent.

Surprisingly, it was a pretty kitchen, neat as a pin and befitting a merchant's daughter with its showy glass figurines decorating every conceivable corner, and the bin laid out with pretty coloured vases and dishes of no inherent value and less possible use except to catch light and brighten the eye of whosoever glanced at them.

"They're my wedding gifts," said Willamena, catching Clair's gaze and trailing a regal finger across a particularly pretty figurine. "A lot of them got sent out from people in Corner Brook and St. John's. When you're a merchant, you gets to know a lot of people everywhere. In there, Nate," she added, stepping around the table in the middle of the room and directing him in through a small doorway with her suitcase.

"I suppose you already knows who you're voting for, do you?" she more said than asked as Nate laid down the suit-case, turning back out.

"Nope, b'ye, can't says I do," said Nate, tossing a wink at Clair as he headed for the door.

"I knows now Luke haven't got ye talked over yet."

"I got ears of me own," said Nate. "See ye's at the meeting." He paused, glancing once more at Clair. "Frankie said you'll be taking her?" he asked Willamena.

"Frankie!" scoffed Willamena. "Sure, it's the youngsters she needs to be meeting, not their mothers, because I dare say they'll try and have some fun with a girl trying to teach them."

"You listen to none of their nonsense, young miss," said Nate. "They're a bit feisty, but nothing a show of the hand or a good threat from the strap won't cure."

"Let's not forget the birds," she offered shyly.

"Geez, don't you go starting on the birds, too." He grinned. "The younger ones are screeching now at the sight of a snipe. See you at the meeting then, and no odds about our grumbling; it's a good bunch you'll find around here." And with a last reassuring wink at Clair, he let himself out the door.

"Yes, ye're a good bunch, ye are," muttered Willamena, her tone turning sour as she shut the door behind him, "as long as ye keeps getting what ye wants, ye're a good bunch." Turning back, she paused, as if wondering at the sight of Clair Gale standing in the middle of her kitchen, and then wrinkling her nose as might a muskrat after getting a good whiff of its own stink, she scurried past her towards a French door, each glass polished to a high glimmer.

"The teacher always stays with me," she said, assuming her royal tilt of a minute ago. "That's why me and Frankie thought it best if you stayed here, too. This in here's the sitting room," she said, the glass door squeaking as she opened it into a larger room, cooler from being closed off from the stove, and heavily furnished with dark oak and a printed chaise. "And this over here," she added, stepping towards a large, hand-hewn desk, tracing a hand carefully across its surface, "is the telegraph machine."

Hooked up to a twelve-volt battery, the raised silver plate sat perfectly centred on a cream-coloured, crocheted doily and was in the direct vision of all who entered the room. "It's the teacher's job to operate it, but I don't look on you as being a real teacher, so I'll keep working it meantime. Besides, the last teacher that come here had me operating it for him. The ones around here feels more comfortable having someone they knows taking and sending their message than a stranger."

"I can't work gadgets, anyway," Clair offered with a discomfited smile, and Willamena, giving the slight bow of one who has just been put upon, whilst the other had no idea a bargain had been in the making, opened another doorway off from the living room, lending Clair a glimpse of frilled bedding and matching curtains.

"We better hurry on, then," she said, snatching a sweater off the bed, "for sure the meeting's started by now—or the arguing, because that's all the Lower Head crowd does is argue, and then loud enough, sir, to burst your drums if you was sitting close enough."

There's truth to them words, Clair thought as she hurried along behind Willamena past Prude's house and around a stack of uncut logs piled high, towards the deep rumblings sounding through the closed door of a small white schoolhouse.

"Humph, Harve," muttered Willamena, as one voice sounded over the rest. Running onto the bridge, she cocked an ear near the door, then without hesitation, pushed it open, stepping inside.

"Everyone," Frankie called out in the sudden hush that fell, "we'll take a minute to meet our new teacher, Clair Gale, from up the Basin. Come, Clair, come on in," and Clair inched uncomfortably inside, awed by Willamena's bluster as she marched before the dozen pairs of eyes, no less cooled by the abruptness of her entry as from the intensity of their meeting, and took a seat atop the teacher's desk, facing them as easily as if it were a room full of school youngsters and she about to give one of her competition speeches. Just as quickly the dozen pairs of eyes fell onto her, sending a flush tinting her cheeks as she stared back, her mind wildly seeking escape from this dreaded force that had laid hold of her life, bringing fear with each intake of breath, and thwarting hope at every turn.

"Lord, Frankie," said Nora, rising from her seat with concern, "you'd have her come meet us in the middle of all this arguing?"

"Arguing? Who's arguing?" asked Frankie, grinning around the room as he took hold of Clair's arm. And noting her reluctance to step forward, he mercifully directed her towards an empty chair besides Nora. "Perhaps we can save the introductions till after," he said as Clair gratefully sat, taking comfort as Nora patted her shoulder.

"Common sense is not one of the things Frankie's known for," whispered Nora, as the fellow, whose loud voice Clair now recognized as Harve's, spoke up directly behind her.

"I don't find fault with the teacher here, but begging your wife's pardon, Frankie, I don't see how we can speak our minds with Willamena here—her father being the merchant and all," he said to a chorus of agreements.

"Youse don't have to worry about that," scoffed Willamena. "I been hearing about cheating merchants all me life, and I can throw on a bit of dirt myself, comes to that—and not only about the merchant, either, so bring it on, I says, and we picks our way through it."

"That's a fine point to make," said Frankie, sauntering to the front of the room, jangling the change in his pockets, "and we can take care of that right now. It's a way of doing things we're going to be talking about—not Saul, and I'm sure Willamena's not going to take anything amiss. Harve, come agin with what you were saying."

"Fine, brother," said Harve loudly, "as long as you thinks it's all right—but what I'd like to know is why you're telling we to vote for a government that never sees us with a cent and always beholden to somebody else. That's what I'd like to know—why you wants us to vote for a government like that—unless you was taking care of your own pocket now." He ended with a loud chuckle. "And by the sounds of that money jangling, you already have."

"Easy to make money," said Frankie amidst more chuckling, "if you're willing to go outside and make it. Is that what you wants—to be travelling around?"

"No, sir, I wants to stay right here," said Harve, "and I wants the coppers, too, right here in me own pocket every month after I straightens up with the merchant. But he don't give we that—and you best be hearing me right, Willameen—but the merchants don't give we nothing but a bill, and sometimes we still owes—after a year's working, we still owes. There's only one way to figure that, sir—"

"Aah, it makes no difference what you owes or don't owe," Aunt Char cut in. "It's only a piece of paper. We gets all the food we can eat, and what kind of stuff do ye want that ye don't already got?"

"That's for we to figure," shouted a bald-headed old fellow over the loud protest greeting Aunt Char's words. "Be geezes, that's for we to figure."

"Aunt Char and Uncle Herm," whispered Nora, leaning towards Clair, "like two cats, they are."

"There's something to what Aunt Char says," said Frankie, holding up his hand for silence, his tone sounding to Clair as surfed up as the merchant's whenever he was meeting and greeting the scattered cash customer. "You'll never have a need, that's for sure, with the way we got things now. There's no guarantee of coppers in your pockets with Confederation. There's no guarantee of even a job with Confederation."

"How you figure that," asked Nate, "when there's talk of the Canadian companies coming in and starting up sawmills—and what about the roads and wharves they're saying they's going to build?"

"That's talk," said Frankie. "No guarantees. And even if they did guarantee it, there's no guarantee they'd hire you. They'll hire whoever they wants, but here's a guarantee for you—and that's it'll be the younger men they hires on, the ones with the strongest backs."

Clair startled at the outcry greeting those words, and Nora patted her knee reassuringly. "Pay no heed; it's how they works out everything."

"The merchant don't have to give you a day's work to know that," shouted Frankie. "He already knows your work. Knows everything about you. Been taking care of you and your'n for years. Them strangers coming into Newfoundland—the're not going to give you a day to watch you work. They don't know about you and your family. They don't know how you lives. Why'd you want to take a chance on them? And suppose they do hire you, and then puts you in a camp you don't like. Calve, how many camps did you shift around to last year looking for good grub?"

"From Faultner's Flat to Pinchgut, buddy," hollered back

Calve, "and I found one, too, brother. Cripes, there's only so much fried dough a stomach can take without his insides starting to stick together," he added loudly to the few titters coming his way.

"There'll be no shifting around when them big companies comes in," said Frankie, his warning softened as he grinned along with Calve. "You might get stuck with toutens for breakfast, dinner and supper, then."

"Now that's a fine thing to figure a vote on," spoke up Nate, "fried dough. What about the fact we might never be in the hole agin, and can buy whatever grub we wants to eat?"

"You can't know that," said Frankie. "Supposing they don't pay you enough to cover your credit? You expect the merchant to keep you on his books if he can't be guaranteed his money? At least with the merchant as boss, he knows he can always take it out in work. Work's always guaranteed."

"Are you saying the merchant'll cut us off if we don't vote for him?" asked Uncle Herm. "Is that what he's threatening to do, cut us off—after all the money he made off our backs?"

"I'm not saying that—"

"That's what you just said then, brother."

"Be geezes, Frankie, you can work for a man who'll cut our throats if you wants," argued another, "but I'd rather eat a bloodthirsty corpse than give the God-damned bastard another cord of wood if that's what he's saying."

"Oh, Lord," groaned Nora, as Willamena hopped off the desk, mindless of Frankie raising a hand to stay her.

"My father never turned his back on a man in his life," she said haughtily to the last speaker, "and it's more than one that stood before our counter looking for credit—even when there wasn't a man in the house to cut a log or bring in a fish. And I wonders that some of you mightn't stand up and speak to that." She took a step back, eyes fixed onto Clair's.

Clair stiffened, her cheeks suffusing with colour. Loud protests greeted Willamena's words, and accusations were hurled against Frankie for his bad judgment in having the merchant's daughter present at their meeting.

"Perhaps you're right, perhaps you're right," he pleaded, holding up his hand for silence as he led Willamena to a seat besides Beth. "Let's just take a minute and pacify Willamena that it's a good man her father is, and she's right in that he's done many a good turn for the people up in the Basin, things you probably wouldn't hear about down here," and then he was seeking Clair, his eyes holding hers as he ran his hand back over his knife-edge part. "And perhaps our teacher might have a word to say about that—after the meetings over and she meets everybody—because for sure her father was a good man, a wonderful man, and he worked for the merchant all his life. And we knows too how the merchant served him and kept serving him." He paused as Clair moved forward, as if to speak. "Clair?" he asked, aiding her.

And as everyone's eyes rested on her, she spoke with the clearness of tone that her father was always so fond of. "Mother always said Father had a big enough kitty with the merchant to do us an extra five years."

"Oh, my," gasped Nora besides her, and murmurs of surprise filled the room.

"It's a funny thing, sir, how nobody calls us cheating merchants when they're standing at the counter looking for charity," said Willamena equally as clearly.

"It's not charity if it's what's owing now, is it?" asked Harve.

"Cripes, if that's charity, then his taking our money must be thievery," cut in another.

"We knows different than that," sighed Frankie, trudging across the front of the room as might a resigned teacher watching his carefully composed school play come tumbling apart. "And if Saul heard us talking like this, he'd have a fit. What Willamena means—but didn't say very well—is there's lots of situations families can find themselves in, and no stranger—a businessman at that—is going to take on them kinds of responsibilities and make amends. It's only them that lives amongst us takes on that, them that knows us, knows our fathers, our youngsters—"

"Be cripes, if it's to have our names slandered after, then I'd rather starve," cried out Beth.

"Let her talk, let her talk," said Uncle Herm, catching the warning look Nora threw at her sister. "That's what we're here for, ain't it—to spake our minds, and I'll not be afeared to spake mine, brother; no sir, be geezes, not when I pays forty fish for every one that comes back on me table. I don't mind one for one, or even two for one, but it's the other thirty-seven I be wanting coppers for."

"How you figuring on that, old man—thirty-seven fish for one, when you haven't been on the water in five year?" snickered Aunt Char.

"Fish, logs, what the hell difference do it make?" shouted Uncle Herm, his face red. "Thirty-seven for one is what I'm on about, thirty-seven for one. Be geezes, you might convince me to vote for one devil over another, but you won't convince me thirty-seven equals one. It's poor I am, not stupid."

"All right, b'ye, all right," said Nate, clapping Uncle Herm's back. "And you keep a distance, old woman," he added to Aunt Char.

"Yes, we said there'd be no arguing now," said Nora, "else we would've left you home with Mother."

"It's not arguing when people spakes their minds," said Aunt Char contrarily.

"It's arguing when you starts calling them names for spaking their minds," countered Uncle Herm.

"I never called nobody names," said Aunt Char. "I'm calling this foolery is all—this talk of government and money—bloody foolery. I remembers how bad things was before the merchant come. Be cripes, I'd like to see one of ye living on seal's fat and rabbits for a year, and I haven't been wanting since Saul come along; no sir, not for one thing have I been wanting. He might be a merchant, but he's never been stingy with his grub, and nobody can argue that."

"And that's what this meeting is about—talking over the good and the bad," Frankie quickly took up. "And you were right, Nora, Nate—it's not fair to expect Willamena to sit here and not get a bit upset when it sounds as though it's her father that's being talked about, for they're close, they are," he added, nodding sympathetically at Willamena. "And who wouldn't come to their own father's defence? And going back to what we said before—it's not Saul we're talking about, but a way of running things. Everybody here can appreciate the good Saul has done—it's the way we're questioning. Perhaps, Willamena, everyone's right and it'd be better if you were to wait at home. Clair? Would you go with her? And then after the meeting we'll send for ye both to come back and Willamena can introduce you around."

"Never mind meeting anybody this evening," said Nora, rising along with Clair. "She'll meet us time enough, and perhaps then we might have a smile for her instead of a scowl. I'll be over at recess in the morning, with a cup of tea." Clair nodded gratefully, casting a glance around the room and hurried after Frankie as he led Willamena outside the door.

"You!" Willamena hissed with the fury of a March wind at Clair as she stepped over the stoop behind them, "You knows nothing about what we done for you since your father died—" But her words were chopped as Frankie grasped hold of her arm, bustling her ahead of him down over the steps and around the corner of the school. Their voices rose and fell on the wind and Clair stood quietly, waiting, till Willamena was running off along the path. She met Frankie coming back around the corner.

"What is it ye've done?" she asked, her voice small.

"Nothing," said Frankie. "Nor the merchant—at least nothing that wouldn't be paid back by the government after the bill was tallied. I expect I owes you an apology. I swear to you, I meant no offence to your father."

"I knows that," she replied, her eyes, she imagined, as hard-caked as his a minute ago while talking to his wife. "I'll take no pay for teaching here."

"Whoa," he exclaimed, catching hold of her shoulder as she was about to disappear along the same path as Willamena, "it wasn't me or Willamena that picked you to come here and teach; we asked the teacher up the Basin and he said you was our best bet. And it's the school board who's paying you—not we."

"After you've taken your board, give the rest to the school," she replied, stepping back from the hand still holding her shoulder. "That'll pay for anything extra Daddy might've owed."

"Your father owes nothing."

"It's his gift, then," she said, "for what was done for him." And turning from him, she followed Willamena's footsteps back along the path, her ears closed to the protests he was calling after her, and her heart inflamed with the potency of her deed.

Her step slowed as she crossed the patch, nearing Willamena's door. Finding it ajar, she crept inside the porch and into the kitchen. Finding no one about, she thankfully let herself into her own tiny room, leaning heavily upon the door as she closed it behind her, and her eyes flitted despondently over the narrow bed, a dresser and her suitcase lodged in the far corner. A window, walled behind a fall of dark cotton, faced out onto the patch. Trailing towards her bed, she sank down, jiggling it a little, more to relieve the tension unnerving her body than to test the bedsprings, and then lay back upon her pillow, watching as twilight dulled the crack of light caught between the curtains. A sheep baaed somewhere a ways away, and the old woman, Prude, could be heard from behind some closed door, bawling out a warning to a youngster. Overcome by fatigue, her body began to lighten, the mattress softening beneath her. Her eyes drooped, then closed, but were startled open as the image of her mother's smile flashed before them, frozen in the curve of a cheek that lay comfortably upon a bed of pink velvety petals. Calming the sudden pounding of her heart, she rolled her head to one side and fought off the vision of her father's eyes, as frozen as her mother's smile, as they stared, shackled, to its unseen phantom.

Sighing, she rolled onto her back, hugging her pillow tight to her cheek, its starched whiteness supplanting the sweet of Missy's hair.

The crack of light betwixt the curtains became darker. Somewhere, the soft strains of an accordion curled through the evening air and she slumbered as it found its way through her wall of curtains, murmuring softly against her ear. After what felt like an eternity of sleep, the whine of a dog, followed by a man's voice soothing it, wakened her.

Another voice sounded—Frankie's—and then a heavy trudging across the kitchen floor. Blinking herself awake, Clair listened as the back door opened, and Willamena called across the patch, "Having another meeting, are ye? I thought with all you got to say about the vote, you'd be the first one there this evening." Her tone, Clair noted, was much more mollifying than it had been inside the schoolhouse earlier, even with the touch of scorn in her chuckle.

"He was coming, but he got lost, wouldn't it, Luke?" said Frankie.

"Yup," said the one who must've been Luke.

"Lost? I thought you knowed the woods like your own door-place?"

"Was a funny thing," said Luke.

"But he's found now," said Frankie.

"My. What a good thing," said Willamena. "And I guess it's a good thing, too, he got you to tell him everything he missed, hey, Frankie?"

"Yup, good thing," said Frankie over the rising sounds of the accordion.

"My, how civilized—helping each other out for the next round," said Willamena.

"Round! Thought we was having a meeting," said Frankie. "What's we doing, Luke, meeting or fighting?"

"Well, b'ye, they says it's only saints that follows the one road," said Luke.

"I guess that's what you are, then," said Willamena, "a saint—at least according to what you're preaching about the vote, because for sure you're only harking on the one path there."

"I think the meeting just ended, Luke," said Frankie, the

stoop creaking as he must've rose. "See you down Chouse tomorrow. Running good, are they?"

"Twelve pounders, b'ye, and sparkling like silver."

"That's Chouse for you, a fisher's dream," said Frankie, and the accordion took up louder as he let himself in the door, snapping it shut.

"You're always sticking up for him," accused Willamena as they entered the kitchen. "He's always preaching against we, and you're always sticking up for him."

"To bed," said Frankie, the French door squeaking open.

"Well, you do," said Willamena, "and what do he know anyway, always in the woods, the way he is."

"He knows the way of things," said Frankie, "and that's why them like your father's not going to have a wharf to tie their punts onto after his vote—because they're too busy scholaring and not thinking."

"You thinks we're going to lose?"

"Yup."

"You acts as if it was nothing," said Willamena. "How can you go fishing with him out there, when it's his addled mouth that's turning people against us?"

Frankie's foot lay heavily on the floor. "You don't ever call him that agin, you hear me?"

"Lord, Frankie, whose side you on, anyway?" whined Willamena.

"The side what wins," said Frankie. "And there's some things you'll follow me on, else you'll be back on the same rotting wharf I took you off, hear it? You don't ever slander him. And you'll be respectful to her whilst she's here." Then footsteps and the sound of the room door snapping shut.

As if to spare Clair further, a fun-filled jig danced its way through her window, causing her to lean forward and lift the corner of her curtain, peering out through it. A dim glow of lamplight dappled through one of Prude's cluttered windows onto a short-haired bitch, squatting on its haunches, looking up at a young man whom she recognized instantly as the one who had sat in his boat with his back to the crowd, and who had appeared on her doorstep that night, looking for her father. He was sitting on the edge of Prude's stoop, his fair hair and the white of his accordion keys barely discernable in the dark, his shoulders doing a dance of their own to the song his fingers were plying into the night. The dog yapped and the young man lifted a foot, rubbing it against the dog's chest, a laugh sounding over his song as the dog yapped twice more, then scuttled beneath the house. Leaning back, he swung the accordion her way, his face shadowed by the night, and she quickly dropped her curtain into place. Lying back down, she stared wide-eyed at her ceiling, one ear tuned to the reel of the accordion, the other to the muted harsh whispers escaping through the high-polished glass of Willamena's French door.

CHAPTER EIGHT

THE NEXT MORNING CLAIR WAS WAKENED by the first crow of the cock. Peering out the corner of her room window, she watched as the men came out their doors, whistling good-morning to one another, and making their way up over the hill, their bucksaws and canvas lunch bags tossed over their shoulders. Likewise, Frankie was out of bed, treading lightly through the kitchen and leaving the house without breakfast. He must've went in boat, perhaps up to the Basin to work with the merchant, thought Clair, as he made no appearance onto the patch. There was no sign of Luke either, and the memory of him sitting on the steps the night before, his fingers dancing over the keys of an accordion, and the bitch yapping at his feet, might well have been a dream.

Climbing out of bed, she hastily washed herself in cold water, combed her hair, then dressed in her stockings and skirt. Thankfully, Willamena didn't emerge from her bedroom till she had finished a slice of bread with a glass of iced tea, and was on her way to the door, hoping to get to the schoolhouse early before the youngsters arrived.

"Leaving awful early, aren't you?" said Willamena, standing puffy-eyed in the French doorway, her tone as accusing as Johnnie Regular's wife, Rose's.

"I don't want to be late," said Clair, brushing the crumbs off her mouth and pulling on her sweater.

"I suppose Luke kept you woke all night, did he?"

Clair shook her head.

"Umph, he kept me woke, then," she muttered, shuffling along to the bin, taking down a teacup.

And Clair, driven by curiosity, asked most casually, "What's—wrong with him, then?" as she did her buttons.

"Low-minded is what," said Willamena, pouring tea. "He was with a fellow who shot hisself when they were youngsters and he got low-minded. Started having fits so he hid out in the woods so's nobody could see him when they took. Now all he does is work in the woods all day and ramble about nighttime," she grumbled, shuffling to the table.

"Does he still have them?"

"Who knows. He's not home long enough for anybody to see."

"Did he die?"

"Who?"

"The fellow that shot hisself."

"He blowed his face off is all. Rather lose your face than your mind, I suppose, although you wouldn't think so by the way they all praises Luke and shits on Gid."

"Gid?"

"The fellow that shot hisself," exclaimed Willamena crossly. "They was a family of no-goods that come here in a storm, but they moved to Corner Brook after the shooting. But you'd do well to leave off talking about it; the ones around here don't like strangers snooping into their business."

And for sure it ought to be school she was thinking about, thought Clair as she let herself out the door into the salty September morning and was besieged by a bunch of youngsters dawdling around the stoop, waiting for her. Partially reassured by their shy smiles, she allowed them to fight over who was going to hold her hand, and prancing by her side, they led her out onto the bank where the sea was washing noisily up over the shore, and the gulls were crying and gliding hungrily overhead.

"Mind you listens to your teacher!" a voice bawled out, raw with threat, and Clair glanced nervously as the old woman, Prude, appeared out of the shadow of the stagehead, her white braids coiled thickly around her head and her skirts flapping in the wind.

"We will, Gram!" said the smaller youngsters. "Go in the house, old woman," muttered one of the older boys, Roddy, with the reddish brush cut, and Clair nodded politely, but Prude was already disappearing beneath the stagehead.

"She's always under the stagehead," said the boy Marty, same height as Roddy and as dark as Roddy was fair.

"Oh, yeah, she's not, my son," said Roddy.

"Yeah, she is," said Marty, "every morning, anyways."

"Saying her prayers to Joey," said a younger one.

"You use the strap, miss?" asked Roddy.

"Hope not," she replied.

"Might have to with them crowd," said Marty, squinting towards a handful of youngsters strolling up from Lower Head.

"They're always late," said Roddy, fingering a rock that appeared to be itching his hand.

"Yeah, they're always late!" chorused the younger ones.

"They're not late this morning," commented Clair.

"Better not put your head too close, miss; they got lice."

"Shh," Clair cautioned them. She squared her shoulders, alarmed at how faint her breathing was, and walked up over the bridge of the little white schoolhouse. Stepping in through its door, she took another deep breath, looking around the one room. The seats had been put back in neat little rows from the meeting the night before, and the pot-bellied stove, with its bucket of coals besides it, was highly polished, and the grey-painted floorboards cleanly swept. A small pile of books, a register and a bell sat tidied to the centre of the teacher's desk, and a black leather strap hung besides the well-buffed blackboard. Someone had written Welcome, miss across the blackboard in large, gay lettering.

Shrieking and squirming, the youngsters clambered ahead of her, finding a seat of choice in the row designated for their grade level, and after much poking and giggling, they gradually quieted, looking to her as she took her place before the blackboard. She looked back, her mouth dry, and her legs beginning to quiver. What now, she asked, her heart beginning to pound, her mind as emptied as a church on Monday mornings.

Foolishness! she thought. Foolishness! They're young-sters, no different from Missy when she used to read to her. And looking to the littlest in the farthest row, she asked in a voice that shook with nerves, "What's your name?"

"Susie."

"And yours?" she asked the next.

"Danny. Susie's my sister."

"And I'm Scottie, miss, and he's my brother, Benny."

"Yup, me and he's brothers," said Benny, "and we and them's cousins."

Thus it went, one after the other, the oldest being Roddy, son of Nate and Nora; second eldest, Marty, son of Beth and Calve; the curious brown eyes beneath the chopped-off bangs staring adoringly into her face, Frannie,

Roddy's sister; and so on till each pair of eyes staring at her became a name, and each name a family. And once they'd all been marked in the register, Clair raised her eyes over their heads, staring at some distant point in her mother's kitchen, and announced in the same clear voice that she'd practised a thousand times with her father that there would be no lessons from their school books this morning, but rather a story about fairies and bluebells that she had learned from her younger sister, Missy, and after which some of them might like to stand before the teacher's desk and tell her a story if they wished. The one who spoke the loudest and clearest would be given the bell to ring at recess, and this would be the way, then, that they would start all their mornings, with stories. Then, noting Willamena strolling by the front of the school, peering curiously in through the windows, "And our stories will be our secret," she added most firmly, "so we can say whatever we wish and nobody will ever hear them but us, right here in this schoolhouse; do ye think ye can keep our stories a secret?"

"Yes, miss," chorused the lot, and perching on the corner of her desk, Clair began her story.

Time moved, and within a blink, most of them were scattering out the door for recess and Nora was sauntering in through, shooing out young Frannie and the others loitering around their desks, cradling a cup of tea in her hands.

"Like I promised," she said, laying the cup before Clair.

A cup of tea, thought Clair, no different from what her mother would make for Alma or those others coming for a visit. It struck her then, as she smiled her appreciation to Nora, that she wasn't young Clair, Sare's girl, any more, dallying with her cereal so's to keep her spot at the table amidst the adult conversations or practising reading to her father from some far corner so's she could make a grand teacher someday. She was now the teacher. Her heart expanded a little, as it had yesterday upon presenting Frankie with her pay to square off any debts owing; yet a sickening crept through her stomach, the same as she had felt upon seeing the first stain of menstrual blood upon her underwear. And as she had then, she sought to understand this new thing that had claimed her body and was now wrestling for her mind.

"The people feels bad about you having to leave the meeting yesterday," Nora was saying, sitting on the seat nearest her, the crinkles around her eyes deepening as she smiled. "Most of us didn't know you were coming—or Willamena—till the door opened. Anyways—" she raised her brow expressively "—whatever Frankie was trying to do in getting ye there, it never worked—you seen to that."

"Me?" asked Clair, startled.

"Well, what you said about the five-year kitty sure struck a chord," Nora grinned. "Frankie wouldn't expecting that one. Anyways," she said more seriously, "the people are proud to hear you thinks along the same lines as some of we about the merchant, and they wants you to know that you're welcomed in their houses anytime you wants, and to let them know right away if their youngsters aren't listening, and they'll take the belt to them."

"Oh—no—they've just been fine," exclaimed Clair. "And tell them—the people—I'm grateful for them having me as their teacher."

"They thinks it's nice—having a woman teacher for a change. How are you finding it?"

Clair glanced around the room with an exaggerated shrug. "I never thought I'd be a teacher this week," she said impulsively, then faltered.

Leaning forward, Nora touched one of her hands. "I pities the poor orphans born into the world without a mother and father," she half whispered, "but my heart breaks for them that loses their mother so young. And may God have mercy on those that brings them more hurt by the carelessness of their tongues."

Clair swallowed. "Was your brother talked about as well?" she asked.

The smile faded on Nora's face, and Clair sat back, recognizing in its place a look akin to hers whenever others had asked after her poor father and her poor, poor mother, when it was their minds they wanted to know about, wanted to see deep down inside of, and pick and scratch and snip at whatever they deemed odd, improper or sick about it. And she had suffered their inquisitions the way a snail suffers the thousand incantations of youngsters playing on the beaches, to detach their jellied bodies from their protective shells and appear before them—that mountain of segmented parts luring them to their doom with sweetly crooning deceptions of their house being on fire and their children all alone. Sitting now, at her teacher's desk, she wished a cure for her cursed tongue as this woman, Nora, with the warmth of her father's eyes, was now set upon to suffer the same.

"I expect you've heard otherwise, but Luke's as sound as any man or woman walking," said Nora.

"No, no. I meant—I meant the one who went to war," Clair said hastily.

Nora's face reddened. Sitting back, she looked at Clair and spoke apologetically. "I expect we're all guilty of listening to tongues wagging, despite our knowing that yarn gets stretched with every washing." She rose, appearing slightly relieved as some of the younger ones started trailing back in. "You're doing fine, then? They're listening?"

Clair nodded, rising along with her.

"That's good, then," said Nora, backing her way to the door. She paused, her foot on the stoop, a trace of her old warmth returning. "Just mind what the people says; they only keeps their door closed on account of the wind. And Frannie and the other girls are already fighting over who gets to name their dolly Clair," and then she was gone, strolling back along the path leading past the woodpile.

The rest of the day passed with ease, and surprisingly, the rest of the week—even mealtimes with Willamena and Frankie on those rare occasions when Frankie took supper with them and wasn't travelling around the island. And each time he returned, he always had much to say about the upcoming vote.

"The Confeds are painting a mighty fine picture, with their promises of old age pensions and family allowances and unemployment cheques," he added one evening over baked mackerel and potato. "Plus all their talk of building new roads and wharves and opening up the island—yup, it's a pretty picture."

Willamena passed him a napkin that matched the yellow of the tablecloth and complimented the lamplight bronzing her face. "Nothing they haven't had in Canada all this time," she replied. "Still for all, it didn't keep them from near starving to death back before the war. It was we, then, sending them fish, wouldn't it? And there's nobody starving around here, that's for sure. Dad was saying last week how he could hardly keep up with the orders coming in for lumber."

"That's because of the war, not the government," said Clair, and immediately took a long drink of water, wishing to wash away her words as Willamena turned to her, a thin veneer of a smile tarnishing the glow of lamplight.

"Where'd you hear that?" she asked. "I thought it was thieving merchants they blamed everything on."

"Willamena's still thinking the vote's either for or agin her father," said Frankie as Clair bent her head over her mackerel. "I hear you've been down Lower Head for dinner?"

And Clair, eager to bypass the merchant, was quick to relate the names of the people she'd met, and the good behaviour of the school youngsters; yet her one concern, she told them, was the Hurlys, who couldn't get their boys to attend school and listen to a woman teacher.

"The Hurlys!" snorted Frankie. "They never listened to anybody in their life—what's they going to start now for? Bar them out if they starts coming; they're too big to be in school, anyway."

"Listen to Frankie," said Willamena, "I suppose they got as much right as anybody to get a education."

"What for—so's they can learn how to pile a cord of wood? Cripes, Willamena, they're either going out in the boat, fishing, or in the woods, cutting; either way, it's the broad of their backs that's going to get them through life, not pencils and scribblers."

"I suppose that's for them to say—"

"Yup, and both the mister and missus had their say—at the meeting," said Frankie, his ear cocking towards a dog's yap outside. "Everyone was in agreement with Clair's coming then, so there'll be no more talk about it."

"Where you going—wait for your tea," said Willamena as he shoved back his chair, rising. "And don't worry about him," she added, rolling her eyes towards the door and the sound of the accordion starting up. "He's been out there every night this week, scrooping that box."

"I'll have it later," said Frankie.

"Sir, you're always running off," cried Willamena, following him to the door, "and I got some gingersnaps made, too."

"I'll have one with tea."

"Frankeee!"

"I'm just checking on the gear—I'll be back in a bit."

"Gear! Where you going—Frankie, you're not going to Chouse agin—you just got home!"

"One night is all. You can come, if you wants," said he impatiently as Willamena put herself between him and the door.

"Right, and spend the night with he in a bough-house."

"Bough-whiffen—and we can make our own if you wants. And don't mind her," he said, tossing a grin to Clair as he moved Willamena aside. "She don't like no one preaching for Confederation. Besides, she got it in for Luke ever since she got a fright once."

"I dare say! Looking through my window, he was—"

"Looking *at* your window, he was," cut in Frankie. And opening the door, he let himself out.

"Lord, Frankie, sir!" cried Willamena with such dejection that Clair turned to her in surprise.

"He often goes fishing?" she asked sympathetically.

"Only with *him*—that's all he can get *him* to do, he's so loony," she ended sourly. And spurred to charity by her moment of humility, she turned to Clair: "I didn't mean nothing," she exclaimed quickly and just as quickly assumed her queenly tilt. "Anyway, Frankie don't like for me to talk about it," she said, rising. And marching into the sitting room, she closed the French doors behind her, leaving Clair alone with the table and the dirty dishes.

Later, after Frankie had his tea and gingersnap, and he and Willamena had retired to their room for the evening, and the patch had been cleared of chickens, sheep and bustling souls, Clair lay back on her bed, her curtains slightly drawn, watching the first stars prickle through the evening sky, and listening to the sea rustling up over the beach rocks.

"IT'S MY TURN," ANNOUNCED RODDY the next morning, rising from his seat, a scribbler in his hand. "Can I, miss?"

"No, I wants to tell," cut in Marty.

"You've already told one, Marty," said Clair. "And it's 'may I,' Roddy, and yes, you may," she added, stepping aside from her desk, and taking Roddy's seat as he stood before the room, hair wet and standing straight up from an horrific morning's brushing, and a smidgen of jam sticking to his bottom lip.

"It's a big story, so I'm going to tell it in bits, all right, miss?" he began. "A bit right now, and a bit tomorrow and the next day—"

"Hope now, my son, you can't do that," protested Marty.

"Sure he can," said Clair. "Whoever wants to tell a story in bits can. Go ahead, Roddy."

Wrinkling his nose at Marty, Roddy took a deep breath and began.

"'Once upon a time there was this contrary boy named Henry who hated and complained and made fun at everything in his house, till one day his mother drove him out.

"'And don't come back here till you gets better manners,' she bawled after him.

"'Ha,' said he, 'it's me own house I'll be getting, and once I finds it, I won't be back here no more, either.'

"'And no you won't be,' called out his mother, 'fore if you goes up that shore, you'll be took by strangers and boiled in hot tar and never be seen or heard from agin, I'll warrant you that.'

"'Cripes, took by strangers,' scoffed Henry, 'big fellow like me, took by strangers. Foolish is what you is, Mother, bloody foolish.'

"So he starts off up the shore, looking for his own house. Well, he was so mad that he never minded going way on up the beach by his self. And he scarcely ever looked back, checking that he could still see the smoke from his mother's chimney curling up over the trees. But after awhile, sir, he started getting a bit tired, and too, he never had nothing to eat yet the day, and he was starting to wish for a slice of bread and some molassey. And then, when he thought he was going to faint he was so starved, he spied another fellow, same age as he, sitting on a rock, munching on a big chunk of scald pudding.

"First he was a bit scared because this other fellow was a stranger, even though he was his own age, and he was always thinking on his mother's stories about strangers carrying boys off and soaking them in boiling tar. But he was *so* starved, he went up to the fellow, anyhow. And besides, this fellow had nice shiny eyes, and a great big smile and didn't look one bit mean.

"'Hey, buddy, you got a piece of scald pudding to spare?' he sings out.

"Now, this young fellow, his name was Conner. And even though he was nice enough, he was lazier than a cut cat and was always looking for a way to con his way in to or out of something. That's why he was called Conner— sly as a conner.

"'What're you doing all by yourself up here?' he asks Henry.

"'I'm leaving me old mother's house,' said Henry, point-ing back to where he could still see her smoke curling up over the trees, 'and I'm going to find me own.'

"'Ooh,' says Conner, 'that's a fine idea.' But that's not what he was thinking at all, because along with being sly and lazy, Conner was just as scared of strangers and stuff as Henry. So he was wanting a nice comfortable house to heave off in. And he was wanting some good grub, too. So he thinks, Mmm, I wouldn't mind living in Henry's mother's house, with the fire going and for sure, there'd be bread baking. So he gives all of his scald pudding to Henry and says, 'Now I got nothing left, so you got to take me with you and let me live in your house when you finds it.' That was fine with Henry.

"'All right, b'ye, that's fine with me. But first you got to help me find one.'

"'Well, that's going to be hard to do,' said Conner with the big frown, as if he was thinking heavy. Then he looks up and says, 'I knows—let's go back to your mother's. I bet she got some good bread baked by now.'

"'I already said I was never going back,' snaps Henry, 'so come with me if you wants.'

"Ol' Conner, he didn't like it, but he figured he'd best go along for awhile, till he got another chance to change Henry's mind. And Henry was glad Conner was coming, because, see, he never let on, but he was starting to feel a bit scared by now, being this far away from his house. So off they went, walking side by side, up the beach, Henry talking about finding his own house, and Conner trying to weasel him back to his mother's by saying things like 'Bet your old mother's worried about you now,' or, 'You think she's out looking for you, yet, Henry?'

"But Henry was caught on to Conner's weasling and just kept on walking up the beach, every now and then, whistling a bit. And that's when they seen this other fellow, same age as them. All curled up, he was, in the root of a big log, just like a baby. And he was skinny and shivering all over, with no socks or boots on, and when he opened his eyes and seen Conner and Henry staring at him, he never even got a fright, he was feeling that miserable. And all he done, when Henry and Conner come right up close to him, was sit up and look. And that's when Henry and Conner seen the gun lying under him. And that's all I'm going to tell ye's the day." Looking proudly at Clair, Roddy marched back to his seat.

"Oh, yeah, my son," said Marty.

"Can't tell it if that's all I got made up, can I, miss?"

"Guess not," said Clair. "Did you make it up all by yourself, Roddy?"

Roddy shrugged. "Henry's making it up, miss."

"Then Henry's a good storyteller," said Clair, nodding her praise.

Missy would like it here, she thought later that afternoon, gazing over the little rows of bent heads, studiously working on their assignments. But then, as always when she thought of Missy, her face darkened and she paced the floor between the rows of desks, wringing her hands and looking for a tardy student she could sit with, or take the dusters outside and beat them together till chalk clouded the air around her, rendering her head and shoulders to that of her father's the morning he had sat at the kitchen window, sheathed in pew dust. And chance she was caught without a pencil, a ruler or a book to occupy her hands, she was running for the mop and broom to sweep, scrub or polish the grey-painted floorboards. And when an unexpected rain threatened the caplin drying on the flakes, she'd lecture her students to stay seated and finish their lessons, and bolt outside with the rest of the women, quickly hauling sheets of canvas over the catch, or layering with boughs those the canvas couldn't reach.

"Like one of our own, you are," Nora exclaimed one breezy Saturday morning as Clair squatted down besides her and Beth on the beach, pipping a bucket of squid.

"Not like some others we knows," said Beth, with a peevish look towards Willamena's house. Catching a warning look from Nora, she chanced a sideways glance at Clair, and fell to muttering, "Well, she knows we're going up the Basin this evening; you'd think she'd help us try and get a head start on the day."

"The smell of squid makes her sick," said Nora. "My, the youngsters loves school this year. You must be making for a grand teacher, Clair—and what's they doing with all the writing? And in secret, too? Sir, I never seen Frannie so quiet before as when she goes in her room with her pencil and scribbler."

Ignoring Nora's questioning look, Clair glanced down the beach to where Marty and Roddy hung over the edge of the stagehead, jigging tom cods, and Frannie and some other girls were scampering around the beach, collecting white rocks. "They're pretty imaginative," she replied with a smile, then turned her attention to the slippery cone-shaped fish near slipping out of her hands, and tried to keep her fingers away from the mass of tentacles dangling from where a mouth ought to be.

"Here, like this, look," said Beth. And taking the squid out of Clair's hand, she slipped her thumb between its head and the jelly-like flesh of its body, then broke the three dots of gum-like sinew connecting them. A good yank on the tentacles, and the head and entrails slid out, neatly detached from the now hollowed body.

"And mind you don't break the sacs," she warned, tossing the pip out over the water to the gulls shrieking and flapping over the bounty, "because there's nothing like squid shit to stain a garment black. Should tell that to the merchant, Saul. He might use it to tone down his halo, because it's shining awful bright them days now, with the vote almost here."

Nora tutted.

"Well, what's wrong with talking to her about him?" argued Beth. "I'm just curious, that's all," she said to Clair, "about what the people up the Basin is saying. One thing to be grumbling agin Saul all the time—we'd do that no matter who the storekeeper is—but are they going to vote for him, that's what I'd like to know; or are they scared of getting cut off the same as we if we don't vote for him and he wins?"

"I don't think Saul would cut anybody off—" began Nora.

"Oh, yes he would," said Clair. "I—heard Mommy talk about it once," she added as both sisters looked at her with surprise.

"What did she say?" asked Beth.

"Well, that this one family had to move to Bonne Bay once, because the merchant wouldn't give him no more work and cut off his store bill."

Both sisters continued to stare at her, their squid lying limp in their hands.

"And they moved?" asked Nora.

"Yup," said Clair.

Nora gazed past Clair towards where Frannie and the other girls were now squatting down by the water's edge, giggling over the smooth white rocks they had found, and were now using gulls' feathers to paint them with water; and to young Roddy and Marty arguing excitedly over a tom cod Roddy was hauling in; and Prude hollering out her warnings to the little ones scampering to and fro the water's edge, their shrieks mingled with the gulls swooping over their heads. "Sure, how can you just move from a home?" she asked quietly of no one. "And what about all your family—your sisters and their youngsters—and your old mother—how can anybody leave their old mother?" She shook her head, turning back to Clair, "I could no more leave here than I could walk out in that water and drown," she half whispered.

And indeed, why should she ever have to leave, thought Clair, for it's how she herself would feel, could she ever find her way back in Cat Arm again, with her mother chattering around the stove as she fried up pork scrunchions, and her father carving the liver out of a moose, and Missy supping back onion strips, giggling over his silly sayings. For it was, as her father had said, perfectly fine to claim one's own small corner and make it a sacrament of God. "If everybody voted against him, there'd be no fear of getting cut off," she said, turning to Nora. "He's got to have some customers, don't he?"

"Ahh, now you're sounding like Luke," said Nora, "but how do you get people rallied together—especially when everybody lives so far apart?"

"And you don't know who to be talking to up the Basin," said Beth. "Some of them's up the merchant's arse, and them who aren't don't bother talking with we most times. If it wouldn't for the bit of news Luke brings home—he goes up the hill high enough to get radio—then we wouldn't know the half of anything, would we, Aunt Char," she added loudly as the scrawny old woman appeared on the bank, her long black skirts rustling around her legs as she bustled down besides them.

"What's ye harping about, now?" she asked in a tone already fixed on arguing as she settled herself on the end of the log besides Beth, reaching into the squid bucket.

"The vote," called out Prude from down the beach. "That's what they's always talking about when they got their heads together, whispering."

"My Lord," groaned Nora, "she don't miss a word."

"Foolishness, that's what ye's be getting on with, foolishness," grumbled Aunt Char, flinging a pip to the gulls, its juices spattering Clair's face as it sailed by but an inch from her nose. "The old ways worked for we, it can work for ye. Sure, ye's getting as grand as the merchants with your want of fancy tablecloths and the like."

"Having a tablecloth don't make for grand ways," said Nora, in the resigned air of one who's been through this argument a dozen times before.

"When it got to match the curtains, it do," said Aunt Char. "Putting yourselves in the hole just to have something nice for the youngsters to spit on."

"Well, sir," said Beth, taking a keen look at the old aunt, "what kind of youngsters did you have, that went around spitting on curtains?"

"What I can't figure," said Nora, "is that they'd get all of our wages, anyway—and then more, if we starts getting money for youngsters and the old and so forth—why wouldn't they be wanting us to have more money?"

"It's not just our wages they're fighting to keep," said Beth, "it's what Luke says—they gets triple for a cord of wood over what they pays us. And if the big companies moves in paying wages, and the men all goes working for them, then they starts losing their fortunes."

"And what's a fartune but something to sit on," said Aunt Char. "We'd still be sitting here, I tell ye, whether it was a money bag or a cantal of fish cushioning your arse. Better the fish, I says; you can eat that when all else is gone."

"Ohh, I gets so mad at Frankie," said Nora. "He's the one out amongst them. He's the one who knows the best way."

"Frankie knows the best way for himself, and he makes no bones about that," said Beth. "But I allows he paid dear for some things," she added, her voice dropping to a whisper as Willamena dodged onto the bank, peering curiously at their bowed heads.

"Ain't that what I been telling ye," said Aunt Char, sitting back, peering at Beth, "that your fartune's what you already got at home, not what you goes out and drags in."

"Shush, now," cautioned Nora. "Some morning," she called up to Willamena.

"A busy one by the looks of ye," said Willamena.

"Bring yourself over and busy yourself, if you've a mind," said Aunt Char.

"Watch out now," said Willamena, taking hold of her nose with an exaggerated pinch. "I told Frankie I couldn't bide here if there was squidding all year round."

"It's not bothering the young teacher none," said Aunt Char, patting Clair's knee with a squid-inked hand.

Nora groaned, brushing at the stain left on Clair's skirt. "Oh, Lord," she groaned louder as Clair punctured the pip she was ripping out of a squid, spurting more of the black, shiny liquid over her lap.

"Ugh." Clair grimaced, then looked up as Beth let out a

whoop and leaping off the log, tore off down the beach,
singing out, "Luukkeee! Luukee!" Clair stared after her,
running and dodging youngsters and gulls, down the beach
towards the fair-haired young man strolling out besides the
stagehead, fishing rod and pack bag slung over one shoulder,
his dog yapping at his heels.

"Going off agin, is he?" commented Willamena, "My,
you must do some worrying with him," she added, glancing
at Nora, "always going off by himself like that."

"I worries more for we," said Nora, watching as he laid
his rod and bag inside a punt pulled up on shore, "that he'd
rather his own company to ours." Suddenly she hollered,
"Roddy! Here, Roddy!"

Her eldest, upon sight of his uncle, was leaping off the
stagehead, the water nearing the top of his boots as he
lunged towards his uncle, calling out, "Uncle Luke, Uncle
Luke, can I come, can I come?"

"Well, sir, I'll kill him if he got his feet wet," cried Nora.
"Here, you young bugger," she yelled, but her cry was lost
amidst a chorus of hails as Frankie strolled out from behind
the same woodshed as Luke, and then Nate alongside of
him. But it was onto Luke Clair's eyes were fastened as Beth
grabbed him by the ear, bringing him to his knees with a
painful yelp. Always there was Luke, or glimpses of him,
vanishing up into the woods each morning with his bucksaw
tossed upon his shoulder, or strolling up alongshore Sunday
mornings with his dog trotting at his heels, or shoving off his
boat, on his way to Chouse.

"Mother, leave him alone, for God's sake," Nora was
yelling as Prude tried to haul Roddy away from the boat by
the back of his shirt. "Sir, she don't let up on the youngsters
for a minute; I allows she'd drive them mental if they paid

heed at all. Luukeee! Luukkeee! You going to take him?"

"What's all the bawling out about?" said Nate, striding towards them. "I say you're going to have sore wrists in the morning, young miss, you don't get them cleaned up," he added as Clair punctured another pip and a wash of ink spread over her hands, running up her sleeves.

"Squid hands—that's what she's going to have then, squid hands, if she's not more careful," said Aunt Char.

"It's—it's nothing," mumbled Clair, wiping her wrists on her skirt.

"Be something when you got to start pissing on them to stop the smarting," said Aunt Char, "because that's the only thing to stop squid hands from smarting, piss—and most times not your own, either."

"Better go wash them," said Nora, nodding sympathetically as Clair turned an alarmed face her way. "That's why poor old mother's not pipping besides us—squid hands. Nate, go get young Roddy out of Luke's boat, because he's going up the Basin with us whether he wants to or not. Clair, you coming, too?"

Squatting by the water's edge, her sleeves rolled up, Clair quieted, feeling the water numbing her skin. "Clair?" said Nora, approaching her from behind. "You haven't gone home for a visit since you come."

"I—perhaps I will," she replied with a tight smile to Nora. "Yes, I think I will." Rising, she walked back to her rock, flicking the water off her hands, and reached into the bucket for another squid.

A great fear fanned itself in her belly as Clair stood on the wharf, looking up at the great white house on the top of the hill, and her foot grew leaden. Trembling, she reached out to a grunt to steady herself, thinking at first she might be ill.

"Are you all right?" asked Nora, appearing besides her. Raising her eyes, Clair nodded weakly, unable to speak. Sensing her distress, Nora sent Nate after Missy and, giving Clair a quick hug, left her alone and went into the store. Clair sat on the grunt, her chest constricting, and clutched her hand to her heart as it started pounding wildly, stifling her breath as if she were breathing through the thick of a pillow. A quick breeze brushed her cheeks and she scarcely felt its coolness, thinking of her father and understanding a little of how he must've felt those times sitting on the stairs, or hiding in his room, choking for breath. A hawk screeched overhead and she startled towards it, watching as it swooped in an arc over her head, then glided towards her house. The hawk screeched again, then dropped from sight, leaving her with her father's screams as he had fought his way through the nights. She was still sitting on the grunt when Nate returned and, assured that she was fine, just a little seasick, he went into the store, leaving her be. He was back and forth to his boat several times, storing boxes of supplies into the cuddy before Missy finally appeared, walking slowly down over the hill, her hair its usual mass of curly abandon, and her figure slight. Mommy's right, she never grows an inch, thought Clair. The tall, reedy shape of the uncle appeared besides Missy, reaching for her hand as might a father to his child at the brink of danger. As quiet as a shadow was Missy as she kept stride besides him, and Clair saw that she had grown after all, surely an inch; but her mouth was as petulant as ever, and her final steps towards Clair were slow, guarded, as were the uncle's as he neared, staring intently through eyes barely discernible beneath the peak of his cap. With a sinking heart Clair saw too that Missy's eyes were guarded, and that she, Clair, was being beheld as a threat by this younger sister, for she had fettered herself to the uncle the way in which an abandoned barnyard kitten suckles the first teat left open to it.

"Let's go for a walk, Missy," she said, reaching for her sister's hand, but was deterred by the uncle as he straightened to his full height, taking Clair back to that last day in her father's house when, once the neighbours had gone, he had lorded it over her. And as then, her distaste grew.

"You'll speak with me here," he said.

"You've no more say over me," she replied.

"And you've no say over her."

"I've a right to talk to her alone. She's my sister."

"You'll not tell her your lies—I'll see to that."

"Lies! You talk to me about lies?" snapped Clair.

"I'll not stand here and argue," he cut in, making to leave, tugging Missy's hand to follow.

"Wait! Wait," said Clair as Missy wrenched her eyes onto her. "I—I just want to tell you something," she pleaded to Missy. "Here, we'll just sit here," and taking a step backwards, she perched on the grunt, as if her sitting might show the uncle she wasn't about to nip his precious pet by the neck and drag her to another roost. The uncle hesitated, then reluctantly allowed Missy to pull her hand from his, and stood watching with both ears perked as she came to stand besides Clair.

"Are you? Are you coming home?" asked Missy.

"Missy, you'd like it where I am," Clair whispered, leaning into the familiarity of her sister's candied scent, mingled with the garden smells of her mother and the spicy smell of her father's pipe. "You must come," she whispered feverishly. "There's a real nice girl—her name's Frannie—and she wants to meet you—"

"No, you must come home," cried Missy, pulling away. "You said you would and then you never."

"That's because I'm teaching—and I'm trying to figure things," said Clair. "Missy, wait—" but Missy was already pulling away.

"Leave her be," the uncle ordered.

"Leave us alone," shouted Clair, coming off the grunt and storming the uncle, but Missy was snatching hold of his hand, half hiding behind him.

"You said you was coming home, Clair!" she cried. "You said!"

"But I'm teaching—"

"There's loonies there!"

"Loonies?" said Clair.

Her mouth dropped as Missy cried out, "Yes there is, Clair, and they lives in the woods and comes out nighttime making up strange songs."

"Who told you such a thing?" she asked incredulously, and immediately cast her eyes upon the uncle.

"There's more than one to think that," he returned. "And you'll not take her amongst the low-minded—she had her fill of that with her father."

"You!" Clair gasped. "You'd say that—when it was you who brought on his screaming—you and your stealing?"

"You was always the liar," replied the uncle, finger pointing, "but there's no one to listen to them now—and you'll not put foot inside my door with your lies."

"Daddy's door, you *bastard!*" she hissed as he turned, starting back up the hill with Missy stumbling over his ankles. And she would've been onto his back like the cat if not for Nate who'd been standing quietly to one side, listening, suddenly darting forward and grabbing hold of her.

"Bastard!" she gasped, throat raw with spite, eyes clawing after the uncle's back and unseeing of Nora, who'd stepped outside the store upon hearing their voices. "Bastard!"

Nora ran to her, whispering, "Oh, my dear, oh, my dear."

"ANYWAYS," SAID RODDY, several mornings later, "Henry was pretty surprised to see the gun lying underneath the young fellow. He asked, 'What's your name?'

"'Sammy,' said the fellow.

"'How come you got a gun?' asked Henry.

"'Me father was going to shoot me, so I took his gun and runned,' said Sammy.

"Well, sir, Henry looked right mad at that. What kind of father would want to shoot his boy?

"But Conner, now, he was seeing his chance. Perhaps if he got Sammy walking along with them, he might help change Henry's mind about going back to live in his mother's house. So he says, 'I suppose, Henry, he can come with us, can't he—although he looks awful weak for walking.'

"First Henry didn't like the idea, because he didn't fussy the chance of running into Sammy's father and perhaps getting shot along with Sammy; but then he felt right bad, seeing how tired Sammy looked. And he was such a sight, with his eyes all drooping like he was half asleep, and he had awfullest hair—striped yellow and brown and frizzed off his head like a haystack. Then Conner seen this scar—like a scab—on Sammy's gut, and put his fingers on it and then screws up his mouth like he was going to throw up.

"'Yuck, squishy. Like a dog's tits after she haves pups,' he says, and then tries to get Henry to feel it; but Henry was seeing how shamefaced Sammy was looking at his scar, so he wouldn't touch it, and he never screwed up his mouth, either, like Sammy. And he was going to walk away, but Conner kept on after him to let Conner come, till he finally said yes. Then all three of them was walking up the shore, and Sammy stuck his hand in his pocket and hauled out a ten-cent piece, and handed it to Henry. Well, sir, Henry and Conner stared at that for a minute—a ten-cent piece—and Henry said, 'Where'd you get it?'

"Sammy said, 'Stole it from me father.'

"'Ooh,' said Conner, 'that's stealing. I bet his father's looking for him right now to shoot him. And we too, seeing how we's with him. We should take him to your mother's house, Henry.'

"Henry gives a big snort. 'Take you to me mother's house,' he says. 'Going up the shore is where we're going, and buying a bottle of orange drinks with that ten cents. What do you say, Sammy?'

"Sammy nods, right proud.

"'Put it back in your pocket, then,' says Henry, 'till we finds a house to live in. Then we'll buy a bottle of orange drinks.'

"And Sammy give a big smile because he liked Henry, he did, because Henry never screwed up his face at his scar. And he was happy as a pup walking up the beach, jumping over brooks and climbing big rocks, only stopping to skip a piece of shale out over the water every now and then. Finally, they come to a big cliff that jutted into the water, cutting off the beach and Conner was right proud.

"'Guess we can't go no farther,' he says.

"'Oh, yes, we can,' says Henry. And he points to a path leading up through the woods. 'We're going up there and see if it takes us down the other side,' he says. And never minding

Conner's grumbling, he walks over to a flat-top rock—like a big table—and hauls hisself on top and looks back down the beach to see how far he'd come. And by geez, he was a long ways off from his mother's house by now. He couldn't even see any smoke at all now, coming over the treetops. He never said nothing, mind you, but he got a little twinge of something in his guts when he couldn't see his mother's smoke no more. So, he sits down on the rock and says to Conner, 'But first we'll take a little spell.' And then he moves over and makes room for Conner and Sammy to climb up alongside of him. And that's all I got made up for today, miss."

Clair stirred. "Well done, Roddy. Have you always told such good stories?" asked Clair as he pranced back to his seat, his red-freckled face looking as proud as could be—like Missy, she thought, whenever she had put together yet another story about fairies and such.

"Yup, he does, miss," answered Marty with a touch of scorn. "They calls him Old Man O'Mara around here for making up stuff, and he was the biggest liar that ever walked."

"Hope now," said Roddy.

"Who's Old Man O'Mara?" asked Clair absently, nodding for the little girl Susie to take her place before the desk.

"A hangashore, miss. Drinked all day and made up lies till they drove him off."

"They never drove him off—they left after Gid got his eye shot out," returned Roddy.

"Gid?" Clair tuned in.

"Gid O'Mara, miss," said Roddy. "He shot his eye out, rabbit catching with Uncle Luke and Uncle Frankie."

"What happened?" asked Clair, feigning attention onto a piece of chalk she was picking up from the floor.

"Gid falled down with the gun." said Marty.

"And it went off," added Roddy.

"Where's Gid now?" asked Clair.

"All the O'Maras went to Corner Brook after Gid went to the hospital," said Marty, "and that's where they ended up staying."

"Not Gid, though," said Roddy. "He was sent with the missionaries down on the Labrador."

"And Uncle Luke won't ever go up the shore no more," said Marty.

"Hope now," said Roddy.

"No he won't," said Marty.

"Because he got no reason to—not because he's scared," said Roddy.

"Yes he is, my son," argued Marty. "Ask Mom."

"No," said Clair quickly. "We don't tell tales out of school. Besides," she added more loudly, cursing her probing tongue, "the O'Maras got nothing to do with schoolwork, so no need for ye to be talking about it." Turning to the little dimple-cheeked girl waiting patiently, she asked, "Susie, you ready?"

"You got a way with them," spoke a voice later that afternoon as Frannie, always the last, was hugging her goodbye. Clair straightened at the sight of Frankie standing in the doorway, lodging his fishing rod against the door jamb.

She smiled, patting Frannie on the bottom and hustling her towards the door. "They're so good," she said, watching through the window as she darted along the path, past the woodpile.

"Bet it helps now that we got the Hurlys out," said Frankie, sauntering to her desk. "Strife breeders, for sure; always getting the teachers worked up and disrupting the lessons. Are the rest attending?" he asked, running a finger down the roll of names listed on the open register.

Clair nodded, wondering at his visit, when Luke strolled in front of her window, his fishing rod tossed across his shoulders, his head so close she could almost touch him. She stared at his hair, cornflower yellow in the afternoon sun, and his skin ruddy. He turned, as if sensing her there, and she caught her breath as she looked into a pair of eyes the colour of blue trapped within the contours of icebergs.

"Haven't missed a day, none of them," Frankie was saying. "I'd say that's a record for this school. Looks like you got a career as a teacher in front of you."

She pulled back from the window, her heart racing, staring blankly at Frankie. "You think so?" she asked, then chanced another look out the window. He was strolling past the woodpile, his back to her, and his shoulders a little stiff, alert to the eyes watching him. Then, with a final glance over his shoulder, he disappeared around the corner of his mother's house.

"Manna from heaven," Frankie was saying. "Trout," he explained, as she turned to him more blankly than before. "From Chouse. Our daily bread, remember?"

She nodded quickly, smiling. "You spend a lot of time there."

"Yup—always did," he replied, turning to the long-division sum she had marked across the board. "The happiest brook in the world."

"Happiest?"

"According to Luke, and for sure he's the gospel on Chouse," replied Frankie, picking up a piece of chalk and working through the sum.

"Does he—really not like people?" Clair ventured.

"Who, Luke? Oh, sure he likes people. It's hisself he don't like, I'm thinking. Course, who knows what another body's thinking half the time. And it's what they don't say sometimes that makes what they're doing look crazy, when most times what they're doing fits right in with whatever it is they're learning." He turned to her with a grin. "I'm starting to sound as crazy as he. Next I'll start living by his thoughts and then Willamena will be right in calling us both addled."

"What does he think that's so crazy?"

"Oh, that everything thinks. Trees, rocks, weeds; everything thinks, according to Luke, right along with the moose, birds and we." He paused, and she felt his eyes watching her as she began straightening some of the desks so's to cover her interest. "And perhaps he is crazy," he added quietly. "Perhaps there's nothing crazy about being crazy. There's times I envies him his lot. It's not easy letting yourself become a part of what's around you, is it?" he asked, forcing her to look at him.

"I—I don't know," she answered.

"Isn't that why you came here—to escape? You're like me," he said so low he was almost whispering, "you got to go changing things. Make a bigger world."

"Luke's for changing the government and you're not," she offered.

He nodded. "And that's what I charges him with; he's no better than me because in the end he goes for what'll serve him best. And as always with me and Luke, it's never the one thing that'll serve us both." The shrieks of a couple of youngsters assailed the air from outside, and Frankie started. Taking a step towards her, he spoke with sudden earnestness. "Clair—I have to leave for Corner Brook in the morning. I may not get back in time for the vote—and chances are I'll have a teacher with me when I comes back."

Her hands fell.

"It's not what I wants to do—" he half whispered, then broke off.

The youngsters' shrieks became louder, more persistent, "Teacher, Teacher—"

"There's a family near Howley," he began again quickly. "The mother's sick—they have five youngsters. They can use a serving girl. The pay wouldn't count for much, but they're good and kind. And they'd give you a comfortable bed and lots to eat. I—would see you," he faltered. "I stays over with them every time I goes to Corner Brook and—if we lose this vote, I'll be going there quite a bit—perhaps moving to Corner Brook."

"Miss, miss, Mommy wants to know if you're going to mop the floors this evening," shouted Frannie, bursting in through the opened doorway. "Are you, miss?" she asked as Clair gazed past her, watching as Frankie lifted his fishing rod away from the door, sliding it across his shoulders.

"Miss?"

"Come, Frannie," said he, taking hold of her arm. And raising his eyes to Clair's, he backed out the door, pulling Frannie with him, oblivious of her protests. Clair stared back, never faltering. And as he disappeared around the corner of the door, she kept staring, hearing from a distance his coaxing Frannie to run along home and tell her mother the teacher was taking a spell and that she'd come for her when she was ready to start the cleaning. She caught sight of him through the window, his shoulders gracing the same path as Luke's had but a few minutes ago, and she drifted towards it, watching till he turned, his eyes colliding briefly with hers, then disappearing around the other side of the woodpile.

Raising her eyes, she stared piercingly through the

cloud-broken blue. "Downhill chance, Daddy?" she asked.

More the weak horse, she thought dismally that evening, pacing the confines of her room. More a weak bloody horse. The accordion started up, and flicking aside a corner of her curtain, she watched as Luke slouched on his stoop, the yellow of his hair heightened by the light of his mother's lamp as he cradled his accordion as one might a newborn babe, his fingers slowly caressing his melody. He turned to her, and caught once more, she dropped the curtain, stepping back, tripping over her suitcase and sitting down hard onto her bed. The tempo of his music picked up.

"Fool!" she exclaimed loudly of herself. "Fool!"

CHAPTER NINE

Now, see, this is what happened," says Roddy. "Henry, Conner and Sammy was all upon the rock and Conner was getting crankier because he wanted to go live in Henry's house. And he was starting to get a bit jealous of how well Henry and Sammy was getting on. So, he tries to turn Henry against Sammy.

"'Brothers, that's some ugly scar,' he said to Sammy. 'How come you won't touch it, Henry—go on, touch it,' he coaxed, taking another poke at the scar. 'Whassa matter, my son,' he bawls when Sammy shoves his hand away, 'it's nothing we ain't seen before, is it, Henry? Go on, feel it, Henry.' And grabbing Sammy by the shoulder, Conner knocked him flat on his back so's Henry could have a good look. And with it right close up like this, Henry couldn't help looking—just a little thing it was, red and soft looking. But Sammy was clenching shut his eyes as if it was his private parts that Henry was staring at.

"'Let him go, my son,' Henry ordered Conner, and lying back, he closed his eyes and made out he was sleeping. And that's what they all did. And because the sun was so warm on their faces, and the water nice, lapping upon the shore, they all forgot about Sammy's birthmark and went to sleep.

"Then, Henry woke up, hearing something. 'Putt-putt-putt,' and he sat up straight. Guaranteed it was Sammy's father come looking for his gun and ten cents. Bawling out to everybody, he jumped off the rock and made for the woods. Sammy was right behind him, but not Conner. No sir, Conner was just sitting up, making out he was still half asleep because, see, he was wanting to get caught, so's Henry would be made to go home.

"'You sliveen, get off the rock!' screamed Henry. The boat was almost in sight by now, and they was almost caught. Running back, Henry grabbed Conner by the scruff and dragged him off the rock and up across the beach into the woods. Then he looked back and seen the gun still lying across the top of the rock in plain sight. Sammy seen it too, and before Henry had a chance to do anything, Sammy was running back to the rock. Grabbing the gun, he pulled it down and ducked with it behind the rock just as the boat cut into sight. And that's when Henry near fainted. It wouldn't Sammy's father after all, coming after them. It was Henry's mother. Sitting up at the bow, she was, staring as hard as she could at the beach, looking for him.

"Henry's stomach started getting bad. She looked right sad, she did, sitting there, leaning over the boat, looking for him. She's gone off head with worry, he was thinking, and she'll be worse if she gets all the ways up the shore and still haven't found me.

"Then he seen Conner staring at him, and no sir, he wouldn't going to let that sliveen see how bad he was feeling. He knowed the kind of fellow Conner was; he'd never let him forget he got mommy-sick. No sir. He wouldn't going to let no sliveen like Conner have that kind of say over him, so after the boat had gone around the cliff,

Henry grabbed Conner by his shirt and they both fell onto the beach rocks.

"'You asshole,' Henry bawled out, 'you ever tries to get me caught agin, you won't be living in no house with me!'

"'Oh yeah, my son, I never tried to get you caught,' said Conner.

"'Yes you did, you asshole, and you tries it agin, I'll womp your arse—'"

"Mind your language, Roddy," said Clair. "No, don't stop," she added as Roddy was about to walk back to his seat, "just watch your language, that's all."

"That's all I'm going to tell," said Roddy. "Except, after he lets Conner stand back up, Henry starts leading them up over the path through the woods, to get past the cliff."

"Perhaps you can tell us a little bit more," coaxed Clair. "What do you think, everyone? Want to hear more of Roddy's story?"

"Don't know it, miss; only Henry knows it," said Roddy. "And he don't know either till the rock tells it to him."

A pang gripped Clair's stomach. "The rock?" she asked, over the guffawing from Marty and the others.

"Yup. It was a rock that told it to Henry."

"He got a talking rock," shouted Marty. "Hey, miss, you hear that—Rod got a talking rock."

"And a mighty fine one," said Clair, fascination mounting in her. "Roddy, does this rock know the rest of the story yet?"

Roddy shrugged, his ears reddening.

"Just a minute, Marty—"

"But it's my turn, miss; Rod had his."

"Roddy—?"

"I don't know it yet, miss."

"My turn, miss?"

"Ohh, go ahead, Marty." And she turned in exasperation to the window at the back of the schoolhouse, looking up over the hills.

Marty scrambled out of his seat, talking excitedly about ". . . . this boy hears a great big grunt under his bed one night, like a—like a beast—a great big beast, and the great big beast was grabbing hold of the fellow's bed-springs and jiggling the bed hard—right hard—so hard that the fellow was knocked right out of his bed, right onto the floor next to where the great big beast was waiting to eat him—"

"It's quite the imagination young Roddy's got," Clair commented to Nora on her way across the patch that afternoon, waving to Frankie's mother peering at her from behind her flapping sheets.

"Nice way of putting it," said Nora, hanging out her window, fiddling with a jammed pulley. "What's he up to, now?"

"I allows you'll have to take the bell away from Marty," called out Beth, stepping onto her bridge with her basket of colours. "I swear to God, he was crawled up under the house this morning, ringing it."

Nora laughed. "Perhaps he thought Roddy was up there, snoozing—and perhaps he was."

"They minds me of Frankie and Luke," said Beth, "when they was younger; never got along for a minute, but always up the other's rear end."

"My oh my, they're going to be drowned, they're going to be drowned," cried out Prude, bustling through her door out on the stoop. "They're skinning the pudding over the stagehead agin—ye won't be standing gabbing when they falls off and drowns," she warned over her daughter's groans.

"They swims like fish, Mother. My Lord, it's addled they're going to be if you don't leave off," said Nora as her mother waddled across the patch, arms swinging.

"They can't swim if their brains is knocked out," cried Prude, "and youse won't be standing gabbing then, they got their brains knocked out—"

"She been sitting all morning, sir, staring straight ahead, thinking up something to worry about," moaned Nora as Prude vanished around her house, her cries sounding over the snipes as she started bawling out to youngsters.

"Clair, what's the youngsters up to—heads in their scribblers every night, writing—and no one's allowed to look. And Frannie, God bless her, got me mesmerized with spelling out words."

"Just little stories we starts off the day with," said Clair. "I was thinking we could plan a school play—get some of them to stand up and tell their stories to everybody. What do you say, Willamena?" she asked politely as Willamena came out on her stoop. "It was fun when we did the speaking contests, wasn't it?"

"Might be something we can take up with the new teacher," said Willamena, her head tilting regally as she drew a telegram out of her apron pocket. "It just come. From Frankie," she added, turning to Nora and Beth. "He'll be home in a couple of days with the new teacher."

No one spoke. The only sound was the gentle flapping of the sheets against the dull rumbling of the sea. Slipping the message back in her pocket, Willamena turned to Clair, her nostrils twitching like a rodent who has ascertained a pending threat harmless and is now free to burrow along its path.

"Well, it was a good turn we done bringing you here," she said, "but I expect your grandmother could be using your help now, for I hear she's not well, and I'm sure it must be hard on poor old Sim having to do for young Missy as well. And I suppose you're longing to see Missy agin, too; for sure you haven't been home since you come—and that's what, five weeks now?"

"She went back once," said Nora, her tone deep with meaning.

"For all the welcoming she got," added Beth. "Clair—you want to stay?"

"Not as a teacher, she can't," said Willamena. "The fellow coming got his grade eleven and is sent by the school board."

"Humph, that last fellow that taught here had his grade eleven," scoffed Beth, "and we doubts if he even knowed his alphabet. I say if Clair wants to stay, she can stay."

"Well, this one must be good," said Willamena, "else, Frankie wouldn't be bothering with him. He said that before he left."

"It's not just Frankie who got a say in this," said Beth. "We all do. When's he getting here, did he say?"

"Not for next week," said Willamena. "And he's bringing the teacher with him."

"Next week!" exclaimed Nora. "He's going to miss the vote?"

"He's going to vote in Corner Brook."

"Then who's going to set us up here?"

"Somebody from Corner Brook is coming out with the box and setting it up in school. We all votes there, then he takes the box up to the Basin and counts them."

"Up to the Basin," said Beth suspiciously. "Who's going to witness the count?"

Willamena shrugged, then with sudden thought spoke out. "Perhaps Clair can. It'll be a good way for her to get home—and she can witness that nobody touches the box till the count."

"I haven't heard her say she's going yet," said Nora. "Clair? Would you stay?"

"Sure you'd like to, wouldn't you?" said Beth, as Clair continued to stand silently. "I know, we can take a vote," exclaimed Beth. "That's what we can do—when the men gets home this evening, we can run around and take a vote—"

"You can't do that," cut in Willamena. "It's the school board who decides things like that—not a vote."

"School board!" scoffed Beth. "We wouldn't have a school if we never went after them, screaming blue murder. Why would they argue if we found our own teachers as well. That's what we'll do, Nora; run around after the men gets home and take a vote. And if we all says yes, you can send Frankie a message tonight, telling him to not bring the teacher," she added to Willamena.

"Clair?" asked Nora. "Clair, you haven't said you wanted to stay yet."

Clair's gaze dropped. In a world where everything good she had ever known had been wiped away by the devilish hand of fate, could she learn to trust it? Even that which was evil—such as the uncle's stealing her home—for had it not brought her here, to this place where she stood before the children, becoming the grand teacher her father believed her of being?

Now, wasn't this a lesson to be lining whatever bed awaited her, she thought grimly, that within the crux of fear is to be found its own comfort. She raised her eyes, casting them onto the questioning faces of Nora, Beth, and the hills beyond, her thoughts drowning amidst the flapping sheets and shrieking youngsters, and the foreverness of the wind and sea. Turning to Willamena, she gave the slightest of nods.

"Now, Nate," Clair heard Willamena saying later that evening as the outside door opened and his voice hailed loudly from the porch, "I already warned the women that it wasn't their say on this one."

"There you are, young miss," said Nate heartily as Clair's room door burst open and she stood staring at him expectantly. "I suppose you're keen to hear what everyone's saying, heh? They says you're most welcome to stay," he said, grinning at the relief overtaking her face. "Now you get on that machine," he added loudly to Willamena, "and tell Frankie to leave that teacher behind—we already got one."

"I'll telegraph him," said Willamena, "but like I'm after saying, it's what the school board says—"

"Ahh, Frankie don't bloody mind what the school board says," said Nate, trailing back out the door, "he got ways of getting what he wants, and I'm sure he wants Clair to stay on as much as the rest of us. See ye in the morning."

"Wait, Nate," said Clair, and running to him, she stood awkwardly for a second, then smiling up into the eyes twinkling down on her, she said breathlessly, "Thank you—and tell everyone I'm—I'm pleased with the vote."

"You got lots of time to do that yourself, miss," he said, and with a wink, let himself out the door. Turning to Willamena, Clair attempted a smile that offered a repose to the strife forever breeding between them. But it's not the mind of a foe to kiss the feet of its victor, and receiving naught but the glitter of two beady eyes hard fixed upon her, she hurried back to her room, closing her door. And as if to champion her tally, the most pleasing of melodies danced through her window that night. Opening her curtain just a little, she lay back on her bed, gazing into the dark.

"LIKE I WAS SAYING," said Roddy, "Henry starts leading Sammy and Conner up over the hill. It was a hard climb, and straight up, and then they were all swooshing down this slippery, grassy path, back out on the beach on the other side of the cliff. And just a ways up was Copy-Cat Cove. And that's a real bad one, miss, Copy-Cat Cove is, like a rock cavern cut right into a cliff and fills right up with water so there's no beach going around her, except when the water's low. And the water's so filled with kelp, it's like soup, and it makes this awful sound when it swishes up agin the sides of the cavern and then echoes back at you—spookier than anything. And when Henry looks inside of it, he gets the jeepers at how darkish it is, and how spooky the kelp sounds swishing in the water agin the rocks. But he seen that the tide was down and that there was a bit of a beach going around the inside. Then he hears this laughing coming from up the beach, on the other side of the cavern.

"Cooping down a bit, he runs with Sammy and Conner down to the edge of the beach as far as the water would let them, straining to see around to the other side of the cavern. They sees a boat, pulled up. Then three men comes out of the woods, laughing and staggering, lugging burlap sacks filled up with something.

"'What'd you think he got in the bag, Henry?' asked Conner. He sounded worried-like.

"Henry looked at him, thinking, You old conner, still trying to con me, is you? So he says, 'I dunno, Conner. Do you think it might be youngsters they's going to fry up for supper? Come on, Sammy, they's just having fun, is all. Not scared like Conner, is you?'

"Sammy shook his head and off Henry goes, back towards the cavern, whistling away and not showing a bit of fright. And he don't walk around the inside of the cavern on the little bit of beach. No sir, he walks right into the water, no matter it was so cold it started freezing his legs the second it struck his skin. Nope, sir, buddy, right through the water, he sloused. Then he looked back and seen Sammy making his way around the bit of beach, holding the gun up so's it don't get wet.

"'Cripes, hide the gun,' Henry sang out to Sammy. And meantime, he screwed up his face at Conner who was creeping behind Sammy, looking right scared.

"'Taking your time, is you, Conner?' he bawled out. 'My son, you're not going to live in my house if you don't hurry up and get your arse over here.' And that's when them fellows turned around and seen him.

"'What're ye little buggers doing here?' one of them snarled—just like a old wolf.

"'We're just going up the Basin,' Henry called back, slousing his way to shore.

"'And what're ye going to be blabbing up there?' asked the surly one.

"'Nothing,' said Henry, starting to figure that these fellows weren't from here, nowhere—not with dirty, long hair like that and scraggly whiskers. Then he thinks— perhaps it's them foreign fishers that stole the youngster off the wharf that time and boiled him in hot tar in the bowels of their boat. And then the strangers started running at him. And that's when Sammy comes out of cavern, and they sees him too. And Henry starts bawling out, 'Sammy, run, run!' And that's all, miss."

"Wait!" said Clair, holding out her hand to stay Roddy. "Wait—can't we hear the end of the story now?"

"Nope. I can only tell it in bits, miss," said Roddy proudly, walking back to his seat.

"Well, I think everyone would like it if you told the rest of the story now," said Clair.

"Can't, miss."

"Why not?"

"The rock won't let him," burst out Marty.

"Oh, yeah, my son," shouted back Roddy.

"Sshh, Marty," said Clair. "That's fine, then, Roddy. You and the rest of the grade sixes take out your history books, and everybody else, I wants you to start reading the next story in your readers, except for the primers; I'm going to give ye a copy. Roddy, it's a really good story, and we're all waiting to hear what happens next. Do you think you might finish it tomorrow?"

Roddy shrugged, taking out his history book.

"It might be nice if you were to finish it tomorrow," Clair insisted, and then smiling to the room at large, she added more softly, "I guess we're all a little concerned as to what happens to Henry at this point."

"DID YOU HEAR BACK FROM FRANKIE YET?" Clair asked Willamena that afternoon, hurrying in through the door after school was finished for the day.

"Matter of fact," said Willamena, dawdling at the bin over a cup of tea, "I just heard a minute ago. Here, you want this cup? I'll make another."

Clair stared at her. Not for nothing had she weathered this woman's scorn the past few weeks. Watching the grace now with which she laid the cup of tea on the table, a dread settled over Clair. "What did he say?" she asked.

"He never said nothing," replied Willamena. "Frankie was already after leaving." She turned to Clair, a smile thinning further the scant line of her lips. "With the teacher. The school board wouldn't have held with what you was asking anyway," she added, "so it's just as well."

"He's on his way?"

"Yup."

"With the teacher?"

"We haves the vote day after tomorrow—Friday. I expects Frankie home on Monday—with the teacher. So, I expects Friday to be your last day as teacher. I shouldn't wonder you'll be wanting to go home after the vote. Like I said, we needs someone to witness the box. You're not old enough, but I'm sure they'll let it pass, seeing's how you've been acting as the teacher here the past weeks."

"But Frankie doesn't know I wants to stay. Perhaps when he—they—gets here—and he learns about the vote . . ." she trailed off as Willamena straightened to her full height.

"I haven't said much," she said loudly, "but I don't think it's fair, you expecting more from us than what we've already done. I should think you'd be grateful for Frankie's asking you in the first place—what with your parents dying and Sim going to hire you out. Yes, that's right; Sim was going to hire you out—to a woman down Bear Cove somewhere. It's no odds my telling you that now, although Frankie won't like it that I did. But I don't think it's right, you playing on people's feelings like this. They needs a real teacher for their youngsters, not someone they feels sorry for. And besides, Sim's not for hiring you out any more. He wants you to help take care of the grandmother and Missy—and him, too, from the sounds of it. There. Frankie won't like it that I've told, but it's only to help him I did—so's he won't have a ruckus on his hands with the new teacher when he gets here."

A sickness had crept into Clair's stomach. "What makes you think Uncle Sim was going to hire me out?"

"Because he come to Dad and asked him to find somebody, that's how. And I told Frankie. And that's when Frankie went to the school—although he says he never pointed you out, but I think he did, just to help Sim."

"Does everyone else know—Nora, Beth—about the uncle hiring me out?" she asked quietly, steadily.

"Frankie said it best not to tell your business."

Clair fell silent, her eyes searching out Willamena's. Then, "Say nothing to Nora and Beth about the new teacher coming," she said firmly, "that will stave off the ruckus," and still wearing her coat, she walked towards her room. Suddenly Clair turned and bolted back across the kitchen and out through the porch and onto the patch. A damp fog met her, and a cold wind. Turning away from the patch, she ran out onto the bank and down on the beach, stumbling a little as she hurried up along shore. Out of sight of the houses, she slowed her step, bundling her coat more tightly against the cold, and allowing the sparse trickling of a tear to mingle with the fog misting her cheeks. Sniffling hard, she sought to wipe it away, but the wind splayed it across her face, numbing her skin even more. She came upon an old, uprooted tree lying across the beach, and searching for warmth, she crouched to its lee. The waves rolled harder upon the shore, the fog thickened, and the wind moaned a little stronger. Yet, she stayed, huddled into the once-strong birch. When it felt as if she might sleep, she rose, her knees stiff, her shoulders sore, and turned back towards the houses.

The patch remained quiet for the rest of the evening with its strong winds and fog. She had said no to Willamena's offering of a late supper, and an invitation extended to her from Nora to come for tea. Lying across her bed, she waited, listening. He was earlier this evening. And when his song began, it was broken, restless, as was his impatient urging for the dog Tricksy to quieten. Then he played no more. She rose, her shadow playing around the edges of her curtain. Silence, still. And finally, when dark had fully draped her window, she succumbed to her pillow and the quiet outside. Where was he then, with his song on this night?

It must've been past midnight when her fitful dreaming was disrupted by Prude's door opening and slamming, and gnashing snarls sounding from Tricksy. The door burst open again, and Prude's cries sounded across the patch: "Luukkeeee! Luukkeee!" Crawling up on her knees, Clair shoved her curtain to one side, catching the last of Luke's back as he disappeared up through the woods. "Mother of God, Luuke, come back!" Prude cried out.

Willamena's French doors squeaked open and her footsteps trod heavily across the kitchen floor. "What's going on? My, what's going on?" she sang out the same instant as Beth flung aside her curtains and hoisted up her bedroom window as Nora ran out on her bridge in her nightdress.

"It's Tricksy!" cried Prude. "She's gone surly, she is, from birthing. Trying to eat it, she was and then went surly when Luke took it from her—my oh my she was snapping at his hand and snarling like the devil—ohh, Nory, I thought she was going for his throat, I did, and now he's gone up the woods after her, he is—Luuukkkeeee!"

"Now, Mother, Luke'll be fine," said Beth, as Nora ran down over her steps and across the patch in her bare feet.

"Come on now, back in the house," coaxed Nora, wrapping an arm around the old woman's shoulders. "He'll be home in a bit."

"He'll be lost, he'll be lost in this dark, mark my words," Prude cried out, raising her fists to the woods.

"My God, sure what's he doing leaving his mother and going off like this?" exclaimed Willamena. "Sure, he knows what she's like for worrying."

"If we give heed to Mother, we'd all still be tied in high chairs," said Beth. "Go on in with Nory, Mother, Luke'll be home when he finds Tricksy."

"I'll go get him," sang out Roddy, appearing in his mother's doorway, buttoning up his shirt.

"You get back inside, you young bugger—get on," ordered Nora. "Nate!" she called out. "Cripes, it's the dead you'd wake before you woke he—Roddy! Get back in that bed."

"The racket," exclaimed Willamena.

"Nothing a pillow over your head wouldn't shut out," snapped Beth, and mindless of Willamena's closing her door with a huff, she called out to her mother, "Go on in with Nory; Luke's going to be fine. Sure, you wouldn't hear him coming anyway with all that bawling out."

"Yes, come in, we listens for him," coaxed Nora, "he'll be home the once, dog or no. Come now, and show me the pup. Poor little thing, how's we going to feed it with his mother gone?"

Inching her mother back inside the house, Nora closed her door, and all fell quiet once again. Leaving her curtains opened, Clair lay back in bed, propping herself upon her pillow, staring through her window up over the darkened woods. But as hard as she tried to stay awake, sleep overcame her. And because of the lateness of the hour, she slept past the men's leaving for work in the morning. Hopping out of bed, she quickly dressed, leaving the house without breakfast and before the youngsters had chance to stir. Aside from Prude saying her prayers to Joey underneath the stagehead, only the gulls stirred the quiet of the morning. Letting herself into the schoolhouse, she heaped some coal into the stove and lit the fire and sat, on this her last day in the little schoolhouse. The door burst open soon enough and Roddy charged in across, his cheeks as red as his ears.

"What're you doing here so early?" asked Clair.

"Luke said to give you this, miss," he said breathlessly, hauling a whimpering ball of fur from beneath his coat and shoving it across the desk at Clair.

"It's—it's Tricksy's pup!"

"Yup. It's for a fellow down Lower Rocky Head. But Luke said you was to feed it till he got back from looking for Tricksy. She come home agin last night, she did, but the minute Luke set his foot up over the hill to go after her, she run off agin. So he's gone to work now, but he'll be looking for her along the way—and Dad and Uncle Calve, too."

"Why did he give it to me to feed?"

"He never said. Just that he wants you to feed him with a bottle dropper, like the one from the peppermint bottle that got the dropper. You got one?"

"No. No—"

"I'll go get Mom's. You got some milk, miss?"

"Milk?"

"I'll get some milk, too."

"Roddy—wait," she called out as he bolted back to the door. "It'll have to be our secret, won't it? I mean—" she stood up, taking a step towards the boy "—it wouldn't be proper having a pup in school, so I'll keep him wrapped nice and warm in the back room, all right?"

"Then who's going to feed him, then?"

"I'll sneak back after I sets the lessons."

Roddy nodded and was about to dart outside, only to catch himself and turn to her again, "And, oh, miss, Luke said you was to name him. And, oh, yeah, he's a boy." Then he was gone, slamming the door so hard the windows rattled. Picking up the pup, Clair held it trembling and whimpering against her breasts as she fished her scarf out of her coat pocket. Wrapping it loosely around the pup, she sat down, rocking with it till Roddy came tearing back along the path, and in through the door with the bottle dropper and a can of milk, lodging them onto her desk.

"Want me to show you how, miss?"

"No, I can do it—Roddy, do you have the rest of your story for this morning?"

"No, miss."

"The—rock hasn't told it to you yet?"

"Nope."

"Roddy, there's another secret I have to tell you," she said urgently, seeing Marty strolling along the bank, firing rocks out over the water. "Promise you won't tell?"

"I won't."

"I won't be teaching here no more after tomorrow— there's another teacher coming. A real nice one, too," she quickly added as Roddy's eyes widened in surprise, "but I'd like to hear the end of your story before I go tomorrow—"

"But I don't know it—"

"Go ask the rock," she interrupted. "Seeing how it's my last day teaching, it might tell you the rest of the story."

Jamming his hands into his pockets, Roddy glanced out the window and up over the hills. "It's a long ways in, miss— where the rock is."

"Oh." Clair's eyes dampened as she followed his glance up over the woods. "Oh dear."

"Not that far, though."

"Can you go by yourself?"

"God, yes. I goes in by meself every day in the summertime. Just that I mightn't be back till recess, is all."

"Ohh—that's fine, that's just fine. It's special schoolwork you're doing, so it don't matter how long it takes—and I needs the rest of your story so's I can give you a mark before I leaves. And a red star to stick on your book. And Roddy," she said with a quick grin as he was setting off, "keep your promise about the new teacher and I'll give you two stars."

"I won't tell, miss."

"Not even the rock," she called after him, but he was gone, the door slamming once more, and the sound of his footsteps stomping down over the steps.

The morning crawled. Keeping everyone occupied with copies and readings, she wandered to the window every two minutes, scaling the hills, searching for Roddy's red-topped head. When she had a free moment, she slipped into the back storage room where she had the pup resting in the top drawer of a discarded desk, soothing him with a few drops of milk from the tip of the bottle dropper.

Recess came—and went. And then lunch. No sign of Roddy. Watching everyone leave for the evening, Clair called after Marty to tell Nora Roddy was doing an errand for the teacher, and then she returned to the window with a leaden stomach, searching for the thousandth time the woods covering the hills. He met with a bear, she thought.

Oh, Lord, suppose he met with a bear. Or fell down and broke his leg. Or he's lost and becoming more lost as she just sat there, waiting, praying—for a boy to come back from talking to a rock. Ohh, what had she done? And what won't Willamena do with this? And everyone else. But wait—there he was coming down through the woods, leaping and jumping, his hair glinting like a new penny. Onto her feet she was and running outside to greet him, near frightening the youngster out of his wits as she swooped down over the steps, grabbing hold of him in a hug. "I thought you'd gotten lost!" she exclaimed. "Oh dear, I thought you'd gotten lost."

"On that old horse road, miss? Sure, you can't get lost on that; it leads right to the brook and back down on the beach."

"Ooh, thank God you're back," sighed Clair, weak with relief, "thank God."

"Yup, I'm back, miss, but the rock never talked."

"Never?"

"Nope, miss," said Roddy, shaking his head.

"Oh." She stared, speechless. "Did you tell it I—I was leaving?"

"You said not to," said Roddy, smiling, the clear grey of his eyes shining, his ears reddening further. And then he burst out, "Nay, miss, the rock talked—I was only joking. And that's how come it took so long, because I was a long time remembering it."

Her release was painful. "I should strap you," she said. "Come, come, tell me," she cried out, grabbing the boy by the arm and dragging him towards the school.

"But it's not school time!" Roddy protested.

"There's no school tomorrow, remember? And I've got to hear your story to give you your mark—hurry now, and the pup wants to hear it, too."

Roddy's eyes brightened as he lit inside the school door. "What'd you call him?"

She stopped. "I haven't thought of it," she replied, and then, "Henry," she burst out. "His name's Henry."

"Hah," Roddy said, laughing, "he'll like that."

"Who'll like that?"

"The rock, miss. And oh," Roddy exclaimed suddenly, "the rock said if you wants to hear any more of the story after I tells you this one last bit, you got to ask it yourself."

"The rock said that?"

"Yup."

"Where—did he say? Or . . . or when?"

"Nope, he never said. Where's Henry?"

"You stand in front of the desk—just like school time," she said, "and I'll get the pup." And letting Roddy nuzzle with it for a minute, she took a seat near the window at the back of the room, holding the pup against the warmth of her throat, and signalled for Roddy to begin.

Shuffling self-consciously with just the teacher as his audience, Roddy dug his hands in his pockets, and began.

"Louder," said Clair.

Clearing his throat, Roddy began again.

"And so, miss, it was like I said before—Henry was just sloused ashore to the other side of the beach across the mouth of the cavern. And he was getting scared because he knowed the way them fellows looked, with their dirty hair and scraggly whiskers, they wouldn't from the Basin, nowhere, but was probably the ones from that foreign fishing boat who stole the youngster off the wharf that time and put him in boiling tar. And he was getting such a fright thinking about it, that his breathing would've stopped if Sammy never come outta the cavern at that minute and stood besides him.

"But then the strangers made a bolt towards him, singing out, 'We're going to get ye'.

"'I'll fight with you, Henry,' Sammy said, but Henry was already jumping back into the water and beating across for the other side.

"'Run, Sammy, run!' he was bawling out, and then he tripped in the kelp and fell, head and eyes in the water. When he come back up, he was choking so hard he could scarcely see, and when he did, he seen Sammy running behind him with the gun hold up so's it wouldn't get wet, and Conner running besides him, screeching out, 'They're coming after us! Run! Run!' And it sounded right weird, it did, with the cavern echoing his words over and over 'Run, Run Run!' And that's what Henry did—started thrashing his way through the water, back to shore. A loud bang went off behind him and when he turned, he seen Sammy falling into the water, and the blood bleeding down his face and Conner screaming like a baby besides him. And then he seen the strange fellows just standing on the other side watching them, and he knowed they wouldn't chase them after all, just playing around. But it was too late to figure that out now, because Conner was hauling Sammy towards the beach and Henry near fainted to see his eye all shot out and the blood pouring down his face. And after he helped Conner haul Sammy up on the beach, he fell onto his knees and started to cry.

"'He's not dead, Henry; he's not dead!' Conner kept saying, and then he saw the ten-cent piece fall out of Sammy's pocket and he picked it up and handed it to Henry. 'Here, you take it, Henry,' he said, 'and perhaps if you goes up the Basin with your mother sometime, you can still buy the orange drinks—you want to buy the orange drinks, Henry?'

"But Henry was shaking his head, still crying and shivering and looking down the shore to where he could see a grey cloud rising over the hills, which he figured was smoke from his mother's chimney. 'It's all right, Conner,' he said. 'I don't want no drinks.' And heisting Sammy onto his shoulder, he started lugging him down the beach towards his mother's house, and where he knowed the fire was always lit on cold days like this."

"CRIPES, YOU'D THINK LUKE WAS TWO YEARS OLD the way Prude was getting on last night," Willamena began the second Clair had entered the door after school. "I swear she gets foolisher. I wouldn't wonder what she's going to be like ten years from now—my, what's wrong? Getting a cold, is you?" she asked as Clair, scarcely looking her way, came in through the porch door and headed straight across the kitchen, head down, sniffling a little. Mumbling something about a bad head, Clair let herself into her room, closing the door.

"Poor little thing," she murmured, pulling the pup, still shivering and whimpering out of her pocket and laying it on her pillow. With the wind blowing a gale, the youngsters were mostly crowded around the patch this evening, adding their charm to that of the scatter piece of clothing flapping on the lines, and the clucking of Aunt Char's hens. Nate stopped to invite her over for tea, but Willamena was quick to meet him at the door, explaining Clair's bad head, but how she'd make sure and tell her of the invite the second she got up.

"And be sure to tell her that Nora and Beth's been down Lower Head all day sitting with the old midwife," he added.

"That I will," said Willamena.

"And that they're not expecting her to make it through the night, but however it goes, Nory's planning to have tea at the school tomorrow, after the vote—so's they can celebrate her staying on as teacher."

"That's a fine idea," said Willamena. "I'll be sure to tell her, soon as she wakes up."

Clair pulled back from her window as Nate traipsed across the patch, calling out warnings to one of the youngsters poking a stick at a cornered hen. And when he'd gone inside, she pulled her suitcase near the window and sat, watching outside as she coaxed the pup into drinking some milk from the bottle dropper. It was growing dark when he at last swung down the path from the woods. The last of the youngsters had been called in for the evening, and taking a quick look around the patch, his glance dallying around her window, he went inside his house. Clair began to rock, stroking the pup more quickly. The clack-clack-clack of the telegraph sounded through the house, as did Willamena's footsteps as she hurried across the kitchen. Her French door squeaked open the same instant as Prude's door swung open and Luke stepped back outside, a fall jacket tossed over his shoulders and his accordion hooked off his thumb by a leather strap. He sat down on the stoop, settling the instrument onto his knee, fiddling with the keys. Clair kept rocking. The French door creaked again and Willamena's footsteps drew nearer.

"Clair. Clair, you got a telegram. Clair?" she called out again, tapping on the door when Clair didn't answer. "My, I thought you was sleeping," she said, her eyes widening questioningly as she nudged open the door, peering in at Clair perched on the edge of her suitcase, staring out her window, her scarf rolled into a ball and held to her throat. "Still got a bad head?"

"I's fine. Who's it from?"

"Maid, it's from Sim. Your grandmother's getting worse. He wants you home tomorrow."

Clair nodded.

"You want a cup of tea?" asked Willamena, lingering.

"No—thank you."

"You want I should go get Nate? Perhaps he might take you up tonight."

"No. Don't do that."

"Well, then," said Willamena, and with nothing else forthcoming from Clair, she withdrew, quietly closing the door. A fleeting melody danced from his fingers outside, then deepened into a long drone that throbbed as though it wore the pressure of the finger plying the key. Clair rose, lifting her coat off the bed.

"Change your mind, did you?" asked Willamena as Clair came out of her room, the drone ripening into a more tender pulse behind her. "Sure, I can go get Nate if you wants."

Clair didn't answer. And ignoring Willamena's eyes burrowing after her, and ignoring the trembling in her knees and the pounding of her heart, she walked across the kitchen and out into the porch, her lips twitching spasmodically, her breathing erratic, and the hollow of her throat quivering at the rate of a hummingbird's. Reaching for the doorknob, she quietly opened the door and stepped out in the cold, salty night, raising her eyes to those of the fair-haired young man rising to greet her.

BOOK TWO

HANNAH

HANNAH SQUATTED BESIDES HER AUNT MISSY, helping her root up the newly budding sweet williams and replace them with the bluebells they'd dug up from the bottom of the yard. "Go, spread them around the fairy ring," said Missy, brushing the sweet williams to one side. "Hurry now, I'm getting too hot."

"It's not hot," chided Hannah, scooping up the flowers.

"Go, get," said the aunt, dropping a kiss onto her niece's nose.

Clutching the flowers to her chest, Hannah ran with them across the yard to a circle of beaten-down grass, and began dropping the pink-and-purple buds around its outer ring. All done, she snatched a seeding dandelion from its stem, blew its fluff into the air and began skipping around the circle, chanting, "Fairies, fairies, one, two, three; fairies, fairies, come to we; banshees, banshees go to hell; little girl sleeps in her little bluebell."

Her aunt turned to her, and the laughter that usually rippled from her throat like a chorus of morning chickadees was subdued this afternoon and, in fact, had been for some weeks now—perhaps even months.

"Come, Aunt Missy, let's go to the thicket," called Hannah, leaping out of the ring, disliking this new quietude.

Missy shook her head, rising, her face flushed with heat. "Your mother'll be here soon," she said, pushing her fingers through her mat of curls and fastening them behind her ears. "Let's get you cleaned up."

"We're going to ask if I can stay, right?" said Hannah, scooting back across the yard.

"We'll ask," said Missy.

"We'll make her let me, won't we?" said Hannah.

After they had washed and fed on raspberry syrup and crackers, Hannah trailed to the door, pleading, "Now, can we go to the thicket?"

"Lord, Hannie, I can't keep up with you these days," said Missy, yawning and settling herself on the divan, her hair puffing up like her cushion beneath her head as she lay back. "Come, lie down with me. Come on," she coaxed as Hannah groaned, dragging her step towards her. "I'll tell you a story."

"A fairy story!" exclaimed Hannah. She hopped onto the divan besides her aunt.

"An old-man story," said Missy. She shifted to one side, cuddling her niece besides her. "He was ugly, very ugly, and he drank some squaw-root tea so's he could see the fairies. At first, the fairies didn't mind that he could see them because he left them alone. But one day, he got greedy and thought he could catch one and sell him for a lot of money. So one night he set a trap in the woods. And the next morning when he went to check his trap—guess what?"

"What?"

"A hundred fairies jumped on him."

"Ooh, what did they do?"

"They stole his eyes."

"They blinded him?"

"Now every day the fairies leaves him bread and butter—fairy butter—so's he won't starve to death. And he won't ever leave them because he waits and waits and waits for them to give back his eyes."

"We won't try to catch one, will we?"

"Noo, never. But tonight's a full moon," said Missy, her eyes bluer than the sea as they poured into Hannah's, "and if Clair lets you stay, we'll scrape some fairy butter and leave it wrapped in a handkerchief besides the huckleberry bushes. If the fairies likes the butter, they'll spread the hanky over a spider's web, and by morning, the dew will have marked in silvery letters the day we're going to die."

"Ooh—" A shuffling sounded at the door, and Hannah sprang up on her elbow. "What's that—it's Uncle Sim," she then shouted, and leapt to her feet, running to greet the uncle as he pushed his way in through the door, his grizzled face partially shadowed by the peak of his cap, and his thin frame hunching forward as he ambled past her towards the bin, reminding Hannah of the old mule her father once told her about, forever needing a mulberry bush to woo him forward.

"She's not come yet?" he asked, his tone more gnarled than the knotted fingers holding a skipper of trout.

"Nope," said Hannah, prancing around to the other side of him, poking her fingers at the frozen fish eyes, "and when she does, Aunt Missy's going to ask if I can stay the night, aren't we, Aunt Missy?"

"Grumpy," chided Missy as the uncle more snorted than sniffed, laying his trout into the dishpan. "You want tea?" she asked, rising, stifling a yawn, but it was Clair's voice that answered—calling out Hannah's name from the front of the house.

"Mommy!" said Hannah. "Come on, Aunt Missy, let's go ask," but her aunt had sunk back down at the sound of Clair's voice.

"Hannah! Missy!" called Clair, and Hannah darted to the door. "Coming, Mommy," she called out. "Aunt Missy, you coming?"

"Go, go," said her aunt impatiently, waving her outside.

"Mommy! Mommy, can I stay the night," sang out Hannah, bursting onto the step. "Aunt Missy said I could and I really wants too. Mommy—?" Her voice faded. Her mother was leaving the roadside, where she always stood whenever she came to collect her, and was now coming down through the gate, her eyes on the uprooted flower bed as if refusing the sight of the bluebells standing there, so preserved in memory were the pink-and-purple sweet williams they had replaced.

"He did this, didn't he?" she declared, as Missy appeared in the doorway besides Hannah.

Hannah inwardly groaned. There was always a tinge of anger riding her mother whenever she came collecting her, reserved for the uncle, no doubt, for stealing her father's house after he died, and putting her mother out to work— leastways that's what Lynn, Uncle Frankie's girl and only two weeks older than she, always told her. And not wanting this anger to spill over onto her aunt before getting consent for the evening's sleepover, Hannah hopped off the stoop. "No, Mommy—we did it—we made a fairy ring," she sang out, skipping towards the trodden-down circle of grass, deco- rated with the wilting pink-and-purple buds. "Come see, Mommy—now the fairies can sleep right here in the blue- bells and we can hear them if they rings." She trailed to a stop, turning back. Her mother was clutching on to the gatepost, gazing at her aunt, who was standing quietly in the doorway, looking as petulant as she, Hannah, when caught in the bigness of a wrong committed with full knowing. But her mother was seeing nothing of her aunt's look. She could tell by the discomfited look in her eyes that her mother had gone to that place again, the one her father told her about once, as she'd sat on the spindle, pouting that her mother had yelled and was mad at her again.

"No, lovie, she's not mad; she's not even here," he'd said, easing his foot on the treadle and pressing the blade of his axe on the mounted grindstone. "Remember I showed you once the big burst of sparks from where Chouse crashes into the sea? Well, them's little fishies making them sparks, and that's where your mother is right now, thrashing with the fishies amidst the waters of Chouse. And best to leave her alone, lovie, when you finds her thrashing the waters of Chouse."

"They were getting root rot, Clair," said Missy, the sullenness of her tone belying the carelessness of her shrug, and had Hannah been older, she would've known that her aunt was not without knowing this place of unquiet within her mother, and that by digging up the sweet williams, she had sought to broaden these waters of unrest and to flood what pools of quiet might be found. But she was neither older nor clever. And seeing her aunt step off the stoop and toe the ground more firmly around one of the bluebells, and knowing from deeds past done that the wait for the hand to fall is far more torturous than any slap it should beget, she ran to her aunt's side.

"We likes the bluebells best—don't we, Aunt Missy." Hoping to persuade her mother of the same, she flashed a quick smile and starting up her prancing again, calling out,

"Come, Mommy, come hear our song." Plucking a dande-lion from its stem and puffing its seeds high over her head, she raised her face to their descent, hopping and skipping around the ring of dead grass, chanting, "Fairies, fairies, one, two, three; fairies, fairies, come to we—come on, Mommy, come on, Aunt Missy—banshees, banshees, go to hell, the little girl's sleeping in her little bluebell." She shrieked in surprise as her mother's hand suddenly snapped around her wrist, pulling her out of the fairy ring. "You don't like our song," she cried out as her mother bent over, picking up one of the dead flowers.

"How could you?" asked Clair, her tone tight with anger, her short, curly dark hair falling away from her forehead as she watched her younger sister trail towards her.

"You've never bothered with them before," said Missy.

Clair rose, palming the flower as one might a dying baby bird, her eyes hard as they beheld Missy's. Then dropping the flower, she marched back towards the gate, her back rigid.

"Mommeee!" Hannah wailed. "I wants to stay the night— you never lets me stay the night," she wailed louder as her mother reached out her hand for her to follow.

"Perhaps she thinks I can't look after you properly," cut in Missy, as Clair kept walking. "Perhaps she thinks I'm mental—like Daddy was—is that what you thinks, Clair— that I'm mental?" she called out, and as her sister's step faltered Missy leapt into the fairy ring and skipped around as Hannah had done. "Perhaps I am. Perhaps I thinks I'm a fairy." And swinging her arms off from her sides, she started hopping and skipping faster and faster around the ring, her hair bouncing around her shoulders, her voice feigning a little girl sound, she half-chanted, half-shouted, "Perhaps I'm a changeling bought by the fairies. Or an angel. Wouldn't that be nice, Clair—to be an angel? Mommy always said I was real little angel, and perhaps that's what I am—not Missy at all but a wee little angel, weee." Leaping into the middle of the ring, she slumped down, looking up at Clair through eyes scarcely visible behind the curtain of curls screening her face.

There is a moment when what is known most comfortably can present itself most queerly if seen through an eye of sudden distortion, like a horse emerging through a dense fog. And in that moment, with Missy slumped before her, the sun flushing out the blue of her eyes through the yellow of her hair, and the bundles of dead flowers scattered around her feet, Clair put her hand to her stomach as in sudden fright.

"It's all right," said Missy, rising, smoothing her hair back from her face. "I'm not mental yet—leastways, I don't think I am." She attempted a laugh as Clair continued staring at her. "It's because of Uncle Sim that you won't let her stay, isn't it?"

"She's—she's too young," said Clair, her voice guttural, her words thick. And with the same weight slowing her movements as thickening her speech, she took hold of Hannah's hand and began walking to the gate. Opening her mouth, Hannah let out the bawl of a bull moose, but it could well have been the mewling of a kitten, so unhearing was her mother as she marched woodenly through the gate.

"She's older than I was when I started sleeping at the grandmother's," Missy called out, her tone more accusing than declaring, but Clair never faltered, despite Hannah's hanging back, fuming against every step that took her farther and farther from the big white house with the bluebells swaying beneath its kitchen window.

"We were going to scrape fairy butter," she cried, near tripping over a ratty-looking cat scooting between her legs. Her mother looked back, and so tightly did her hand clutch Hannah's it were as if she saw the ghost of the father that her aunt Missy sometimes told her about, who'd sit in the window, watching through blackened eyes that were horribly wrinkled, making noises in his throat, and screaming horrid demon screams. Turning back to the road, she began walking faster and faster down towards the wharf until Hannah was almost running to keep up with her.

"Mommeee!" she wailed in protest, but then shut her mouth and snatched back her hand as she spotted Lynn hanging around a grunt, lending half an ear to whatever it was her father was hollering up at her from down in his boat.

"Just a minute, Hannah," said Clair, her tone as heavy as the hand she laid upon her daughter's shoulder, holding her back. Bending towards the child, she raised a finger, stroking her cheek. "Perhaps when you're a little older, you can stay," she half whispered, her mouth working as though it were trying to say many things.

"I'm nine!" stated Hannah loudly.

"Yes, I knows, and almost as tall as Aunt Missy," said Clair, pulling a hanky out of her bosom and wiping at Hannah's chin.

"Lynn stays with her aunt."

"She got grandparents watching after her as well—"

"Uncle Sim looks after me too," shouted Hannah, knowing full well the foul sound the uncle's name made in her mother's ear, and then darted forward with the same skewed look as her aunt had, ripping up the sweet williams and replacing them with bluebells. Ignoring her mother's warning cry, she ran past the old rotting-down building that

used to be Lynn's grandfather's store, and to the grunt where
Lynn was saucing her father. Lynn turned in greeting as
Hannah approached, her tongue protruding from her mouth
like a fat wriggling slug. Exhibiting a fine-looking slug of her
own, Hannah jumped over the grunt and scampered down
the ladder into the boat.

"What's the matter—someone steal your money?" asked
Frankie as she landed with both feet into the boat, rocking it
noisily. Glowering his way, and wanting to rock the boat
harder, she trotted heavily to the stern, throwing herself
against the side of the boat, leaning out over.

Lynn's face reflected up from the darkened depths of the
sea. "Hannah's not allowed to sta-aay."

"Pass her down. I bars her in the cuddy," sang out
Frankie, and the look on Clair's face suggested she just
might; but Lynn was already tandering off the wharf, up
over the hill.

"Best buddies one minute, and savages the next—like
their fathers, heh," said Frankie, helping Clair aboard.
"Want's to stay agin, do she?" he asked, coiling the painter at
his feet as Clair, sighing in agreement, fixed herself away on
a wooden bench.

"I swear, they gets more hardening as the day is long,"
she said. And Hannah, knowing the futility now of finding
her way back to her aunt, turned to this mother who was
always spoiling things and yelled, "I'm not hardening!"

"Ohh, Hannah."

"Tell you what, Hannah," said Frankie, shoving them off
from the wharf, "how's about you steering us straight to
Rocky Head and I'll bring you back agin next time I comes."

"You never means nothing you says, Frankie!"

"Hannah," warned Clair.

"Well, that's what Uncle Calve says."

"Hannah!" And her mother shot to her feet. "You take that tiller this minute, young lady, else you'll be floating home on a log."

Flinging herself around, Hannah grabbed hold of the wooden lever, the noise of her anger clouding reason. Blue-bells, spiders webs, fairies all became part of the undertow that grew stronger and stronger with each fathom of sea buoying her onward. She heard little of the talk about a new road coming through, and Frankie's new job as member of some house, or her mother's asking something about a new store. Scowling her face to such contortions that the muscles supporting it began to ache, she burrowed her eyes into the sea—the one place that hoarded none of the silly scorns of people, only fish that fed them their flesh. Leastways, that's what her father always said whenever he took her fishing down at Chouse, and his was a word that once rooted in his girl's mind shadowed all else in the rightness of its bloom.

She spotted him first as they neared Rocky Head. On the beach, his hair catching the sun's sheen, he stood as he always did whenever she and her mother returned from the Basin, arms out, reaching, eyes searching, and the broad easy smile appearing last, the flutter of a snipe's wings when the last of her chicks return to roost in the down of her underwing. She hung back as he lifted her mother out of the boat, setting her down gently, cautioning her to be careful as he shook his head at Frankie, commenting on how blousy the wind had gotten, and raising his brow at Clair as she brushed down her skirts, chiding him for becoming more and more like his mother for worrying. And as Frankie teased his fear over a little lop, and threatened to put a road down to Chouse someday, he tugged on one of her mother's dark curls, saying in his warm, easy tones, "Yup, now there's a thought—a truck and a road—bet that might get you fishing with us, lovey. Didn't think so," he added at the sight of Clair's nose wrinkling. Turning to Frankie, he said, "Guess I'm just going to have to start baiting her hooks like she asks. A bit proud is what the Basin women are, what'd do you say, buddy?"

"Yup. The pickle barrel, sir, is what them women likes," agreed Frankie. "Not something fresh off the hook."

"Whoa, now, what's wrong here?" asked Luke, as Hannah rose from her slouch and started unsteadily towards him, holding tight to her pout.

"Mommy won't let me stay at Aunt Missy's."

"Now, where have I heard that before?" said Luke as he lifted her out of the boat. "Did you remember to invite her down to see Brother?"

"She don't like babies."

"Sure she do; perhaps when you goes up agin—"

"Don't set her up," cut in Clair. And as Luke raised his brow to the sharpness of her tone, she turned from him, yoked once more by the heaviness that had laid hold of her earlier.

"Hey," said Luke, reaching for her, but he was cut short by Prude's cries as she scurried onto the bank, wisps of white from her loosely plaited hair clouding her face, and red splotches marking her throat.

"Luuke! Luke, did you tell him? There's a stranger come ashore down Gold Cove," she cried out to Frankie as Luke shook his head with a groan. "You mind now, Luke," she warned, shaking her fist, "there was a time when you'd be in the woods by now, trying to catch your breath with the thoughts of a stranger coming—"

"For God's sake, Mother, can't a stranger come ashore without you thinking it's Satan?"

"You'll mock me one day," cried Prude. "He's wearing the devil's coat is what I said—all black skin and full of silver zippers and chains. It's the road he's on about, I knows because I seen it in my tea, and what's that if it's not the devil's work, putting through roads where the people don't want them?"

"He'd be coming by way of the Basin if it was the road he was about," said Frankie, "not down the bay somewhere. Luke, climb in and have a look at the piston—she's been skipping."

"I'm fine—go ahead," said Clair, catching Luke's look of concern as she made her way up over the bank towards Prude. "Hannah, where's Hannah?"

"Hiding out, is what," said Luke, pulling her from where she was nearly concealed besides the boat. "Go get Brother for your mother, now," he ordered, boosting her up over the bank with a pat on the behind, "and then come help me chop splits. Hurry on, now."

"What's she, sick?" asked Prude as Hannah trudged up over the bank, scarcely able to see over the ridge of her brow.

"She likes her pout, is all," said Clair. "Show, let me see your knee—is the swelling gone down?"

"Hardening, that's what they is, then," said Prude, "not like when I was a girl and your mother spoke. Go on," she scolded Hannah, "and get the baby like your father told you. My oh my, they got faces like a boiled boot—the whole lot of them, not like when I was a girl and the old mother spoke. Go on, now like your father says."

Glowering more deeply, Hannah plodded towards the string of houses and woodsheds before her, dully hearing her father calling out, reminding her again to come help him cleave splits. On other days his offer might have sent her feet racing from the lashings coming from the tongues of the elders like rocks rattling down a cliff face. But on this day— this day of being wrenched from the scent of the fairy ring, the intrigue of her aunt's stories and the swaying heads of the bluebells, she wanted no comfort. Rather, she wanted to stand before them, gathering around her the grey launched forward by the houses and woodsheds, and to wear it as a cloak that grew thicker with each scolding word buckling her knees.

She turned to them, deepening the sulk that had taken over from the pout. Her father was hunched over the engine house with her uncle Frankie, and her mother was feeling around her grammy Prude's knee, checking for water under the cap; and Grammy was back to ranting about the stranger, bringing worry to her door.

They weren't even watching. They didn't care. How was it, then, that they could stand all knowingly before a youngster over some misfortune or unjust deed when they were so oblivious of a pair of knees, naked to the cold and buckling in sorrow?

"Mind you tells her it's his feeding time," her aunt Nora called after her as she walked unsteadily across the patch, balancing her three-month-old brother in her arms, her face held aside from the sight of his slobbering all over his fists. "And that he was the prince, the real little prince, and his bowels heartier than Grammy Prude's now with the bit of squawroot I fed him this morning. And mind you tells her to burn some flour—his bum's getting another rash—perhaps because of the agueweed."

Her mother had the door closed, mindless of the heat kicking out of the wood stove as Hannah traipsed back in, bearing Brother. She turned from where she'd been standing by the window watching Luke busying himself around the woodpile, and gazed at Brother, unhearing of his fussing, Hannah knew, for she was back at Chouse agin, thrashing waters—had been ever since she'd left Missy's.

"Was he good?" she asked absently as Hannah kicked shut the door behind her.

"He got vomit on him," she replied, dumping the baby into his crib.

"Mercy," exclaimed Clair. Hurrying towards the crib, she clicked her tongue disapprovingly, pulling the ever-present handkerchief out of her bosom. "You got to be more gentle, Hannah," she scolded, dabbing at the baby's mouth, but her firstborn was already snatching open the door and scooting across the patch to the side of the house.

Luke was straddling the spindle, the blade of his axe held against the mounted, round grindstone, and his face screwed up against the wailing of stone cutting steel. Hannah straddled the spindle opposite side of him, taking care to keep her feet away from the treadle as he worked it with his. It was always warmer here to the lee of the house with the easterlies being blocked. And with the woodshed barring Frankie's windows, and the woodpile blocking most of the opening onto the beach, it felt sheltered from prying eyes as well—and that's how her father liked it, he always told her—feeling sheltered and alone. Except for Hannah, he'd quickly add. She was his best buddy, and being with a best buddy was like being by yourself, for you never, ever had to talk, and you never, ever had to listen.

"Got Brother, did you?" he asked, lifting the axe from the stone, squinting closer at the blade.

She nodded.

"Hey?" he asked.

"You knows," she answered irritably.

Wetting down the stone from a bucket hanging off the spindle, he flicked a drop at her face. "Wasn't bawling, was he?"

"Stop," she said sulkily, wiping the water off her face.

"Was he bawling?"

"He's always bawling."

"Gets on your nerves, do he? Watch your knees, lovey," he cautioned, working the treadle again, and laying the axe against the spinning stone. "Did you get your candies at the store?"

She nodded, fingering a piece she held in her pocket for him.

"That's good. And you gave a piece to Aunt Missy? Yup, you're a real nice girl," he said after she nodded some more. "Your mother's of a different mind."

"I didn't do nothing."

"Nope, nope, never thought you did." He lifted the axe for another look. "Just wondering what put her there, is all."

She kicked at the treadle with the toe of her boot.

"Yup, a strange way," her father repeated. "Reminds me of poor old Father the time he lost hisself in the woods, chasing the fairy."

"Granda seen a fairy?!"

"Yup."

"Thought it was only mentals seen fairies."

"Nope, nope, it's the other way around; people goes mental after they *sees* the fairies."

"Granda went mental?"

"Nope."

"You just said—"

"I said he went chasing after the fairies. I never said he seen one."

"He must've seen one to go chasing after one."

Her father looked up, sniffing at the air as he pulled a rock file out of the pocket of his work pants. "Smell that?" he asked, sniffing some more.

"Smell what?"

"Horseshit, ain't it?"

"Yeah."

"See any?"

"It's from Uncle Nate's barn."

"Do you see it?"

"Can't see it if it's in the barn."

"That figures, then. Guess you don't have to see something to know it's there. Like poor old Father, I guess. He knowed they was there and that's why he went after them. And they took him so far in the woods, he almost never got out. I tell you, he never went to bed agin without the dandelion seed on his tongue."

"He eat dandelions?"

"Yup. The only way he'd go to sleep."

"What about the wintertime?"

"Saved them up all summer. Course, he never liked anyone knowing about his chasing the fairies—or about the dandelions beneath his mattress. People would think he was foolish."

"Or loony—that's what they says of Aunt Missy—that's she's loony for believing in fairies."

He raised a cautioning finger to the window above their heads. "I expect that's what got her troubled is it—Missy?"

"Yeah! But mostly about her plucking the sweet williams."

He stopped filing. "She plucked the sweet williams?"

"They was root rotted. So we used them to make the fairy ring. But we planted bluebells in their place so's Aunt Missy can hear them ringing if they rings."

He nodded, the file idle as he took a long look at the window, then groaned as the sound of his mother's voice cut across the patch, calling his name. "What wrong now?" he asked in the tone of one who already knew, scarcely glancing up as Prude come marching around the side of the house, arms tightly folded.

"Frankie's going down Gold Cove to buy some jiggers. Go with him, Luke, and see about the stranger."

"Frankie will see about the stranger."

"I don't trust Frankie," Prude said. "He's liable to say anything, he is, to keep us quiet about the road."

"There's not going to be no road," said Luke, holding his axe blade to the tip of his nose for a clearer look.

"We don't want no road, Luke."

"I already said there won't be no road."

"Frankie says it, then. They'll blast it through the woods, he says; that's what they're doing in the country behind the Basin—blasting it through the woods."

"Woods is a far cry from a bit of beach, walled in by cliff and sea."

"I don't trust Frankie putting a stop to it—he's the bloody hangashore, he is—singing hymns on a Sunday, and making with the devil on a Monday. You go with him, Luke; you go see what that stranger wants. You wasn't always this calm," she cried out as Luke exclaimed impatiently, heaving himself off the spindle and sinking the axe blade into a junk of wood. "I minds a time when you wasn't so calm."

"Christ, Mother, be done with it," said Luke, swinging towards her.

"Away with ye, then. You'll be singing a different tune soon enough, for I seen it in me cup I did; twice now, I seen it in me cup—there's no good coming from that stranger—mark my words, Luke Osmond; mark my words!"

"One of them days I allows I'm going to wrap her up in canvas and banish her off from shore," muttered Luke, turning back to the woodpile as his mother marched back whence she came, her arguing resounding around the patch. "Come on, lovey," he ordered Hannah, dragging the junk of wood onto the chopping block, "else it'll be dark before we sups this evening."

Shuffling off the spindle, Hannah sat at the foot of the woodpile, picking up the splits he had chopped earlier, listening to her aunt Beth bawling out at her mother to go in the house, and she wondered at the old woman's fear. Hard it was to hold on to a pout around such elderly upheaval, and in years to come she would think back to this moment and ponder that whether to fate or chance, life oftentimes offers up circumstance that attests to the most lowly of prophecies, raising them to the sublime, as was with her grammy Prude's concerning the stranger rowed ashore down Gold Cove that day. But a seed just planted grows slowly in the womb, and whilst all of its readiness is tendered in flesh, there is a time before it unleashes itself into the world, and another time again before it finds itself aligning the same footpath as those others it will soon collide with. And oftentimes in looking back, she was never sure that the circumstance was its starting point, or, like the stranger's arrival at Rocky Head, merely a moment that arises out of the ordinariness, calling attention to a process that had already started with the virgin breath of all those others in collision with it.

CHAPTER ELEVEN

THE STRANGER WAS AN OLD VET, Frankie reported upon his return that evening, from the First World War, and who was now spending his time rowing around the bay, visiting old acquaintances and making new ones. After several weeks' speculations and the odd snippet of a tale brought up the bay from a visiting fisher or logger, it was the liquor cellars whose acquaintances the old vet appeared to be more interested in making, and after a while even Prude stopped standing on the bank, squinting down the shore, keeping watch.

"I swear, I don't know how she'd manage if we do get a road and got people driving back and forth every day," said Clair one evening at supper, after Prude had just been for tea, fretting over more news about the possibilities of a road coming through.

"She's fretting for nothing, is what," grumbled Luke, scruffing the back of Hannah's head as he took his seat besides her.

"You're worse than your mother for shutting things out, Luke," said Clair, spooning dumplings into his soup bowl. "If the petition goes through, they could be blasting by next fall."

"Petition," scoffed Luke. "We got ten thousand miles of

coastline around this island, and peppered with outports, some no bigger than ourn—and they're all sending petitions. I allows now they're all going to be getting roads—they might be a big government, but they haven't got that much money."

"According to Frankie they do. And he ought to know; he's been travelling around enough since he got voted member for parliament. Hannah, pass your bowl."

"If we gets a car, can I go see Aunt Missy?"

"Promise you won't keep pouting every time you got to leave," said Clair.

"Geezes, lovey, how can you encourage her about things like that—they're never going to get a road down here, no matter how much blasting they does—the sea'll flood it out in a day. I seen combers ten feet high crashing along that shore."

"You sounds like a hangashore, Luke, tossing a squall into his boat so's he won't have to go to sea today. Sometimes I don't think you wants the road any more than your mother does."

"Matters none to me."

"It mattered once."

"Now who's starting to sound like the old woman," said Luke irritably. "Be cripes if she's not always harping back twenty years."

Clair smiled apologetically. "You're too good a man to deserve that, Luke Osmond."

He softened. "Been a spell since I thought about going to Africa, that's all, lovey—or going anywhere out there. It's a funny thought, this notion of going out there," he carried on, halving a dumpling with the side of his spoon and settling more comfortably into his talk. "Think about it, Clair—if all the ones out there comes over here, and all the ones over here goes out there, then where in kingdom come is 'out there' or 'over here'? No, no, listen," he said, as Clair rolled her eyes towards Hannah in recognition of another of his ongoing suppositions about life, "I thinks, sir, that 'out there' and 'over here' is just one spot, and it's right here where I'm sitting. What'd you think, lovey?" he asked, cracking Hannah across the knuckles with his dirty spoon.

"Ouch. I thinks it's at Aunt Missy's," said Hannah, licking her knuckle and slewing a look at her mother.

"I swear, you're both like Prude for holding on to things. But I suppose it's just as well she thinks that way, because if they builds the new school up the Basin, that's where she'll be spending her days," said Clair.

Hannah snapped to attention, as did her father. "I'll be going to school up the Basin?"

"What talk is this?" followed Luke, his voice suddenly quiet.

"More than just talk," said Clair. "The government's already starting to build bigger schools in some of the larger outports. They're going to drive the higher grades back and forth every day—them that got roads, that is. Some places will be boarding their youngsters near the schools—"

Hannah gasped with excitement. "I can live with Aunt Missy?"

"Ooh, eat your soup," chided Clair. "It'll be years yet should such a thing happen—if it happens at all."

"How long have you known this?" asked Luke.

"Known what?" asked Clair. "Goodness, there's nothing to know," she quickly added as Luke shoved back his chair, ready to rise. "As I said, it'd be years should it happen—and then, only to those who have roads."

"It's what you'd want, isn't it?" he said evenly.

She shrugged. "A better school for Hannah is what I'd want. Whether it's up the Basin or no, I haven't given thought."

"Haven't you?"

"What's there to think about—as I said, it'll be years—"

"I wants to go," said Hannah.

"I'll tell you one thing right now," said Luke as Clair shushed Hannah into silence, "when either of mine leaves this house, it'll be when they've minds of their own, and not what a government thinks up for them—nor their mother."

Clair turned to him. "What does that mean?"

"That it's not right to put grand plans in the head of another, that's all—even if it is your own youngsters. If she wants to be a teacher, let her think of it—I'm not saying that's what you're doing, Clair," he said deeply as her face took on the look of a youngster, who in a moment of largesse, shares her most prized blanket, only to have it taken and waved before her as a matador's cape before a bull. "I'm just saying its something you might be wanting."

"My wanting her to have a good education is no different than you wanting her—or all of us, comes to that—living at Chouse in a bough-whiffen," replied Clair.

"The worse kind of thievery is to steal a youngster's thoughts, and replace them with your own," said Luke. "Perhaps I expects us both to bide our tongues."

Clair rose, her eyes hard fastened onto him. "If making sure my daughter gets a good education and a chance to do something with her life is stealing her thoughts, then that's what I aim to be, Luke, a thief." And stacking her bowl and spoon onto a dirtied plate, she marched with them towards the bin. Luke rose to follow, but noting Hannah's wide-eyed silence, he sat back down, his shoulders slumping like a melting candle.

"Finish your soup," he said, beckoning her attention to the spoon lying limp in her hands, "and mind you helps your mother with the dishes." Rising once again, he walked out the door.

His fingers lay heavily on the keys of his accordion that evening as he sat on the stoop. Hannah was in bed, listening, wanting to go out and sit besides him as she sometimes did, but sleep came relatively quickly that evening. And when next she awakened, it was to Frankie's voice speaking quietly to her father out on the patch.

"I was down Gold Cove this evening," he was saying, "having another word with the old vet. Seems he served in the second war as well. By the sight of him, I'd say he's still serving; drunker than old man O'Mara, and just as sly. But he's still keeping the ones in Gold Cove entertained with his stories. And they keeps paying him with another shot of shine. But I allows they'll soon be getting sick of him—like everyone else up and down the shore, and then I allows he'll be making his way up here."

"Did he say he knowed Joey?"

"Says he got a problem remembering names, but he's thinking on it." Frankie gave a short laugh. "I hears them words often enough, talking to other politicians. Uses them myself when I wants to get away from something. I wouldn't trust him for a copper, Luke. He's liable to say anything for a swig of shine. Minding you of someone?"

She missed what her father said, so low was his voice, then Frankie's took up again. "Speaking of the O'Maras, I saw Gid in Corner Brook last week. He was up from the Labrador— the old man died. He—you were the first thing he asked about.

"He's different," added Frankie, as Luke didn't speak. "Educated. The missionaries done him good. Said he was going to spend some time with his mother and the rest of them. He carries it well, Luke—his scar. He don't suffer none with it."

"No one knows a man's suffering, Frankie, unless he wants to show it."

The accordion grew louder, covering the rest of their words and feeding Hannah's ear with a rhythm that finally lulled her back to sleep. In what felt like seconds later, she was being roused awake by her father, leaning over her bed, whispering for her to get dressed, they were going to Chouse.

"Why isn't Mommy coming?" she asked after they'd breakfasted on toast and tea and were standing on the beach, stowing the gear into the punt.

"Brother's fussing this morning—pass me the worms." He turned towards the house as the door opened and Clair stood out on the step in her nightdress and stocking feet, her hair ruffled prettily around her face, and her eyes puffy with sleep.

"You'll be back for supper?" she called out.

"Yup. Go back to bed, lovey—you'll catch cold," he said as she left off the stoop, starting towards them.

"Here, you'll be cold on the water," she said, bending before Hannah and buttoning her sweater. "Mind you don't go wandering, now."

"I won't."

"You warm enough?"

Hannah nodded, her mother's sleepy warmth a fine wrap against the chill of the morning. And as she finished buttoning her sweater, she lifted her face as she might to her aunt, for a quick kiss on the top of her nose. But her mother was already straightening, minding her father again to watch for the wind, and to be back in time for supper and to be sure and bring back no trout that weren't already gutted.

"Squeamish," said her father, "and getting worse." Picking up Hannah, he dumped her into the punt like a sack of spuds. And assuring her mother that he'd watch for the wind, he shoved off the punt and leaped aboard, grabbing for the paddle to steer them off from shore. Gazing down into the ever-deepening water, Hannah trailed her fingers through its icy coldness, watching a caplin dart here, there, and then towards shore.

"Don't go leaning over," her mother called. "And mind you don't go wandering either; Luke, mind she don't go wandering."

"She won't," her father called back, dipping the oars into the sea, the thole-pins creaking as he plied them, gliding them over the water. The sun tipped a ray over the hills, turning the black face of the sea into a milky brown, the colour of her mother's eyes watching after them.

Leaning over the stern, Hannah watched as a flatfish swam straight up, straight up, straight, straight up, its nose appearing to break through the surface any second, yet still it kept swimming straight up, then ducking sideways, disappearing under the boat.

"Some deep, hey, Daddy," she'd once called out to her father, a little anxious with a sudden wind.

"Yup, lovey, that's what she is," he'd called back. "You've a right to be scared, for it's our birthing waters, she is, and she'll feed us and wash us and rock us, but you don't ever challenge her, lovey, you don't ever challenge her; there's centuries of ribs littering her floors, and there's room for centuries more. Yup, she's one to watch, lovey, for she might be a breast forever full, but she's one forever searching, she is, and God help the mortal who gets caught sleeping in her thrashings."

She turned now, to this man plying his paddles against the sea. The smile that usually lifted the corners of his mouth as he leaned back and forth, steadily heaving to and fro, to and fro, was absent this morning, and in its stead was the worried look of her mother whenever she was thrashing the waters of Chouse.

"Are you still mad at Mommy?" she asked.

"Nope, lovey, I was never mad at your mommy. I was just mad, that's all."

"What were you mad at, then?"

"Never mind, lovey, never mind." And seeing the smile return to his face, she took the plunge and asked the question forever burning Lynn's tongue.

"Are you scared of strangers?"

"Yup, I sure am."

"Noo you're not!"

"That's what I am then, lovey, and you ought to be, too."

"No, I oughtn't be."

"Yup, you ought to be. Like that caplin you seen swimming back there. Not often you sees a caplin swimming all by himself. They's usually swimming in schools, thousands of them. And that's what people are like most times—caplin swimming in schools. One takes a little left turn here, they all do. One takes a little turn there, they all do. And the next thing they knows, they're all aground and beating their heads agin rocks trying to get back to sea. Yup, that's what happens when you swims in crowds. And you know why fish swims in crowds? I'll tell you why fish swims in crowds," he said, taking a rest, "because they're scared. That's why fish swims in crowds. And that lone caplin back there? He's scared too—scared of following the crowd, and that's what I'm saying to you, lovey; everybody's scared. And if I'm going to get caught flicking my head agin a rock on a beach, then it'll be my own doing, not somebody's else's senseless-ness." He went on, heaving back on the paddles again. "Yup, I'd rather be a lone fish, I would; wouldn't you, lovey?"

"Yup! Like Aunt Missy."

The grin vanished. "Like Aunt Missy? Well, it's not too good to be alone all the time, either—"

"You just said—"

"I knows what I just said, lovey, and now I'm saying something else. *All* fish swims in schools sometime or another—they got to, for that's how they multiplies. It's only when people don't take a little time for their own—think about things—that they ends up on the rocks. It's a fine thing most times to live in a nice place and share it with others."

"Like the stranger down Gold Cove?"

"We don't know what he got to share yet, do we?"

"But we still got to share what we got, right?"

"All accordance. Perhaps he's not a good person and got kicked off his own shores and that's why he's on ourn. Grammy Prude might be a worrywart, lovey, but she deserves to be. She seen a few things in her lifetime, so don't go snorting at everything she warns you about."

"How come you keeps telling her to go in the house, then?"

"Because most times it's fright she's offering, not warn-ings," he said, his face souring, "and when she does that, she's no different than a school of caplin offering direction; one bloody path till you're beating your head against a rock."

He snatched back his smile and leaning forward on his oars, peered strongly into her eyes. "You can do with a bit of both is what I'm saying, lovey, being off by yourself sometimes, and swimming with the crowd other times. That way you always got time to think, and always got something to think about. Will you remember that?"

"Yup." And then she was on her feet, shouting, "There's Chouse!"

"Careful now—sit down. Yup, there she is," he added, looking over his shoulder straightaway to the churning waters of Chouse thundering into the sea. Nearing the shoreline, he stood with an oar, steering them towards another more quiet opening that led through a stand of aspens and poplars trembling in the breeze and lowering like an archway over the water. Ducking beneath the branches, he drove the oar deeper, pushing them forward till the waterway suddenly widened and there was Chouse, more river than brook, pouring down the gorge it had beaten through the hills over the years, its waters spreading out and enclosing dozens of turf-covered boulders—some with a tree or bushes growing out of them—and large rocks as it rumbled across country and into a large shimmering pool before thundering into the sea.

"It's like a secret hideaway," exclaimed Hannah, leaping out of the punt as Luke put ashore into the natural harbour formed by the curving of the pool, for indeed, once inside the waterway, the beach banked up, concealing all sight of the ocean from view, leaving them surrounded by giant leafy birches and aspens that buffeted the sounds of the wind and sea, enclosing them with the roar of Chouse and the chirping of a dozen songbirds as they flitted from bush to bush.

"Daddy," asked Hannah, after he'd moored the punt to a rock, and they were sitting untangling their lines besides the brook, "how come Mommy won't ever go inside Aunt Missy's house?"

"It's the uncle I think she steers clear of."

"But he's never, ever there when she comes."

"Perhaps it's because she misses her mother and father too much to see their things."

"She liked the flower bed—and that was her mother's thing."

Her father paused, the string dangling from his fingers. "You know something, lovey—that's a right smart thing you just said."

"That she likes the flower bed?"

"Yup. So it must be her father's things she don't want to see, heh?"

"Lynn says Grandfather Job still haunts his room."

"Now there'd be a real good reason to steer clear."

"Aunt Missy says Lynn's nosier than her mother."

"Sounds like a smart woman, your aunt Missy."

"Lynn says we're all a bit loony, with you never going up the Basin, and Aunt Missy never coming down here, and Mommy never going inside her own house, and me never wanting to leave once I'm there."

"A good thinker is young Lynn; like her father, I'd say. Pass me your hook."

"She said she dreamed one night what you looked like taking the fits."

"Cripes—must've been some awful night."

"She said you looked like this." And turning to him, she started snorting and holding her breath and crossing her eyes.

"Yup—some awful night. But it was more like this, lovey," and saying so, he flung himself upon her, eyes crossed, snorting and grunting like a pig gone mad.

He dug his fingers into her ribs till she was screaming, "Stoopppp, Stooooppp!!!" And then when she was senseless with laughing, he stopped tickling her and stuck out his tongue, huge and wet like a big puppy's, and slapped a lick on the side of her face.

"Daaddeee!!"

"Now then, you ready to start working?" he asked, squatting back on his haunches, digging into the worm can.

"Yuuulllkkk!" she grimaced, sitting back up, wiping her face with her sleeve. "Lynn said you was the one drove Grammy Prude foolish like she is."

"I think her father had a hand in that. Where's your hook?—got your hook?"

"There was three of ye, and ye was always together, robbing eggs."

"Yup, that's right."

"And Lynn said the other fellow, Gid, was ugly."

The hand piercing the worm onto her hook stilled. "You oughtn't be listening to Lynn all the time," he said so quietly, so very, very quietly she had to strain over Chouse to hear him. "Here, take your rod."

Standing side by side, they tossed their lines into Chouse and, loathing the tongue that followed Lynn's, she watched as he wandered off by himself, the water swirling around his thigh-rubbers and the spray dampening his hair. She followed as far as her knee-rubbers would take her, and after a spell, as he wandered farther and farther to the centre of the pool, she sloused ashore, tossing down her rod and taking the little path that trailed up along the river. Patches of orange on a tall spruce caught her attention. Fairy butter. Picking up a sharp-edged rock, she scraped the bark clean and, wrapping the fairy butter in a fern, lodged it in her pocket. Then she went looking for more. Catching hold of a bare tree root, she swung past a rock wall made smooth by running water, then step-stoned to where the river had spread out, ankle deep in some places, six feet in others. Coming upon a clump of boulders near the middle of the river, she climbed atop one. Looking back, she watched as her father, standing knee deep in his favourite fishing hole, swung his line to an eddy nearer the far side. He'd stand for hours at the mouth of Chouse, hooking saltwater trout. And once, a year ago, when she'd sat on this very spot looking back at him, and he was sitting on an old log lodged between two rocks, she had thought he was a shrub growing out of it.

"That's it," he had exclaimed with glee when she'd told him later, "that's exactly what I am, lovey, a part of this whole blessed spot. I eats the trout, grows its flesh and grunts it back out to feed the gulls. Blessed is he, my lovey, who fishes a river."

"Daddy?" she called out, running back along the trail.

"Over here," he replied from below a knoll, a fire already started. And coming out onto the beach, she squatted besides him, watching as the cone-shaped slut kettle started boiling, and he tossed a good six-pounder into the frying pan sitting on the rocks besides him, wearing the satisfied look of Brother after a good suckling, chasing away the last of the morning's shadow.

IT WAS HER AUNT WILLAMENA waiting on the shore to greet them as her father rowed them ashore later that afternoon. Prude was standing on the bank, wringing her hands, and the young fellows, Roddy and Marty, were waiting to haul up the punt as Luke leaped over the side, up to his knees in water, calling out, "What's happened?"

"Clair got a message, Luke, b'ye," said Willamena, taking the piece of orange-rimmed paper out of her pocket, "from the office clerk, Alma, and it don't say nothing, only Clair got to come up and see her right away. It just come— about ten minutes ago and she's in some way, Clair is."

"Something's happened to her sister, I allows," cried out Prude, hurrying along besides Luke as he made for the house, "else they wouldn't send a message like that, they wouldn't."

"You wait out here, old woman," ordered Luke. "She won't need to hear your worrying." Darting past her, he tore in through the door, Hannah besides him. A hand grabbed at the back of Hannah's coat and she turned with a snarl as Willamena tried to haul her back, saying, "Your mother don't need youngsters—wait here with Grammy."

"I won't," snapped Hannah, tearing away and bolting after her father, Williamena's scandalized tuttings following her. Her mother was sitting in her rocker, her face paler than the bare skin of Brother's bottom as she held on to his flailing legs, diapering him. Nora stood besides her, ready to catch the baby should her trembling hands fail.

"She won't let me take the baby for a second," cried Nora as Luke hurried in across. "I don't know why some-body would send a message like that; Lord, better if they just out with it—whatever it is."

"Clair, if something happened to Missy, they wouldn't sent a message," said Luke, holding on to her hands and letting Nora take the baby. "They would've come themselves. Come—let's get ready—I'll go with you."

"You must think it bad," she cried out, "else you wouldn't offer to come like this."

"No, lovey, don't," said Luke, helping her up from the chair. "Nothing's happened with Missy; the message would've said so. Come on, now. Let's go get dressed."

"Praise be," said Prude, wringing her hands in the doorway.

"Now, Mother, come on with me," said Nora, wrapping a blanket around the baby. "Hannah, pass me some of them diapers in the basket there, and look in the crib for his bottle and dumb-tit. You're going up with her?" she asked Willamena, who had inched in ahead of Prude.

"Yes, maid, I'll go with her. Frankie's in the shed, getting some oil for the boat." She turned to Luke. "Unless you wants to take her—" But Clair was shaking her head.

"It'll be fine, Luke; you watch over Hannah."

"I'm going too," Hannah cried out, but her mother was shaking her head. "You stay with your father," she replied and turned impatiently from the splutter of protest rising to Hannah's lips.

"Go rock Brother for Aunt Nory," said her father, lending an encouraging smile over his shoulder as he led her mother to the stairs. "Go on, now," he said more loudly as Frankie's voice sounded from outside.

"Yes, you come rock Brother," coaxed Nora. "Pass me the diapers—hurry now," she said, balancing the baby in one arm. Lifting some of the diapers onto her aunt's arm, Hannah backed towards the stairs. "I'll come in a minute, Aunt Nory," she said soberly, and after the aunts and Prude had left, she closed the door behind them, and bolted to the washstand. Lathering up a froth on her hands, she scrubbed her face and neck, and reaching blindly for the towel, dried it well with both hands. Snagging a comb through her hair, she took to the stairs, ducking into her room the same instant her father came out of his. She held her breath, listening as he walked with her mother down the stairs, murmuring encouragements to not go worrying, that everything was fine. Finally the door closed behind them, leaving the house in silence. Tearing off her dirty clothes, Hannah pulled on a clean pair of socks, a skirt and a nice sweater. Lifting the fairy butter out of her dirtied pants pocket, she very carefully placed it inside her skirt pocket. Fixing her sweater down over the bulge, she peered out the window. They were all there—Frankie standing in his boat, helping Willamena aboard, Prude tutting on the bank and Luke leading Clair, as if she'd suddenly become crippled, down over the bank. When at last her father was helping her mother aboard the boat, Hannah sped down over the stairs, through the front door and out onto the bank.

"Mommy!"

"I wants to go, Mommy—I wants to go," she cried out, clinging to her mother's skirt.

"Hannah!" snapped Clair and it were as though she'd lashed her daughter with a strap, so sharp was her tone and so quick did Hannah withdraw. And then her father was taking her by the hand, leading her towards the bank and Grammy Prude's chastising, and Nora's cajoling her to come rock Brother, and was that not Willamena's tsking sounding over the wind, the lop and the gulls?

"She's not mad, lovey; she's just upset," said her father, bending to one knee, stroking her shiny red cheek as the tears welled up. "She'll take you with her next time she goes—I knows she will. Just go with Aunt Nory now, till I comes for you, and perhaps Frankie will make a special trip to take you next week—"

Frankie. The tears dried in Hannah's eyes. Tearing away from her father, she darted back to the boat, her eyes narrowed and her mouth open, bellowing, "You said, Frankie! You said!"

Frankie looked to her as speechless as her father. Then smoothing back his hair, he shrugged, raising a brow towards Clair. "I did say," he said. Lifting his hand to quiet Willamena's protest, he added abruptly, "Throw her aboard. We can look after her while Clair's doing her business. Lynn will be there. What's one more?"

Getting a nod from her mother, her father scooped her off her feet, his coarse warnings to be good subduing any feelings of gratitude she might like to have expressed to Frankie as he reached down, lifting her into the boat. Shivering past her mother and Willamena, she scurried to the stern, taking up seat besides the tiller.

"Be sure you steers us straight," called out Frankie as the piston caught fire and they started forward, "else we'll be meeting with the folk on Miller's Island."

She managed a grateful look for him, and turning guiltily from her mother's brooding eyes, and ignoring the tutting of Willamena's tongue, she raised her eyes towards the Basin, one hand wrapped tightly around the tiller, the other pressed against the fairy butter soaking through the cotton of her skirt and dampening the skin beneath.

The postmistress, Alma, was standing besides the rotting-down old store on the wharf, watching as they drew closer. "I been out on the road every five minutes since I sent the message," she said as Clair climbed up on the wharf behind Willamena. "I suppose I got you scared to death, do I?"

"Is it Missy?" asked Clair, her voice quavering.

"Missy's fine," said Alma, taking Clair's hand. "I should've made sure and said that on the message, I should've. And perhaps I shouldn't have sent the message at all, just waited till you come back up agin and called you in—"

"It's not just Clair you got worried," said Willamena. "We're all worrying about what could be wrong."

"Well, ye can all stop," said Alma, "because it's Clair's concern, and nothing that can be settled in a day." She directed Clair towards the road, saying, "Come, my dear. We goes up to the house and haves a cup of tea. You'll be going up to your mother's, I suppose?" she asked Willamena. "Perhaps you can take Hannah with you till we sends for her."

But Hannah was already inching her way from the group, edging towards the road. "I'm—I'm going to Aunt Missy's," she faltered, a careful look at her mother.

"I suppose that's fine," said Alma, waving Hannah onward. "Tell her your mother will be along after tea— because she knows I've sent for her, poor thing—" Brushing away the concerns her words welled up once more in Clair, she led her towards the post office with stout reassurances that everything was fine, truly, everything was fine. Receiving a nod from her mother, Hannah kicked up heels, racing towards her aunt.

The door was shut and the curtains drawn on this fine summer's evening. Quieting her step, Hannah inched open the door, peering inside. Missy was sitting besides the table, her hair tightly pulled back and clipped, and her face greyed by the curtained light. A dark shawl of sorts lay around her shoulders, and she looked to Hannah as if she were a hundred years old and as if she'd been cast in stone. She didn't move as Hannah entered, but remained sitting with a straight back on her chair, eyes cast down and her hands clasped in her lap like a child's in prayer. More surprising to Hannah was the sight of him, the uncle, sitting there; this man who was always rabbit catching or fishing or woodcutting whenever her mother was expected. He turned to her, his face shrivelling further with the weight of the evening shadow, and his shirt wrinkling around the thin shoulders supporting it.

It wasn't till Hannah dashed to her knees did Missy turn, the liquid black of her pupils hardening like coal as she stared transfixed at the door Hannah had left open behind her.

"What's wrong, Aunt Missy?"

"Did she come?" she asked, her tone sullen, heavy.

"Who, Mommy?"

"Where is she?"

"She's talking with Alma. Are you sick? How come you looks sick?"

"Do I?" she asked, her eyes letting go of the door, her fingers cool as she touched them to Hannah's cheek and then her own. "Come," and rising, she led Hannah across the stairwell into the sitting room. "She shouldn't have brought you," she said woodenly, giving Hannah a little hug. "You sit in here till she comes—"

"But she's having tea with Alma."

"She won't be long—you sit here, now—ooh," she added with a sudden rush, dropping her arms around Hannah's shoulders and hugging her tight. "She shouldn't have brought you—why did she bring you?"

"Because I made her," said Hannah proudly, snuggling her cheek against the tightly clipped hair. "I know," she exclaimed, pulling back, "we can wait in the garden—ohh, Aunt Missy—I got some fairy butter."

"Leave it there," said Missy, laying a hand on Hannah's as she reached it into her pocket. "Just—leave it there for now. And stay here till I sends for you. Promise," she said more tightly, cutting off further protests. At Hannah's nod, she dropped a kiss on her forehead and rose, backing into the stairwell, a ghost of a smile quivering her bottom lip, leaving an imprint upon Hannah's mind of a frightened youngster too far gone astray. Hannah strained, listening as Missy ran across the kitchen, her chair creaking beneath her weight, and the uncle's voice mumbling about something—as it mostly did. Then, silence.

Looking around the sitting room, she perched on the edge of a wooden chair, the sense of wrongdoing permeating the air too heavy for the feather-softness of the daybed. The house sighed. She heard it, along with that of her aunt, and the moaning of the half-boiling kettle. Her mother would fix it. Despite all, and no matter what, her mother would fix it. Her mother fixed all things. That she knew. If only she would hurry. Sitting back on her chair, her fingers gripping its edges, she allowed herself to breathe, praying for her mother to come. Ohh, was there ever a moment that took so long in the fortitude of a child's prayer?

Finally, the door opened and she clutched onto her chair as her mother spoke Missy's name, her tone hushed. Then it was the uncle she was speaking to, and her voice dropped, hardened, becoming cold. Hannah crept into the stairwell, wanting to hear, to share with them the sorrow so levied upon this precious aunt; but anger born out of yesterday's malice brings with it a vengeance far more frightful than that following a cheeky tongue or disobeyed command. Thus when she crept into the stairwell, inching towards the kitchen, and her mother spun towards her, her features trembling with a rage that was scarcely suppressing itself, and bade her wait upstairs in Missy's room till she was called, Hannah gave up any further notions of challenging her mother on this day and trailed dutifully upstairs, sitting onto the bed that her aunt and mother had slept in as girls.

Their voices were low, and she scarcely breathed with wanting to hear. Then the sound of Missy sobbing. Leaping to her feet, she ran back to the door, pressing her ear against it. Missy's cries sounded louder, and Hannah bit onto her fists for fear of crying alongside of her.

"She'll stay here," said Sim loudly, accusingly.

"She'll stay where she wants," snapped Clair, more angrily, more accusingly. And then beseechingly, she begged, "Missy, please, please come with me; I wants you to come with me—"

"No! Don't make me, Clair; I won't, I won't ever," shouted Missy, her voice weak despite its loudness, and then her footsteps running into the stairwell and up over the stairs. Hannah ran back to the bed, sitting down as Missy burst in through, slamming the door behind her, and turning a key in the lock. Looking at Hannah, her cheeks glistening with tears, and her lips puckered like a dried rosebud, she clasped her hand to her mouth, trying to keep from crying further.

"You have to go now," she said, darting to the side of the bed and wrapping her arms so hard around Hannah that neither of them could scarcely breathe. "You have to go. Ooh," and a sob tore from her, and her heart beating wildly against Hannah's. Knowing with a child's simplicity that it wasn't she, Hannah, the aunt was seeking to comfort in that moment but a soul seeking its own solace, she grasped her arms around her aunt's neck, hugging so tight, she feared her arms would crack like matchsticks.

"Missy," she heard her mother call, her footsteps sounding urgently on the stairs. "Missy." Then a gentle tapping on the door. "Missy, please come out."

Rising from the bed, Missy pulled Hannah to the door, dropping a dozen kisses onto her face, whispering, "Be a good girl, Hannie; you be a good girl, now." Unlocking the door, she quickly pushed Hannah through and just as quickly closed it behind her, locking it, ignoring her sister's pleas to wait, wait, please, wait.

"Leave her be," growled the uncle from the bottom of the stairs as Clair's cries grew louder, her knocks more insistent. "She knows her mind."

Taking hold of Hannah's hand, Clair flounced down over the stairs.

"You've turned her from me," she said scornfully, chasing the uncle into the kitchen. "From since she was little, you've been turning her from me."

"You been always blaming me, still for all. You wouldn't set step inside the door when she was bawling after you. Even when her grandmother died and she was bawling, you wouldn't come. You was always brazen, and you've yourself to blame."

"You kept her from coming to me!"

"Think what you wants—but you'll not do it in this house—I'll ask you to leave," he ordered. And as if worn by his anger, he shuffled past them, crumpling like Luke's accordion onto the chair besides the window. Clair watched. Even as he reached for his pipe, she watched. He flared a match, and as if forgetting that the thing she was holding on to was her daughter's hand, she lurched forward, wrenching Hannah along with her, near running out the door.

CHAPTER TWELVE

THE SCREECHING OF THE CLOTHESLINE pulleys and the screaming of the gulls and the roaring of the wind made nary a sound to Hannah's ears as she tore up over the hill the next morning, lying flat-belly across the cliff, and looking down upon the weather-beaten grey of the houses, barns, woodsheds and chicken coops circling the patch. It was the women's chatter her ears sought, their scandalizing tongues that made common knowledge of the most private thought or deed, rendering each soul that strolled across the patch as bare as the yellow staining the seat of their underwear as it flapped over their heads on the clotheslines. And with her mother just gone with Frankie to see Missy again, forbidding Hannah to put a leg on the beach till she was gone, and Willamena dodging back onto the patch from calling out goodbye to Frankie, she shouldn't wonder whose stains were going to be aired this morning. And indeed her ears cupped forward like a baby elephant's as Willamena started right in: "It's not much good going after Missy now. I always said Clair shouldn't have left her in the first place. My God, sure she never even went back for a visit—not even when her grandmother died, except for the burying, and even then she showed up late."

"Why would she," spoke up her aunt Nora, shoving out

her clothesline, "when her uncle was trying to hire her off the same day her mother died?"

"There wouldn't much Sim could do with her," countered Willamena. "Clair was always stubborn; I knows that from serving her in the store. And now this with young Missy—poor Sim is who I thinks about."

"He's not that poor," cut in Beth, "he got a good house out of it, and what sounds to be a right nice young girl who's been caring for him like a daughter the past ten years. It's Clair I thinks about; she's worried out of her mind."

"No good to worry now, the gander's come and gone," said Prude, heaving out a bowl of slops for the hens. "They be getting more wild by the day, the young is; she should mind her own foolishness and move down here with Clair."

"I'm sure I wouldn't know what to do with her," said Willamena, in the tired tongue of one who ought to. "Missy was never one for acting sensible, all that running around and singing about fairies and stuff. Made me shiver, sir, when I heard her once—a streak from her father, they says."

"And what's sensible?" asked Nora. "She's not the first young girl to fall down, and I don't see nothing wrong with her wanting to stay in her own house and rearing it, either."

"She's the first to be six and half months and not know about it, though," said Willamena. "That says the kind of mind she got."

"I don't stand by that," said Beth. "That young one down Sop's Arm was giving birth before she even knowed she was pregnant—and there was another one—what was her name, Nory? She was eight months before she put on a pound. And sure look at Nory; seven months, wasn't it, sis—before you started popping with young Rod? And look at the size of him now."

"Seven pounds the day he was born," said Nora.

"Well, sir, at least you knowed you was pregnant," exclaimed Willamena. "I can't bide by her saying she never knew."

"Aah, sure we never knowed about none of that stuff," said Prude, coming out of her woodshed with her hoe. "I was further on than she before I caught on. And it wasn't till the cramps started did old Winnie Brett tell me how it was coming out. I near fainted, I did; thought it was through the belly button they come out."

"Cripes, Mother," said Beth, "didn't any of ye's talk to the other?"

"What other?" asked Prude. "There was none here then, only me and Mother, and Hope and poor old Char, and for sure we wouldn't going to ask Mother. And as for them crowd down Lower Head, I never could talk to them—still can't."

"I still says, sir, it's only just starting," said Willamena, as Prude vanished around the corner of her house with the hoe. "She's a strange one, young Missy is, with her talk of fairies and stuff. We'll see what's going to happen now, when she starts raising a youngster; we'll see."

"Heh, she's one for talk, she is," muttered Beth, as Willamena went inside, "when her own youngster's a bloody merry-begot."

"Shh, now," warned Nora, her tone torn between a titter and a tut.

"Shh, nothing," said Beth, "jealous as a cat, she is, over Clair."

"Yes, and talk to me about the uncle," said Nora. "I seen him for what he was that first time she went back for a visit. Not even a minute would he give her with her sister that day.

And I remembers the funeral, too. Sure, she was only after giving birth three days before—what would anybody expect—for her to come and lay her out? Enough she got there at all. And it wasn't just the uncle she was mad at that day—she was mad at Missy too, whatever it was Missy done or said to her, I don't know—Alma, the postmistress, was talking in my ear. But I don't forget her face the day we walked out of that cemetery. And I haven't heard her talk much of Missy since. Till now. She's not one for talking, Clair isn't, but I sees on her face how hard this is for her. She'd raise that youngster like her own if Missy let her; I knows she would. But that's it now. Missy's determined she's going to raise it herself, and that's all anybody can do about it—stand back and let her be a mother."

A mother. Hannah rolled onto her back, sickened to her stomach. Her Aunt Missy was going to be a mother. The divinity of the blue above her might well have been grey, and the gentle June breeze a tiresome squall, for the lack of splendor beholding her world in that moment. A mother. Gone were the days of dancing around the fairy ring, of chanting songs to little girlies lying sleeping in the bluebells at night. Gone were the stories of blinded old men and gathering fairy butter and hankies written with dew in the mornings.

Of what use now were visits when her aunt Missy would be a mother, sitting and rocking all morning long, with a baby slobbering at her breasts? She closed her eyes to the sun, the wind and the shimmer of her aunt's hair rippling behind her like rays of sunshine as she danced around the fairy ring. Unable to bear her heartsickness alone, she rose, doddering down the hill.

The women had gone inside to start on the colours, and

she thought to go help her grammy Prude with the hoeing. Lynn came out on her stoop, her bangs sheared near to their roots, brazening a face already saucy with piercing button eyes and nostrils that twitched on sight. Screwing up her mouth, Hannah traipsed by, not wanting her company on this day.

"Missy's a trollop," hissed Lynn.

"You're a merry-begot," hissed back Hannah, then took to her heels as Lynn snorted like a horse, tearing around the corner of Prude's house after her.

"Here, here, stop that, stop that," Prude bawled as Hannah fell to her knees, scrambling behind the grandmother as she knelt besides a bed of greens.

"She's mocking me," shouted Lynn, skidding to a halt.

"No I never!"

"Yeah you did! You called me a merry-begot!"

"Get on, get on with your blackguarding; you're the devil's imp," cried Prude, wagging her hoe at Lynn, "and your father'll hear about this; mark my words."

"Hope now I was blackguarding—she was the one blackguarding," cried Lynn. "I'm telling Mom she called me a merry-begot!"

"Tell her what you wants—it's the logan's tongue you got; get home, get home!" yelled Prude.

"Trallop!" Lynn spat out to Hannah and vanished as Prude come to her feet, going after her with a hoe.

"Brazen as the devil, that's what they is, brazen as the devil," cried Prude, turning back onto Hannah. "Get up there, go on, get up there," she ordered, jabbing at her feet with the hoe, nudging her farther and farther up the furrow between the two beds of greens. "The tarment, the tarment; I allows your mother will tan your arse she gets home this evening—show, is that a shoot? Is that a shoot you're plucking out there? Name a God, they don't know a weed from a shoot."

"Yes I do, I knows," protested Hannah. "He was already plucked. There, I got it planted agin, now—see, it's growing."

"Fine chance it'll have; if not for ye, it'll be the sheep—it's a fool's job trying to grow a green these days—show, what's that, what's that you got there?"

"That's a weed; it got a yellow top—that's what the weeds are, right—the ones with the yellow top?"

"Show, I can't see, I can't see that—pass it here." Content that it was indeed a weed, Prude tossed it to one side, ordering Hannah onward with the plucking.

And after the old woman laid down the hoe and was sitting for rest besides her beds, Hannah paused in her weeding and asked, "Grammy, what's a merry-begot?"

The weight of her grandmother's hand whacking her on the behind jarred her a foot farther along the bed. "You bloody young thing; the dirt! I allows you'll feel the warmth of my hand on your arse afore your mother gets home on this tarmenting day—sure, ye haven't got a lick, not a lick of sense—your poor, poor mother; I allows she got her hands full with you, I allows she do. I wonder she don't take a strip off your hide one of these days."

No doubt the fates might've been more accommodating of Prude's warning if they weren't busy bringing about the greater of her prophecies. Four weeks had passed since the discovery of Missy's pregnancy, four weeks in which Clair had made several trips up the Basin, but was met by a closed door and Missy's refusal to see her. On this particular morning the wind had risen, a cold easterly, bringing with it an offshore fog that lay low on the sea, touching Hannah's cheeks with the coolness of mint as she loitered on the beach with some other youngsters and Grammy Prude hollering warnings from the bank. She heard before she saw Harve's boat as he put ashore to the stagehead, and watched as her mother climbed on top. Despite her knowing that her mother hadn't been gone long enough to do much more than walk up over the hill and then back down again, Hannah started towards her, hoping for some tidbit of news about her aunt. Her step was deterred, however, by a dark hulk coming through the fog—another fisher from Lower Head, confused by the whiteout, she thought, letting go with the last skiddy rock she held in her hand.

"Mind the rocks, mind the rocks; there's a boat coming," Prude cried out, and then let out the yelp of a frightened dog as the boat popped into sight. The war vet, no doubt, his greying hair, uncommonly long and made damp by the fog, hanging in strands across his face, his eyes sunken into his skull and encircled in a misery of red, and his skin as cracked and peeled as the age-old paint blistering the punt he sat in. But it was his coat that gripped Hannah's and the eyes of all others the way silver grips a crow's. Made of black leather, thicker than the hide of an old harp seal, and with large silver zippers gashing both sides across the breast and jutting up and down the sleeves, and with patches of fog still clinging to him, he appeared the one flung from the heavens and falling to the shores of Rocky Head on his way to hell.

"Get off the beach, get off the beach!" cried Prude, her voice rising to the pitch of the gulls screaming overhead. And as if wearing the one boot, the crowd of them took a step back as the stranger lifted his oars out of the water, rising before them as his boat drifted to shore.

"Good day to ye," called he in a rough voice, and as he

made to climb out of his boat, the youngsters scattered like flankers shooting out of a blazy bough.

"Clair! Clair—tell he to wait, tell he to wait," Prude was bawling out, the flesh quivering on her bones as she caught sight of Clair on the stagehead and Harve shoving himself off again.

Too late was her cry and within seconds Harve's boat was swallowed by the fog, leaving Prude freezing in her tracks as the leather-zipped apparition wheezed, "Is there a Prudence Osmond amongst ye?" Climbing out of his boat, he made his way up over the bank with the drunken gait of a sailor. "My name's Roland Ouncill, missus," he huffed, a belly that had heretofore been hidden behind his coat spilling over the waist of his pants as he leaned over, giving himself a last shove to the top of the bank. Doffing an imaginary hat, he bowed before the old woman's stricken figure, and never had she been so joyous at the sight of Willamena scurrying towards her, her bread-making bandanna wrapped and knotted around the front of her head, and her eyes narrowing slits as she took in the sight of the stranger.

"Yes, sir?" asked Willamena, the gravity of her voice signalling her own authority.

"Sergeant Roland Ouncill, ma'am," said the stranger with the same bow towards Willamena.

"That's Prude you just met," said Willamena, offering her hand, "and I'm Willamena, from up the Basin—my father, Saul Rice, he used to be the merchant, and this is my girl, Lynn," she added, as Lynn, as owl-eyed as the rest of the youngsters, came running up and curled an arm around her mother's waist as a means of propping herself before the stranger.

"It's a pleasure, ma'am, a pleasure," said the stranger, shaking the proffered hand. "I was about to tell this fine woman here," he added, turning towards Prude who was quivering on the brink of flight, "that I come from L'Anse aux Meadows, on the Great Northern—two hours from here as the crow flies, but a fair trip in punt. Took me a while, but I allowed some years ago I was going to make this trip, come meet the folks I heard so much about." Clearing his throat, he lowered his head towards Prude and spoke in quietude of prayer, "I knowed your boy—Joey."

"I'll not hear it," she wailed, and breaking from her stance, she started running towards Beth, who had appeared at that moment from behind the woodshed, a youngster in hand. "He's the devil, Betty," she cried, "he's the devil; I seen him in my tea, I did, I seen him in my tea."

"Ohh now, Mother," cried Beth, staring wide-eyed at the stranger as she wrapped her arms around her mother.

"He says he knowed Joey, but I'll not hear it, I'll not hear it. You stay put, too, Clair; you don't listen to his yarns neither," the old woman begged as Clair touched her shoulder reassuringly, approaching the stranger.

"Sergeant Roland Ouncill," said Willamena as the stranger reached for Clair's hand. "He knowed Joey in the war. I suppose you knowed Job Gale as well, then? Clair's his daughter. She married Luke, Joey's brother."

The smile fell from Sergeant Roland Ouncill's face, as did the hand holding Clair's. "Indeed," said he, wiping it oddly on the side of his pants. "I should've seen it right off; you're his likeness."

"I suppose you'll come in for a cup of tea, won't you?" asked Willamena, brushing Lynn off from heaving another hug around her waist. "The men won't be home from the woods camp till Friday evening, and Frankie—that's my husband—he's the politician for White Bay—should be home by then, too. He's in Cormack, seeing to business. For sure he'll want to talk with you once he gets here."

"You'll spread no yarns about his doings," Prude sang out as Willamena started leading the stranger towards her door. "'Twas a dark day he left, and darker ever since. Take yourself home; we've no need a strangers here."

"Sir, she's always in a thither about something," said Willamena with a grimace. "I suppose, Clair, you're coming for tea?"

"I sees to the baby first," said Clair, breaking off from the group, her eyes upon the stranger as ill at ease as Prude's.

Hannah dragged her step, watching after the war vet and his mighty coat as he followed Willamena towards her house, and then her mother as she took the baby and was walking with Nora towards home. Whom to follow? The worried look on her mother's face won, and tearing around the woodpile to the far side of the house, she let herself in through the door and was scooting up behind the stove a full minute before Nora and her mother entered. Laying her head on a pillow, a token from cold days where she sought more precious heat, she closed her eyes, feigning sleep, her ear pinned to the door squeaking shut and Brother fussing.

"For sure Mother's nervous," said Nora. "My stomach's jittery, too—do you think he come to tell us things, Clair—about Joey? Perhaps Mother's right—perhaps we don't need to know nothing more. Frankie said he's a drunk, just wanting our liquor—perhaps we should drive him off like Mother says."

"He's probably just wanting to be friendly," said Clair, the floor creaking as she walked, soothing Brother. "Who knows what he might have to say—" her voice trailed off wearily.

"Would she see you?" asked Nora.

"She won't even open the door, Nory. And—she never goes outside. Leastways, not during the day."

"She shouldn't be cooping herself up like that. The Lord knows she's not the first young one to fall down. Is she showing much?"

"According to Alma, she is. Lord, the thought of her suffering—"

"She won't—there's smaller than her after giving birth— and younger, too. And once the baby's born, she'll want to see you—I knows she will."

"You don't know her," whispered Clair. "She's always been so stubborn. And him—but that's it," she added more strongly. "No sense in crying—we'll just have to wait and see. You go on now, and see to Prude."

All too quickly her aunt was gone, the door closing behind her, leaving Hannah trapped behind the stove. The rocker groaned, taking her mother's weight, and a series of snorting and suckling as Brother latched on to the bottle's nipple. A silence fell, loud and heavy. And she knew without looking that her mother had gone to that place again. She lay there, listening. She'd never felt before the heaviness of this place that her mother sat in, what with Father clumping around, and the baby gurgling or fussing, and the noise she made herself, scampering from room to room, searching for things. She listened now to how her mother never rocked, never made soothing sounds to Brother, never hummed or whispered comforts to herself. Yet, she felt the maelstrom within her; knew it because she felt it herself—this undertow, sucking the silence more heavily around them, the burden of its weight crushing her lungs as she ached to breathe. And a fear grew within her for that place of unrest that sent emotions churning worse than the waters of Chouse, yet it fitted the sickness in her belly somehow, this silence that overlay a house, stifling all but the scattered creak of a rocker and the drone of the outside sea, for was she not sharing in this place of unrest, too, now? Was not the loss of her aunt hers to grieve as well?

Since the first that she could remember, she felt kindred with her mother.

"FIFTEEN HUNDRED OF US CROSSED OVER, but it wasn't till '41 I met Joey," said the vet to the few women and older boys allowed inside Willamena's kitchen that evening. "Part of the 166 Nfld. Regiment, we was then—heavy artillery, defending the mother's shores. Till the bombing, and that's when she went to war, b'yes; that's when she went to war. But we was a long ways from war yet, the 166th was. From heavy artillery to field we went, and for that we was moved to Scotland. Yup, Scotland, sirs, the heart of the world, she is. In all the places I tucked in, it was there we were treated the best. No matter your name, you were a Newfoundlander, and what they knowed of us was what our forefathers showed them during the first great war. And they done us proud, our forefathers did; they done us proud, for wouldn't nary a door that don't open to a Newfoundlander in that prized land of Scotland. And the girls—" Raising his face with the bliss of a sleeping infant, he'd slip into more yarns of what sounded more like an excursion around the world than a sojourn into war as he traipsed from kitchen to kitchen, sipping tea with the women. And after he'd warmed them with story, and evening was drawing nigh, he'd stroll out onto the bank, talking more serious talk with the older boys, Roddy and Marty, and coaxing them to build a fire so's he could sit, watching the sea, he'd say, and mind himself that it was over them waters that he had bathed in blood, and not till the journey back home did he wash himself clean of its stench. "And a little nip, b'yes, if you can find one, for it pains me, it do, to think on that stench—it's still there," he'd say, holding out his stubby, callused hands. "Every time I looks, I sees it, staining me flesh. And it's only when I talks of it do it fade a bit, and I prays the day will come that if I tells it enough times, and if I dreams it enough times, they might start coming clean, b'yes; they might start coming clean."

And they clung to his every word, did the folk from Rocky and Lower Head. Aside from Prude and Clair, that was. Neither woman was to be seen out on the bank during the next few days. But still they heard. From the mouths of Nora and Beth and Hannah and every other youngster that could string ten words together, they heard. And with keen interest, too, they listened to the growing yarn the old vet was spinning about how Joey was the spit of his own boy— the one he'd lost to the sea once, and his bones nibbled clean by the fish when he was found five years later in a water cave. So, he'd taken to Joey, he had, treating him as if he was his own, and it was good that he'd done so, for he showed him all the fine secrets of the Scottish towns, and sat with him in a great many pubs, clapping their hands to song, and Joey tossing his hat to the pretty girls with nicely set hair and lips as red as darkest ochre.

"Yes, he was my boy," said Sergeant Roland Ouncill, sitting on the bank, sharing a nip of shine with Beth and the fisher Harve. "I nourished him, I did, with food, wine, warm socks, anything that struck his fancy—even an old accordion he found in a junk shop. And Lucifer, could he play. 'Twas times he made us bawl like babies, he stroked that accordion so pretty—especially when he'd play 'Oh Mary of the Cold, Cold Moors.'"

The stranger smiled. He didn't look as devil-like in his common plaid shirt rolled up at the elbows, and his thinning grey hair brushed behind his ears, and his belly pouching out over his pants; more the aging old-timer—if not for the sunken red eyes, and purplish spots splotching the pallor behind the stubble greying his cheeks. "It's odd you never met Job Gale," said Beth. "That's all Joey talked about in his letters he wrote."

"I never said I didn't meet him," said the old vet. "I said I didn't know him. Difference between meeting a man and knowing a man. We never got on, we never—aye, his weren't the ways of Joey. 'Tis another world over them waters—another world." And he closed his eyes to the breeze and the lapping water. A snipe screeched and his eyes startled open. "Damn snipes," he muttered. "Damn snipes," and he began to drift again. "My boy," he croaked, not so's anyone could hear, but sitting as close as Hannah was, she heard. She saw, too, as he lifted the tumbler of shine to his mouth, his lip beginning to quiver and wondered why neither her mother nor her grammy Prude had yet to sit with this stranger, and listen themselves to the stories they were hungering to hear. For neither of them shushed Nora or Beth or the youngsters when they went running to and fro, repeating for them each word that fell from the stranger's mouth. And more confounding was her father's refusal to listen to her yarns as he sat at the table, just home from camp, finishing off a late supper of tea and baked salmon.

"But he knowed Uncle Joey, Daddy," said Hannah,

climbing down off the bin with a bottle cap filled with flour. "Is this enough?" she asked her mother, who was sitting in the rocker, washing Brother from a pan near her feet, and him laid naked across her knees.

"That's enough—keep stirring so's not to burn it—just a little brown is all," she added as Hannah pushed the high chair, which used to be hers and was now waiting for Brother, nearer the stove and laid the cap onto the stove top.

"That don't look too good," said Luke, peering at the baby's bare bottom, peppered in a red rash.

"He's forever with a rash," said Clair. "He—the vet— says he wants to meet you. There's always so many people about—I thought we'd have him in some evening."

"Do it after I'm gone, lovey, because I knows all I needs to know about Sergeant Roland Ouncill."

"What do you know? What a few people are after saying—"

"I knows he's an old bastard, that's what I knows," said Luke, and Hannah glanced over her shoulder, as surprised as her mother by her father's words. "And how do I know that?" he asked, calm as anything. "I knows that by the way he's sitting out there on our shores, sniffing our brew and peddling out yarns to keep our liquor flowing, that's how I knows that. I met his kind before; liquor-addled they are, and they'd tap their own bodies for their own spirit if they could—just in case it was the drinking kind. And that's why I'm proud the old woman out there is having nothing to do with him. But what I'm more interested in knowing is how come you haven't already been talking to him?"

Clair shrugged. "He didn't know my father."

"How come he knowed Joey, then, if he didn't know your father?"

"It's a big war, Luke."

"Is that what he said—he didn't know your father?"

"He said he met him, but he didn't know him."

"What's that mean?"

"What do I know what it means! That's why I'd like to have him in—to talk to him about it."

"Why have him in?"

"Why not? He's been everywhere else—except Grammy's. It's only fitting we'd have him here, too."

"Suppertime tomorrow."

"No. Everybody else would come too."

"Thought so," said Luke, with a deep nod.

"Thought what?"

"You don't want nobody else listening when you asks him about your father. You listen to me, lovey," he said as Clair rose with a sharp sigh, "you got nothing to be frightened of with your father; he was a brave man—"

"Leave it be, Luke," she warned, laying Brother in his crib.

"I met your father. I knows his stock. He was a good man, he was, and if that old bastard out there was to say anything but, I'd throw him overboard, you hear that?"

"Ohh, for God's sakes," sighed Clair, stacking the dishes in front of him, "you're bellowing as if you was in the woods."

"Bloody yarns," muttered Luke.

"And who's to say they're bloody yarns?" asked Clair, the forks clanging from her hands. "He was a sergeant—Joey's sergeant. He just might have something to say."

"Yup, he might," said Luke, "but I was already told; he died with courage, your father said, and that's what I carries with me—he died with courage. How many bullets or bombs or whatever tore at him, matters none."

"It mattered to Daddy, then," Clair whispered. Gathering up the dropped forks, she carried them to the sink. Luke was quick behind her.

"Lovey, I don't make light of your father's suffering. No, no, listen to me," he said, as she turned her back to him, "I knows you don't like to talk about him, but damn it, Clair, I thought I walked in hell once, till I met him, but, 'twas a different hell I seen in his eyes—one that's been scaring me ever since, and all I can ever think is he must've been a helluva man to carry around whatever it was he was carrying around—a helluva man."

"But he didn't," Clair croaked, twisting around to face him. "He let it kill him—his way of thinking on it, day after day—"

"His *way* of thinking? Geezes cripes, you think it was a *way* of thinking that broke a man like your father? Lovey, it weren't no bloody way of thinking that took Job Gale. When a man walks that deep in hell, taking off a uniform ain't going to bring him out of it. It was nothing but guts that brought him back. He could've stayed if it wasn't for ye and your mother, and he would've found peace a lot damn sight earlier if he'd gone with Joey."

"Then let me know that!" Clair cried out, her face as stark as death.

Luke quietened. "Tell you what, Clair," he said finally. "Let me take you to Cat Arm tomorrow." As she tried to walk away, he argued, "I told you once I'd take you back. Maybe it would be good for you to go back. I've always felt you should."

Suddenly her eyes swooped onto Hannah standing on the high chair, motionless as she stared at them, and smoke from the burning flour oozing up from the stove. She startled as her mother darted towards her and snatched the spoon from her hand, pushing the bottle cap to the back of the stove.

"Now, look," exclaimed Clair, staring at the burnt flour, her voice quavering. "Rock him, Luke," she ordered as the baby started up bawling, "and Hannah, you start with the dishes, I browns more flour. And there'll be no more talk this night," she added sharply to Luke, helping Hannah off the high chair. "There's enough filling her ears these days, without having to listen to us."

Scruffing the back of Hannah's head, her father picked up Brother and sat himself in the rocking chair as Hannah began scraping bones off the plates, each casting chastened glances the other's way, whilst sneaking glances at Clair as she busied herself scraping the burnt flour out of the bottle cap. Brother's cries fretted into silence and all might have ended well enough had Willamena not felt the need to vindicate herself from a similar deed perhaps done eight years before. But as with Prude's prophecy, mere circumstance is ignorant of the greater seed it comes from, as was Willamena's visit that evening.

"I'm not one for arguing, but there's some talk I won't stand for," she announced as both Clair and Luke turned to her in surprise. "Hannah called Lynn a bastard!"

"Hope now!" exclaimed Hannah, mind frantically seeking backwards.

"I checked it with Grammy Prude before I come here," said Willamena in a no-nonsense voice.

"Hannah?" asked Clair, her tone already laying out punishment.

"I never! Lynn's a liar!"

"Prude heard you—I asked her—you called Lynn a merry-begot, you did, and you called her it twice."

"So?" challenged Hannah.

"I—don't think she knows what that means," said Clair as Luke turned to one side with a soft groan.

"Yes I do," said Hannah, "I heard Aunt Beth—"

"Hannah!"

Hannah jumped, clattering a saucer onto the floor as her father came out of the rocker, and still holding Brother, scooped her up with one arm and lodged her down in the hall. "Bedtime," he said, patting her bottom, nudging her towards the stairs.

"She called Aunt Missy a trollop," Hannah yelled, then winced as her father's hand gripped her shoulder, boosting her up over the first couple of steps.

"Not another word," threatened Luke. "You hear me?"

She tensed against the stairs, but moved no farther as her father strolled back into the kitchen, speaking with a controlled quiet to Willamena. "Perhaps it's Clair who ought to be knocking on your door, if we was to pay heed to youngsters."

"It's not from other youngsters they're picking up this talk," said Willamena, in full view of Hannah as she inched back down the stairs, listening. "Lynn oughtn't to have said what she did, but it's only what she's hearing, and I won't have the same said about me. I wasn't tarred with that brush—" She paused as the door opened and Frankie stepped inside, letting in the evening breeze and the guffaws from the old war vet and others as they sat around a fire on the beach.

"There you are," he said, turning to Willamena. "Someone from Lower Head wants to send a message—it's important," he added, holding the door for her.

Willamena stared from Clair to Luke, then, tilting her head, walked back out the door. Frankie closed it quietly behind her and with an invite from Luke, drew out a chair at the table.

"Is what they're saying true—that Missy was running around?" asked Clair.

"God, no," said Frankie, shaking his head. "She's got a good name. She was only doing what they were all doing—prancing around the hills on starry nights with the boys—it's what we all done, wasn't it? They says she got caught first time. And who's to know who is or isn't a merry-begot—weddings took care of that."

"Nobody's saying who?" asked Luke.

"Not a word," said Frankie. "She won't say, either."

Clair shook her head, and Hannah flattened herself out, scarcely breathing as her mother took the baby from her father and bent over the crib with the burnt flour, diapering him. Her face was taut, pale, even as her father lit the lamp, yellowing the evening light.

"Have you thought about sending her to Corner Brook till the baby's born?" asked Frankie. "There's a place there for young girls."

"She's not giving the baby up," said Clair.

"Even still. Some goes just to have privacy whilst they're pregnant."

"Damn foolishness they're made to feel this way," said Luke. "Must be a way of making her think differently rather than running off and hiding."

"None that's going to settle itself soon," said Clair. "Perhaps she might like to go to Corner Brook till the baby's born—and it won't be that far with the road coming through to the Basin—two hours' drive, Frankie?"

"If that," said Frankie. "And with the road, I'll be going back and forth more often—and you, too, if ye goes ahead with your plan." Frankie paused at the quizzical look from Luke. Scrooping back his chair, he rose. "Think I'll mosey out there, see what they're on about this evening. Coming out, Luke?"

"In a bit."

"Yup, see you, then. Never mind nothing Willamena says," he added on his way out the door to Clair. "Youngsters exaggerates everything. I'll have a word with Lynn, the young bugger."

It was her chance to scramble up over the stairs, but her father was onto his feet the second the latch clicked in the door.

"What's he talking about?" he asked, striding before her mother.

"Nothing I wants to talk about right now," said Clair, trying to move around him.

"Tell me, Clair; what the hell's he talking about?" he asked more loudly.

Clair sighed, starting to gather the dishes. "This isn't how I wanted to tell you—and I don't want to argue any more this evening, either—"

"Tell me, Clair."

"I'm thinking of starting up a small store. I won't need anything from you," she added quickly, toppling over cups in her haste. "With Hannah's help, it won't be much to serve the few people around here, and it would certainly save having everyone going up to the Basin every time they needs some little thing. We could set it up in the front room—we don't use it for anything, and the extra money will help with Hannah's education—" She faltered as Luke stared at her, shaking his head speechlessly. "I'm not going to argue it," she began, raising a hand to silence him. "We've already had enough this night."

"First, you answer me this one thing," he asked quietly. "How is it you got plans to change the roof over our heads and you goes to Frankie first?"

"It's just that he knows about such things—"

"About whether or not we should have a store?"

"About how to go about starting it. He knows the right people, and he's offered to put his name on a bill for us—but it was my idea," she said loudly, "and it's a damn fine idea. And I would've told you, but I thought you'd say no."

"Yup, and that's just what I thought," he said. "Go talk to somebody else because Luke's scared of change, right? Well, it's funny you thinks I'm scared of going out and meeting change, lovey, because that's what I thinks about you—"

"Me!"

"Yup, you. All the time sitting and waiting, sitting and waiting. I heard you say it once," he said as she stared at him in sheer astonishment, "about how you was always waiting for either your father to come home or your mother to get better. And now it's Missy you're waiting for—for her to come to you. And barring that, for the uncle to die, and then you thinks you can go right in there and scoop her up. But I expects it's more than a road or a dead uncle that's going to bring Missy to where you wants her. It's a nasty thing to sit and wait on life, lovey, when all the time it's flowing right past where you're sitting."

"You dare talk to me about going out to meet life," she said in a near whisper, "when you've been up the shore once since the day of a shooting accident thirteen years ago."

He stared at her for a second. Then, "You spends too much time thinking in fear, lovey; you're starting to see it everywhere you looks." And as if he'd turned to stone, he remained staring at the spot she'd been standing whilst she snatched her sweater off the rocker and walked out the door.

Too late she heard her father treading towards her. Scooping her into the curve of his arm, he trudged tiredly up over the stairs, lugging her into her room and tossing her onto her bed. "And mind you says your prayers," he warned, turning back into the hall and down over the stairs again.

Springing onto her knees, she pushed her face against the window, staring out into the darkening evening. Her mother was standing in the shadow near their woodpile, looking down on the old war vet as he sat, legs splayed out in front of him, besides a fire, guffawing loudly and passing around the brew jug to Marty, Roddy and some others from Lower Head. Her uncle Nate was out there as well, she saw, along with her uncle Calve. Shoving open the window, she leaned out through, shivering as a shaft of night air washed over her face.

"You can't think cold on a desert, b'yes, no sirree, you can't think cold on a desert. And I allows every Newfoundlander there suffered more in that whore's oven than he did lying in mud, dodging bullets. Eight months we was in Africa, eight months of swapping flies and spitting out sand and sweating. Be God, we cursed the night we crossed over them seas, swinging in hammocks."

A movement near the woodpile, and her mother had vanished. Hearing nothing more from the old vet but yarns about Italy and Cassino and some monk's place on a mountaintop, she pulled down the window, lying back on her bed. A gust of wind rattled the pane, and her stomach tightened again as she thought of her mother out in the night, wearing only her sweater. She lay there for what felt like a long time, refusing the blanket. Later, when she heard the door open, she shed her clothes and then covered herself, pretending to be asleep when her mother came up over the stairs with Brother in her arms. Scarcely opening her eyes, she watched as her mother paused at doorway, looking in on her. And for the first time that she could think, she wanted her to come and tuck her in as she sometimes did on real cold nights. She didn't. Instead, she turned into her own room. The sound of her father's accordion took up from out on the stoop. Rolling onto her back, she lay awake till long after the old vet's yarns and the crackling of their fire had dulled, listening to her father playing out his song to the quiet of the patch.

CHAPTER THIRTEEN

THE NEXT MORNING HER FATHER WAS UP and gone to Salt Water Pond on an overnight hunting trip, and her mother too might just as well be gone, given her scarcity of attention as she wandered about the house, attending to the baby and her cleaning. A quiet followed his return, a quiet that served them well as they took care not to be caught alone with each other, Clair going to bed before Luke, and Luke spending most of his time out by the woodpile, sitting on the sandstone, filing down the blade on an old bucksaw rusted by the winter's snow. But it was a quiet that did little to mask Luke's unease, or the sense of urgency aggravating Clair's movements. And while it was her father Hannah traipsed behind the most, it was her mother that her eyes continuously sought, knowing with a child's heart that it was within her that past deeds were now colliding, and as with those things that catches up with you from the inside, there is no uncle to slew one's eyes upon, no sick mother or dying father, or burrowing-eyed store clerks, only the self, and those innocents who may be wise enough to remain at bay, yet are caught like suns in a field of gravity.

Her mother's turmoil grew after Luke left for another two weeks in the camps and she stood at the window, watching the old vet wander off down Lower Head, abandoning

the beach to the youngsters and the gulls. Hannah took to
the hills, rambling old paths and despairing that she'd ever
see her aunt again, except as a mother, which brought about
as much comfort as the sourness of Brother's spit as she tried
to rock him to sleep one evening, and her mother stood
washing dishes at the bin. It was turning into September, and
light was fading early. Striking a match, her mother lit the
lamp, turning the wick high and wiping at the baby's mouth
with the corner of her handkerchief.

"I'm sending you up with Missy for a couple of days," she
said, lifting him out of her arms, "before school starts."

Hannah simply gawked. "To sleep?"

"I heard from Willamena that Sim has to go in the
country for a few days. She'll be glad for the company.
Frankie's going up tomorrow—he'll take you. You want to
go, don't you?"

Hannah nodded forcefully, the joy she'd normally feel at
a time like this tethered to the paleness of her mother's hand
as she caressed Brother's bottom. But the first rays of the
morning sun dispersed the gloom of the past weeks, and
licking the butter off her fingers and dragging the comb
through her hair, she bounced across the kitchen with her
usual quickness at the sound of Frankie's voice, even stopping
on her way out the door to smack a kiss atop of Brother's head
as he gurgled in his crib. Her mother followed behind with a
carrying bag packed with a few garments of clothes and an
offering of wild strawberry jam—Missy's favourite—tucked
in besides them. Miss Tattle-Tale, Blabbermouth, Forever
Running to Her Mother with Lies Lynn skipped onto the
bank, a bag of her own tucked beneath her arm, and her
bangs plastered wet across her forehead. She scowled at
Hannah and Hannah scowled back, but then Frankie was

hoisting them aboard the boat, and Hannah sprawled flat-belly across the cuddy, leaning over the bow, her insides seized with excitement. Lynn flattened out besides her as Frankie shoved off the boat, and the fact that Lynn was a tattletale blabber fell into the backwater like yesterday's rain. And that Hannah had bloodied her head once with a sharp-edged rock, and she'd bloodied Hannah's twice in return became part of the sea, buoying them from shore. The putt-putt of the piston cracked through the air, and with the morning sun warming their backs, and the sea wind spraying their faces, and the vibrations of the motor reverberating through their bellies, and their throats bleating "M-i-i-l-l-e-e-r-r-s-s—I-s-s-l-l-a-a-n-n-d" as they motored passed the tombstone with the mother and her little girl buried side by side, they were best friends forever. And upon arriving at the Basin and Frankie boosting them up on the wharf, and Lynn's cousin come running down over the hill to greet her, the lambs became two long-horned rams, heads down and ready to butt as one sallied forth towards an aging old merchant with boxes of candy still hidden in his cupboards, and the other towards the enchant-ing sweet of a fairy-like aunt.

Johnnie's wife, Rose, and others called out to Frankie from their doorways as he walked along behind Hannah, carrying her bag, and he'd slow his step, commenting on the road coming through the following week, and the wood trucks along with it, to start trucking wood from the boons to the pulp and paper mill in Corner Brook. Hannah skipped ahead impatiently, hearing none of their greetings, except when Alma stepped off the post office steps, blocking her path.

"She's letting you stay this time, is she?" she asked, glancing at the bag Frankie was toting behind her.

"Till Sim gets back, day after tomorrow," said Frankie. "Is Les going in the woods with him?"

"He got to—to get his stuff from the camp. They says whatever's not took is going to be ploughed over. I says it'd be some road, sir, if they ploughed over my new saw."

"They had their time—is he taking his horse?"

"He got to—all the stuff they got to bring back. And he said he was going to take apart the camp and haul some of the wood closer to Rushie Pond. That's good wood they got there in that camp."

"A day's work, for sure," said Frankie.

"I allows Sim'll have a fit, seeing Clair's maid back agin— he's frightened to death, he is, Clair's going to come and take Missy from him. Do he know you're coming?" she asked Hannah, but Hannah was already running off, leaving Frankie to satisfy Alma's curiosity.

Coming upon the house, she ducked through the gate and down the path. The bluebells stood merry, their heads nodding in the breeze, but the fairy ring was grossly over-grown, and no dead flowers in sight. And too, the kitchen window was curtained. Her step lagged, as did her spirits, before this maimed frontage, returning to the gloom of her last visit. Taking hold of the door handle, she quietly opened it and stepped inside, a hush falling on her ears as when step-ping through the doors of a church already in service. It was as if she had never left, as if the clock hanging resolute upon the kitchen wall were withholding time. And her footstep was no release for its pendulum, for the uncle never so much as laid down his pipe and rose from his seat as Frankie pushed open the door to his own knock and followed her inside.

"Is she come for her agin?" he asked contrarily, his eyes falling onto the bag beneath Frankie's arm.

"Mommy said I can stay the night," said Hannah, glancing around eagerly for her aunt as Frankie laid her bag on the table.

"It's Hannah she'll be coming for," said Frankie, "day after tomorrow. She thought it'd be good for Missy to have some company the next few days you're in the country."

"Missy's not wanting company," said the uncle, coming forward in his chair. "She's resting in her room."

"Ahh, she ought to be getting out more," said Frankie, "and perhaps she will now, with Hannah here. What time in the morning are you leaving?"

Unhearing of the uncle's response, Hannah darted into the stairwell, feeling his eyes snapping at her heels as she ran up over the stairs. The door to her aunt's room opened as she bolted across the landing, stopping her dead upon sight of the lithe, slender body that had twirled and bent like a willow in the wind now all bloated and fat inside a hideous dark dress, and looking as dejected as a sawed-off stump as it half hid behind the door, looking out at Hannah. But it was her aunt's face that stunned Hannah; her hair, all dulled from lack of sun, was tightly drawn back into a ponytail that consumed the gentleness of her features, producing a tautness that snapped the second she opened her mouth to speak.

"You can't stay, Hannah!"

"Mommy said I could—"

"She got no right to say you could. Now, listen to me," she said, taking hold of Hannah's arm as her mouth began to pucker, and pulling her inside the room. "I'm not well—you can see—and I can't be playing with you."

"Mommy said we could just walk—"

"No, we can't."

"But Mommy said!"

"Mommy!" Missy twirled on her heel like the young sapling again. "She thinks she can just send you—well, she can't. And you've got to go. Now. And don't go crying about it, either—it's no good crying."

Hannah shook her head, staring at the dark encircling her aunt's eyes and wanting to touch it, to wipe it from her skin. Her aunt turned from her, wringing her hands and pacing the room worse than her mother the past few weeks.

"Listen to me, Hannie," Missy whispered. "I needs to be alone for the next day or so. Come back after if you like—but not now; you can't stay now. Don't be mad, all right? Just give me a couple of days and then I'll be much better and you can stay." She peered into Hannah's eyes, the crystalline blue of hers all clouded and dark as she attempted a smile. "You'll see," she whispered, "everything will be fine soon. But right now, you got to go home. Will you go home like I asks you, and come back next week?"

Hannah dropped her eyes from her aunt's begging.

"You're such a good girl," said Missy with relief. "And when you come back, I got something to show you—a place, a secret place—and it's all mine," she whispered, hugging Hannah to her side, walking her to the door. "I goes there by myself when it's dark; that way nobody can see me and talk about me looking the way I am—big mouths, all of them, always gawking and talking. Promise you won't tell anybody, now," she coaxed, stopping at the room door. "You promise?"

Hannah nodded and Missy gave her a quick hug, dropping a kiss on her nose. "That's a good girl. Better hurry, then—catch Frankie before he leaves. Go, hurry, and next week you'll be back."

One step, two steps across the landing. "Go," Missy urged. "Hurry, now." One step down, two—and as might a sleepwalker awaking on the edge of a cliff, Hannah suddenly stopped, and throwing back her head she cut loose with a wail that sent the uncle's chair scrooping across the kitchen floor, and her aunt swooping across the landing and down over the stairs behind her.

"What's wrong with her?" bawled out the uncle, thumping into the stairwell.

"Nothing, shhh, Hannie, shhh, ooh," cried Missy, leading her back up the stairs. "She's fine, she's fine," she called down to the uncle.

"Send her home, that's what," ordered the uncle. "We can't look after her here—her mother should've knowed that."

Hannah wailed harder and Missy led her into the room, shutting the door on the uncle's orders. "Shush, Hannie, you can stay the night—till tomorrow. Stop crying. Ohh," she sighed unhappily, and raining kisses across Hannah's forehead, she led her to the bed, lying down with her, kissing and rocking her till Hannah's wails subsided into shuddering sobs. "There now, let's just rest for a bit," she said quietly, "then we'll have supper, and you can come with me when I—when I goes for a walk, all right?"

"T-to the fairy ring?"

"If that's what you wants. But only this evening; like I told you, I don't go outside these days."

"Only at night?"

"Yes, only at night because everybody talks and stares during the day."

"Don't it get t-too hot?"

"I haves my window open and there's always a breeze. Shh, now, I'm tired again. See? I told you, I'm tired all the time, and that's why I don't go out. Perhaps we can just be quiet and nap a little. Is that all right? Can you nap a little right now?" she coaxed, her hair brushing soft against Hannah's cheek.

Hannah nodded, laying her head carefully upon her aunt's chest, feeling it swell with each breath she drew.

AFTER SUPPER WAS DONE and the evening shadow was beginning to fill the room, the uncle ordered, "You'll not take her prowling."

"I'm just going out the backyard, that's all—breathe some air," said Missy, pulling on a sweater at the door. "Hannah, you ready?"

"She ought to be in bed."

"Will you check on the wharf in the morning, for someone going down Rocky Head?"

"Thought she was staying till I got back?"

"Thought you wanted her sent back?"

"That don't fit," said the uncle, his tone becoming more querulous with surprise, "all the time wanting her to stay, and now sending her back."

"Ooh, light your pipe," said Missy, patting his shoulder. "Come, Hannah, got your boots on?"

"You're up to something," he said, rising. "I knows when you're up to something—and I been feeling it for a while now. Either she stays whilst I'm gone, or I ask Alma to keep watch over you."

"You dare!" snapped Missy, turning on him. "I swear, I'll leave and never come back agin if you goes asking that busy-body to come watching over me."

"Then the girl stays. And you mind as well," he warned Hannah, "else you'll never put another leg back here agin, if I finds you up to no good with her."

Shaking her head impatiently, Missy opened the door, ushering Hannah outside. "I swear, I'd like to leave here and never come back," she muttered.

"You mind what you says," called out the uncle, but she was already slamming the door.

"Worse than having Daddy back," she said as the uncle pulled apart the curtains, staring after them, "At least he never seen or heard nobody." Cramming her hands in her pockets, she stared disdainfully at the houses of the Basin, flushed with lamplight, staring back at her.

"How come your daddy never seen nothing or nobody?" asked Hannah, keeping step besides her as she hurried into the dark of the backyard.

"Too busy thinking on his own things, I imagine. Sometimes I finds myself wondering what it was that kept him sitting like that—now that I've been sitting there myself, most days." She gave a little shiver. "I used to be frightened to death when I was a youngster, coming through that gate, with him sitting in the window, his eyes all hollow and black and his face white—like a skull, I used to think."

"Is Uncle Sim like a skull?"

"No. He don't sit in torment like Daddy did. He just sits, is all, grumbling at whoever happens to be walking up the road. I got used to that—his grumbling for hours on end. Funny, but that's what makes me know now that Daddy wasn't just sitting there, waiting for me to come home and be glared at. Lord, I thinks of the times I used to run home through the backyard and sneak around the corner of the house so's he wouldn't see me with his skull-like eyes. Poor Daddy. It must've been awful living all alone like that, and with everyone staring all the time. I thanks God for Uncle Sim and his foolish grumbling and our arguing." Reaching out, she tightened her hand around Hannah's. "Does Clair and Luke argue—or grumble?"

"Only since the old vet come ashore."

"What old vet?"

"From over the hills somewhere. He was with Uncle Joey in the war. How come there's no stars?" she asked, tossing back her head as they reached the bottom of the yard, gazing at the last trace of blue ebbing from the sky.

"Not dark enough. Did the vet know Daddy, too?"

"Don't know."

"Hasn't Clair asked him?"

"No, and that's why she's fighting with Daddy—because he won't go talk to him either."

"Why won't she go talk to him?"

"Don't know."

"Then why won't he go talk to him?"

"Because he says he's a bastard."

"Luke says he's a bastard? Why does he say he's a bastard?"

"Because he drinks liquor. Are we going in?" asked Hannah as they come to the gate leading into a thicket.

"Not scared, are you?"

"No," said Hannah, staring hard at the dark woods before her, trying to imagine it in its daylight foliage of aspen, brooks and squawking bluejays. "I—I can't see," she protested, fumbling with her foot for the path, hands reaching before her as Missy creaked open the gate, ushering her through.

"You'll see better in a minute—here, hold my hand." With the clarity of a nighthawk, Missy led them straight onto the path through the wood.

"Daddy said a fairy led Grandy into the woods once and got him lost," said Hannah.

"Ouch," exclaimed Missy as Hannah stumbled over her ankles. "What else did he say?"

"That Grandy ate dandelion seeds every day from then on so's to protect himself so's he'd never see another fairy."

"Did it work?"

"I don't know. I think so—" A sudden rush of air struck her cheek and she leaped back with a shriek.

"Shh, it's a bird; it's just a bird," soothed Missy.

"It's a bat!" cried Hannah.

"Bats don't hurt you. Hear the brook? It'll be lighter in the clearing. There's no bats there, and they don't hurt you, anyhow. Lord knows, I'd be dead by now if they did. Come on."

Holding up a hand to ward off further bat attacks, Hannah allowed her aunt to lead her off the path and alongside a brook choking its way free of the underbrush and sliding across a grassy clearing. It was lighter here, as Missy had promised, and taking courage, Hannah shoved herself more boldly through a grouping of huckleberry and alder bushes, closing her eyes against the branches flicking at her face. Finally they broke through, meeting up with the brook again as it tumbled down an embankment, joining with a river onto the gorge floor. But it was impossible to see the river on this night, with the floor of the gorge as black as tar, and Hannah turned her eyes instead towards the pearly grey of the ocean, scarcely visible at the mouth of the gorge, reflecting the final traces of the evening's light.

Missy was brushing off a place to sit besides the brook and Hannah fell to her knees, scrambling to sit besides her.

"Mmm, I loves the sounds of running water," murmured Missy, resting her chin on the crown of Hannah's head and trailing her hand through the brook as it splashed down over the grade. Hannah nodded, closing her eyes to the dark of the gorge, and feeling instead the warmth of her aunt's throat on her forehead.

"Where do you think the stars go in the daytime?" her aunt asked softly.

"Nowhere. The sun makes it hard to see them."

"Getting smart, aren't you?"

"Daddy told me. And he said you can't ever reach them, not even if you piled every house in the world on top of each other, and every ladder and every log, not even then can you reach them—that's how far away they are."

"He must be right, else we'd be lying on a star this evening."

"And he said once he was thinking so hard about it that he made a star fall right across the sky."

"Mmm. Once I believed my daddy could make the heavens dance."

"That's silly."

"Maybe so. Some things are too big to think about." And she lapsed into silence, gently swaying, her chin nuzzling Hannah's crown. They sat like that for some time, Missy much calmer than earlier, except for the strength of her fingers as she more fidgeted than stroked Hannah's shoulders, and Hannah a little uncomfortable because of the damp of the ground penetrating the thin cotton of her slacks, yet remaining still, not wanting to disrupt the aunt's quiet. Despite herself, a shiver ran through her and her aunt immediately rose.

The horizon had given way to full darkness by now, and Hannah clung tightly to her aunt's hand as they fought their way back through the huckleberries and alders. The gurglings of the little brook sounded more like a rushing river in the quiet of the night, and with relief Hannah found herself on the path leading back through the aspens and the glimmer of a lamplight twinkling through the dark. Another glimmer, and another, and they were back besides the gate again, and windows from the Basin burnishing the night.

"See that," sniffed Missy, coming up across the yard and staring up at the upstairs window and the uncle, his hands cupped to the pane, peering down at them. "That's what it's like all the time now—everybody staring at me. You'd think they never seen anybody this way before, and don't let them windows that's dark fool you; that's the ones they're most likely looking through," she added as they made their way up over the garden.

"You can get to bed now," she shouted the second they were inside the house and she had strolled to the foot of the stairs. "We didn't turn into fairies and fly away." Rolling her eyes, she patted the back of the divan for Hannah to sit and, raising the wick, made them each a cup of hot cocoa. "Don't spill," she cautioned as Hannah crept up over the stairs behind her, their shadows looming on the wall from the lamp the uncle had left burning on the landing.

Laying her cup on the bedstand, Hannah stripped off her clothes and snatched up the end of the curtain, covering the opening to the closet, looking for her bag. "You got some squawroot?" she asked, dropping to her knees besides some dried roots gnarled around each other, and leaves shrivelled up like hay drying on a piece of brown paper.

"Get away from that," said Missy loudly, pulling Hannah away from the closet and letting the curtain fall back in place. And seeing Hannah's stung look, she quickly smiled. "Yes, yes, it's squawroot. I dries them for Uncle Sim."

"That's a lot," said Hannah. "Too much makes you really sick, Granny Prude says."

"Never mind," said Missy. "And tell no one about it. There, underneath the bed is your bag. Hurry now, get undressed."

"Is it too hot?" she asked, after they were both gowned and had crawled into bed, sitting up on their pillows, sipping their cocoa.

Hannah shook her head, taking a gulp of the sweetened liquid.

"Bet Clair don't let you drink cocoa in bed."

"Nope."

"Is Brother laughing yet?"

"Just bawls."

"All the time?"

"Yup."

"Nothing else?"

"He slobbers."

"I hates slobber. Do Luke rock him?"

"Yup."

"What else did Luke say to Clair—when they were fighting about the vet?"

"That she's waiting for something."

"What's she waiting for?"

"Don't know."

"And what do he say?"

"That he's scared."

"Of what?"

"Of walking up the beach."

"Since the shooting?"

"Yup."

"Do you think he is?"

"Daddy's not scared of nothing."

Missy laid her partially emptied cup on the dresser, reaching for Hannah's. "Everybody's scared of something, Hannie," she said, leaning over and blowing out the lamp. "Only difference is, some people knows what they're scared of, and some don't. I'd say Luke's one of them that knows exactly what he's scared of, and I'd say Clair's one of them that don't."

"I'm scared of thunder," said Hannah, sinking beneath the blankets.

"And I'm scared of lightning," whispered Missy into her ear, making it all shivery.

"Is this how you and Mommy slept?" asked Hannah, after her aunt had tucked around the curve of her back.

"Uh-huh."

"Did you turn in to her back—or did she turn in to yours?"

"She turned in to mine. She used to say my hair felt like bird's feathers."

"Bird's feathers!"

"Beneath her cheek."

"Let me feel," said Hannah. Reaching beneath her head for a fistful of her aunt's hair, she pulled it across her pillow as had her mother when she was just a girl.

CHAPTER FOURTEEN

T HE FOLLOWING MORNING HANNAH AWAKENED with the robins, shifting wide-eyed on her pillow, waiting for her aunt to stir. Missy had turned from her during the night, and was curled onto her other side, facing the window.

Inching her head off her pillow, Hannah leaned over and whispered, "Are you awake?"

"Ummm."

"Are we getting up?"

"In a bit."

"Is Uncle Sim gone?"

"Ummm. Ooh, Hannie, I don't feel good in the mornings."

"Why don't I go stoke the fire?"

"Don't burn yourself, then."

Scrambling out of bed, Hannah pulled on her clothes from the night before and, hopping onto the bannister, swooshed down the railing, landing off balance and staggering against the stairwell wall.

"Hannah?"

"I'm just going to stoke the fire." Shoving in a junk of wood, she pulled the kettle forward, humming a little, as her mother sometimes did when she was making breakfast, and pulled open the curtains, letting in the morning sun. She found a knife in the drawer and cut off a slice of bread.

"Hannah?"

"Be up in a second."

Pouring some milk into a cup of tea, she then stirred in some sugar, and rescued the toast before it was too badly burnt. Lapping on lots of butter, she laid it on a tray, along with the cup of tea, and crept up over the stairs, proudly bearing it before her aunt.

"Ohh, Hannie," said Missy, as she shoved herself up on her pillow. "You're such a good girl."

Hannah stood back, beaming. "Now, I'm going to get mine. You can rest some more, if you wants," and swooshing once more down the bannister, this time landing on her feet. She hacked off another slice of bread and poured another cup of tea. It was going to be a grand day, after all, especially with the uncle gone and no one to watch and grumble as she took care of Missy. And after breakfast, perhaps they'd wander about the thicket, scrape some fairy butter and find a good spiderweb to lay their handkerchiefs on come evening. And perhaps tomorrow she could stay again, seeing's how she was being more help than hindrance. Frankie was right; Aunt Missy really did need more fresh air and walking, and in no time at all, she mused, wolfing down the last of her burnt toast, the dark would leave her aunt's eyes, and her cheeks would be pink again from the sun.

It was close to mid-afternoon when Missy came down over the stairs. Her cheeks weren't so pale, but the pained look still pinched her mouth, and her hair looked so much darker, tied back as it was in its tight ponytail.

"You want more tea?" asked Hannah, watching her anxiously.

She nodded, then took the uncle's seat at the table, looking out the window. "It's a nice day," she said simply.

"You want to go for a walk?"

She shook her head and, rising, began pacing the kitchen and looking as if she didn't know what to be doing with herself.

"It'll be good to go for a walk," coaxed Hannah.

Missy sighed, walking briskly to the door, opening it.

"If it wouldn't for their tutting tongues, I might," she said, peering out through. Then, pressing the door shut, she marched over to where Hannah stood pouring her tea. "But the last thing I needs to hear on this day is their tutting. Lord, they thinks I can't hear them, but I hears them—even when I'm not listening, I hears them."

"Let's go down in the thicket then. No one can see us there."

"You're forgetting something," said Missy, sitting on the uncle's chair. "You got to go home today."

Hannah stepped away from the stove as if she'd been burnt. "But—Uncle Sim said—"

"I knows what Uncle Sim said," exclaimed Missy. She laid her cup on the table, beckoning Hannah towards her. "It's—just that I'm sick, and there are—things I have to do."

"I'll help you," cried Hannah, "I been helping all morning, haven't I? You said I was a good girl. I've not been a bad girl, have I?"

"Come here, Hannie," said Missy, holding out her arms, and when Hannah shuffled hesitantly towards her, she leaned forward, pulling her close.

"You couldn't ever be bad," she whispered, "not ever. Not even if it's a bad thing you've done, that's all it is—a bad thing. That don't make you bad. You listening, Hannie?

You're a good girl, the best." And pulling away, she peered into Hannah's eyes. "Tell you what," she exclaimed, the pallor of her face belying her sudden enthusiasm, "I'm going to take you to a secret place—a real secret place. You thought I was making it up yesterday, didn't you? Well, I wasn't, and this evening, if you promise never, never, ever to tell—not ever—I'll take you there."

Hannah nodded. "I won't tell."

"But you must promise not to be afraid," said Missy. "Do you promise—even though it'll be dark? It won't be like last night," she warned as Hannah shook her head. "We'll be walking a lot farther—and it'll get a lot darker. You sure you won't get scared?"

Hannah shook her head vigorously, basking in the sun's brightness against the windows.

"Then we'll leave soon as it gets dark," said Missy. "Be sure to dress warm, and Hannie—" she leaned back, staring fixedly into Hannah's eyes "—you're never to tell!" she whispered strongly.

"I won't."

"Not ever!"

"Not ever!"

Evening came. And after a supper of bread and cheese and cold meat, Missy tied a dark bandanna around her hair and, gathering jackets and boots and bundling some other things together, they dressed and went outside. The blue-bells rustled with a sudden breeze. Tightening her bundle more securely beneath her sweater, Missy took Hannah's hand and, checking the lamplit windows, hurriedly retraced her steps from the night before down over the backyard, through the gate and onto the path leading through the thicket. They spoke little, for there is a silence in the forest at night, no different from that of a darkened bedroom; and unlike the night before when Missy had been full of assurances and content to dawdle along the pathways and visit the little brook, tonight she stole like a thief through the dark-covered path, skirting the brook and keeping out of the way of the full moon as she half-crept, half-slid down the side of the embankment, Hannah tight to her heels. The moon tucked behind cloud and the dark was smouldering as they began their trek alongside the river.

"Careful," Missy cautioned as Hannah tripped on something, nearly slipping into the river, "and, Hannie, we can't talk now, not till we're out on the beach on the other side of the wharf, because there's always people out and about—that's why we're going down the gorge to the shore; nobody walks down here much at night. Careful," she urged as Hannah tripped again in the tangled grass hedging the path, and then again and again as she hurried to keep step with her aunt. Twice they crouched amongst the bushes as voices no more than twenty feet away rang through the night, and once they shrieked with fright as a weasel or a lynx darted across their path, slipping into the river. When finally they came onto the beach, their step brightened once more by the glorious full moon and the sea lapping softly upon shore, Hannah almost sobbed with relief. But holding tight to her pounding heart and her earlier pledge not to be scared, she kept her quiet and watched as her aunt checked carefully up over the road, then beckoned her to follow as she darted across the wharf, ducking down its other side. Crouching for a moment in its shadow, and neither seeing nor hearing anything, she rose, gathering her bundle more securely to her side and started down the shore. The lights from the houses quickly receded behind the growing hills, making brighter the moon lighting the beach and turning greyish white the pieces of driftwood vomited up by the sea, reminding Hannah of the ribs of her father's ancient boats.

"Would that I was a fish," Missy sighed once they were clear of the houses, and a school of mackerel fluttered to the top of the water, the tips of their fins and tails flicking silver in the moonlight.

"That's what Daddy says."

"That he was a fish?"

"Yup—a caplin. Moseying by hisself and not running aground like when they swims in schools."

"Sounds like I'd like your daddy," said Missy, checking over her shoulder.

"How come you never comes visit, then?"

"Ohh, I don't know."

"Because you're mad at Mommy?"

"Is that what she says?"

"No."

"Who says, then?"

Hannah shrugged. "I says."

Missy laughed her old fun laugh, wrapping an arm around Hannah's shoulder, hugging her as they walked. "It's the little marm, you are," she said, "and I'm glad Clair sent you, no matter what; it's been lonely all by myself, and I haven't been much fun, have I?"

"Yes you have."

"No I haven't. But tomorrow I'll be really good fun, and perhaps tomorrow evening we can scout through the thicket, hunting fairy butter; you want to do that?"

"Uh-huh."

"That's good, then," said Missy. "Not scared, are you?"

"Nope."

"It's nice here on the beach, don't you think?"

"Not too dark."

"I'll warn you now—it's dark in the cavern," said Missy.

"The cavern?"

"Not a real cavern. It's just a rock wall, shaped like a horseshoe, but it sinks in a bit like a cave, and the walls are smooth right down into the water, so it feels like a cave—and it's called Copy-Cat Cove. It's—it's spooky in there, but only till you comes around the other side, and then we're right at my secret spot. It's just a little shack that must've belonged to an old fisher or somebody once, but nobody goes there no more. It's out of sight behind a bunch of trees—nobody in the world knows it's there." Her voice trailed off.

"How come you found it?"

"I remembered it from when I was young—I found it with a bunch of others. It's a good place to go sometimes. I stays inside so much during the day that I'd die if I didn't get out at night, Hannie. And I likes it, really, being by myself, walking on the beach. And I can sleep there."

"You sleeps there?"

"Sometimes. That's what makes the uncle so worried. But I always wakes up and gets home before the fishers go out—so's they won't see me and have more to talk about."

"Are we going to sleep there tonight?"

"Sure. Tomorrow's Sunday, so the fishers won't be up as early. Nobody'll see us, and if they do—" she paused "—I won't care any more."

Hannah looked about. The water was ink black despite the moon, and she felt that same unease she felt in the thicket, as if she were venturing somewhere that she ought not to be. And things sounded louder at night, more pressing with its need to be immediately understood.

"There's the cove—just up ahead," said Missy. "Mind, there's nothing in there—just water and rocks and kelp—lots of it. And I brought a flashlight so's we can see where we're going. First, let's get inside the cove before I lights it; that way nobody can see the light and come snooping. Here, take my hand."

Catching hold of her hand, Hannah followed her aunt around the outcropping of rock, and into what appeared to be a giant mouth of black against the greater black of the hills. More eerie was a rustling, sludging sound, echoing from within its jowls.

"It's the kelp," said Missy as Hannah pulled back timidly. "See?" She flashed on the light, flicking it around the cavern walls open to the sky and its black water glistening as sprigs of kelp slithered above its surface, brushing against large rocks that dotted the narrow, broken beach skirting the base of the cavern walls. "Everything echoes in here—that's why it sounds so loud," added Missy, her voice faltering despite the sureness of her step as she inched her way before Hannah deeper into the cavern. "Listen," she said, hugging the rock wall besides her so's to keep her feet from slipping into the water, "I'll make it echo for you—Baa aaaa aaaa!"

"BAA AAAA AAAA!" the walls echoed back, and Hannah clasped her hands to her ears, shutting out the ghastly sounds reverberating madly in return.

"Aunt Missy—"

"Ohh, don't be scared, silly," said Missy, laughing. "Go on, you try it." But there was a timidness to her laugh, and a falsity of tone that sounded to Hannah like her mother's whenever Brother had gas and she was trying to cajole him into sleep. Yet despite the added fear rising within her, she felt sadness too, that her aunt needed so much to comfort her, and taking a little breath, she bleated "Baaa" into the chamber.

It barely registered back, but Missy oo'd and aahh'd so much, you'd think the cave was singing just for her. "Come on, now; we're almost halfway," she coaxed, as they crept deeper and deeper into the dark, "and once we're in the little shack, everything will be fine, because you know something, Hannie, it's a good feeling I have about bringing you here, and now that Clair's letting you come overnight, we can come back agin sometime, perhaps during the day and we can comb the beach and find lots of things. There, now, halfway," she exclaimed, and Hannah clung more tightly to her aunt's hand as she walked her around the inside of that cove whose thickened waters hissed like snakes around her feet and whose walls brayed phantom cries all around her. With relief they reached the far side, and Hannah ran out onto the beach with the moon shining bright, and the waves breaking white upon the shores.

"Do we have to go back there?" she cried out, her sense of release painful.

"It'll be morning when we do, and lots of light," said Missy, "and you'll see then that it's not scary at all. Come now, just up through here." Leading the way towards the treeline, she shoved aside some brambles and came upon a battered old door, tied shut with a piece of string.

"See—here we are." As she pulled away the loosely tied knot, the door fell open, letting out a smell of rot. "It's not very big, but comfy," she said, stepping inside, her flashlight flitting over a broken window, a pile of boughs made into a bed with blankets and a rusted oil drum, cut in half and serving as a stove. Stepping farther inside, she tossed her bag onto a rickety wooden table standing in the corner, with several candle stubs sitting in clam shells decorating its centre. Hannah spotted the flowers the second Missy did, a bouquet of Queen Anne's lace, bluebells and daisies—wild flowers that grew everywhere around the Basin. But there were some other things mixed in with it, ferns that grew deep in the woods that she'd seen way inside of Chouse sometimes, walking with her father, and a kind of berry that grew only on the barrens. And more intriguing was the piece of leather that tied them, wide enough for a hairband and hemmed with red and purple stitching.

"It's beautiful," whispered Missy, grasping the bouquet to her breasts. Her eyes swung widely around the shack, as did Hannah's, settling on the open door. Darting back, Hannah pulled it shut, staring half fearful at her aunt and the bunch of flowers.

"He—don't mean us no harm," said Missy, sitting on the makeshift bed and making room for Hannah to come sit besides her.

"Who don't?" whispered Hannah.

"I'll tell you, but you must keep your promise—you won't be scared."

"I—I'm not."

"Then listen really well," said Missy, wrapping her arm around Hannah's shoulders. "It's—it's a fairy who leaves me the flowers."

"A fairy!?"

"I seen him."

"But—how do you know he won't hurt us?"

"Because he leaves nice things."

"But fairies trick you."

"No, no, not unless you try to hurt them—or lead other people to look for them. And we've done neither. He—he's found us. I was just sitting here, not looking for anyone, and he found me. And he means no harm, I can tell."

"But—perhaps this is his house."

"No, silly; fairies don't live in houses. It's an old fisher's shack; I remembers from the time when I was young, there was nets and stuff lying about. You see? Instead of us looking for him, he's looking for us. So he don't feel no threat; just a little company is all he wants—or—" and her voice lowered whimsically "—perhaps he knows that it's me that's been needing a little company the past while. Anyhow, it's only a bit more than a week that he's been here. I think he likes it that I'm here—why else would he leave me berries and things?"

"What did he look like?"

"I just got a glimpse. He—he got curly hair, real long curly hair—in a ponytail—and it's yellow in the sunlight. And that's all I seen—just a glimpse, peeping in through the window over there. I don't think he knows I seen him."

"But what was he standing on—was he bigger than your finger?"

"Nope—not this fairy. He was as big as me."

"Then perhaps he's not a fairy—perhaps he's a banshee!"

"Don't be scared," replied the aunt as fear crept into Hannah's tone. "I've learned not to be scared—either being by myself or alone in the dark. Like your daddy says, it's all right to mosey alone sometimes. Didn't your daddy say that? Didn't he?" she coaxed, tightening her arm around Hannah's shoulders.

"There, then," she soothed as Hannah gave a little nod. "I bet he'd say that even lone fish runs aground sometimes, too; but you don't always end up in the fisher's net, either. An old bear ambles about day after day after day, doing nothing but eating and prowling. But the minute he knows he's being tracked—he changes everything he does. Well, that's like me. I'm not going to sit home, feeling scared and waiting and waiting for whatever it is I'm scared of to catch up with me. And I'm not going to be scared, either, of its waiting out there for me. Mommy said we were nothing more than walking roots, and that's what I feels like; no more than a walking root, and the most important part of me is hidden in the ground somewhere, all nice and safe and getting only what I feeds it. First, I used to think I was feeding it all bad things; but I don't think that no more. I believe I'm feeding it good stuff, too—like coming here and thinking things through. And that's why I don't get scared no more; not really, because I'm nothing more than an old root, anyhow. There now," she said with a little laugh, rocking Hannah comfortably, "you got a caplin for a father, and a root for an aunt. Poor thing, you. And you got me prattling, you do— worse than Mommy used to. Lord, she prattled so. Does Clair prattle?"

Hannah shook her head, and Missy was quiet for a minute. "I didn't think so," she said. "She could never have borne the grandmother, anyways. Lord, now there was a root that could prattle; like an old weedy vine that just went on and on and on, strangling everything it come across till it wore itself out."

Something scratched at the side of the shack and Hannah started. "Nothing, it's nothing," soothed Missy, "just the brambles, is all. It used to make me jump all the time too when I first come here. Here, lie down and get comfy. It's the nicest thing, sleeping here—feels like you're wrapped up in a wave, they sounds so loud, and you'll be asleep before you knows it." Lifting her flashlight and bundle off the table, she snuggled down, her cheek resting coolly against Hannah's. "Warm enough?"

Hannah nodded. "Were you lying here when you seen the fairy?"

Missy nodded, her hair scratching Hannah's cheek.

"Weren't you scared at all?"

"I knowed before I glimpsed him he was good."

"How did you know?"

"Same way the old bear knows he's being tracked; I felt him. But I didn't feel no fear, only safer; like he was watching over me whilst I slept."

"Do you think he's watching now?"

"Uh-huh. Not scared, are you?"

"I'm not scared."

"Good, let's go to sleep. And we'll be up in no time, walking home, and perhaps we can find some fairy butter on the way—oh, dear—"

"What?"

"Oh, nothing. Just that my stomach gets bad sometimes. Just cramps. Don't go worrying if they gets worse; they always goes away. It's just being this way, that does it—you know."

Hannah didn't know. But she knew enough about women and babies and stuff to know not to ask questions and was content for a while, to lie quietly, eyes glued to the window, more fearful than hopeful, despite the assurances she gave her aunt. One thing for a fairy to be no bigger than a finger, but tall enough to look through a window? But as was promised, she didn't know she was sleeping till she felt her aunt rising.

"Aunt Missy?"

"Shh, it's the cramps, is all. Lie back down, I goes outside for a minute."

"I'll come with you," she said, instantly awake in the darkened room.

"No, no, Hannie, I'm just going by the door."

"I don't want to stay by myself."

"Ohh, don't be silly. I already told you, there's nothing to be afraid of, else why would I come here all by myself?"

Hannah lay back down as her aunt flicked on the flashlight and, with a reassuring smile, untied the string holding the door.

"See, I won't even leave the stoop," she whispered. "It's just a bit of fresh air I needs. Keep watching the window now, in case you sees a fairy."

Hannah sat up. It didn't fit that her aunt should be talking to her about fairies, not with her sick with a pregnant belly out on the stoop, and she, Hannah, just a youngster, lying on a berth of rot in an old fisher's shack on the far side of a cavern screaming with phantoms. And for once, she wished this favoured aunt might start sounding more like her mother, and order her to leave off the foolishness of fairies and banshees, and tuck her in tightly and shush her to sleep. Thinking of her mother brought a lonelier feeling to the queerness of the night. These nights were the first she had ever slept without her mother a scant ten feet away, and when her aunt finally came back in, closing the door behind her, she lay back down with a sense of relief.

"There, that feels a bit better," said Missy, snuggling in again. "You warm enough?"

Hannah nodded, wrinkling her nose. "What's that smell?"

"Shh, I don't smell nothing."

"Is it the squawroot?"

"No, it's nothing. Go to sleep."

"But I smells squawroot."

"You smells the boughs you were sleeping on—they smells like squawroot. Now go to sleep."

Twice more Hannah drifted, only to be wakened by the sea washing upon the shore, or a gull crying out into the night. Each time she hugged more tightly against her aunt and dozed again. Then, after what felt as if she'd been sleeping for a long, long time, she awakened fully. There was a coldness around her. The aunt was gone, and with her, one of the blankets keeping them warm. She sat up, looking around the darkened shack. "Aunt Missy?"

The wind grew louder, creaking the loosely held boards of the old shack, and washing the sea noisily up over the shore. The window rattled and her eyes flew to it in terror. There was nothing, nothing, only the black of the night. Scrambling out of the makeshift bed, she felt her way to the door, pulling it free from the string tying it from the outside, and ran through the brambles and out on the moonlit beach.

It was empty. Then came a chorus of devils wailing from the cavern, and she turned wildly, hearing her aunt Missy's voice in the mad distortion of echoes. She backstepped, a frightened whimper growing in her throat. Another cry from her aunt, more urging, more pressing, and Hannah whimpered again, fear binding her feet. How she wished now for her mother and her father to come running up the shore. But only the wind answered her prayer, heaving the sea more forcefully upon the beach. She jumped to one side as it washed up over her feet, soaking them. And then she bounded for the cavern. Carefully at first, her feet slipping on the wet rocks, and then more recklessly as the echoes of her aunt's voice vanished in the roar of the sea. Scrambling over the outcropping of rocks, she rounded the mouth of the cavern and stood rooted in fear. Her aunt was there, lying crumpled on the beach, the flashlight burning steadily besides her and someone—something—half lying over her. It moved, the flashlight catching its face and a rippling of screams tore from her throat as a monstrous, mutilated creature with one eye raised its head her way.

"Aunt Missy!" she screamed.

"AUNT MISSSY AUNT MISSSY AUNT MISSY!!" the cavern screamed back, and she fell to her knees, squeezing shut her eyes against the long, thin banshee with the mangled face and hair hurtling towards her. Two bony hands clasped her shoulders and she went rigid with shock, her breath stuck with her screams in the thick of her throat. It struck her across the face, and she opened her eyes, choking and rasping.

"I'm not going to hurt you," it—he—said, his voice almost gentle. "She's sick—we'll get her inside."

Closing her eyes, she screamed again, shaking her head senselessly as the cavern screamed more loudly, wildly all around her. Still holding her shoulders, he shook her gently.

"Don't be frightened—I'm not going to hurt you. Missy's sick; we have to help her inside."

"Hannie!" Missy's voice sounded weakly. "Hannie—" and then the sound of her retching.

"Come," the creature said kindly. "I need you to carry the light." Then, letting go of her, he started back to Missy. "Hannie's fine," he said, bending over her, "she's fine. Come now, Hannie, and take the light."

Hannah hadn't moved, was staring at him, frozen. His back was to her and barely discernible in the dark as he managed to hold on to the flashlight whilst rolling Missy into his arms, her face ghostly white, her hair all messed around her face and her arms dangling like a broken doll's.

"Hannie," she whimpered, then convulsed, her knees drawing up to her stomach. Breaking free of fear, Hannah ran to her.

"I'm right here, Aunt Missy," she cried, her throat raw from screaming, "I'm right here." Taking the light he held out to her, she lit their way along the wall of the cavern, holding on to one of the hands dangling lifelessly besides her.

"Everything's going to be fine," he reassured her, and she followed, her insides quaking with a fear she'd never known, despite the softness of his voice as he coaxed her along besides him outside the cavern and onto the beach. Once there he quickly knelt as Missy started retching again, and Hannah turned from the sight of her being so sick, and yet wanting to drag her away from this hideous thing from the cave, believing sorely that it was he and the cave itself responsible for the sickness. She stole a glance at him but saw only the unscarred cheek, his one drooping eye and a thin-lipped smile.

"Can we go get Mommy?" she cried out.

The drooping eye raised itself onto her. "She's been sick for a while now. She's getting better. Best if you lie down with her and help her sleep. By morning, she'll be good as new. Go first," he said as Missy's retching subsided and he rose, still carrying her.

Clearing the branches aside, Hannah led the way to the shack, the foolish thought crossing her mind that there was no need to tie the door now, for the worst that a night could offer was squatting besides her bed, tucking in her aunt. He turned to her, speaking softly. "I think I dropped her bag.

Will you check the path near the door? Just the path, that's all. Go on."

As she stepped back outside, Hannah hesitated, fearing the night. She walked along the path, but in the dark she could see nothing, so returned to the shack. He was leaning over Missy, speaking quietly but sternly.

"It's too late for that now. You'd kill yourself as well." His voice faded as Missy caught sight of Hannah appearing in the doorway and glanced up at him worriedly.

"Come," he said, turning to Hannah. Your aunt took sick, but she's going to be fine. Come sit with her."

Hannah stepped towards her aunt, watching him as he sat back, cross-legged, on the floor. And with a gesture that spoke of a familiarity established by time, or, as in this case, germinated by the grimness of a shared moment, he brushed a lock of hair away from Missy's cheek. And when she opened her eyes to him, they were soft upon the empty socket and the ragged scar on his cheek.

Not so gracious was Hannah. Gaping wide-eyed, she looked from the scar to a silver medallion with black letter-ing etched across it, hanging from a strap of leather around his neck. Strung onto the same strap was a round stone, the size of an infant's fist, which he absent-mindedly rubbed with long, thin fingers as she shifted her glance onto his one brown eye, large and drooping, as if from the weight of its wide, flat lid. He looked no older than her father, but there was a settling around the corners of his mouth, puckering it down, as if time had rested heavily there. He smiled, as if used to such scrutiny as hers, and patiently allowed for it.

"When I'm not woke so early, I usually do like this," he said, a faint lilt of foreignness softening further his words, and taking hold of a printed scarf looped around his neck, he hauled it up as a band around his forehead and covered the scarred socket. Untying a piece of rawhide from around his wrist, he flattened back his unruly hair, and grasping a fistful, secured it into a grizzled ponytail.

"Is he the fairy?" whispered Hannie to Missy.

"Ohh, Hannie—"

"My name's Gideon, and I'm nobody special, I fear."

"Pity then, if that scar was for nothing," said Missy, reaching out a finger as if to trace the ravaged cheek. The exertion proved too much and she let her arm fall to her side, her mouth quivering as if she might cry—or smile. "Where do you come from?"

"The Labrador, mostly. I've been camping by a pond just up over the hill. I'm looking to meet an old friend—but first, I just wanted to camp out for a bit. Then I saw you and—" he inhaled deeply "—I thought you'd feel safer knowing there was someone about. So I've stayed a little longer than I intended."

"You're very kind."

He smiled. "I know when it's more loneliness than solitude a person's feeling. Lie with her," he said to Hannah as Missy's eyes lids began to weigh heavy. "It'll help keep her warm. I'll be outside the door if she gets sick again."

"Please—take a blanket," said Missy as he rose.

"I have one. Rest now." And the door closed behind him. Crawling in besides Missy, Hannah scarcely had time to pull the blanket around her shoulders before she felt her aunt's breathing deepening on her nape.

"He's nice, isn't he, Hannie?" she murmured, almost in sleep.

Hannah nodded, saying nothing, her eyes fastened to the window. Missy's body tightened behind her and it felt as if

she might get sick again. But she turned towards the wall,
bringing her knees up to her stomach, and became calm
again. Several times during the rest of the night Hannah was
wakened by her aunt's dry retching, but each time Missy
soothed her back to sleep, assuring her that all would be fine
by morning—it was just being this way that made her sick,
and she would soon be over it.

Finally, morning came. Hannah awakened, smelling
smoke. Glancing around the empty shack, she bolted
outside and through the brambles. Missy was sitting on a
log besides a fire Gideon was feeding, a steaming cup of tea
held between her hands. They looked kindred for a second,
and far from the world in which they sat, he with his grizzly
fair hair springing out in disarray around his head, and her
hair, half freed as well from her ponytail like a cloud around
her tiny, wan face. She wore a blanket, wrapped shawl-like
around her shoulders. With his white shirt hung far down
over his trousers, he stood over her, fanning with his hands
a gust of smoke spiralling around her face, as she reached
towards him, waving back the same. When they heard the
rocks crunch beneath Hannah's feet, they turned to her, and
Hannah noticed the same touch of sadness that so comfortably puckered the corners of his mouth now nestling around
hers.

No picture could have been more unsettling. This aunt
had been alone, pacing the floor of her room, bemoaning the
fate fallen upon her, but she had found comfort in Hannah. It
was Hannah she sat besides, listening to the wanderings of
the brook, and Hannah who took the midnight trek along a
moonlit beach in search of a place she could feel safe. Then
he appeared, like Jonah out of the mouth of the whale,
holding her soul. He had walked tall out of that cavity, his

step sure upon the rocks protruding from the cavern's mouth. And now it was to him she looked—she, whose ankles were still mired in the kelp strangling the cove's waters.

"Come, Hannie," she said, holding out her hand. "We'll have tea before we leaves."

"Won't the fishers be up soon?" asked Hannah, dragging her step.

"We've time—it's Sunday, remember?"

"A spoonful?" asked he.

She slewed her eyes towards him, his bony fingers slow as he measured the sweet molasses into a cup of black tea. Crouching besides her aunt, she accepted the cup.

"Her name's Hannah, but I calls her Hannie," said Missy, finger-combing a lock of hair off Hannah's cheek.

"That's a strong name, Hannah," said Gideon. "I like Hannie, too. It's soft and easy to the tongue. What name will your child carry?" he asked, turning to Missy, his brown eye drooping onto the blanket concealing her belly.

Missy's eyes startled onto his face as he brought forth this thing that had thus far remained a sinful deed. And slowly shaking her head, she slouched forward, her arms instinctively wrapping around what was now a child in want of a name.

"It's a merry-begot," exclaimed Hannah, in a desperate urge to push the thing back in, then cringed as her aunt's cheeks suffused with colour.

"I've always wished to be that," said Gideon, busying himself with feeding the fire, "and to carry the charm of such a night."

Hannah chanced a sideways glance at her aunt, but the words were already sliding from her tongue. "What's a merry-begot?"

"Lord, Hannie—!"

"See that?" cut in Gideon, directing her attention towards a slender, transparent-winged dragonfly as it flew before them and lit upon a pool of still water. "See it? Would you think that just last night, that was a grey slug, living under the water, eating fly spit? And now look at it—it floated to surface this morning and became that—a blue damsel. See the blue in its wings?" he asked, his words so lilting it sounded as though he were singing. "In the moonlight, fluttering merrily over the meadows, it's even bluer. And then—" he sat back on his haunches, peering keenly at Hannah over the fire "—it meets up with another damsel, a boy damsel, and they touch in a certain way—and—" PUFF!! Flames shot up from the fire with a rattling hiss, sending Hannah and Missy drawing back in fright and turning wide-eyed onto Gideon as he whispered, "Another damsel is begotten. And that, Hannie, is how a merry-begot is gotten."

"How'd you do that?" Hannah demanded.

"Do what?"

"You knows—with the fire."

"I only have one eye, you know," he said, pouring more tea, "and it was busy seeing how pretty your aunt would look dancing around the meadow." The orange danced brightly off his eye as he turned it onto Missy. "This merry-begot must have the prettiest name. What do you think?" he asked, flashing the queerily lit eye onto Hannah.

"I think you're strange," accused Hannah.

"Hannah!" exclaimed Missy.

"Most people thinks that—when they first see me," said Gideon, touching his scarred cheek. "But they gets used to it."

"Don't it bother you?" asked Missy. "That other people stares so, I mean."

"Nay, not once I got past seeing it myself."

"Daddy seen a boy shoot his eye out once," offered Hannah. "It was up here somewhere on the beach, and he haven't been back up since." She paused, not having noticed the calm of Gideon's face till she watched it ebb away; but then he balanced forward on his toes, leaning closer to the fire, so's only his scarred side showed.

"What's your daddy's name?" he asked.

"His name is Luke Osmond. Lynn says he's too scared to come back up the shore ever since, but Daddy's not scared of nothing. He says some things is a man's own damn business."

"Shh, Hannie," cautioned Missy, and then began to rise, the blanket sipping from her shoulder. "It's time we left. Hannie, will you go get my things?"

"I'll walk you around the cavern," offered Gideon after Hannah had come back out with the bundle and flashlight, and the bouquet of flowers crushed amongst them.

"Ooh," exclaimed Missy, lifting out the flowers. And as he dampened the fire with sand and rock, she pressed them against her breasts, trying to straighten them. The cavern didn't look so scary in the light of morning, but even with the sun rising and the gulls and snipes calling out hungrily over breakfast, shadows loomed in that place. And too, the endless shifting of kelp and the braying of the walls sounded as ill-boding as it had the night before.

"You might come to supper—at our house," said Missy to Gideon as they came out of the cavern on the far side.

He gazed at her for a second, then draping his hands into the baggy pockets of his trousers, looked back over the kelp-choked waters of the cove. "There's reasons why we travel in the dark," he said quietly. "I need to sit in this place for a while longer. I would hope no one hears of me just yet."

"We won't tell. Will we, Hannah?"

Hannah shook her head, edging away from the cavern.

"Hannie," said Gideon, untying the rawhide around his neck, "the people I lived with down on the Labrador give gifts to show their friendship." Removing the rock from the rawhide, he held the medallion towards her. She hesitated, lured by its strange etchings. Then, bowing her head, she allowed him to tie it around her neck, the rawhide cool against her skin, the medallion heavy around her neck. Lifting it, she stared at the etchings.

"It says it will protect you," said Gideon. "For now, it might be best to wear it inside your sweater."

Fingering it curiously, she dropped it inside her sweater, and offered him a bit of a smile. Yet it was with a sense of pride that she walked along besides her aunt, feeling the adornment sliding cooly across her chest.

She looked back many times as her aunt led her along the beach. Each time, he was crouched by the mouth of the cavern, watching after them.

CHAPTER FIFTEEN

WITHIN A SHORT TIME THEY WERE STRIKING across the wharf towards the far side of the beach. The houses were quiet this early morning, and aside from an old tom scooting along the beach and the gulls and the wind forever rustling the air around them, they were left alone during the rest of the trek up the gorge and through the thicket. The same quiet had fallen upon both Hannah and her aunt, and a comfort it was as opposed to the brooding nature of last evening. And each time Hannah snuck a glance towards her aunt, she couldn't help feeling the glow from the flush on her cheeks, despite the pallor that hung upon her face.

Missy begged off for a nap after they arrived home, leaving Hannah with strict instructions to stay put and not bother lighting the fire. "Hannie, you won't say nothing, will you?" she asked, halfways up the stairs.

"I won't," promised Hannah, her hand upon the medallion. "Are you sending me home today?"

"Tomorrow. Frankie said Clair would be coming for you tomorrow." She flashed her smile of old, and vanished up over the stairs.

It was towards late in the afternoon when the uncle arrived home with his bucksaw, an assortment of work clothes, a brace of skinned rabbits and some tools. Arising from a long nap, Missy cut up and fried one of the rabbits for supper, and then paced the kitchen restlessly after she had washed the dishes and cleaned the table. Hannah sat waiting to be signalled to slip into a sweater and out the door and wander off down over the yard again, and through the thicket. But there was such discontent within her aunt's pacing this evening that she felt that nothing, not even another trek along the beach and around the cavern to her secret spot, could curb such restlessness. It was her mother again, battling the waters of Chouse.

The uncle watched too as Missy brushed down the curtains with her hands, complaining of the dust, and running a cloth across the bin each time she passed it. Yet he said nothing, sitting there as he was with his cap forever pulled across the ridge of his brow, and his pipe sending clouds of smoke towering above him. Come late, he lit the lamp and sat back again, watching her from beneath the overhang of his brows, his face so furrowed with brooding it could hold a day's rain.

"I'm not going nowhere," she snapped at him once when it looked as if he might speak, and tossing a disgruntled look Hannah's way as if she, too, might be the source of her idleness, she hauled the kettle onto the front top of the stove and began heaping spoonfuls of cocoa into a cup. Making one for each of them, and with a final scowl at the uncle, she headed for the stairwell.

Once they were into their nightdresses and propped upon their pillows, she calmed a little, sipping her cocoa. Still, she wanted no chatter on this evening. And when finally they went to sleep, the blankets were twisted and turned into knots around both of them, so uncomfortable and long did they lie, waiting for sleep.

It was scarcely dawn when Hannah was startled awake. She sat up as Missy began thrashing wildly, singing out, "The bluebells, the bluebells. Stop them—ohh, stop!" And then she was sitting upright, her eyes staring into Hannah's with fright.

"Are you going to die?" cried Hannah.

"I was dreaming," she gasped, staring wide-eyed around the room.

"The bluebells were ringing?"

"Yes—no—I was just dreaming."

"But somebody dies when they rings—"

"I was *dreaming*, Hannie!"

"But I heard them too."

"Hush now, silly, it's the wind—listen." And they listened to the wind, always the wind, rustling the grass, bushes, trees and no doubt the bluebells sleeping way down beneath their bedroom window. They lay back, sleeping fitfully, their ears pinned awake.

Morning found Hannah sitting moodily at the table, toying with a pencil and scribbler as her aunt veered betwixt anxious looks at the uncle and absent, dreamy looks at the mop, broom or dusting rag she held in her hands.

"You'd think I was a cripple the way you been doing for me this morning," Sim grumbled once as she poured him his third cup of tea and straightened his shirt collar for the fourth or fifth time.

"You've not been looking well."

"You've always been saying that."

"Ohh, you're such a grump," she sighed, smacking the peak of his cap. "Wonder how it would sound if you should laugh. Hey, Hannie?"

Hannah shrugged, as uninterested in the uncle as he was in her, and wandered outside, hoping to lure her aunt as well.

But no matter how many times she drummed on the stoop or poked her head inside the door, looking like an expectant pup, Missy pretended not to notice, pacing as she was, and making yet more tea for the uncle. And worse, that dewy look was growing stronger, as if the tea towel she kept fondling was a thing of wonder.

Dinner came around. After feeding them a good scoff of stewed beans and bread, Missy readied the few garments of clothes Hannah had brought with her, and laid the bag on the table for when it was time to go. Bidding Hannah to stay put, she darted up the stairs, and when next she emerged, both the uncle and Hannah gaped at the hair released from its ponytail and brushed to a sheen around her shoulders, and a sky blue dress that bared her arms from the elbows down and pleated nicely around her swollen belly.

"Get ready, it's time to go," she said, bustling forward as Hannah reached out, fingering the cotton of her dress.

"Where you going?" asked the uncle, as she slipped her feet into a pair of shoes.

"Walking Hannah down to meet Clair. Got your boots on, Hannie?"

"You don't know yet that she's here," said the uncle.

"There's a boat docking. I seen it from the window. It'd be her."

"You've no need to go—I'll walk her," said the uncle, shoving back his chair.

"She's big enough to walk herself, come to that," chided Missy. "Besides, I'm capable of taking a walk—it's birthing I'll soon be doing, not dying, and given there's going to be a youngster bawling out in these rooms soon enough, it's time everyone around here learned that. Come, Hannah." And taking Hannah's bag off the table, she marched out the door, her step fraught with purpose.

"But you don't go out during the day," Hannah called out, scurrying after her.

"It's a nice day to start, don't you think?" she answered, her tone almost gay. And indeed it was, thought Hannah, liking this new vigour and breaking into a skip besides her aunt. The morning breeze had risen with the sun, adding lustre to the brightness of the day, and perking the steps of the youngsters darting about the road, shrieking to one another, or giving chase to a cat or dog prowling underfoot. Owing to Sunday, there was no one about on the wharf, only the boat Missy had seen from her room window, just putting ashore.

"My, you're out and at it today," called out Alma from her stoop as they walked by.

Missy waved, returning some such civility, her hair shining like gold in the noonday sun and giving vent to a dream within Hannah that her own dark locks might grow and ripple down her back and perhaps shine like coal beneath a miner's lamp someday. The wind gusted harder as they neared the wharf, and upon seeing Clair climbing up the ladder from her uncle Nate's boat, Missy halted her step, turning to Hannah.

"You're getting to be a big girl, Hannie," she said quietly, "and someday, no matter what happens with Clair and me, you can come visit me on your own, no matter what anybody says. You remember that."

"I'll come, Aunt Missy—"

"And I want you to run off now, after Clair gets here, because I'd like to have a few words with her—alone. So, mind you does that?"

"I will."

"And don't go running back, no matter what you hears, all right? And Hannie," she said, "do you remember what Gideon said—about a name being strong? Well, it's whoever's wearing the name that makes it strong, and if my baby's a girl, I'm going to call her Hannah, after you, because you're the strongest little woman I know." As Hannah clasped her arms around her aunt's neck, Missy exclaimed, "Ohh, listen now, promise you'll say nothing of Gideon?"

"I promise."

"Swear," she said, pulling Hannah's arms from around her neck, "for Clair might think bad things about him and not let you come back again."

"I'll never tell," Hannah whispered fiercely.

"And you're not to let anyone see the medallion."

"Not even Daddy."

"Because it's a friendship token, and it holds a power, friendship tokens do, so mind you never tattles, because tattling is the worst."

"I won't ever tattle, I promise."

"And don't worry none about me and Clair; everything's going to be fine—someday. All right? All right," she whispered as Hannah nodded, and taking hold of her hand, she led her towards Clair climbing onto the wharf.

"You look so well," Clair called out, slightly breathless as she ran towards them, her own dark curls escaping from her scarf and dancing around her face in the breeze. Perhaps because her mother looked so dear at that moment, smiling as she hurried towards them, a surge of affection broadened Hannah's heart. And she might've skipped to meet her, surprising them both with the abandon of a huge hug, had not the tightening of her aunt's hand held her back. "Was she good, Missy?" Clair asked, smoothing a lock of hair behind Hannah's ear.

Missy nodded. "A blessing. Thank you, Clair, for sending her."

"Can I come back agin, Mommy?"

"Let's get you home, first. Daddy's off from the camps for a week and he's got the canvas worn off the floor with missing you. And besides," she added, cocking her head towards Missy, "perhaps now Aunt Missy might come visit us. What do you say, Missy, will you come—just for a few days? Luke's longing to meet his girl's favourite aunt."

"Ooh, will you, Aunt Missy?"

"I just might," said Missy, patting Hannah's behind, urging her towards the boat, "if some people we know were to keep their promises." And Hannah skipped ahead with delight, hopping around a grunt as her aunt said laughingly to her mother, "She reminds me of myself, always impatient and hopping." Then the smile left Missy's face, and Hannah's skip faltered as she saw it replaced with the same air of certitude that had accosted the uncle minutes before leaving the house.

"But first, I'm inviting you back to the house with me, Clair—to take tea with me and the uncle."

Clair hesitated. "You know I won't," she then said. "But that's not to do with you—I want you to come home with me, Missy—just for a few days; meet Luke and—and the baby—"

"His life is mine; scorn him and you scorn me," said Missy. "Is it such a monster who cared for me all these years?" she asked as Clair stared at her in silence.

Clair's lip curled contemptuously. "He cared for hisself."

"No more than you," whispered Missy. "You never come back. And now you offer your own youngster as a bribe—as

Mother done with me. I wasn't so young that I didn't know," she added at Clair's look of astonishment. "Every youngster knows when its banished by its mother."

"Oh, no, Missy, she—she wasn't herself—she was sick."

"She was dead—at least to me," said Missy, her face paling as she stood facing down this older sister, their privacy assumed by a grunt that Hannah had inched behind, sickened now, as a blast of wind swiped the hair back off her mother's face, and that of her aunt's, baring the starkness of old pain. "And you too, Clair," Missy said evenly, "you were both dead to me—long before Mommy lay down on a flower bed."

"What're you saying?" cried Clair.

"I'm saying I don't blame you for how things were," said Missy, her voice rising. "You were a girl like me, but don't think me bad for not paying your notion of homage to a dead woman. I hated him. I hated her. And I welcomed the door she kept shoving me out through—anything to escape those screams—"

"Missy!"

"Ooh, don't worry, Clair," said Missy with a shrill little laugh. "I counts them as a blessing, for all that. He was only screaming what we all felt. Ohh, Lord, I don't know what I hated the most, his screaming, or her shushing," she exclaimed, raising her hands to her ears, shaking her head. "Even now, the slightest sound I hears, I tries to shush it—even when it's the wind blowing—"

"Missy, stop it!"

"I won't. I won't stop it. I've things to say, Clair. I'm having a baby. And I swear to God, when it's born I hope it screams with the lungs of a hawk. I hope it shatters the font when the christening waters hits its head. I'll never shush it.

And I'll not walk in shame with it no more, either. No one talked to me as a woman. I was banished with the old and the sick, and I learned from ignorance."

"And so was I!" said Clair. "So was I banished. Ask him— go ask him that sits at our mother's table. He stole from us, he did. And he sleeps in our mother's bed. I'll never enter that house as long as he sleeps in our mother's bed."

"And me," asked Missy, "am I less of a daughter because I do?"

"No. You were young—you didn't know—"

"I did know!" she shouted. "I felt everything you felt." Her words fell quiet. "He don't sit in torment, Clair. He's just an old man, sputtering about. Anything he had, he give to me, and Lord knows, I needed it. I don't hate her now— or Daddy. And I've learned not to hate my life. And that's why I'm asking you to come sit with me. I'll come with you, then—and meet you and yours. But, first, I'm asking you— come with me, Clair; come sit with me at our mother's table—at my table."

But Clair was slowly backing away. "He brought our father shame," she whispered. "I can never bide by him that brought our daddy shame. I've never told you," she cried, "I've never told you the things he done—"

"It's not what he done that torments you, Clair; it's what Daddy done. I seen it. The day you left, I seen it. I carries it with me all the time. Only all this time I thought it was hurt, and it's not; you just said it—it's shame, or pity." Her mouth soured. "For in the end I think that's what killed him—her pity. And yours. Shun the old uncle if you wants, but at least he took me away from all that. And I don't look back pitying Daddy, either, sitting on that pew-chair and not able to get off it. You're still back there, Clair," she called out, tears running down her cheeks as her sister moved away from her, "still sitting with a dead man. And Luke's right; you're too scared to go ask what killed him."

"Luke—what do you know of what Luke thinks?" asked Clair in surprise. Her eyes fell onto Hannah who, at her aunt's words, had already risen from behind the grunt, a look of guilt on her face.

With one last passionate look at Missy, she marched towards Hannah and, taking her hand, walked with her none too gently towards the boat and Nate, who was by now standing on top of the wharf, eyes fixed on the two sisters.

Settled down in the stern, Hannah chanced a glance at her mother and sorrowed at the sight of the single tear as translucent as a drop of rain sitting on her cheek. Her aunt stood on the wharf, watching after them, sobbing freely.

Had she been older, she would've known that a life lived only once is a life unlived. And far more tormenting is its reliving as felt by her mother setting forth from the wharf, leaving behind again her younger sister watching after her, eyes like two squashed blueberries, and their house rising behind like a far-reaching tombstone, resurrecting the parting she'd made all these years ago, and forcing her to reach back and touch the woman-child who had set out so bravely, seeking her father's words over the wind. And had she not hidden her fears the bestest, this mother who had been touched by death when she was but a girl, and her sister, Missy, still running through the grass? But how best to hide fears now when it's the road already travelled, a pair of eyes reaches back to see.

As they neared the shores of Rocky Head and her father stood waving at them, it was onto the old war vet that Clair's eyes focused. Dodging up from Lower Head, he came towards the older boys, who were crouched down besides the stagehead, picking apart an old motor. Young Roddy and Marty were his only audience—as most of the elders had tired of his stories and plies for shine and were more in keeping with Prude as she prowled behind her woodpile, hollering at him to get home because there was drinking enough on their shores that they didn't need him and his devil's greed.

It was with the restlessness of a caged cat that her mother paced the floors that evening, covering and recovering the baby in his crib, and circling the table, and fixing things straight on the stove, the washstand, the bin. Her father knew. He'd already enticed her out to the woodpile, wheedling out of her snippets of the conversation that had taken place on the wharf between the two sisters. And she'd told him enough—leaving out the part about her own tattling. And now piecing together what his own senses told him, he sat at the table, sharpening the teeth to his bucksaw, and looking as troubled as her mother as he kept darting glances at her pacing. Her steps quieted as Hannah traipsed across the kitchen towards the door, buttoning her sweater.

"Where you going this hour?" she asked.

"Playing spotlight," said Hannah, touching the flashlight under her arm.

"Bit late for that, isn't it?"

"I can stay in if you wants me to," said Hannah, her hand hesitating on the doorknob.

Her mother looked at her confusedly for a second, then shook her head, brushing her away. "No, no, it's all right. Just don't be too late, that's all."

"I won't, Mommy." Glancing at her father's bowed head as he continued to apply the file to the teeth of his saw, she went out into the cool of the darkening evening. A shriek from the bank told her Lynn and the others had already started the game, and clicking on her flashlight, she walked across the patch towards her father's woodpile, past the sandstone and out onto the bank. Somebody moved over in the dark and she flicked off her light, yet made no attempt to run and hide. The weight of the medallion swinging around her neck, her aunt's sobs and her mother's tear were proving too much to heave off in a single evening and run pell-mell, wielding a flashlight at shadows in the dark. Young Roddy and Marty appeared a little farther down the bank, tossing armloads of dried slabs and birch rind onto the beach, building a fire. The old vet staggered behind them, singing drunkenly, "She had her apron wrapped around her, and I shot her for a swan."

"Lynn's it! Lynn's it!" a chorus of shrieks sounded from no more than ten feet away from her, and Hannah started, about to duck and tear into hiding, if not for the sight of her father strolling out of the house with a jug of brew swinging from his hand. Much to the astonishment of Roddy and Marty, he headed down onto the beach, sitting amongst them, the firelight glowing on his face as Roddy struck a match to the birch rind. Thoughts of Lynn vanished with the rest of the evening light, and crouching almost into the overhang of the bank, Hannah crept forward till she was a scant couple of feet from the fire, listening as her father exchanged greetings with the old vet and commended Roddy on the purity of his spirits as he took a swig from the jug Marty passed him.

"She's a fine batch," agreed Roddy. "I cooked it myself with Dad watching on, although he's not too proud of it." Taking a swig himself, he passed the jug back to Marty, coughing and spitting, "although I've done better, buddy, I've done better."

"Never mind the shine; here's what ye ought to be drinking," said the old vet, taking a sip of Luke's brew, "a mother's milk is what, a mother's milk."

"Yup, and I suppose that's why you sucks it like the tit," jeered Marty.

"No doubt," said Roddy, "and he'll be sleeping like the baby any minute now." He grinned, holding out a hand to steady the old vet as he swayed too far to the wayside. "I allows he got Les Ouncill from Lower Head sucked dry since this morning, and buddy, he had vats of it hidden away."

"Aye, I'll be leaving ye in the morning, me boys," sang the old vet. "I'll be leaving ye in the morning."

"I allows if you don't, Gram'll soon have your scalp nailed to her door," chuckled Marty.

"Gram!" groaned Roddy, turning to Luke. "Cripes, I heard ye's this morning—no more than five o'clock, was it?—and Gram out on her stoop, a bit of rain coming down, and she bawling out, 'Luukeee, Luukee, we're going to have a flood, we're going to have a flood, we'll be drowned, we'll be drowned,'" Roddy mimicked amidst much chortling, Luke's included. "And then I hears Luke scroop open his window, roaring out, 'What's going to flood, old woman, the water's not even up' and she's hollering back, 'The laakes, the laakes, Luuke, in over the hills, they're going to flood, mark my words, they're going to flood,' and then Luke's roaring back, 'Then go moor off in the punt, old woman, for gawd's sake, go moor off in the punt,'" and Roddy convulsed with the others in a proxy of laughter as Luke shook his head, grinning.

"Poor old Mother," he said, "she was bad enough when the old man was kicking." He raised his eyes to meet those of the old vet. "Course, with Joey getting killed, that didn't help her none."

The boys' laughter quieted as the moment they'd been expecting since Luke sat amongst them presented itself. Through his drunkenness the old vet, too, recognized the importance of this moment, and propping his hands onto his knees to keep himself from tottering, he sought to keep focus on Luke.

"Aye," he said thickly, "he was my boy, he was; my boy. And that's why I come here, to meet his folk; his old mother and his brother, Luke—he was always on about his old mother and his brother, Luke. Course she won't have ne'er to do with me, but I understands it, I do. I lost my own boy and it plays, it do; it plays. And perhaps it was my fault I lost him—there's those that says so—but I was no more drunk than a preacher when that boat capsized." He dropped his head, his mouth screwing up like a hungry baby's. "But I found him agin, I did, in Joey—aye, he was so gentle, so gentle. . . ." His voice trailed off, his head sagging near onto his chest.

"The last letter he wrote he was at Cassino, Italy," said Luke, "fighting the Gustav Line."

"Aye, Cassino. Not even in war can you think a hell like Cassino, b'yes. Aye, that's why we needs our comforts, we do, for it's not a mother's lap that'll give you that, not after you been in hell, no sir—not even the lap of God can bring you any rest after that—not if you finds Him out there—for the thought becomes a plague, b'yes, if you find Him in hell, for then you starts thinking—perhaps He's a part of that, too—aye, they'll hang me for saying it, but it's too sublime, too sublime. He'd have a hand in it, else it wouldn't be there, and that's when I falls down—thinking He has a hand in hell as well. A man needs his comforts, he do." His voice babbled off as he raised the shine bottle to his mouth, slobbering more of the liquid down his chest than into his mouth.

"No doubt she's a hard truth," said Luke, nodding slowly. "I figured myself, a long time ago, God was too smart for a snake."

"And it's not for figuring, it's not, when it's coming at you in all evil; bullets and gas, ripping up your buddies lying alongside you, filling your boots with their vomit. Aye, there's no time for figuring then—only for shooting it and gutting it and biting it back. And that's when you sees that it's not rot rupturing outta their guts at all, but life, my b'yes, life; redder than the morning sun. Aye, the closest I been to God is lying in me own vomit, yes sir, that's what it is then, to be in war, and it's not to be spoken, it's not, not to them who's never seen it; for how can a man tell such a thing to them that kills only what they eats?"

"Tell me," said Luke as the boys held their silence, nodding over the vet's words, "about the church on top of that mountain—"

"Satan's church," snarled the vet, his eyes fevered with a sudden heat. "A monastery; grey it was without the sun, and towering out of the smoke and fog like hell's castle and with hundreds of little black eyes searching out our every move. Aye, there was no bells sounding from her towers; the moaning of the dead is all we heard. And the bloody snipes."

"Snipes?" asked Roddy.

"Aye, snipes. I can hear them now, screeching worse than the dying over our heads. He liked them, Joey did; he'd close his eyes to their screeching and feel like he was home. And so did I—once. Now, I hates them. There's mornings they wakes me and I thinks I'm back there agin. Mind you leaves it with me, sonny," he said to Roddy, clasping more tightly the shine jug as Roddy tried passing him the brew instead. "'Tis not milk them old insides needs, my b'yes, for it's jellied, they are, and if you was to poke, your finger would go straight through, they would, aye, straight through."

"Tell me about the bombing," said Luke, "when the Americans bombed the monastery."

The vet hung his head. "It's enough I've said—enough—"

"That's when Joey got killed, wasn't it; when the American's were bombing the monastery? Evacuating men, wasn't he?" Luke persisted as the old vet nodded. "Were you with him?"

"Aye, that's what I was."

"Tell me then, how did he get this?" asked Luke, reaching inside his shirt pocket. And when he pulled out the bronze war medal with its striped ribbon and dangled it over the fire, the vet pulled back as if it were a stingray.

"Is that what he come back saying?" he roared, his mouth twisting sideways as his head reared upwards. "Be God, is that what he come back saying—it was Joey's?" His face contorted further as he leaned towards Luke, hissing, "And well it is he screeched hisself to death; well it is, for it's the devil's torment he was feeling if he come home saying such a thing; the devil's torment, and he'll not rise on judgment day, I'll grant ye that. Job Gale won't do no rising on judgment day; I'll wager me own soul on that one," and he slumped, the effort of sustaining such speech proving too much.

"It was Job's medal?" asked Luke, staring quietly at the old vet.

"'Twas hard for my boy," he whimpered, "gentle like he was. And I knowed it from the first war, I did, what it was like. That's why I tried to keep him with me, you see, that's why I tried to keep him with me, but he wouldn't listen, no he wouldn't listen. It was to him he listened—to him who was just as soft." His face soured. "I could've helped Joey, I could've, but not him—not Job Gale. He was fit for no war. War ain't no place for a thinking man! That's what I told him more than enough. War is about this—" and the old vet near tumbled as he surged forward, clenching his fists and knocking his knuckles together "—it's about listening to your bones; it's about running, shooting and diving and listening to your bones telling you when—when to run, when to shoot and when to dive. It's like land birds leaving a beach laden with bounty and flying thousands of miles over water because something in their bones tells them to. And that's what Job Gale never done—listened to his bones. Instead he kept looking up at that church and thinking about souls," he snarled, "when all he was getting back was evil. And it should've killed him, aye, it should've. And it's well he screeched his self to death, for it's Joey that paid for his thinking—and in the end it still got him, didn't it? Aye, it's a hard pillow when you sleeps with the devil."

"The last letter from Joey said he was part of Britain's Eighth Army," said Luke, his tone remaining steady despite the tensing of his mouth, "and under command of the New Zealanders—artillery division. I've since learned some things—that a corps was formed to take Monastery Hill, but it never included the Newfoundlanders. How did Joey die on that mountain if the Newfoundlanders were never there?"

"Him," said the vet, vigour growing along with the heat in his eyes. "It was him, Job, that took him there. Volunteered, he did, volunteered to go up the mountain to help evacuate the front line. We was close by, laying line; we was never supposed to go up that mountain. But not Job, sir. He was going up that mountainside, readying for the Allies to start bombing the top. 'Downhill chance, by'es,' he kept saying; 'we gets that monastery, we got a downhill chance,' the kind of stuff he was always spouting off with, and on he went, disobeying orders and joining with them crawling up the mountain with stretchers. Aye, he was the man, he was, going to win the war on his own—"

"And Joe?" cut in Luke.

"Joey. He wouldn't listen, he wouldn't. He followed Job and so I followed him—I wouldn't let him go, I wouldn't; no sir, they blamed me for drowning my boy, but I never; it was the wind that capsized that boat, and I was no more than a youngster in that wind. And that's what them men were on that mountainside, on that front line, helpless as youngsters. Not even the ones who weren't wounded could walk; that's how helpless and sickened they was." The old vet's body began to quiver. "I tell you, b'yes, it's a hard thing to see a man too emptied to walk. And that's what they were by the time we got to them. Days they were, clinging to that rock with no food, water or blankets—nothing but guns they couldn't shoot. In full view on all sides to the Jerries, they were; and every move brought a sheet of bullets cutting over their heads. Aye, half-alive, they were—and those that wouldn't wounded was too emptied to walk—we had to carry them; aye, full-grown men without a scratch, and we had to carry them, they was so emptied." His voice trailed off and his head slumped and it looked as if he were passing out, so far did he sway to the side, but then he jolted upright, as if sensing Luke about to reach out and prod him.

"They bombed us, they did," he slurred. "Our own men—bombed the monastery on top of the mountain whilst we were still there, lying on our guts, carrying men down the side. Near killed us they did, their own men. Near blasted us along with the Jerries and that damned church of a place. Oh, it's a awful thing, b'yes, to feel the earth shaking and quivering beneath you, an awful thing—"

"Joey," whispered Luke.

"Ahh, it's too much, too much—"

"Tell me," said Luke softly. "The Allies were bombing—you got caught—"

"Aye, we was supposed to be out of there—but they come early, they did, and we was caught—we was never suppose to be there, not me and Joey—"

"What did you do?"

"What'd we do? We cowered," he snarled, "like bloody animals in a bloody landslide. And we lost sight of him, Job. Aye, it took some doing, but I finally got Joey away from him. We couldn't see—smoke, dust—couldn't see nothing. And shooting coming from all sides. On our bellies we crawled, me and my boy, bit by bit, and if it wasn't for the youngsters, I would've got him down, I would've, and he'd be sitting with us tonight, aye, he'd be sitting with us tonight."

"What youngsters?" asked Luke.

The old vet's eyes flashed open, then lowered. "I'll not say more," he said, his hand shaking as he reached for the shine jug. "I'll not say more." Lifting the jug, he squinched his eyes shut and took a long, hard swallow, sputtering and choking and nearly falling to the wayside if not for Roddy's hand staying him once more.

And when finally he opened his eyes again it was to see

Luke's aflame with the same fire burning within his own as he repeated: "What youngsters?"

He might've wished then that he had fallen to the wayside and been sucked into the black hole of the drunken sleep; but, as was with Grammy Prude's prophecy, fate resides within time as life within the seed that impregnates it.

"It's not what I come here for to tell things," he moaned piteously. "We've all done things—it's not why I come here—"

"Give over, old man—what youngsters?"

"Not ours," he cried as Luke came before him, kneeling. "Italians. Hiding in the mountain—in caves they were— and the bombing drove them out." A crazy laugh spurted out of him. "I thought they was ghosts—covered with dirt and coming through the fog. But they was no ghosts. They was youngsters—five, six of them—quiet as anything and scared. I knows it was wrong, but I tried to get Joey away— to protect him. But no, no, he wouldn't leave them—he couldn't. I knows that. He was soft, too soft. It was Job's thinking that got him; I could hear it clear as if he was thinking out loud—how to save hisself—for resurrection—the bloody young fool! But he was only a boy, only a boy and he was as scared as the youngsters and he drove them back in the cave and crawled in after them. And I fell behind a rock, I did. I could've left, but I never; I couldn't leave my boy, and I'm glad I stayed, for I seen his madness, I did; I seen Job Gale's madness, the old bastard, the old bastard— may he rot in hell—"

"Stop it!" Clair's voice screamed through the night. Wrapped in a shawl, she appeared on the bank, her fist raised towards the vet, and her face greyish white. "It was to save the children!" she cried out. "Why do you call him mad? Tell me, why do you call him mad?"

The old vet had risen along with Luke at the sound of Clair's voice, and now with her standing before him and shrieking, he raised both hands, stumbling and near falling backwards, roaring as if she were the devil himself, "Get her away, get her way—for he's in her, Job Gale is—I seen it, I seen it—'Twas he that murdered them, murdered all of them."

"How?" cried Clair, stumbling along with the vet, and falling to one knee. "How did Joey die? How did he die?" she shouted, grasping hold of his pant leg and staring up at him.

"God willed it, is how, God willed it—to teach him. No man bargains with God. It was the devil that got him in the end, the devil—oh, the devil liked Job Gale, he did, and he tracked him—up here, see in the mind," he sneered down at Clair, tapping his skull with a shaking finger. "Oh yes, he must've liked him right fine, he did, to have followed him all the way here—because he knowed the vermin crawling around Job Gale's spine; he wouldn't going to allow for no cross awaiting his return—not with Joey blowed to hell behind him." Staggering forward, he threw off her hands, staring wildly down at her, the fire flashing off his zippers, making darker the holes his eyes had sunken into as he hissed, "Oh yes, I knows a man's mind, I do, I knows a man's mind—"

"Leave over, old man," Luke roared, and shoving past Roddy as he tried to stop him, he grabbed hold of the old vet's coat collar and heaved him back onto the beach rocks, falling besides him. "You tell it now, you tell it—how'd Joey die?" he snarled with such savagery that it brought forth a cry from Hannah, and in fear, she ran to her mother, grasping her from behind as her father repeated over and over again, "Tell it! Tell it!"

"It killed them," said the old vet, "every last one of them—"

"What killed them?" roared Luke.

"The grenade. Job's grenade. He throwed it in the cave."

"Why'd he throw a grenade in the cave?"

"Joey started shooting, he did; from the cave. I don't know what for—fear, perhaps, for he was mad with fear—and Job!" The old vet spat as if he had the rot of Satan on his tongue. "He throwed a grenade, he did—I seen him, fool that he was, and I tried to call out, but Joey was shooting agin and a bullet skinned the side of my head, and I seen Job with his grenade—I was going to shoot him—but I was too late—too late, for I seen it sailing through the air—into the cave—and I stood up screaming for Joey to get out, but it was too late. He killed them, Job did; he killed the youngsters and my boy. And he knowed, Job did. Soon as he seen me rise up from behind the rocks, he knowed, and 'tis music to my ears, it is, when I sleeps at night and hears his screaming—"

Hannah heard no more, for her mother had laid her head on her lap and was sobbing brokenly. Her father turned, his own face streaked with tears as he reached for Clair. Only then did he see Hannah, and a small groan escaped him as he pulled himself to his feet, then her mother and then Hannah. Nora and Beth had appeared on the bank, along with Lynn and the other youngsters who had gathered out of the dark, staring hard at the commotion taking place, and Roddy was ushering them home, whilst Marty kept soothing the old vet to say no more, no more, as Luke was leading Clair and Hannah up over the bank and towards their door. They spilled inside and Hannah watched in silence as her mother collapsed into her rocker, chewing on her fists to cease her sobbing, and her father on a chair besides her, pulling Hannah onto his lap, jiggling his foot, rocking her as he would the baby.

"How much did she hear, Luke?" cried Clair, her eyes falling onto Hannah.

"Not much, I don't think," he said, rocking her harder. "And you're not to pay attention, Hannah, you're not to pay attention, for it's a sickness that makes the old vet say things like he did. A sickening of his mind by the shine that he drinks. And you never mind what Lynn or anybody says about your grandfather Job after this. It's what your uncle Joey wrote that says the most, and he said Grandfather Job saved his life so many times he was starting to bow every time he seen him coming towards him. That's what you remembers about Grandfather Job, all right, my lovey?"

"Take her to bed, Luke," said Clair, her gaze falling onto her daughter. And putting her arms around her, she kissed her on the cheek, her lips cold, dry, scarcely moving. "You won't have bad dreams, will you?" she whispered as Hannah kissed her in return.

"No, Mommy."

"That's good," she said quietly. "Aunt Missy used to have bad dreams."

"Clair," said Luke, "Nory, Beth, they'll be sitting over there—waiting for us."

She looked to him with eyes too fatigued. "I can't talk, Luke. I can't even feel. I don't know how you can either—it was your brother that Daddy—"

"Shh," said Luke, and she bit off her words as another flood of tears swamped her eyes. "I already told you, lovey. Joey walked them foreign soils with courage, and he fought as brave as any of them. It matters nothing to me whose bullets tore at him—it was an act of war. He died with courage, that's what brings me peace. And it was Job Gale that helped him find that courage. Nothing said tonight changes that. Now I'm putting Hannah and you to bed and I'm going to go have a word with Nory and Beth. Pray Jesus the old woman slept through it. Come morning I'll take you for a boat ride. It'll give you some time. Perhaps—" He hesitated. "Clair, I told you once we ought to go to Cat Arm—" He broke off as she looked to him.

"Perhaps," she murmured. "Perhaps."

CHAPTER SIXTEEN

A S IN TIMES OF LOSS, her aunts made salads instead of the usual cooked Sunday dinner, and everyone gathered at Prude's to eat, their forks clicking on their plates as they commented quietly about the southerlies dying down, and for sure the wind would be up eastern before the day was done, bringing with it the fog, no doubt, and drizzle. And as if awaiting the boat bearing the coffin, Roddy kept looking out the window towards Cat Arm, saying what everyone must've been wondering—was Clair and Luke on their way back yet, and for sure, they must be by now, getting late as it was, and no, Prude, it's not a wind, but a breeze coming off the water, and Luke would be home before the wind hit.

As in most times of adult needs, Hannah and the younger ones went unnoticed, freed really, to roam farther afield, to brave more with one another, to curse, knowing they were paid less heed. Thus scant attention was paid to Hannah's moping around their stoops, or sitting long-faced on the bank, staring out towards Cat Arm. And even when upon traipsing into her aunt Nora's and opting to sit and rock Brother for a spell, the most she received was a caution not to drop him.

It was nearing evening when the telegram came. Luke and Clair still hadn't returned, and Hannah was lugging the baby around the patch behind Nora as she unpinned her pudding bags off the line.

"More bad news, I'm sorry to say," sighed Willamena, coming out on her stoop, holding aloft the orange-trimmed piece of paper.

"What is it now?" cried Nora.

"It's for Clair, maid, and I can't say I haven't been expecting this—but young Missy's disappeared."

"Oh my Lord," exclaimed Nora.

"What's it say?" shouted Beth, poking her head out around her door.

"Missy's disappeared," said Nora.

"Last seen standing on the wharf yesterday evening," read Willamena.

"Oh my Lord, they don't think—" Her words trailed off as she dropped the pudding bag and ran out onto the bank.

Hannah stood there for a minute, digesting this latest. Surely they didn't think Missy jumped into the water—and drowned!

No—I bet I knows where she is, she wanted to yell, running after her aunt, but Brother was beginning to wriggle in her arms, pressing the medallion hard against her chest, and with a sudden remembrance of Missy's warnings to say nothing ever, ever, about the shack and the stranger, she slowed her step, biting down on her tongue. Immediately she was struck by another thought: Missy would never spend all night and day at the shack. She'd be home before the fishers went out, so's they wouldn't talk. Unless she hadn't come home from the night before. Why hadn't she, then? She'd never leave the uncle on his own this long—especially if he was sick—no, she'd never do that. Where was she, then?

Nora's voice cut through her thoughts, singing out, "Calve, Calve," as she ran down on the beach towards where Roddy was helping Calve put his motor back together, "for God's sakes, get ready and go get Clair—we just got a message her sister is lost."

"My, my, oh my," cried Prude, hurrying onto the bank, "the wind, the wind is coming in; ye can't go to Cat Arm with the wind coming in."

"We'll take Nate's motorboat," said Calve, and he hurried with Roddy towards the boat tied on to the stagehead.

"Here, you get back here, Roddy, you get back," called out Prude, "we needs someone left behind; he might come back, the old vet might come back."

"Never mind that, Mother," said Nora, taking her mother's arm as the men were climbing aboard. "We can take care of him if he comes back."

"She's drowned; the poor thing's drowned," cried Prude, and a trickle of fear crept coldly into Hannah's stomach.

"For God's sake, Mother, don't go going on like that in front of Clair," warned Nora. "That's all she needs to hear—young Missy's gone off and drowned herself. Come on in the house; bring in Brother, Hannah—it's time for his feeding."

Hannah traipsed behind her, the cold in her belly creeping up her spine as she thought of her aunt lying in the water somewhere, crying—and yes, that was it! She'd be crying, not dead, for she could no more imagine Missy dead than she could imagine summer without sunshine. In the cavern most likely, having slipped on the kelp and broken her leg on her way home that morning—and suffering, she would be, like her uncle Calve the time he was stung so bad by hornets and he had crawled, swollen and crying, out of the woods, near dead. And now something had happened to Missy.

Turning the baby over to Nora, she walked with a quickness in her step towards home.

"Where you going?" Nora called after her.

"To find Lynn," she called back. But her path veered from Lynn's house. Absently grasping the medallion beneath her shirt, she found comfort in its round fit into her hand, and the warmth that it held against the cold sweat of her palm lent a strengthening to her step as she darted across the path, checking to make sure no one was watching, before ducking inside her house. The morning's languor had lifted, making room for work that had to be done, delighting her heart at the prospect of easing some of the grief befalling her mother by rescuing Missy from her sufferings within the cavern, for it were no longer a possibility now, that her aunt sat alone with a broken leg, awaiting rescue, but a thing of reason. And what she would do once she found her there, she never gave thought. Enough to figure the journey that would take her to her aunt.

Digging into the closet, she pulled out her warmest fall jacket, for despite the blue of the summer's sky outside, and the warmth of the breeze, she knew the cold accompanying the easterlies, and judging by the ridge of dark creasing the distant skyline, she wouldn't be long into her walk before they hit. Snatching a pair of mittens out of a cardboard box her mother had stored beneath a shelf for winter, she stuffed them into the pocket of her red-plaid coat, feeling rather proud of her thoughtfulness. Her father always said there was no such thing as bad weather, just bad clothing. Peering out the door to ensure no one was about, she darted out onto the bank and, leaping down over, qualled down and ran up along the shore.

A couple of minutes and she was around the curve of shoreline and out of sight of the houses, but still she kept running, leapfrogging over a couple of brooks, running across the beach and hugging the treeline whenever the beach became too narrow. The thought that she'd never been this far up the shore by herself crossed her mind, bringing with it a tinge of unease, but she pushed back silliness, for even with the wind almost at her back now, and a fogbank soon to follow, no doubt, it was still early evening, with the sun sparkling upon the water, and it was difficult to conjure up darkness on a shoreline softened with babbling brooks and sparkling seawater.

According to talk it was a two-hour trek up to the Basin, and with Copy-Cat Cove being an half-hour to this side, that would shorten the walk to an hour and a half—and she was already well on her way. Everything would be fine, and she was almost glad, she was, for this chance to undo some of her mother's sadness, for her mother would be proud that she had found Missy and helped her to safety. And Missy would be proud too that she hadn't told anyone of her secret place, or the stranger. Remembering the stranger, she felt a tingle of excitement as the medallion slid coolly across her chest, for it added to her adventure, this foreign object around her neck, and how nice to have something else occupying her mind aside from fairies and stuff.

Thinking about fairies caused her to glance quickly at the woods crowding the hills, but no, they didn't hold the same curiosity somehow, the fairies didn't, not after meeting the stranger with the scarred face who looked more odd than any fairy she could imagine—except for size. Fairies were no bigger than your little finger, except for banshees who were supposed to be the size of women.

Pick a healthy stride, her father had said more than once as she trekked behind him down at Chouse, and lean into it

like you might a good wind; that way you covers a fair
distance without getting winded from all them baby steps
and meandering about. And keep to the small rocks, not the
big ones, when you're walking on the beach, so's you won't
roll on one and twist your ankle.

She was walking close on half an hour, she figured, when
the wind hit. Riding a dark blue on the face of the sea, it
curled the waves forward, raising dust and twigs and
anything else of like that was strewn around the beach, and
tumbling it along as easy as it might a ball of duck's down.
Pulling on her jacket, she quickly buttoned it, abandoning
the pebbly shoreline for the larger, more cumbersome rocks
nearer the woods, and seeking what shelter the trees might
afford from the wind. A bit of ground patched with grass
extended along the treeline, making for a sort of path, allowing her to steer clear of the cumbersome larger rocks and
keep the healthy stride she had started out with. And despite
the sudden chill, the wind was more help than hindrance as
it lifted her step, buoying her along. Surely she would be
there more quickly than the hour and a half she had allotted,
and won't Aunt Missy be happy, she thought, when she looks
up and sees her coming. And her mother too, when she got
home and found her missing, and they all come looking for
her and found her walking down the shore with Missy
leaning on her—for that would be the best thing—for Missy
to come down to Rocky Head, finally, and sit with her
mother, and meet her father and brother and Grammy
Prude. Course, it would be hard for Missy to walk with a
broken leg, but they'd manage somehow, for the first part of
the walk anyway, till she got tired; but by then, her mother
would have seen them from the boat, because she would sure
to be in the boat watching the shoreline as some of the

uncles walked. And then they'd all climb aboard the boat and her father would carry Missy into the house, because her father was strong and it would be easy for him to carry Missy; she'd seen him carry her mother up over the stairs more than once when he'd been teasing her and she was trying her best to feed Brother or do some housework and he was wont to leave her alone. She smiled, thinking back on her mother and her father. It was always hard to tell if they were playing at first, because her mother would never smile or act silly like her father, and she'd always try to get around him whenever he blocked her way coming out of her room, or down the stairs, or in the kitchen, even; but she had learned that her mother seldom smiled anyway, and when she was having none of her father's silly ways, she had her own means of jousting him out of the house.

She had travelled perhaps another twenty minutes when her step began to lag. Stopping for a breather, she looked back to see how far she had come and was startled to recognize nothing behind her—even the brooks had fallen behind a point of land. How dreary everything now looked with the fog drifting in over the water, gathering the grey of the evening into its folds as it banked the sun, swiping the colour from the land around her. Well, she'd tramped around in overcast skies before, and looking up towards the Basin was heartened to see a few dots of light, like far-off stars, twinkling. Another ten minutes or so and the lay of the land would conceal those twinkling lights from the Basin, but the fogbank beat even that, and within minutes, the little lights vanished in shrouds of grey, along with the path before her. But it was more over the water the fog hung, and she was still able to see a good distance ahead and behind her.

Funny how the shoreline looked so different now that she walked along it, for she had motored past here a hundred times in boat, yet nothing seemed familiar. It would be good to get to her aunt soon, and she wished she had a way of knowing the time, for it would help to know how close she was, and when, perhaps, to start calling out and letting Missy know she was coming. And she wished, too, she had thought to take some bread, for hunger pangs were making themselves felt, reminding her that aside from a couple forkfuls of salad, she hadn't really eaten much the whole day. Thinking about the salad made her feel hungrier, and before long it felt as though a giant hole was gnawing its way through her stomach. She tripped on a stick embedded in the ground, and with her hands in her pockets and nothing to brace herself, she fell flat, smacking her face onto the hard-packed ground, and bringing a stream of blood from her nose.

Ohh, Lord, was there anything as frightening as blood streaming from one's face? Pulling her mitts out of her pocket, she pressed one of them against her nose and sat back on her haunches, holding back her head as Grammy Prude would have her do, waiting for it to stop. Thankfully, it soon held, and tossing the blood-soaked mitt to one side, she used the other to wipe her face clean of any more dirt and blood, then stuffed it in her pocket, should she need it further. Keeping her head held back, she got to her feet and began walking once more, much more slowly, so's to not start it bleeding again.

Her feet were becoming cold, and a chill crept up her back. Despite the warmth of the fall jacket, her thin cotton slacks and sneakers were no match for the fog-driven easterlies. Too, light was beginning to fall now with the fog, and she still couldn't see any signs of Copy-Cat Cove. Would that be it up there—where a clump of trees nearly reached down to the waterline?

She quickened her step, emboldened by the thought of her journey's end, but no, it was nothing more than a clump of trees, beyond which was more grey, rocky beach, made more difficult to walk now as the rocks became larger and larger, giving way to boulders, some too big to even climb upon. This took some getting used to, leapfrogging, one rock at a time, and then having to walk around some, and in no time her breathing was harsh and the back of her throat dry for want of water.

Water. She wished she had taken some water. There was the brook besides the shack, she remembered, consoling herself, but she was becoming more and more tired now, and her stomach almost sick from hunger. And how fast the light was going with the fog darkening the sky. She ought to be getting close by now. She'd been walking for a long, long time, most certainly an hour, and that's how long it would take to walk in over the barrens with her father to the caribou herd—an hour. And she never became tired with her father. But then, he would take little spells along the way, pointing out tracks of rabbits or moose, and lifting her onto his shoulders over boggy areas so's to keep her feet dry and save her sneakers. Oh, how she longed for her father now, and crouching behind a boulder for a little spell, she huddled inside her coat for warmth, wishing upon wishing for the warmth of his strong arms around her, and the calm of his voice as he talked to her about caplin and stuff. Even to be in the kitchen with Brother bawling, and the rocking chair creaking as her mother tried rocking him to sleep, and he with his bottom all sore from the rash, and her burning flour on the stove so's to heal it. Even Willamena's voice would be a blessing right now, she thought, staring miserably back along shore, anything other than the wind creaking and rustling the trees, and the waves drowning out even that, sometimes. But no, she'd gone too far now to turn back. The thought of all these boulders and the long stretch of beach behind it, and with the easterlies blasting like ice into her face—no, it was too much. Easier now to keep going, because for sure she must soon be there. No fear of getting lost, as her father often said—as long as you stick to the shoreline, you'll be sure to come out somewhere; it's only in the woods that a man becomes a fool and starts walking around in circles till he drops from dizziness.

Onward then, she thought, rising. The medallion moved coldly across her chest, and she shivered. Slipping her hand beneath her blouse, she grasped hold of it, but gone was its warmth she had felt earlier today as she had walked besides her aunt Nora, carrying her brother, and gone was the sense of adventure it stirred within her. Moreover, she was beginning to feel a chafing from where the rawhide strung around her neck.

A faint spray of sea mist dampened her face from the waves surging upon shore. The sea had become quite choppy, broken with whitecaps—fairy horses, Prude called them, horses that the fairies used to steer ships to shore whenever they became lost upon the sea in stormy weather. I should hope they don't steer Mommy's boat to shore, then, she thought, as a particularly nasty wave sloused farther up over the beach than its predecessors. And in this dismally greying evening, with the cold becoming more and more numbing, the thoughts of her mother suddenly appearing in boat, calling out to her, became more and more insistent, almost a prayer inside of her. But there were no signs of anybody out on the water this evening.

Pulling the one mitt out of her pocket, she shoved her hand into it, and trying to keep the other hand in her pocket for warmth, she started leapfrogging again, much slower now, as her legs had become a little numb, and with her feet becoming quite soaked from trapped pools of water peppering her path, she could no longer feel her toes and was not sure of her footing. Then suddenly what she thought was a point of land jutting out into the sea was a cliff, studded with trees and cutting off any means of getting around it. She stood there, so shocked that she near sat down and cried. How was she to get around this? Then she saw the footpath leading through the trees, up over the darkening hillside, and her heart leaped with fear. Fairies! Had not her Grandy seen one in the woods once, late in the evening, and been led astray till he became lost? And had not her father said the woods was where men became fools and walked in circles, becoming so dizzy they walked over cliffs?

The wind pummelled her back, and the cold of her hand was becoming unbearable. There was nothing for it; she had to take the path. It was a relief, almost, to be rid of the wind, for the trees buckled all around her, buffeting her from its onslaught, and the ground was at least dry under her feet. If only it wouldn't go too far inland, she prayed; if only it would take her around to the other side of the cliff before she had time to become lost, for it was much darker here in the woods, and easy to see how one might get lost. Oh, how comforting now were thoughts of her father's fires at Chouse as he cooked the trout and boiled the slut kettle for tea. Even without milk and sugar, she would've drunk every drop at this minute, with her hands wrapped around the heat of the mug. And how tasty the trout when her father fried its skin to a crisp in pork scrunchions, and traces of wood smoke flavoured the pink flesh beneath.

The hill became steeper, and huffing and puffing, both hands out, climbing like a monkey, she grasped at underlying branches to pull herself onward, digging both feet into the dirt, shoving upward, moving farther and farther away from the roar of the sea. Her slacks snagged on a stick, and she grimaced to hear the material ripping, but never once looked down to inspect the damage. What fear had she now of her mother's wrath over a ripped pair of slacks when all of her fingernails were broken and caked with dirt, and her hands scratched and bleeding, and her hair knotted and sticking to the snot on her face and her sneakers in ruins upon her feet. In fact, the farther she climbed, the more meaningless it all became: her mother, the tear and even her aunt Missy. None of it seemed real any more, only the cold, the wet, the hunger—and the fear. And when finally the hill levelled off, beginning an immediate downward slope, she began to cry. She wasn't to become lost, after all! And surely they were in their boat by now, scouring the shoreline looking for her. And if she could only hurry, because it was all downhill now.

"Ohh, Mommy will find me," she said, her thoughts becoming entangled with her voice, "I know she will, and once she sees I'm all right, and wraps me up in a blanket and feeds me, I'll take her to Aunt Missy and she'll be so proud." Then without warning her foot reached into emptiness and suddenly with a shriek of shock, she was swooshing down a grassy incline, and coming out with wonder onto the beach again, the cliff besides her, its lee a shelter from the wind, and the sky much brighter. And looking up the shore, she wept aloud. Ohh, blessed Lord, but there was Copy-Cat Cove, only a few hundred yards away, and was that not a light she saw flickering through the woods? Ohh, sweet Christ, it was her aunt Missy after all, and she wasn't suffering inside the cavern with a broken leg, but nursing it inside the shack, all warm beneath the blankets, and nibbling, no doubt, on some berries the stranger might've left. Ohh, scarcely able to contain her pleasure, she picked herself up, running, singing out, "Aunt Missy! Aunt Missy!"

IT WAS HER DAUGHTER'S CRY as she plunged down the incline that prodded Clair onward, for she hadn't been far behind. Luke had spotted the black ridge creeping forward from the horizon, and within minutes they were stowed into the boat, her sitting midway for balance, facing him, and he hunched over the tiller, peering past her shoulder, attempting to gauge the wind's velocity as they raced full throttle up the bay from Cat Arm en route to Rocky Head. She liked it, Clair did, this urgency in racing the wind, for it suited the sense of immediacy within her to get home to Missy and tell all that she'd discovered in their old abandoned cabin.

"Won't be scared, will you, lovey?" asked Luke as the southerlies died around them, making room for the full-blown easterlies drawing closer.

"No," she answered, and strangely she wasn't, not with him rising as he was, squinting back at the approaching wind, guiding the tiller with his foot as he took them to the middle of the bay to avoid the groundswells. She watched as he flicked a stray lock of hair aside with an ease born out of recklessness in that he wasn't concerned about the coming winds, merely putt-putting along, assuming his boat's stability. Indeed, many times during the past nine years Clair wondered, along with Prude, how he hadn't plunged to his death or drowned or become lost in his faith of his habitat, for no matter what he was doing, he took his thoughts with him, moulding them to the rhythm of his swinging axe, the push and pull of his bucksaw, the keys of his accordion. And there was always a calmness about him, brought on, no doubt, by the harmonizing of his thoughts with the cadence of his deeds over the years. And now as he glanced towards her, his eyes sombre yet intent upon her face as he smiled, the indolence around the curve of his mouth was as if it held the time of the universe.

Leaning towards her, he held out his hand. "Come sit with me," he said. Gripping her hand, he guided her past the engine house and sat with his arms around her as they leaned against the stern, the wind to their backs and the sun full in their faces.

She remembered those first days. Much to Willamena's glee, even Nora and Beth took up talk when she donned a pair of men's pants and accompanied him in the woods most days, or across the bay when he went fishing at Chouse. He showed her where he stood on the cliff overlooking the patch that first moment he seen her coming around the corner of his mother's house, nearly getting trampled by a sheep, and looking taller than a doorpost, despite her shrinking at the sight of Nate lugging her suitcase inside Willamena's. And he showed her the path Roddy had taken to find him that final day of school, and how he'd followed Roddy home and watched her from the woods as she ran out the door, swooping before him, needling him for his talk with a rock, and then sat in the window with the pup to her throat, listening as Roddy repeated the story he had so painstakingly taught him. And he showed her from where he had watched her despairing besides the old, dead log the day she discovered she would be leaving Rocky Head. Once, he confessed, sitting across a campfire from her, boiling the kettle for lunch, that when the light was just so, he could sit on the cliff and see through her room window before she closed her curtains for the evening, and watch as she rocked on the edge of her bed, or just sat.

The cold spray of a breaker dampened her neck, and she cuddled to him. "Remember when you used to imagine me breaking my ankle?" she asked.

"Yup. That's what I'd imagine; you slipping on a rock and breaking both ankles and I'd find you and lift you into my arms, and carry you off into the woods and keep you in a bough-whiffen close by wherever I was cutting."

"*Both* ankles!"

He grinned. "Case you tried to get away."

"What else did you imagine?"

"Nothing else," he said with a grin, "for I'd always go to sleep with you in the whiffen, and when I woke up, it was time to go work and start thinking about you slipping down all over agin. Remember the first time I took you to Chouse?"

She remembered. "Go back in the house," he had roared, pushing the punt off from shore and springing aboard, his mother's cries assailing him from beneath the stagehead to "watch the wind, Luuke! Watch the wind." And she, Clair, had waved reassuringly back at Prude as a breeze crinkled the smooth surface of the sea, the expression of his mother's face worrying after them. "Aren't you glad I've such a place?" he had asked, swinging out his arms after he had rowed them in through the tree-covered entrance to Chouse. She'd smiled and told him of her father standing at the bottom of the snow-covered hills in Cat Arm, swinging open his arms and declaring it Eden, and how she wished she could be there again. And he touched her cheek and whispered he would take her there again someday, whenever she was wanting to go back. Later, as they stood with their fishing lines floating past them, he had leaned over, nuzzling her cheek, his attentions growing more and more persistent till finally he'd thrown his rod into the water. Lifting her into his arms, he carried her to shore, lying with her on a grassy knoll, his eyes shining through a sheen of hair as he whispered to her about the time he forgot to hook the wood sled to the horse one day whilst thinking about her, and come all the ways home out of the woods with the horse towing nothing. And how he'd walked around foolish for the rest of the day, spying on through the part in her curtains as she peeled off her stockings, readying for bed that evening, and how he then slouched on the stoop and played and played his accordion till his fingers numbed and his mind numbed. And then he'd gone to bed and thrashed and thrashed so much he drove his poor mother nuts. And his dog too went nuts because his dog used to sleep with him; and despite having a pup, Tricksy ran away that night because she didn't want to live with a lunatic no more. And if he could've, he would've ran away with his dog, because his blood was seething so furiously he couldn't rest, work or think—only mesmerize himself with pictures of her peeling off her stockings through half-parted curtains.

She listened as he talked, her eyes closed, feeling the softness of his mouth as he grazed her cheek, her brow, her throat, drinking deeply of her mouth till she became all soft and moved with him as his hands searched out her nakedness.

"Clair," he said, after they lay quietly and he had covered her with his shirt, "I've come to learn that it'll always be the same song, no matter the river. And strange as it is, I've still to hear every ditty of Chouse's, despite the years I've spent listening. I think, lovey (as he had taken to calling her), that it's himself a man has to learn about, and hard enough to do that in the noise of his own quiet—much less everybody else's. But perhaps you hear it differently—perhaps you need to be out there, somewhere—have something more—"

"A house," she replied instantly. "I want a house." She said no more, but his face wore the question she was not ready to answer right then, for who can tell how much of a life is to be taken with the re-creating of another? And if such a thing could be completed, should the river finally end its song, what could she know today of tomorrow's accord?

As if he had already known and was frightened of its coming, he pulled her tight against him, running his hands through the darkness of her hair, whispering fervently, "Someday I'll take you back to Cat Arm. For that's another thing Chouse has taught me; our pining for another time or place is a squandering of life because Eden's a place in your mind, lovey; it's a place in your mind."

Would that she had heeded his words. For unbeknownst to herself was that her father had been the crucible of her Eden. And upon approaching the cabin once they'd come ashore in Cat Arm, and she stared in dismay at the curtains, colourless and frayed to ribbons by the rain and sun, blowing lifelessly through broken panes, and the roof collapsed at places, its debris embedded into the floor with a green moss creeping over it, she felt the same coldness of death that her mother had lain upon the night her father died.

"It's dead," she whispered. "Like Mommy's flower patch." Despite the sun, she shivered as she took a step towards the rotting-down cabin and pushed aside the door half hanging on a hinge. It was shadowed and damp inside, and smelled like rot. The top bunk that had been hers and Missy's had given way and was imbedded into her parents'. Sheltered by the two walls cornering it and the roof intact overhead was the wooden table they had sat around, Missy slurping back strips of onion and whining over her father's making fun of her, and her mother chiding her father, and she, Clair, giggling into her cup and kicking her father's leg under the table as he rolled his eyes towards her in astonishment that he should be accused of such a thing as lying and teasing. And resting in a cupboard to the side of it, its door a partial protection to the weather, was the Bible her mother used to read from, its pages merged as one, the colours long since swept from the angels in the tunnel of light arcing down from the heavens.

"She used to read to us," she said softly, sensing Luke behind her. "I hardly ever heard her, so wanting was I of a doll. It sounds silly but I used to think God took Daddy because I prayed for a doll instead of listening to my prayers—" She raised her eyes to Luke, her face pale.

"That's what we all do, lovey—think about things according to ourselves," said Luke, checking to see the bench would hold up, then laying his hands on her shoulders, seating her. "Especially when everything gets changed overnight," he added, sitting besides her. "I never looked up the beach the same agin after Gid shot hisself. That's why I goes the other way—down Chouse and Salt Water Pond—because everything still feels the same down there. But that's not right, either. I thought about that—the first time I took you to Chouse—when right off you said you wanted the house built. I knowed right then and there you can't pretend everything is the same when you've been to hell and back. And I been watching you ever since fighting to get back everything that was took from you."

"You think I'm a schemer—like Uncle Sim?"

"Urchin is what I thought you were. A scared urchin— with no place to grieve. I thought if I built you a house, you'd find that place. Only you never. You keeps wanting more—and there's nothing wrong with wanting a big house and a good education, or a store to help get things. Only you can't know peace, lovey, when you've known war. And you can't get back peace till you lays it all down, because it's all part of the same thing, somehow. And I don't mean to make big of myself, Clair, for I'm no more than your father, carrying around a piece of hell as though it were separate from the other. But I've not lost sight of it, lovey, like your father did. He lost sight of his good and became caught in the other. And that's what killed him. I've not done that. For reasons I've yet to figure, hell resides in a man's heart right next to Eden. And one's as potent as the other for bringing about good. It must be. Why else would a baby robin peck its brothers to death?"

"It wouldn't do for Prude to hear such a thing, Luke," said Clair, laying her head against his chest, "but perhaps that's what religion is for, the faint of heart. And shame it is I've looked no further, either." Warming her cheek to his throat, she whispered, "Missy's right, I've always kept Daddy here—the way he used to be. I never tried to understand him. Or Missy, either." She pulled back, looking to him.

"I've not been right, have I?" she whispered hoarsely. Shaking her head as he was about to soothe her, she rose, pulling him alongside her. "It's time to go," she urged, leading him to the door. "I've got to see her. I've got to see her now, Luke."

She looked past him as he shoved them from shore, at the tree-coated hills towering green above the cove; the slope they used to slide down during those wintry evenings; their cabin as it still half stood, nestled from the wind amongst the evergreens.

"Tell me again what Joey said in his letters," she pleaded as Luke leaned over the engine house, easing back on the throttle, cutting their speed as the boat began to rise and fall with the growing swells.

"He said your father was a saint amongst men, lovey," said Luke, settling back besides her, steering around the breakers cresting white in front of them, "and that he'd squat with them who was scared in the hell they were caught in, and he'd coax them into talking about their small corners. And after a while of talking about it, he'd say 'Put it in your hearts, lads, and feed on it, for it's a blessed path your walking, no matter the hell it's taking you through.'"

"He believed it, didn't he?"

"And he made Joey—and others, too—believe it."

"Luke," she whispered, "he killed your brother."

"No, lovey. The war killed him. It killed them both."

"You don't hate him?"

He shook his head, his cheek gentle against hers. "I thinks of the guilt he carried—I loves him more. Nothing can hinder a man more than guilt and shame, and they're useless, them feelings are; useless. And you'll do well not to carry it for long, lovey, for it's a crippling weight." He paused, then rose, a heaviness settling around his shoulders as he stared off into the fog that was beginning to gather around them.

She wanted to reach out, to take his hand, bid him to sit with her again, but the same weight of mood that had taken him was now pinning her as she heard again her own voice singing out, "He stole from us, Daddy; he stole from us." How foolish it all seemed now; her bowed head the night she had looked down upon her father's; her belief that it was her and the uncle's doing that had rendered him so—that a mere act of thievery could've lowered the head of a man whose world had been bombed and strewn around him like the entrails of a gutted moose. A pebble on a growing rock slide is what her and the uncle's deeds had been. And had she but kept her shame—bowed in deference to it as her father had done his—she might've more easily have slipped her neck from its yoke once her father's self-crucifixion was made known to her. But so hidden had it become within her hatred of the uncle that it now kicked and squirmed, its roots withering from being unearthed, and the harsh light of day blinding the soul burrowing within.

"Luke!" she cried out, but the wind took her voice and she sat up farther, a little unnerved by a wave breaking over the bow. "Luke, can we go see Missy?" she cried out again as he leaned over the engine house, cutting back on the throttle.

"Not with this wind," he replied over his shoulder, spreading his legs for balance as the boat lurched and rocked beneath them. "We'll veer with the lop and slew around in Brown's Cove if we overshoots. Is that a boat?" he asked, cocking an ear to the faint putt-putt of a motor, straining to see through the ever-whitening fog. "Dammit, lovey, she's rough; but we'll soon be home—come, sit in the middle agin. Not scared, are you?"

She shook her head, a little pale, holding tight to his hand as he guided her past the engine house, the wind buffeting her back. Sitting midship end, she huddled deeper inside her coat from the dampness of the fog, and clung tightly to the seat that rocked and buckled beneath her. But Missy kept drawing her attention. It was Missy she was wanting to be with right now. And perhaps she might, she thought, as Luke steered them closer to shore and the black line of the beach appeared. The hills loomed a wall more black than green, its trees swaying to the wind as one. Soon they were bobbing like a cork up over the slate grey ground swells, and dipping quickly down their other side, chorused on all sides by the breakers peaking into foam and splashing white across their paths. "Always worse close to shore," said Luke. "See the houses—there's the houses. A little bit farther—"

No doubt the sea was rough as they put ashore, but the fog was thin and there were a few hours yet before dark. Summer squalls were as likely to blow themselves out in an hour as well as an evening, and as young Roddy called to them from shore to "run her aground, Luke," Clair was already planning on feeding and bathing Brother and Hannah as soon as she got ashore in preparation for the earliest possible leaving. Thus when Roddy had helped her out of the boat and up on the bank, and Beth ran out in greeting, informing her of Missy's disappearance, Clair, with a cry of fear, immediately tried to climb back in.

"No, lovey; you're not going," Luke had said, pulling her back.

"I'm going," she cried.

"No—I'm the one who's going," said Luke, beckoning Beth to take her, "and you'll wait here till you hears some-thing—I'll not risk it," he hollered over her cries of protests. "Enough we've Missy to worry about—not you along with her. Now you listen to me, Clair," he ordered, "Missy's fine. Hiding out somewhere, is all—you've said it yourself—she's always going off these days, hiding out. We'll find her. In a shack in the woods somewhere, most likely, enjoying the storm like I does myself a thousand times. Rod, climb aboard—Beth, take her in the house." Beckoning Roddy aboard the boat, he shoved it back out to sea, hopping aboard, ignoring her protest.

"Come now, like Luke says," coaxed Beth, catching up with her as she ran along the shoreline, calling after him. "He'll handle the boat easier without you to worry about. And Missy's shown she can look after herself. It's you we've been worrying about. Come now, in the house for tea and we haves a sensible talk before Mother wakes up—she got in such a way when the wind struck and ye weren't back yet, we had to put roots in her tea. And Hannah's sitting at Nory's rocking Brother—she'll be happy to see you safe."

Hannah. Her daughter's name drew her in another direction. She'd not felt good about leaving her this morning; not after the wretchedness she'd seen on the beach the night before.

"Go make the tea, Beth," she said to her sister-in-law. "I'll have a word with Hannah, and be right over." But Hannah wasn't sitting in the rocker at Nory's. Nor was she with Frannie at Nora's—or at Beth's. Her own house turned up empty—and aside from the box of winter's clothes half dumped onto the floor, no trace of her having been home all day. A quick word with Lynn revealed that she'd been seen ducking up the shore playing some kind of game all by herself. Frannie had also spotted her coming out of her house with her jacket on and stuffing a pair of mitts into her pockets and ducking onto the beach.

"Hannah!" Clair sang out, peering inside the stagehead and then the woodhouse. "Hannah!" Somewhere between Prude's garden and the woodpile her step faltered. Comes a moment—once providence strikes repeatedly—a heart ceases to pound from fright and prepares itself instead for this newest intruder into its already crowded chambers. She knew where Hannah had gone. Running out onto the beach, she stared up along the shore, at the dirty grey sea, foaming white up over the shore, and the fog settling damply upon the land.

"Lynn! Lynn!" she yelled at Willamena's daughter who was cornering one of Prude's chickens beneath her mother's front stoop. "Go tell Nora I'm gone after Hannah. Go on, now," she ordered, and without stalling a second more, she started running. She would find her daughter. And when she did, she would find Missy, too. She was dressed warm enough, and she took hope from knowing that Hannah, too, had taken time to wear her jacket and a pair of mitts. Perhaps she'd also worn a sweater—and stockings. Twenty minutes wasn't a long time. If she wasted not a step, she'd overtake her—pray Nora would care for Brother till she got back. And that Luke might've spotted them both by now and was already putting ashore, bringing them to safety.

But no, the fog was too thick on the water to see anything on shore. Blissfully, she could see a good distance ahead, and the light was good. If she hurried, she'd overtake her before she got to Copy-Cat Cove. God forbid if she tried to scale around the inside of the cove. With the water this high—but no, she couldn't think like that. Hannah wouldn't be stupid enough to try and scale a cove that was flooded with water. She was a smart girl, her Hannah, and her heart cried out as fear once more assailed her, sending her near racing up the beach, her feet slipping on the pebbly rocks till finally she spotted the narrow footpath up by the treeline. And there, wasn't that her child's footprint embedded in the softened

ground? Her heart quickened, and thankful for the wind
buoying her forward, she ran harder, picking her step over
the uneven ground, her eyes burning through the dampening
grey, straining for a glimpse of the red-plaid jacket, zipped
all the way up, she prayed, and with the hood tucked tight
around her throat.

"Hannah!" she shouted, cupping her mouth to the wind
as she ran, and then her ear with an urgency for her baby's
return call—for that's what she was, a baby, no more than a
baby. Her Hannah, or her offering, as Missy had called her
on the wharf yesterday.

Her heart cringed as her ear found naught but the echo
of her own voice amidst the wind and the sea and Missy's
cries all those years ago at the grandmother's graveside, for
she'd been right, Missy had; she did make an offering of her
child—and not for the first time either, but a mere three days
after her birth. Ignoring Prude's hollering that an unbap-
tized baby shouldn't be taken on the water, she'd set aboard
with the fisher Harve, Hannah bundled at her breasts. Nora
had come with her and a chill grew as she climbed atop the
wharf up the Basin and started up the hill. Quickly she
walked past her father's house, his face shadowed in the
window, and her mother's cheek imprinted upon the dirt
below. A chorus of voices sounded from the graveyard upon
the hill and could well have been the hymnals sung for her
father and her mother, so fabled was the moment. And upon
entering the graveyard she almost crumpled, so weak did her
legs become at the sight of the two sagging mounds of ground
to the far corner of the cemetery marked with a small white
cross some charitable soul had erected. She turned towards the
group of parishioners, searching frantically for Missy and
found her standing besides a fresher dug mound; the one

golden ringlet of her ponytail lending relief to the black of her dress and hat, the same as what she'd worn to their mother's funeral a mere one year ago.

"Watch yourself," cautioned Nora as Clair faltered besides her, but at that moment the congregation had parted, disclosing the uncle standing besides Missy, and her father's good wool jacket spanning his stooped shoulders. A snort sounded from Clair and it were as if the uncle heard her, for he turned ever so slightly, his back stiffening at the sight of her, and laid a hand protectively across Missy's shoulders. The parishioners stirred again and Alma, the postmistress, popped from among them, shaking her head in disbelief as she hurried towards them.

"Out on the water with the baby already—your poor old grandmother's turning in her box," Alma tsked, taking the baby from Nora and peering through the bundle of blankets. "There—the spit of her mother, she is—not that we've ever laid eyes on Luke to make a proper judgment— you're his sister, aren't you?"

"Missy," Clair called as the last amen had been said and the congregation was gathering around the uncle for their final words of comfort, "Missy."

She'd turned to Clair with surprise, her eyes wet with crying, and ran to her.

"I knew you'd come," she wept, throwing her arms around Clair's neck, her body quivering with grief.

"I've brought someone, Missy," she'd whispered, holding her tightly and leading her towards Nora's as the uncle's eyes turned their way. "Look," she urged, taking the bundle from Nora, "look at your godchild, Missy, look at her; I haven't named her yet, I'm waiting for you to name her," and she'd bent to one knee, pulling the blanket from the wee little face sleeping within. "Isn't she beautiful? She looks like you—and the same size, no doubt, as when you were small. What do you think, Missy—do you want to be her godmother?" she asked, her tone becoming more urgent as the uncle started towards them. "Here, lift her— she's so light—lift her."

"Are you coming home, Clair?" Missy had asked, staring sullenly at the baby's face.

"Silly, I'm married. I can't come back now—not to live anyways. I want you to come with me—just for awhile—I have a house; a big house, and you can have your very own room whenever you stay, please, Missy," she begged as the younger girl began backing away.

"I don't want to come," cried Missy. "I wants to stay with Uncle Sim. He's lonely now with grandmother gone. And I helps him, Clair; I does all the things he asks me to, and he tells me I'm a good girl—"

"But wait, Missy—you don't have to stay—just come for a little visit is all I'm asking."

"No! I won't go—I looks after Uncle Sim and he says I'm a good girl, Clair."

"It's not a good girl that won't come visit her sister," Clair had hissed. And Missy had shrunk from her. Casting a defiant, almost fearful look at the two sagging mounds to the far corner of the graveyard, she grasped her uncle's hand and turned with him back to the grandmother's grave. Clair's anger grew. And when her sister's golden ringlet started bobbing against her shoulders as she gave vent to a bout of sobbing that she'd never shared over their own dead mother, Clair turned, marching out of the graveyard. It wasn't till she was back down on the wharf did she think to check that Nora was behind her with the baby.

And it wasn't till now, eight years following the deed, did she falter in her step, staring unseeingly at the cold, grey Atlantic heaving itself ashore, pausing to consider that day. Small wonder her sister clung to the uncle's hand instead of hers. Small wonder her daughter forsook the safety of her home for that of another.

Had she been a hard mother, too? No. No—not a hard mother. Not a fun mother, is all. Not a fun mother. And turning from the sea, she began running again the way her daughter had gone; her step heavy, yet fuelled with the urgency of wanting more; of taking back all that she had laid on those she held most dear, and freeing them—freeing herself—for it wasn't her father she'd found in the cabin at Cat Arm, but herself, nailed to a cross that she'd thought had been his all these years. And now she had to find them; find Hannah, find Missy, and love them as fiercely in her arms as she had in her heart. A child's mitt caught her eye. Hannah's mitt. And it was bloodied. She'd fallen. She'd hurt herself. Grasping the wool mitt, she searched the ground, finding only more blood and sat down, struggling for breath. How? How had she been hurt? There was a stick across the path. Fresh ground to one end. She'd tripped, that's all. Tripped and fell. And cut herself—on a rock. The blood was fresh. She wasn't far ahead, not far at all.

"Hannah!" Bolting to her feet, she called out again and again, cupping her ear from the wind as she ran. The rocks grew larger, and shoving the mitt into her pocket, she began leapfrogging, then slowed as more and more boulders took up the beach. Nosebleed is what, she assured herself, breathing heavily as she clambered around one boulder after another. Nosebleed. She'd seen enough of those, Hannah had. And Prude had told her enough times what to do—hold back her head and nip her nose. That's why her mitt was bloodied. She'd held back her head and nipped her nose. Then thrown away her mitt.

What was this, then? She'd come to the cliff protruding into the sea, cutting off the beach. She turned wildly. But no—no she wouldn't have to tried to walk around the cliff. She was smart, her Hannah was. She wouldn't walk into icy cold water, soaking herself in a easterly wind. "Common sense," Luke said often enough as she sat fretting about Hannah's wandering away whilst he paid more attention to fishing than his daughter's rambling. "Credit the girl with common sense. She's not going to trample through the bush and lose herself when she can follow the river home."

A cry. Clair turned towards the hills. The light was falling and she scarcely saw the glimmer of a path leading up through the trees. There, she heard it again—faint and far away. "Hannah!" she screamed, and scarcely listening for a reply, tore at the bushes, dragging herself up over the path, her breathing ragged, her heart pounding. Twice her foot slipped and she fell flat to her face, and thrice a snapping alder near blinded her as it struck across her face. And whilst she cursed herself for the first time upon leaving home for not taking somebody with her, she faltered not a step in her determination to get to wherever it was this path was taking her. "Hannah!" she yelled whilst staggering to her feet as the hill levelled off, then bolted ahead, only to have her footing give way in front of her and she tumbled helplessly down the steep incline buried beneath the canopy of bushes.

Coming to her feet, she stared at the darkening stretch of beach before her, her heart sinking. Copy-Cat Cove already. She'd hoped to have overtaken her daughter by now. The cove would be flooded with the water this high. Staving off further thought, she hoisted her skirt and started running. A light. There was a light—shining through the trees. A cabin—was there a cabin? The light disappeared and she skirted the treeline, ploughing at the brambles, searching for an opening. Finding one, she plunged through and found herself before a half-opened door, and through it, Hannah's voice, and that of Missy's.

Ohh, Lord. Closing her eyes, she repeated her silent prayer of gratitude, then snapped them open. Missy was shrieking—in pain. She shoved open the door and stared wordlessly at the muddied, bloodied face of her daughter, and her fear-stricken eyes as she crouched besides a make-shift bed and Missy, lying upon it, her breathing coming hard and rapid.

"Mommy!!" Breaking into sobs, Hannah flung herself at her mother as Missy twisted and a moan escaped her lips. "Mommy, what's wrong with her, what's wrong with her?"

Wrapping her arms around her daughter, Clair kissed her repeatedly whilst stumbling with her to Missy's bedside. "Shoo, now, it's the baby coming; Aunt Missy's baby is coming," she said, striving to quieten her voice despite her own growing fear as Missy's moan turned to a cry of pain. "It's going to be fine," she soothed, grabbing hold of Missy's hand as she looked around the shack. A lit flashlight propping onto the window was giving off the only light, and although she could tell from the mess of ashes around the front of the stove that a fire had been lit, the shack was getting cold.

"Gideon!" gasped Missy, falling back, her eyes rolling with fatigue. "Gideon."

"Gideon?"

"He's up the woods, Mommy, in his bough-whiffen."

"He—he can born babies," whispered Missy.

"Then go—sing out—sing out hard," said Clair, kissing Hannah's face urgently. "Hurry, now—hurry!" And as Hannah bolted out the door, tearing through the brambles, screaming, "Giidddeeoonnnn!!!! Giidddeeooonnnnn!!!" Clair leaned over her sister. "How long, Missy—how long have the pains been coming—oh, Lord, you're almost there," she whispered in both fear and surprise as her sister's breathing deepened. As Clair folded back the blankets, her surprise gave wholly to fear as the glistening crown of the baby's head appeared between her sister's legs. "It's—I can see it—don't push, Missy—don't push—"

"I can't stop," gasped Missy, "I've been holding back, Clair—now it just does it—" and her words gave way as her breathing tightened and her body tensed. Curling back her lips, she squeezed shut her eyes and uttered a low moan, drawing her knees up to her stomach. Clair fumbled helplessly, reaching for the baby's head that was slowly easing itself outside of Missy. "It's—it's coming—oh my Lord— Shut the door! Shut the door!" she shouted as Hannah bolted back inside with a gust of wind.

"He didn't answer, Mommy."

"Bide there, child!" Clair cried out, and positioned herself closer as Missy let out a long, low moan. The bluish, bloodied head slipped out between her sister's loins—and then the rest of the infant, no bigger than the doll of her dreams, eons ago. "Mercy," she whispered, unsure of how to touch the now mewling infant.

"Clair!" cried out Missy.

"Shh, it's all right," said Clair. "It's—it's born. Ooh! Oh, Lord, it's so small!" She raised her eyes, searching frantically around the shack.

"Is it—is it all right?" cried Missy.

"Yes—yes, I think so. Hannah, go sing out agin, louder this time, louder!" But her daughter was staring transfixed at the muddle of flesh and blood between her aunt's legs.

"Hannah!" said Clair strongly, but the infant's mewling claimed her attention. The cord. She had to do something with the cord. Lifting it gingerly between her two fingers, then more firmly as it slipped from her, she then tugged on it, easily at first, then harder, harder, till another piece of Missy gushed out from within her, glistening and brown like a piece of moose liver.

"Clair!"

"That's all right, it's fine. It's fine," whispered Clair, meeting her sister's anxious eyes. But things weren't fine; they weren't fine at all—she scarcely knew what to do now, and this baby was small, really small, and the shack was cold and getting colder—"Hannah, go call!" she ordered almost angrily.

"But—he's not there, Mommy," whispered Hannah, and Clair turned, the fear in her heart resounding in her daughter's voice. She was still standing by the door, her eyes darkened further by the greyish evening light, her face wan beneath its layer of mud and blood and her eyes frozen onto the mewling creature as though it were a changeling planted by a no-good banshee who had come and gone in her wake. Along with the panic in Missy's eyes and the mewlings now growing fainter from the infant, it was this need upon her daughter's face to fashion the sickness before her into something of solace that struck Clair. She glanced around the room, her eyes quick, seeing nothing, then focused, not for the first time, on the rawhide string around Hannah's neck.

"Give me that," she commanded quietly, "and you get the fire going, Hannah. Maybe there's matches—or a spark—hurry now," she urged as her daughter pulled off the rawhide and passed it to her.

"Let—let me see," said Missy, raising her head, trying to get a glimpse of her child.

"Keep still, Missy—I've got to fix her first."

"Her?"

"Her—yes, her; it's a girl." Clair sat back, drawing a deep breath. "She's tiny," she said more calmly, "scarcely eight months. We've got to keep her warm—hurry, Hannah; that's a good girl," she coaxed, as Hannah lit a match, her tone softening and her words babbling on their own accord, easing her own nerves as well as her sister's and her daughter's. Slipping the medallion off the rawhide, she cast it aside and began wrapping the rawhide once, twice, thrice around the umbilical cord. "But she's perfect, Missy— a perfect little girl. Born a wee bit too early is all, and that's why she's blue and funny looking and not fat and pink like Brother," she added more loudly as Hannah chanced another glance over her shoulder. "There, that's the girl," she went on as a sudden flare of light burst from Hannah's fire. "A fire is the most important thing right now." Knotting the rawhide as tight as she could, she leaned over the infant, placing her mouth over its nose and mouth and sucked hard. Gagging, she turned aside and spat. A more lusty cry replaced the baby's mewling and she turned to it with as much wonder as relief.

"There you go," she said softly, lifting the baby onto Missy's belly and covering it with a blanket.

"Lord," gasped Missy, her eyes widening in fright.

"That's how they look at first," said Clair. "She'll be all pretty and pink in no time. We can leave the cord— I've nothing to cut it with—as long as it's tied tight. But you've got to start breastfeeding her—it keeps you from hemorrhaging."

"Am I hemorrhaging?"

"No, but you could start. Don't ask me how, but you must breastfeed so's it don't start. Here." Fumbling with her sister's clothing, she lifted the baby closer to her breast. "Help me, Missy."

"How?"

"Poke at her mouth—with your nipple. Just poke it—there you go," she exclaimed softly as the infant's mouth, no bigger than a freckle, opened, groping blindly. "There—it's in—is she sucking?"

"I—I think so."

"Can you feel it?"

"Yes, I can feel it. Lord, she's so small—"

"Like one of your fairies. Hannah, come see," said Clair, noting her daughter's stalled movements before the stove door. "Come," she urged as Hannah dragged her step, casting a reluctant glance at the baby. "Ooh, come here." Reaching for her daughter, Clair pulled her into her lap, cradling her head onto her shoulder, rocking her. They were quiet for some time, Clair, calming her breathing through the tangled mess of Hannah's hair, and Missy, lines of fatigue drawing her face as she gazed from the baby suckling her breast to Hannah to Clair.

"They'll find us, Clair."

Clair raised her chin to the top of Hannah's head, still rocking her. "Of course they will," she whispered. "And till they do, we're fine—as long as we keeps warm. At least we've all found each other. I swear I've died a thousand times this night," she sighed, kissing the top of Hannah's head. "Why'd you run off like that, Hannah? Why didn't you tell somebody?" urged Clair as Hannah burrowed deeper into her shoulder.

"I promised I wouldn't tell," said Hannah.

"Ooh, Hannie," sighed Missy. "It's my fault, Clair; I should never have made her promise."

"We should never have left you this morning," Clair whispered into her daughter's ear. "But I'm glad we did now, for you saved Missy's baby, you did." Cupping Hannah's chin, Clair tipped her face back and stared into the pair of dark, murky eyes. "You're a strong, wonderful girl," she whispered.

"And a cousin," said Missy, reaching out a hand and jiggling Hannah's foot. "Come on, Hannie," she coaxed as Hannah gave a sideways glance at the splotch of red no bigger than an apple suckling her breast. And when her girl grinned, her face brightening onto Missy, Clair dropped a kiss on her nose.

"There, sit besides Aunt Missy whilst I checks the fire," said Clair, shifting Hannah off her lap onto the bed. "I might have to get more wood, Missy—Hannah will stay with you—" Clair paused, bending over the stove, her eye quickening onto the door at what sounded like someone pushing through the brambles. Just as quickly Missy half rose from her pillow.

"Gideon," she cried out, and Clair drew back in alarm as the door slowly opened and a grizzled head appeared, a scarf covering his right eye and partially concealing a scarred cheek. A wild look marked the eye that took in the sight of Hannah's bloodied face and Clair's startled eyes and the babe suckling at Missy's breast. Gideon. Gid. Immediately she knew. And saw, too, the excitement tinting Missy's cheeks as she pulled the blankets off the infant for Gideon to see, and the gentleness with which he stroked a finger across

Hannah's cheek as she babbled, "I found her—I found Aunt Missy first, and then Mommy found us and she borned the baby."

"I was to the other side of the cove when my water broke," said Missy. "I come back but you were gone. I—I was frightened, but I lit a fire and waited—and prayed—but then—"

"Your sister came," finished Gideon as Missy turned to Clair, her smile growing more feeble as her bout of excitement faded.

"But first it was Hannah," said Clair, kneeling back down, cradling Hannah against her. Yet it was onto Gideon her eyes were fastened. And the look of awe he cast upon the infant as he felt along the umbilical cord with a doctor's fingers, was akin to that of Luke's the first time he had knelt besides her, gazing at Hannah, and then at Brother, telling himself that he was a father, he was a father. Murmuring words of comfort to the fretting infant, he fished into his pocket, pulling out a pocket knife. He struck a match, and drew the blade slowly and easily across the flame, his eye warming with fire, gazing onto Hannah.

"I thought I heard you sing out, but then I thought I was dreaming. But I kept waking up, puzzling whether it was a dream or not." Slicing the cord beyond the rawhide knot on the baby's belly, he said, "No doubt you've earned your namesake, and that's a far greater gift than a piece of rawhide." Wrapping the baby, he patted Missy's hand, then rose, looking to Clair. "I'll take the woods road to the Basin before it gets too dark. You'll see that the fire keeps burning. They need to be warm—real warm."

"Find Luke," said Clair, following him to the door. "He's up the Basin somewhere with his boat."

Gideon paused, then with a slight nod, stepped off the stoop and disappeared through the brambles.

"Hannah," said Clair, and giving her daughter a quick hug, she ushered her towards the door. "Go gather as much driftwood as you can—hurry now, before it's too dark. The sea's rough and it might be a while before anyone can reach us. Just gather a pile, and I'll come help bring it in," she called, leaning off the stoop as Hannah ducked through the brambles. Fixing the door in place, she turned back to Missy. There was a calmness around her sister since Gideon had come and gone, and despite her wearied look, her eyes were still bright.

"He seems nice," she said, shoving more wood into the oil drum.

"He's not the father."

"I'm not prying."

"A silly boy is the father. I never think of him. Do you think me bad, Clair?"

"Bad?" Clair heaved a sigh, staring into the fire. "I was wrong to say those things I said at the grandmother's funeral, Missy. You've never been bad." She gave a short laugh. "What's that anyway, and who's to say what bad is? Only youngsters can say what bad is. We become too guilty as we leave off them days to judge what bad is—or even what good is, for that matter."

"I've always felt bad, Clair. From the moment Daddy left, I felt bad; that it was my fault—because of my dreams."

"Ooh, Missy, you were a little girl."

"She turned from us."

"Our mother? But she was sick."

"She turned from us. She was our mother and she turned from us."

"She didn't mean to hurt you."

Missy smiled sadly. "Not just me, Clair. She left you, too."

Clair became quiet, looking at her younger sister. Closing the door to the drum, she rose, sitting besides her bedside.

"I always remember how Daddy found her," she said softly, "fallen down on a wet plank and crying from the cut in her knee. He saved her, he did, and she built everything around him. And when he left, she was just a scared little girl agin. That's how I sees it, Missy. I can't bear it any other way."

"I was scared, too. I was always scared—more so when he come back. It was only because you weren't scared of him, that you liked to sit next him and read and stuff, that I was able to come home at all. And then when you left—even with him dead—I was still scared; scared of waking at night and hearing him scream—and there's times I thought I did. And I could never go in the kitchen by myself at night to—to get a glass of water, or something; and one night I even wet the bed because I was too scared to get up in the dark."

This last was spoken in such anguish that Clair simply hung her head. "I should never have left you."

"It was Mommy who left. Not you. Not even him. I know," she added tiredly as Clair opened her mouth in protest. "I know it was because she couldn't get over him. Nor could you," she whispered, touching Clair's hand.

Clair spoke tonelessly. "I was scared, too. Scared he wouldn't come home, and that Mommy would just get sicker. And then when he did come home . . ." She paused.

"It must've been hard for you," Missy whispered, "seeing him like that. You always loved him more."

"He was a wonderful father. Don't you remember?"

"Not like you."

Clair's lips quivered. "I did love him," she whispered deeply. "And I tried so hard when he come home. But I just wanted him better. You were right; it was pity I felt. But not any more. You've given him back to me. I swear to God, you did, Missy, for I found the courage to go find him agin. And I'm glad he went. No matter what, I'm glad he went, for he was a father to all those others. And they needed him more than me. He left enough of himself inside of me for a thousand lifetimes." She became quiet, wiping the wet that had seeped into her eyes. "Can you remember nothing of them days, Missy?" she asked almost pleadingly. Missy sighed, her eyes closing tiredly.

"Yes. I do. At least, enough to feel that they were there. Perhaps I was too much for myself to feel what you felt, Clair," she added, opening her eyes and looking back at her sister. "You always felt too much. That's why you couldn't come back. I always knew that about you, even when I felt it was because I was bad."

"I was wrong," cried Clair. "I never meant any of those things I said!"

"Ohh, you were right in everything you said about the grandmother—and Uncle Sim, too. He was wrong in his ways to you, Clair; I know that. And Lord, bad as it was, it would've been worse if you hadn't gone—the way you and the uncle fought. But I can't imagine how it felt having to go off teaching like that and Mommy and Daddy both gone. You're strong-willed, Clair. You're like him. Ohh, sure, you're strong," she managed as Clair shook her head, trying to speak. "Like Daddy, you came back, didn't you? And I know it's more hurt than mad I'm feeling with Mommy. It'll go away someday, especially now," she murmured, casting her eyes down on the sleeping infant.

"Missy, I can't feel in my heart for the uncle, but I feels for you," said Clair, stroking the little hand clenched tight upon Missy's breast. "He was there for you—like Daddy was for these men. I'll—I'll try to get along. To come visit."

"He's not long left; I've seen that. And I don't want much—tea, is all."

"It'll be good to sit at our mother's table agin," said Clair as Missy's eyes closed. "And I long to hear this youngster's screams fill the rafters." She smiled as Missy's eyes opened onto her. "There, you're so tired. You sleep now, whilst I goes and checks on Hannah. Listen—I think I hears a boat already—ooh," she murmured as a tiny hole appeared on the little red face lying upon Missy's breast, and the faintest wail in the world sounded, bringing Missy's eyes onto her baby in new-found wonder. Leaving her, Clair crept outside, quietly closing the door. Pushing through the brambles, she spotted Hannah down by the water's edge calling out to her father who was still a ways off shore. It had been a long day, she thought, smiling as Hannah danced and chanted, "Over here, Daddy, over here." A long, long day. And for him too, no doubt, she thought, spotting Luke standing at the bow of the boat, and the grizzle-headed Gideon behind him. She glanced upwards. The fog was thinning and a flush of stars shone through a patch in the night sky above them. A ghoulish sound came from the mouth of the cove and she turned to it, remembering Henry's fear in the story that Roddy had spilled out. Luke's fear. "It's the strongest man who hides his fear the bestest." Her father's words came to her, and she closed her eyes, remembering him standing so tall in their boat, as Luke was now, eyes squinting from the sun as he smiled down at her. In a flash she remembered too his fright when he had steered them into the piece of pan ice, and his chastizing her mother and Missy for their talk of the dead and the bluebells. And perhaps it wasn't brave of us, Daddy, to hide our fears behind bluebells and dreams and rivers, she thought. But in the end we create our own saviours, don't we? And far more easier to imagine a fairy than He who can make the Heavens dance.

THE FEAR CAME AS HE KNEW IT WOULD. Till now it had been kept at bay by the ordeal of motoring to the Basin in the fog and sea looking for Missy. They'd just done searching the ravine and he was climbing onto the wharf when Gid appeared. It had circled his belly then, but the joy of Gid's news drove it off, beat it back like a strong wind against a bird in flight. For that's what it felt like, a bird in flight, a vulture shadowing him overhead, falling back sometimes, so's that he was scarcely aware it was there—scarcely. He always knew. Always sensed that it was hiding behind some cloud, waiting for a soft moment to come swooping over him, casting him into the darkness of its shadow. He could never trust it. From the moment he dragged Gid onto the bank of Rocky Head and met it, he could never trust. It was right after Nate had bedded Gid into the bow of his boat and was putting off to the doctor up the Basin that it showed itself. Right in front of his mother, sisters, aunts, uncles, as they stood on the bank watching after the boat, it had appeared; beating at his face with its wings, stealing his life's breath till he was gaping like a beached fish, his lungs bursting, his face reddening, and his heart beating faster and faster and faster till he thought it would burst. And then it flew off, leaving him leaning onto his frightened old mother, panting with exhaustion as his lungs slowly took back what was left him, and his heart slowed and his breathing calmed.

It tricked him at first. Watching the O'Maras pack and leave for Corner Brook during the next few days (to be near his beloved firstborn whilst he healed in the hospital, O'Mara had announced), and then going about his daily chores of chopping wood and cleaving splits and bringing water, he nearly forgot. It was whilst he stood in front of the teacher's desk, reading out a poem to the teacher, Mr. Bissel, and the rest of the school, when it came again. No different from the first time, only harder; beating at his face, taking his breath till his lungs sucked and sucked as if breathing through plastic, and his face reddened and his heart pounded like the surf upon the rocks of Copy-Cat Cove. Like the fits, they said, only not quite. Like what that fellow down Conche used to have. And he got so bad he never come out of his house for thirty years—and then it was in a box.

No fear had Luke of spending thirty years in a house. For it became a dread to be walled in, and only the woods offered him solace from the ever-threatening demon that ruled overhead; the bird of prey that took from him when it pleased, whether he was spooning back a bowl of soup before his mother and father, or chopping down a spruce in the thick of the woods with only himself as witness. Out of the two, it was the woods he chose. At least there it was only himself looking skyward to gauge when his next fit would be.

In time when he learned that his lungs would always refill, and his heart would never burst, he turned to this demon flying low, and with nothing in his hands, challenged it to attack whenever it wanted, for here, alone with the birds, the trees, the rocks, the rivers, he had begun creating a cloister that contained him in his torment. For he had shivered his way through the cold of winter's night on the downs, and learned to burrow for warmth like a dog into the very thing that threatens it. And he had seen the terror of innocence as a young caribou is mauled by a bear. And he learned not to question why pricklebacks eat their young, and weasels eat each other, and the beauty of a morning glory lies in its ability to choke the lily whilst climbing towards the sun. And it marred not the perfection of a bead of dew, clinging like a silver teardrop to the tip of a dandelion. Nor did it taint the flesh of the young caribou that he roasted after the bear had gone, and feasted upon as the sun crimsoned beyond yonder hills. One day whilst the wind rocked the trees as one, three crows flew overhead. He watched as two found shelter in the branches and one perched on the highest treetop, flapping its wings as it fought for footing, and never resting. He watched it for a while, this crow that braved the wind that forever kept him struggling. He marvelled it should continue to do so, when all others roosted more comfortably below him. And he learned, too, to brave that which threatened him.

Then she came, like a dove over the seas, bringing with her a twig from a world he'd washed asunder, and perched with it on her windowsill, taunting him to come closer, closer; stroking, caressing him with her wing till his heart pounded with a new rhythm, and his face reddened with a new dawn. Sitting on the stoop with his accordion, pleading through the rhythm of his lament that she come sit with him, he allowed not a muscle to tense as she opened the door, her sweater clutched tight around her as she slowly walked towards him. And when he shifted aside to make room for her to sit, it was with the quiet of a pond that the blood sat in his veins. For those things were within him now, the calm, the fierceness, the strength and much, much more. He had sown himself into the earth, and had grown himself an anchor that would find sanctuary in any port—except one. And that was the one he found himself before this cold fall night with just a spattering of stars above him for warmth. For it was more than his heart, his lungs, his mind even, that he had lost in this cave—and those things he had retrieved. It was his soul that he'd never fully recaptured, that was now braying out to him from the pit of this rocky cavern.

"Luke! I'll fight with you, Luke! I'm not scared! I'm not scared!" He had stood there, fear swamping him like a leaky boat as the three strangers bolted towards him. He swung around and plunged back into the water. "Run, Gid! Run! Run!"

"They're coming after you, Luke, they're coming after you!" roared Frankie. "Run! Run!" Like yesterday he felt the cold of the water freezing his legs, his feet slipping on the kelp-covered rocks, the kelp tangling around his legs, pulling him, pulling him till he felt nothing but the cold wet darkness of the cavern's water swallowing him, smothering him, its roar deafening his ears. Gagging for breath he surfaced, clawing the kelp from across his face and staring around him blindly. There was Frankie, slousing through the water behind him, holding the gun, his eyes wide with fright. Stumbling behind Frankie was Gid, flailing at the air for balance. The strangers—where were they? There they were, standing on the beach near the opening to the cove. They weren't running or chasing after them; just standing there. One of them was calling out—who to? Frankie. He was calling out to Frankie and there was caution in his tone. "Watch out! Watch out, buddy, careful with that gun!"

"Frankie, Frankie, they're not chasing us, Frankie—be careful, Frankie—the gun; don't run with the gun," and slousing back through the water, he grabbed the gun from Frankie and swung around to face Gid. "It's all right," he was to shout, "it's all right!" but a loud shot split through the air, deafening Luke. Gid's eye exploded, the white showing all around the brown before breaking into red and running down his cheek as he started falling, slowly, slowly, into the sea—his one eye frozen onto Luke, the other like a ruptured jellyfish.

He closed his eyes, blinded by sight, then opened them to darkness. The yellow gold of the kelp seeped through and he stared unblinkingly. He couldn't see Gid at first, his hair the same browny gold of the kelp and floating amongst it. Then he saw where the blood was reddest and mixing amongst the kelp like sprigs of berries on a sea of autumn leaves. Frankie appeared, grabbing hold of Gid's shirt and pulling him to the surface. "Help me, Luke; help me," he cried, but Luke's hands were frozen around the gun, his finger still pressed against its trigger. He looked skyward, and at the black rock walls surrounding him. He was cold, shivering. And his knee hurt from where he had fallen. He thought to move, to start lunging through the water, to help Frankie drag Gid to shore. But he couldn't. Wouldn't. Maybe in a while, if he waited, Gid would awaken, his one eye looking up at him, and the other just a little hurt. He heard Frankie saying something about the men being gone now, but he couldn't hear clearly, labouring, as he was, to drag air into his lungs. The rock wall of the cavern loomed dream-like in front of him, all wavering and ballooning, and then the sun burst over the cliffs, its colours too sharp. Letting slip the gun, he ploughed through the water towards the beach where Frankie was bending over Gid, turning him onto his back. And there was Gid, his one eye closed and the other shattered amongst chards of bone, yet trembling still, willing him to touch it, and the colours broke, all running together and with a wrenching cry, he dropped onto his haunches, burying his face in his hands.

"We'll tell them he did it, right, Luke?" Frankie was crying. "We'll tell them he took the gun and fell down with it, that he shot hisself, right, Luke? Luke?"

"LUKE?"

Luke started. He was hunched down at the mouth of the cove, staring into the cavern, locked into its darkness. He closed his eyes as Gideon hunched down besides him and bowed his head.

"I'm so ashamed," he whispered.

"What shames you, Luke?"

Luke shook his head, burrowing deeper into his palms. "It was me that shot you, Gid. It was me that had the gun."

Gid fell silent, lost in the cavern's darkness as Luke had been a few minutes earlier. When finally he spoke, his tone was quiet. "Over the years I've made myself believe it was no accident. That I didn't trip and fall. That I turned the gun onto myself." He paused. "And I've credited you with the courage it took for me to pull that trigger, Luke."

Luke turned to him. "Courage?" he asked incredulously. "I ran like chickenshit."

"Yeah. We were all running. Before I met you, I was running. Rocky Head wasn't going to be no final stop for we—not with our old man. But then it was. And that's to do with you." Gid smiled at Luke and clasped his hands as though to keep from reaching out. "You showed me what it was to be a boy. And to feel love. I haven't run since. But I fear what it might've took from you. They say you've never been back. How come you've never been back?"

Luke turned to the dark of the cavern, the rustling of the kelp and sea. "Fear," he said quietly.

"Fear?"

"Of finding I got no courage. That I'm still the same chickenshit that ran. And I am," he said with a short laugh. "A part of me will always be chickenshit. I'm learning not to run, is all." He turned back to Gid. "It's one thing for a man to stand strong in the wake of his own follies, but it's for them he hurt to cast the final say."

"It was a good bullet, my friend. And a good lie at the time. I'm chickenshit, too, Luke. All this time sitting here, too scared to go visit with you. Yeah, scared," he added. "I've been protecting them memories of you—running around the way we used to do, building bough-whiffens." He smiled, bowing his head in the manner of Luke earlier. "Guess I've been scared of finding that you wouldn't be the same now. That you wouldn't remember things the same way as I do."

Luke turned to the scarred face partially hidden beneath the scarf. Reaching, haltingly at first, he pulled the scarf back over Gid's forehead, gazing over his head somewhere. Then slowly he brought his eyes back to the scarred cheek, the ravaged socket, long since healed, but its flesh now purple with the cold of the night air. A drooping brown eye bored into his, but he refused it, focusing instead onto his fingers as he raised them and laid their tips onto the bottom of Gid's cheek where the scar began. Slowly, gently, he traced along the path of the bullet as one might a lover's mouth. And when finally he reached the socket, a finger strayed to its corner, and he pressed it there, allowing himself to look now, into the one brown eye staring back at him.

"You won't find me the same," he whispered.

"Nor would I want to," said Gideon. "I'd rather the man who can now touch me."

A glimpse of a smile touched the corner of Luke's mouth, and he lowered his head once more, as did Gideon, their foreheads touching, their hands grasping the other's shoulders. "It's good you've come back," said Luke. "Cripes," he then mumbled, pulling back and stuffing his hands into his pockets, "there's time I've wished to be Frankie, going and doing whatever he pleases, nothing bothering him, nothing sticking."

"Nay," said Gideon, "rather the soul that suffers love than the one who baits it."

Luke looked to the one drooping eye. "We could've done more," he half whispered. "Your mother—the rest of the youngsters—we could've done more."

"He was a Godless man, my father. Nobody can carry the weight of a Godless man, Luke." He grinned. "That's something I learned from Prude, although it took me some time to put it in place." His grin broadened and he was about to say more but quieted as Clair's voice cut through the dark.

"We're ready to go," she called out to them, appearing onto the beach before the brambles. "Gideon, she wants to speak with you."

Gideon was already rising. Touching Luke's arm, he spoke with a sense of urgency. "I've a confession too, Luke. It's not just you that's kept me here all this time, camped out by a dirty pond on a boggy hillside. Yeah," he added, and leaving Luke staring after him with a drawn brow, he strolled off towards the shack, pulling his scarf down over his scar, and fitting his grizzled hair more tightly into a ponytail. He stopped to have a word with Clair.

Luke made to follow, but a faint scratching sound drew his eyes back to the black mouth of the cavern. The wind was dying out now, and the sky had cleared considerably. By morning the land and sea would be quiet. And once the tide was out and the sun broke over the treetops, the cavern would be flooded with light, the mussel bed glistening like a field of goldenrod after a heavy rain. He thought of Job's desperate search for a downhill chance out of hell back to the peaceful waters of Cat Arm and he shivered. It's the one garden, Job, b'ye, he thought, it's all the one garden. And as he turned back to the beach and Clair walking towards him, her chin tilted proud as she watched him, his heart swelled. His dove. "Aye," he said in the words of the old vet, "it's too sublime, too sublime."